# complicate me

the good ol' boys series

## USA TODAY BESTSELLING AUTHOR
# M. ROBINSON

CW01418480

Complicate Me

Copyright © 2015 M. Robinson

All rights Reserved.
No part of this book may be used or reproduced in any manner whatsoever without written permission of the author.

This book is a work of fiction. References to real people, events, establishments, organizations, or locations are intended only to provide a sense of authenticity, and are used fictitiously. All other characters, dead or alive are a figment of my imagination and all incidents and dialogue, are drawn from the author's mind's eye and are not to be interpreted as real.

M. Robinson

# Dedication

Boss man. My husband. Best friend.
Thank you for always supporting me in everything I do. I love you.

# *acknowledgements*

Dad: Thank you for always showing me what hard work is and what it can accomplish. For always telling me that I can do anything I put my mind to.

Mom: Thank you for ALWAYS being there for me no matter what. You are my best friend.

Julissa Rios: I love you and I am proud of you. Thank you for being a pain in my ass and for being my sister. I know you are always there for me when I need you.

Ysabelle & Gianna: Love you my babies.

Rebecca Marie: THANK YOU for an AMAZING cover. I wouldn't know what to do without you and your fabulous creativity.
Heather Moss: Thank you for everything that you do!! XO
Silla Webb: Thank you so much for your edits and formatting! I love it and you!

Michelle Tan: Best beta ever! Jen Dirty Girl: I love your voice! And you. Tammy McGowan: Thank you for all your support and boo boo's you find! You love to give me heart attacks. Michele Henderson McMullen: LOVE LOVE LOVE you!! Dee Montoya: We're are some sexy bitches. Just saying... Roxie Madar: Thank you for your honesty and your friendship. Jessica Winstead: You're amazing!! Thank you! Rebeka Christine Perales: You always make me smile. Adrian Culbreth Perkins: Your feedback means so much to me!! Mary Jo Toth: Your boo-boos are always great! Argie Sokoli: Thank you for coming in like a boss and getting it done! Ella

Gram: You're such a sweet and amazing person! Thank you for your kindness. Michelle Kubik Follis: You always make me laugh!! Kimmie Kim: Your friendship means everything to me. Tricia Bartley: Your comments and voice always make me smile!! Isabel Montes: Thank you so much for helping me find a title for this book! I appreciate it so much!

To all my author buddies: T.M. Frazier: I love you, you Ginger. Jettie Woodruff: You're my sister from another mister. K. Webster: I love your face! Stevie J. Cole: You're a whore. The end.

The C.O.P.A Cabana Girls: I love you!!

To all the blogs A HUGE THANK YOU for all the love and support you have shown me. I have made some amazing friendships with you that I hold dear to my heart. I know that without you I would be nothing!! I cannot THANK YOU enough!! Special thanks to Totally Booked for sharing my exclusive prologue reveal and Like A Boss Book Promotions for hosting my tours!

Last, but most definitely not least, to my VIP GROUP. Oh my God ladies...words cannot describe how much I love and appreciate every last one of you. The friendships and relationships that I have made with you are one of the best things that have ever happened to me. I wish I could name each one of you but it would take forever, just please know that you hold a very special place in my heart. You VIPs make my day, every single day. THANK YOU!!!

# Prologue

## Alex

"You look beautiful, Alex," Lucas whispered from behind me, his voice broken and torn. The errors of his ways finally catching up with him, it was evident in his tone. It pained me to hear him sound like that, no longer the carefree boy I grew up with.

"I'm sorry you had to see that," I replied, trying to keep my own voice from breaking. The physical ache surrounding and consuming me in ways I never thought possible. The gravitational pull we had toward each other wreaking havoc on our souls.

This wasn't supposed to be this hard. Today was supposed to be one of the happiest days of my life. I should be celebrating, not wallowing in the memories that I hold so deeply in my heart and soul. I hadn't seen him all night and then he just appeared out of nowhere.

I blinked and he was there.

I felt him from across the room before I even found his stare. I didn't think he would show up, I should have known better. He always did what he wanted, since we were kids there was no telling him what to do. It's one of the things I hated the most about him.

"I'm not," he simply stated, the fervor of his voice radiating from behind me and burning a hole in my back.

"Are you happy?" he added.

I closed my eyes as a single tear fell down the side of my face. I had spent endless nights crying over him.

Over us.

"I just want you to be happy, Half-Pint." He hadn't called me that in years. Not since we were kids.

"Are you happy, Bo?" I countered, throwing his question and nickname back at him, knowing it would have the same effect as it had on me.

"Only you would be standing out on the sand in a dress like that," he brushed me off, changing the subject.

"I was never afraid to get dirty," I reminded him, digging my feet into the sand and dragging my dress along with it.

"Always trying to be like one of the boys. What are you doing out here on the beach? You looked so happy until you saw me. What took away your happiness?"

I scoffed. "Do you even have to ask me that? Does it make it easier for you? To be here? To see me like this? Is that why you're here?"

"It's never been easy," he softly spoke.

"What did you expect from me? What did you want me to do, Lucas?"

"You know what I wanted. You've known since we were kids and I carried you around on the handlebars of my bike. It hasn't changed, it never changes between us. You know that as much as I do."

I wrapped my arms around my torso in a comforting gesture, it didn't help. Nothing was more comforting than his arms around me.

"Why didn't you use the abandoned house, Alex?" he quickly followed.

I hated that he knew so much about me, our childhood entwined together like the weaving of a tight rope. Our names being synonyms of each other, there was no Half-Pint without Bo. Except now we weren't kids, we were just Alex and Lucas.

"You know why," I softly hinted, my voice catching in the wind and the waves of the ocean.

It was a soothing calm to the chaos all around me, everywhere he went he brought his hurricane with him. He was always the eye of the storm. When we were kids I loved it, I wanted to be pulled into his winds and let him take me wherever he wanted to go. I'd follow him anywhere. But as we got older I realized it was too late for me to seek refuge. He was already my destruction and there was no way to get past the heavy gusts of our complicated love.

"Tell me anyway."

I shook my head. That was Lucas, true to his nature, wanting what he wanted when he wanted it. "It's ours," I admitted, giving in to what he needed to hear from me. I could never lie to him.

"Damn, you look so beautiful. So damn beautiful," he murmured into my ear, engulfing me with his scent. I couldn't move if I wanted to and he didn't falter. "I know, Alex, I have to live with the fact that I messed up. I lost you."

"It's not your fault."

"You're lying, Half-Pint. I know you, so stop pretending like I don't. Do you love him?"

I took in a deep reassuring breath and nodded, not being able to say the words.

"More than me?"

"That's not fair," I argued, trying to control the emotions that were threatening to take over by hugging myself harder.

"I never said life was fair." He brushed my hair to the side of my neck and softly kissed my bare shoulder. I tried not to shudder from the feel of his lips on me.

"You should get back in there, Alex."

"I know."

"You know I can't go in there before you. I can't walk away from you again. I've done that too many times and it nearly killed me the last time."

"And what makes you think that I can, Lucas? What makes you think that it's any different for me?"

He turned me to face him and his hand immediately grazed my cheek, gently easing my chin up to look at him. There it was...

Our connection.

Along with all our stolen moments placed in between us.

Then came a cold, distant allure in his eyes when he said...

"I wasn't the one that said 'Yes.'"

# LUCAS

*I love her.*

I debated for weeks on whether to attend her engagement party or not. I looked at the invitation so many damn times I had memorized every word.

I sat in my truck for hours, debating on going inside or driving back home. It was near 10 PM when I finally managed to pull myself together enough to walk through the doors and into her future.

A future that didn't include me.

At least not in the way that I had once hoped it would. We would always be best friends though, over the last few years our conversations and interactions became less frequent, shorter and almost non-existent. I knew every time she looked at me that I had broken her heart. I had hurt her in the worst ways possible and I had to live with knowing I did that. My hand was firmly placed in my pocket, holding the necklace that I had bought her after our first kiss. She wore it for years, until one day she didn't.

It produced a false illusion that she was still mine.

The second I walked inside I saw her. I stopped dead in my tracks just to take her in, she was a vision. There was no beauty in this world like Alex. She was wrapped around her fiancé, his hands firmly locked in place on the woman that belonged to me. I claimed her a long time ago. She looked breathtaking, smiling at everyone with her long brown hair framing her mousy face and her big brown eyes that always made my heart skip a beat. She wore a long white dress that hung loosely on her body, always a tomboy at heart but still managing to make it look sexy. I remembered a time when she hated dresses, fighting with her mom because she kept buying them for her.

I couldn't take my eyes off her, it took everything inside me not to make a scene. I couldn't control the internal battle that surfaced in the forefront of my mind, it was a tsunami of emotions. I loved her, I knew I loved her, I always have and I always will. She owned every part of me. My heart was hers since before I knew what her having it even meant. But she deserved to be happy, so I had to let her go.

It wasn't fair to either of us.

Especially her.

She suddenly looked down at the ground as if she felt me. The look on her face exposed the girl I grew up with, the same girl that couldn't hide her emotions from me. Her face frowned and her mouth parted, instinctively pulling away from her fiancé who didn't pay her any mind. I didn't know if she did it for my benefit or hers. Then she looked up and right at me. There was no wandering in her stare as she found mine from the corner of the room. We stood on the dance floor gazing at one another like there was no one else around us, like the room wasn't filled with our friends and family. I didn't care if anyone saw us. We had spent over two and a half decades worrying about everyone else's feelings.

I saw nothing but pure unadulterated fear as she placed her hand on her heart, as if she were trying to hold it together. Slowly breaking her gaze from mine, our connection was broken. It mirrored our love. My feet moved of their own accord as I followed her out to the beach.

Our beach.

Grasping the necklace tighter in my pocket.

We exchanged words that will forever haunt me, adding to the pile of endless confessions, secrets, and betrayals. I inhaled the sweet and tantalizing smell of Alex, the lingering scent of her vanilla shampoo and the sunscreen that I knew she still put on every morning. The smell of her cherry lip-gloss brought me right back to childhood when she used to be mine.

I kissed her because I couldn't *not* kiss her.

I pecked my lips on the only spot I knew wouldn't be crossing the line, even though a line was never drawn.

She belonged to me.

*Plain and simple.*

Our emotions were running wild, trying to accept the bond our hearts will forever have. We laid our love out for each other years ago. I fought a battle I knew I could never win. The emotional turmoil ate away at me the closer we got to saying goodbye. That's what happened when two halves of a heart come together and become one.

We would always be linked.

We were destined to be soul mates.

Star-crossed lovers.

When I spun her to look at me, the little girl with pigtails wearing boy clothes was gone and all that was left was…

The woman getting married to a man that wasn't me.

# Chapter 1

## Alex

"Guys, this isn't fair!" I shouted from below.

"Life's not fair, Half-Pint," Lucas called out.

"But I want to play in the tree house, too."

"Can't you read?" Jacob yelled, pointing to the crappy sign that looked like it was drawn with women's lipstick. The bright red, boy handwriting clearly stated, "No Girls Allowed."

"That's a stupid rule if I ever heard one. I'm not a girl, I'm one of the boys, exactly how I've always been. I'm one of you."

I put on my best boy stance, as they peered down at me, leaning all my weight on one leg and crossing my arms, giving them one hell of a standoff. If they didn't let me up there, I would find my own way. Even if that meant I had to climb the tree all by myself. By the look on all four of their faces, they knew it, too.

We grew up in the small town of Oak Island, North Carolina. Our families had all been friends growing up in this Southern beach town. My parents, Nathanial, and Jana owned a restaurant right on the water where I spent most of my childhood along with my four best friends, who all happened to be boys.

Jacob Foster was the oldest. He took on the "Big Brother" role before all of us could even walk. He was thirteen and tall for his age, nearly six foot. He was still a gangly kid, all skin and bones, but with the sweetest smile and vibrant green eyes. He always had a ball cap permanently glued on his head. He was like the poster child for surfing, always wearing all kinds of different surf brands. He protected me fearlessly, but I didn't need any protection, I could carry my own weight and I often reminded him of that. His parents, Ginger and Lee owned a grocery store up the road, where they sold all kinds of tourist crap and food. They preserved a farm on his grandparent's old plantation in South Port that they only opened on Sundays. The church folk would gather together and go to town just to get the freshest produce near us. He had two younger sisters, Jessie, and Amanda, who bored me to no wits end.

*Why would I want to play with dolls when I could be climbing trees and building forts?*

Dylan McGraw was thirteen, just a few months shy of Jacob. They were always the closest to one another. I think it's because their personalities were somewhat the same, both acting as if we owned the beach whenever kids passed through town on vacation. He was also tall, almost the same height as Jacob, with hazel eyes and skin that tanned like the best of them. He had long blonde hair that went past his ears. His mom was always on his butt to get it trimmed but he refused, saying it was his style. During the summer the sun and salt water would bleach his hair almost white. His parents, McKenzie and Steve mostly worked from home. They had an act for refurbishing old furniture and turning it into something modern, new, and unique. Some of the items were sold in local shops, some from their online store, and some were loaded up and hauled to flea markets, where tourists flocked and overpaid for the quality work. Dylan and I both had the only child syndrome.

Austin Taylor was eleven and the shortest among the boys, although he would punch you in the face if you ever told him that. He was a rambunctious kid that was always trying to make up for the fact that the other boys were bigger than him. He was a cute kid with red hair and green eyes. His mom said he had some Scottish bloodline, hence the red hair. He hated it growing up, but once we reached high school, it had its perks. The freckles on his face became more prominent, which were very enticing to the girls at Oak Island high school. They fawned over him because he looked so different from the other boys around here. He had a baby brother named Hunter, who was five years younger than him.

Last, but definitely not least was Lucas Ryder or Bo, as I called him. It meant commander and that was him to a T— born to lead, not to follow. He was twelve, almost thirteen, and had a temper like no one else I had ever met before though he was always the sweetest boy to me. No one could tell him no and if you did, he would do it anyway just to spite you. We're the closest to one another. He always looked out for me and defended me when the boys called me a girl. I hated when they pointed out I couldn't do something they could do, just because I didn't have something dangling between my legs.

*Who would want that anyway?*

Nothing pissed me off more than being called a girl.

I was constantly showing them up because I had to. I was always covered in bruises, skinned knees, and dirty clothes. My hair tied up high on my head, either in pigtails or a ponytail. When I was four years old I took a pair of scissors that I found in my mama's nightstand and walloped off all my hair, cutting it short just like the boys. From then on out they hid the scissors from me and always tied my hair up, fearing that I would do it again if given the chance.

Lucas was secretly my favorite out of all the boys. You could even go as far as saying that I loved him a little bit more than the rest of them. I didn't know why, I just did. It had always been that way for me and I often felt like the feeling was mutual. Though we never spoke about it until we were older and understood the emotions that circulated through the years. He was always the most handsome out of all the boys and girls were pining over him since the day he was born. He had dark hair that complemented his baby blue eyes that resembled the ocean water on a warm summer day. He had prominent facial features that I never got tired of looking at, and even at that young of an age, he knew it.

Lucas was just as tall as Jacob, maybe slightly taller. He was built broader than the other boys because he surfed like crazy. All the boys did, but Lucas was obsessed with it. You could always find him on the waves whether it was night or day. He wanted to grow up to be a professional surfer, often riding waves that no one else dropped into and making all of us nervous.

The boy had no fear.

He had a baby sister, Lily, she was a few years younger than me, but we didn't become friends until much later in life. I swear the girl came out singing with a guitar in her hand, they put her in lessons by the time she was five. Their dad, Dr. Robert Ryder was one of the only doctors we had in town, often seeing patients that weren't even part of his medical degree, while his mom Savannah was a housewife.

I couldn't tell you how many times Dr. Ryder stitched us up right in his very own living room, not bothering to take us to his office. Bringing home medical supplies became a thing of the norm since we were constantly getting hurt. I remembered the first time I needed stitches. I was six years old and tried to jump off the riverbank like Dylan and my knee caught the rock at the bottom of the river. It hurt like hell, but I didn't cry, I never cried. I bit my lip as hard as I could to keep the damn tears from falling down the sides of my face. Lucas tried to sit me on his handlebars, but it hurt too much to bend my knee. So I sat facing him on his lap as he rode his bike home.

I wrapped my arms around his neck and held on as tight as I could, while my good leg draped over his lower back and my hurt one sat stiff as a board in the air. I laid my head on his shoulder and closed my eyes, but I couldn't hold back the tears. I cried the entire way to his house. His shirt was covered in nothing but my sissy tears by the time he parked his bike on his front lawn. He didn't say a word about it when he kissed my forehead, telling me everything was going to be alright and that he would never let anything happen to me. He carried me inside while the rest of the boys patiently waited for the wrath of our mothers, knowing they would be yelled at for letting me do something so careless.

Lucas held my hand the entire time his dad stitched me up and not once made me feel bad about crying. The rest of the month, while my knee healed, I rode on the handlebars of his bike. The boys continuously offered me to hitch a ride with them, but Lucas was adamant that I was only riding on his handlebars. If they thought he was being possessive over me, they never shared it.

That's just how we were with each other and they knew it.

And then there was little ol' me, Alexandra Collins. The truth was everyone thought I was supposed to be a boy, even the doctor. Much to my parents and families surprise I came out a girl, screaming like a bat outta hell to put me back in. My parents already had a name picked out for me. They were going to call me Alexander, Alex for short. Seeing as they didn't have much time to decide on another name, they wrote down Alexandra on my birth certificate and still called me Alex for short. I grew up with these boys, at ten years old I was a Half-Pint compared to all of them. They had been calling me that since the day we watched an episode of Little House on the Prairie and the dad called Laura Ingalls, Half-Pint.

I never crawled, I went right to walking and my first word was, "Shit." My mom slapped my dad on the back of the head the moment it came out of my mouth, at least that's what they told me. Like I said before, I was the only child, Dylan and I had that in common. I never wished for siblings, I didn't need to I had my boys. I stuck to them like gum did on the bottom of your shoe. One way or another they were my big brothers. I loved each one of them in my own way. The feelings were very much mutual, I would do anything for them and vice-versa. We were best friends, day in and day out.

I stomped my foot on the ground to emphasize my words. "You let me up there! Before I… before I…" I stumbled on my words.

"Before you what, Half-Pint? Go running to mommy and daddy and tellin'," Dylan shouted.

My mouth dropped open. "I would do no such thing! I ain't no tattle tale. Now you let me up there, ya hear?"

"Come on, guys, just let her come up," Lucas reasoned, looking from me to them.

I nodded in agreement. "Yeah come on, guys, just let me up there," I repeated.

Sometimes they would get a stick up their ass and just want to pick on me for no good reason. I hated when they did this, I think they got a kick out of me not backing down. They wanted to see my feisty spirit, the same one they so proudly claimed was due to them.

Austin rolled his eyes. "I knew you would be the first one to cave!" He pushed Jacob in the chest. "Told ya! You owe me five dollars."

Jacob glared at him and then back at me. "Fine! We were just teasing you, we were going to let you up here anyway. You're so easy to tease, being a Half-Pint and all."

"Yeah, whatever." I shrugged, brushing him off. "I could take you on any day, just tell me when and where, Jacob Foster."

"You and what army, *Alexandra!*"

"Don't call me that! My name's Half-Pint."

Lucas laughed and threw down the ladder for me to climb. As soon as my foot touched the last step he held out his hand for me to take and I smiled as he pulled me up the rest of the way.

"Wow! This is awesome!" I said, looking all around me. They had made it into our own little fort, but their heads barely cleared the roof. I opened the lid of one of the compartments near the front entrance.

"No!" Lucas shouted, shutting it forcefully behind me, making the floor rattle.

The rest of the boys broke out into laughter.

I cocked my head to the side, confused. "What?"

"Nothin'. You don't need to go in there is all," Lucas justified.

I put my hands on my hips. "Why not?"

I caught Austin blushing. Jacob and Dylan were grinning like two fools. I thought their faces might get stuck like that.

"What?" I repeated, wanting to know what the big deal was about.

"Just let her look, Lucas, she's going to find out eventually what's going to happen to her," Jacob interjected, making Lucas scowl over at him.

"What's going to happen to me?" I asked, even more curious than I was before.

Lucas sighed, knowing I wouldn't back down until I got my answer. He stepped aside and let me open the lid again. I looked down below and all I saw were women's faces looking back at me. They were barely dressed and posing like something you would see Jessica Rabbit do.

# LUCAS

I told them over and over again not to bring those magazines up here. They knew that our Half-Pint shadow would get her way and be up here hanging out with us. Everywhere we went she wasn't that far behind us. I swear the boys did it on purpose, constantly wanting her to admit that she was a girl and not one of us. We all loved her in our own way, it wasn't coming from a bad place but she was just a girl, and we never let her live that down.

I loved picking on her as much as the other boys did. I believed it was in my blood to do it. My dad picked on my mom relentlessly, and my grandfather did the same with my grandmother. It was a Ryder trait. If we didn't pick on our girls, then we didn't love them enough. My dad constantly reminded my mom that the day he stopped picking on her would be the day he stopped loving her.

I watched her bright brown eyes widen as she picked up the July issue of one of the magazines. She opened the first few pages and gasped letting it go. It fell to the ground at our feet. The guys all busted out laughing and it took everything in me not to kick them each in the balls for what I knew she must have seen.

"Why are they doing that?" she quickly questioned, the subtle red approaching her cheekbones while her stare remained on the magazine laying open on the floor again.

"They're posing," I simply replied, knowing it wouldn't be enough of an answer for her.

"Yeah but why they posin' like that? They're naked." She wouldn't look up at me and I knew why. She didn't want us to see her looking embarrassed and insecure. The pigtails on top of her head already made her appear like a child.

I glared at the guys, they all cockily held my penetrating gaze, not paying any mind at how pissed off I was. I had a bit of a temper. I could go from zero to ten in nanoseconds. That was also a Ryder trait.

Dylan patted my back. "It's alright, Lucas, I'll tell her. Those women are posing like that." He nodded toward the ground. "Because men use those magazines to play with their—"

I shoved him and his back hit the wall. He bounced off of it and laughed so hard that he nearly fell over. "Oh come on, Lucas, stop being such a pansy and just tell her. She has a right to know what happens when we all grow up," he justified, infuriating me further.

"What happens?" her soft voice trailed, making her pouty lips pucker out.

Jacob smiled. "Nothin' to worry your pint-sized head about. It's just boy stuff, and one day when Lucas doesn't get his panties all in a bunch about it we will tell you."

17

"But I want to know now," she replied, looking over at him. I'm not going to lie, it stung like hell that she looked at Jacob but wouldn't look at me.

*Why didn't she look at me?*

"Of course you do. Can I tell her, Lucas? Or are you going to push me again if I do?" Dylan asked, watching me like a hawk.

I shrugged, sweeping the hair back from my face and walking toward the back of the tree house away from all of them. "Whatever." I leaned against the wooden wall and placed one foot in front of the other, getting comfortable and crossing my arms.

I tried to ignore the feeling in the pit of my stomach. I wanted Alex to stay innocent. We were all changing — our bodies, our needs, our emotions. They were evolving into something I didn't quite understand yet. It terrified me that she might think less of me if I wasn't the boy she had grown up beside and loved.

He stepped closer to her and reached for the magazine. "This, Half-Pint, is a nudie magazine. These girls get paid a shit ton of money to show men their bodies."

Her face frowned, taking in his words. "Why?"

"Why not?"

"I understand why men would want to look at them, I'm not stupid."

She didn't get it. She was just trying to save face.

"But why would the women want to be looked at like that?"

"Some women want the attention. One day you'll look like that and you will understand."

Her head jerked back, offended. "I will never look like that, Dylan, you're dead wrong about that one."

*Damn straight she wouldn't. I'd never let her.*

He chuckled. "You will and Lucas over there is going to use you to play with his di—"

"Shut your hole!" I yelled, my fists clenching at my sides.

He cunningly grinned. "You're too easy, Lucas." He threw the magazine back in the cubby and put his arm around Alex, tugging her closer to him and kissing the top of her head. "One day you won't be our Half-Pint. Let's keep you just the way you are for as long as we can, huh?"

She looked up at him with complete adoration and love. "I'll always be your Half-Pint," she whispered, nestling in close to his chest.

I nodded.

She took the words right out of my mouth.

# Chapter 2

## LUCAS

We spent the rest of the summer riding our bikes and getting into trouble. My thirteenth birthday was a few days ago and I hated making a big deal out of it. I wasn't much for being the center of attention, unless I was on a wave, riding it on my surfboard. The adrenaline in my system beat out the anxiety of being watched in my mind. I was definitely an adrenaline junkie, but I hopelessly tried to keep it on lock down. Alex wanted to do everything I did and there was no telling her she couldn't do it. She swore that was my personality, not hers.

But the truth was, we were one and the same.

She waited until we were alone to hand me my gift. Since our parents were the closest to each other, she was constantly staying late. Sometimes they even stayed overnight from drinking too much and shooting the shit. I had bunk beds in my room, I slept on the bottom and the top was hers. She always wanted to sleep on the bottom, but I wouldn't let her. I knew the beds were sturdy and nothing would happen, but I still couldn't get over the fear that if it broke it would crush her.

And I'd never let anything happen to her.

As I rode my bike, I remembered the look on her face when I opened my present. She sat on my bed with her legs crossed and the nervousness oozing off of her. It was a picture of her holding up my surfboard, dressed in my board shorts and gray Quicksilver t-shirt I'd given her. She posed in a funny yet adorable way. When I smiled and raised my eyes to her she said, *"It's so you don't have to look at them magazines anymore."*

"Come on, Half-Pint, pedal faster like we taught you," Austin shouted from a distance, taking me away from my thoughts. It didn't matter how fast she pedaled, she would never be able to catch up to us. Her legs were much shorter than ours.

Again, she was just a girl.

"I am!" she yelled back, out of breath.

I peered behind me and saw her still far behind, so I decided to stop and wait for her on the side of the street. A bright orange flower by my foot caught my attention.

I reached down and tore it from the ground.

She halted right beside me, panting. "It doesn't matter how fast I pedal, I can't catch up with you boys," she sadly whispered, bowing her head. I knew it took a lot for her to admit that and I hated seeing her look so defeated.

It wasn't in her nature.

I placed the flower under her nose and her eyes brightened, quickly replacing the sadness. Gazing up at me with joy for something so minuscule. She grinned and grabbed the flower from my fingers, tucking it behind her ear.

Right then and there, I learned that it was all about the little things when it came to her.

"Come on." I nodded toward her feet.

She took another exaggerated breath and started to pedal down the road with me alongside her. We rode in comfortable silence for a few minutes, going a lot slower now and I started getting a bit bored. I let go of my handlebars and balanced on the bike with my arms out to my sides to maintain my stability. I leaned my body to the side to hold my bike in place, as we were taking a curve.

"Show off," she teased.

I smiled, she was partially right. I always tried to impress her, when you're that young you don't understand the reasons behind it. You just do it. By the time we made it down to the river the guys were already in the water, horsing around. I helped her off her bike and securely placed it next to mine, locking them together around a tree. I grabbed her hand and she followed close behind me.

The woods were murky and muggy. It rained that morning and left a humid atmosphere in its wake. They weren't too far from where we had parked the bikes, but you needed to be careful where you stepped. I knew Alex would tread where I had, without even having to tell her to do so, it was always that way between us. When we were older, I realized that we had this unspoken bond that neither

21

of us understood or talked about and it was only then that I wished we had.

The closer we drew to the river, the louder it became. The trees finally cleared off and all that was left was a field of water with trees surrounding it. It smelled awful and part of me doubted that Alex would actually go into the river. I knew better than to ask her, though.

"I know what you're thinking, Lucas Ryder, and I'm going to punch you."

I spun around, meeting her deep glare. "It's not gonna hurt even if you do."

She punched me anyway.

# Alex

"Come on, you slowpokes, hurry it up already," Austin called out from the tire swing, hanging off of it like a monkey.

Dylan and Jacob were already in the river rough housing, seeing who could hold the other under water the longest and gasping once they came up for air. I took off my shirt and shorts, throwing them onto a tree branch by the water. I wore my black one-piece bathing suit while the boys were wearing swim trunks with no shirts on. I wanted to wear that too, but my mom was adamant that I needed to wear what little girls wore. I hated my bathing suit but they never paid me any mind that I wasn't dressed like them.

I heard Lucas take off from behind me, jumping head first into the river. I knew that there were alligators swimming among them, and I silently prayed they couldn't smell my fear. Lucas came up from under the water and whipped his hair back away from his face with a sudden jolt of his neck. He swam closer to the bank waiting for me.

"Did you know gators only come out into the open when they feel threatened? Otherwise they scurry away from the chaos and noise," Lucas said out loud for all of us to hear, but truly it was just for me.

I smirked and tottered through the grass, my feet sinking to the bottom of the river. Lucas swam in a bit and jerked his head to the side. It was a silent agreement for me to hang off his back. I smiled and swam up behind him, putting my arms around his neck and my legs around his torso. He paddled us out to the rest of the boys and we stayed like that for the entire day.

\*\*\*

School was back in full swing and my birthday was a few days away. I was about to be eleven. It was my last year in elementary school — one more year and I would finally be back in the same school with my boys. They were in seventh grade and Austin in sixth. Their bodies started to fill out and they ate more than ever. Our parents constantly complained about how they couldn't keep them fed. Lucas's mom started stocking the pantry with peanut butter, Ritz crackers, and raisins. I loved them individually, but he would pile it all together on a cracker and eat it. I swear the boy lived off of it. Pizza Rolls, Hot Pockets, Pop Tarts and Sunny D were also some of their favorites. Drinking milk by the gallons became a thing of the norm, always chugging it right from the cartons, much to our mothers' disapproval. I had watched them get slapped so many times on the back of the head that I started to do it, too. Their voices started to change and began getting deeper which made it hard for me to recognize who I talked to from day to day.

There were also girls that started to hang out with them and I hated that, too. It was probably what I hated the most about them growing up and being so good looking. The older we got, the more the girls flocked around them. In my mind, they weren't anyone else's, especially some stupid girls. They were mine and I didn't want to share them. I expressed my possessive feelings to them often and they always laughed me off and reassured me that I fussed over nothing.

All the girls looked completely different from me. They wore makeup, dresses, and their hair was always down and blowing in the wind. They appeared to be Barbies, looking like the girls that I had seen in their magazines. I would catch all of their wandering eyes anytime one of those girls stepped foot around us.

Even Lucas.

And I definitely hated that more than anything. "Hey, Luke," some big boobed blonde said, walking toward us on the beach.

Complicate Me

We were sitting near my parents' restaurant, and she wore the tiniest bikini I had ever seen. I subconsciously glared down at my worn out t-shirt that happened to be two sizes too big on me, and my jean shorts that went down past my knees. I begged my mom for months to let me buy a few pairs, even though they were technically boy cargo shorts. I didn't own any girl clothes. I loathed them as much as I did those stupid girls.

"Lucas, my name's Lucas, not Luke," he replied, as I peeked up through my lashes.

"Oh, I'm sorry," she flirted, sitting beside him on the sand.

I played with the sand out in front of me, piling handfuls of it on top of each other, pretending that I wasn't listening to every word they were saying.

"Are you ready for Mr. Smith's test tomorrow?"

He shrugged, watching me from the corner of his eyes.

"Oh! Well, I'm ready for it. Maybe I could help you. I wouldn't mind. I'm very good with numbers."

He started piling sand on top of each other with me, interlocking his with mine, our fingers brushing up against each other.

"Nah, I don't need any help," he simply stated, tearing down my sand tower and grinning at me with a satisfied look on his face.

"Are you sure?" She leaned over and pressed her gigantic boobs on his arm. She smelled like the honey my mom put in her tea.

*Why would anyone want to smell like food?*

I now hated that smell.

"I'm sure." He brushed her off.

She made some comment about also being good at Chemistry. I didn't understand what she implied, but Lucas grinned like a fool. When she walked away, he bumped his shoulder with mine.

"I think one of her boobs are as big as my head," I blurted while watching her confidently stride away from him, swaying her hips with each step she took.

*How did she walk like that?*

He burst out laughing not following my gaze that was promptly placed on her perfect body.

*Would I ever look like that?*

"I think you might not be too far off from that one," he admitted.

"Do you like her?" I asked, not being able to look him in the eye.

"She's nice," was all he replied.

"She seems like she likes you."

He smiled. "Lots of girls like me."

I rolled my eyes.

"Do you like me, Half-Pint?" he teased, standing up and clearing off the sand from his board shorts.

I rolled my eyes again. "No. I love you."

It wasn't the first time I had said that to him. I would say it to all of them. It was never a big deal...

Until it was.

# LUCAS

I nodded and held out my hand to pull her up. "I love you, too," I repeated, bringing her toward me.

We had been saying I love you to each other for God knows how long and I meant it every time I said it to her.

"She's just a girl," I stated, holding her in place by her shoulders in front of me.

She cocked her head, lifting her eyes to me with an inquisitive stare I didn't recognize.

"What am I?"

I smiled. "One of us. You'll always be one of us, Half-Pint."

"Good." She nodded, seeming pleased by my answer and reassurance.

"Now! Today is the day..."

"For what?"

I spun her to face the ocean, leveling myself behind her. "You're going to surf."

She shook her head. "Nah, I'm not ready yet."

This was the only thing that she never showed any interest in. We lived on the east coast, Oak Island was known for sharks swimming near the shoreline, getting lost in the inlet chasing their prey. They didn't scare me. I'd been around them for what seemed like forever and it went hand-in-hand with surfing. We'd lost count of how many times we'd seen one. It was a natural occurrence for me to be sitting out on my board watching them somewhere in the ocean.

I grabbed my board, giving her the familiar stern look that meant I would get my way, with or without her consent, even though I wanted the latter. She took a deep breath, rolling her eyes as she removed her shirt and shorts that left her in her black one-piece bathing suit she hated so much. I personally thought she looked adorable, especially when her hair was up in pigtails.

"You weigh nothing, it will be so easy for you to ride a wave, and then you will understand the feeling of being one with the water." I thought I could feel her shaking her head behind me or maybe I just knew she'd be doing it.

"That makes absolutely no sense."

"Exactly! It's hard to describe, there is nothing like it and it's time you experience it. I have spent a ridiculous amount of time on the beach, teaching you how to keep your balance on the board and how to pop up once the wave hits." I dragged her to the shoreline.

"I don't want to, Bo."

I laid my board on the water. "I would never let anything happen to you," I stated, locking my eyes with hers, knowing that she could see the sincerity in my stare.

Gawking from me to the board and back at me again, she finally sighed, "Okay."

I strapped the leash around her ankle, as she positioned the upper half of her body in the middle of the board. I gave the fin a little push and she started to paddle out into the waves. I stood there, my arms crossed over my chest with my feet planted in the water, as the receding waves pulled the sand from beneath my feet. I would be lying if I said I wasn't fixated on watching her tiny butt, more than her effort on paddling out against the current. Her bathing suit rode up her cheeks, making it easy for me to do so.

I didn't think much about it, being that young. I just chalked it up to normal boy hormones.

She paddled past the break and awkwardly tried to sit up on the board, still trying to maintain her balance and not flip over. She sat there for a bit once she was comfortable. Dragging her legs back and forth in the water, enjoying the way it felt on her feet and in-between her toes. She started drumming on my board, swaying her body side-to-side, her lips moving, singing Brown Eyed Girl by Van Morrison, I was sure, I sang it to her constantly. Completely oblivious to anything around her, including when she should be catching a wave, but I couldn't help the huge smile that crept on my face.

She always had that effect on me. I loved her carefree, childlike personality, making lemonade out of lemons wherever she went. She captivated me all the time, enveloping me with her mannerisms and demeanor that was just plain Alex. A part of me knew she was aware of it, the effect she had on me. It didn't matter what she'd be doing, my eyes followed her everywhere, constantly waiting for her to do something else that would make me fall in love with her just a little bit more.

I thought it was normal…

The feelings I had for her. I thought all the boys felt that way, assuming she had a gravitational pull on all of us. I learned later that I was wrong.

I couldn't have been more wrong had I tried.

She finally paddled for a few waves here and there with no luck and I saw it before it happened, a shark skimming through the waves. I knew if I yelled for her to paddle in she would freak the hell out and probably flip my board, ending up in the water.

So I waited, dreading the reaction from her that I knew would come. She sat back up and not even a minute later the shark bumped the board with its nose. It hit hard enough to make her aware of what was going on, what had happened. Even from the shoreline I could see her panicked expression. I ran out into the waves, far enough to where she could hear me.

"Half-Pint! Lay on the board and hold onto the sides and let the white water drag you back in!" I watched for the right wave and time. "Do it now!"

She immediately did as she was told. I waited until I could grab the nose of the board and helped her in. I could see the tears falling down the sides of her face before we were back on land and I knew I was in trouble. Alex didn't cry.

Ever.

"I told you! I told you I didn't want to go out there! Why would you do that to me?" she bellowed, yelling at me in an unfamiliar tone before she was even off the board.

"Half-Pint, I'm sorry. Calm down," I reasoned, grabbing her arms to help her off the board while trying to comfort and hold her up at the same time.

"No! You didn't listen to me! I'm so mad at you! Let go of me!"

I held her tighter, pulling her toward me. "Half-Pint," I coaxed. "You're okay. I'm sorry. I would never hurt you. I would never let anything happen to you. You know that, please. I'm sorry," I apologized with desperation and frustration filling my eyes and voice.

She thrashed in my arms, desperately wanting to pull away from me and it broke my heart.

"Lucas Ryder, let go of me! Let go of me this instant before I kick you where the sun don't shine! Do you hear me? I want nothing to do with you! Now let go!"

I tried not to laugh, amused with her banter and feisty spirit. "No, not until you forgive me."

She screamed, heaving back far enough that I had to grip her wrists. "Stop screaming."

"Then let go of me!" she argued through gritted teeth near my face.

"Are you going to forgive me?" I replied not backing down.

"Hell. No."

"You stubborn lil' thang." I jerked her forward, closer to my face and she lost her footing.

She wouldn't stop fighting while I just held onto her, barely breaking a sweat or using any of my strength. She knew her efforts wouldn't matter. She would never be able to overpower me and get away. I was bigger, she wouldn't be able to go unless I wanted her to, and I knew that pissed her off more than anything.

"Stop being such a girl," I simply stated.

Her eyes widened, gasping loudly. "Oh my God! Let go! Let go before I really hurt you. I'm not kidding, Lucas!" she yelled out directly in my face.

Thank God the beach was secluded or we definitely would have attracted a crowd. Her parents' restaurant wasn't far from us.

"You and what army, *Alexandra*."

And then she screamed again. She screamed so damn loud you would think I was killing her. My ears felt like they were bleeding and I worried that someone would hear her and then shit would really hit the fan. If my mom knew I let her go out on my board, she would have my ass. Our parents were always grateful that she didn't care for surfing, saying it was enough to worry about those treacherous waves and me. She was violently whipping around and screaming bloody murder, if I used any force, then I could hurt her, and I definitely didn't want to do that. Before I gave it any thought, I did the only thing I could think of to shut her up.

I yanked her toward me.

And I kissed her.

## Alex

He kissed me.

His lips touched mine.

Our mouths became one.

My eyes tightly shut, my heart stopped beating, and all the fight in me was gone. His grip moved from my wrists to my hands. Holding them. It wasn't one of those movie kisses that we watched on TV, but it was enough to have me paralyzed from the sudden feel of his lips on mine. I had no clue what to do, so I awkwardly froze from the unexpected turn of events in the last few seconds. My mind wasn't even wandering, it went blank as if my body wanted to live in the moment and be with him. We just stood there, neither one of us moving with our mouths glued to each other. Encased in nothing but bewilderment and something else?

Something I couldn't put my finger on...

Something that had me weak in the knees and dizzy in the head...

Something I'd never felt before but wanted to hold onto...

We were waiting...

For what?

Who the hell knows.

As if reading my mind he pulled away first, and I quickly followed suit. Our eyes slowly opened at the exact same time and I saw something in his I'd never seen before. They were dilated, and the sapphire blues that I had become so accustomed to and loved throughout the years were gone. They were replaced with two big, black rings that held so much emotion that it was overwhelming, and yet I didn't know what it meant. But there was also a familiarity that was still present, and it calmed the confusion that was rapidly forming in my mind. That alarmed me more than anything else. It scared me that momentarily I didn't know the boy standing in front of me.

Still a little part of me, a small part of my heart, it soared for the first time.

I removed one of my hands from his, and lightly touched my lips. I was breathless as I swiped my fingers back and forth on the top and the bottom. They felt so different.

I felt so different.

*Why?*

He watched my every move with an intense glare that had me gasping for breath while trying to understand what had just happened between us. Unspoken questions ricocheted but stayed unvoiced. His stare so penetrating, so consuming that I couldn't break it. I couldn't move my eyes from his. They were glued together just as our lips had just been. With air slowly returning to my lungs, it restored blood flow into my unbelievably fast beating heart that I swear he could hear.

*Or maybe it was his that I heard?*

I watched him swallow deeply and profusely, and then his lips parted like he tried to catch air that wasn't circulating fast enough so he needed to open his mouth to breathe. He slowly reached up and touched his own lips, repeating the same gesture he'd seen me do, mimicking me in every way. But right after he removed his fingers he did something completely different, he licked his lips.

I think my heart may have burst. It was now lying on the sand in between us for him to see, secretly hoping it was beside his. Right then and there I knew I wanted that feeling to stay forever. I wanted to bundle up whatever emotion coursed through me, and *that* stare that was just for me. Bring it home with me, and bottle it up, where I could cherish it and relive it whenever I wanted to. A futile hope, that for just one second I may have had an effect on him and it wasn't an illusion.

It was real.

For a young girl...

That meant everything.

I was about to be eleven years old in a few days and I had known Lucas all my life, but it was the first time I truly felt something different, something more than just friendship for him, and I knew it was very much mutual. Even though what I felt for him, what we felt for each other, it wouldn't be defined till a few years later. This is where it all started.

Our first kiss was our beginning and in some ways our end.

*This* is where our complicated love began.

"Why did you do that?" I whispered, our frenzied gazes still locked.

He shrugged. "Your eyes look funny," he murmured, confirming my thoughts.

"So do yours," I breathed out, swallowing the saliva that had pooled in my mouth. "Now what?"

He shrugged again.

*Well if he didn't know what to do and I didn't know what to do?*

*Then what?*

"Why did you kiss me?" I blurted, needing to know.

"To get you to hush up."

"Oh." I lowered my eyes that mirrored his. *Maybe I read it all wrong.*

I kicked the sand below my feet for a few seconds, neither one of us talking, but his hand grabbed mine with the other one still tightly entwined.

"Alex."

As soon as I heard my name I raised my eyes to him. He never called me by my name. With our gazes once again connected, his eyes still dark and daunting, but a warm, loving smile now appeared on his face, making my heart skip a beat. He tucked a piece of my hair behind my ear, leaving a deep fluttering feeling in my belly.

"Are you still mad at me?"

31

I shook my head no, unable to find the words to express what I felt.

"Good," was all he replied.

"I'm sorry I snapped at you," I said, changing the subject but not dismissing the emotions that now lay between us.

"I'm sorry that shark hit my board."

"It's not your fault."

He nodded. "You know I would never let anything happen to you."

I smiled. "I know."

"You did a really good job, though."

"Not really," I chuckled.

"I think you singing Brown Eyed Girl attracted that shark to come see you."

I slanted my head to the side, my curiosity eating me up. "How do you know that?"

"You're my brown eyed girl." He grinned. "Come on, Half-Pint, I'll walk you back to your house. It's getting late."

"Okay."

He grabbed his board and we walked beside each other, barely talking the entire hike back to my house. He normally waited until I was on my front porch to leave. My house was three stories high and had a wooden deck leading to the front door. I slowly opened the door, but before I stepped into the foyer, I found myself doing something I never had before.

I turned around.

He was still there, watching me.

I shyly smiled and he waved goodbye. I ran up to my room, closing the door behind me, leaning against it. I caressed my lips one last time and then...

I licked them.

The same fluttering feeling I felt that entire afternoon stayed with me for the rest of the night.

# Chapter 3

## Alex

A few days went by and then it was my 11th birthday. My parents threw an intimate birthday party for me at their restaurant, inviting close family and friends. I wasn't one for big extravagant things. I learned later in life that I really was just a small town girl. All the boys spoiled me with gifts. I had more boy clothes than I knew what to do with, much to my mama's dismay.

"Did you have a good birthday party, Half-Pint?" Dylan asked, putting his arm around my shoulder.

"I did."

"My gift was the best, wasn't it?" Jacob chimed in, tugging me away from Dylan.

I giggled. "I loved all of them."

"It's okay to be honest, Half-Pint, you can tell them that my gift was your favorite," Austin added, smiling and throwing the football up in the air, Lucas intercepting it.

We threw the football for the next hour and soon it was time for everyone to go home. It was Sunday night and we all had school the following morning.

Lucas' family was the last to leave, like always.

"Come on," he directed with a nod to follow him.

"You're leaving."

"My dad just opened up another beer, you know what that means."

I trailed behind him to the same spot we were at the other day with the nervousness bubbling up from my belly to my throat.

*Is he going to kiss me again?*

He turned. "Here," he said, handing me another wrapped present.

"I already opened your gift."

33

"Nah, my mom got that. This one is from me. I bought it with the money I made from mowing lawns this past summer."

"Oh." I slowly unwrapped the long rectangle box and slid the lid off. "Bo," I whispered out loud, surprised and looking back up at him.

He reached for the shark tooth necklace from the box and moved behind me. "I found it in Old Pa's antique store. To be honest, I don't even know why I went in there. I hate that store. Old Pa says it's legit. It's from a baby shark that got lost in the inlet a few years back. He saved the shark, but it left behind this tooth. He found it a few weeks ago in his nightstand, he completely forgot about it and decided to turn it into a necklace." He paused. "Maybe it was the same shark that bumped my board so I had to get it for you."

"Was it expensive?"

I could feel him smiling as he clasped the silver chain into place. It hung right in between my breastbone.

"Only you would ask that." He spun me, placing his fingers on the tooth. It appeared smaller in his grasp. "The chain is white gold." His knuckles brushed against my skin, making me feel warm all over.

*What is happening to me?*

It was my favorite gift. "I love it, thank you, Bo, I'll never take it off."

And I didn't.

Until one day…

I did.

# LUCAS

I spent all my money on that necklace and didn't think twice about it. I wanted her to have it. I wish I could tell you why. All I knew was the moment I saw it, I had to make it hers. I chucked it up to the fact that it could have been the same shark that hit my board, not realizing that maybe it was because that same day we shared our first kiss and I wanted her to remember it, always.

Carry it around with her.

A memory ingrained.

The symbolism behind it wasn't something I realized till I was older.

By that time, it was too late.

"I love you, Half-Pint, you're my best friend," was all I could say.

It was natural, normal. I wanted us to stay exactly that way. Losing her wasn't an option for me and I knew that at thirteen years old.

Shit I knew it even before then.

She smiled, big and wide. "I love you, too."

\*\*\*

The rest of the school year went flying by, and it was once again summer, our favorite time of the year. The island was packed with tourists and the high season had begun. There were only two months out of the year where Oak Island was crowded with random people from all over the world. Living in a small Southern beach town, everyone knew everybody, you couldn't walk anywhere without someone knowing your name. Town gossip ran rapid and everyone knew everyone's drama and business, nothing stayed behind closed doors. I never paid any attention to it.

None of us did.

"Come on, Lucas, just take her out for a burger. She's been fawning all over you since the beginning of the school year and that was almost a year ago. She's hot. Why you keep ignoring her?" Jacob asked as we pedaled from the beach to Alex's house.

"Because she's dated every guy in our grade, the girl's been ridden more than my damn bike."

"That's the point."

"Not for me."

"Lucas, don't you want to do something? I mean your hand must be gettin' tired," he laughed.

I glared at him.

"Whatever, man, it's your dick. I'm just trying to help you. That's what friends do for each other. You know I got to third base with Lesley and Dylan is almost to second with Riley. Austin is still young but shit, man, he's already tongue kissed a girl. What have you done, Lucas? Jack shit."

My mind went to Alex, it wasn't a tongue kiss, but it was still a kiss. I never told any of them what happened and neither did she. That should have been the first giveaway that it meant something, but how much can something mean when you're that damn young?

Surfing, the boys, and Alex, that was my life. That's all I understood. That's all I knew.

It was the first time we hid something from them, but it definitely wouldn't be the last. We never brought it up again either.

We didn't have to.

The truth hung around her neck.

"How do you know that?" I asked, breaking away from my thoughts.

"Are you for real? Unless you done something with Alex that we don't know about, then the only action you've seen is what you find in them nudie magazines. We all love Alex. You know that. But she's a kid. You're thirteen, not far from being fourteen. Man up!"

I sighed, annoyed with his stammer and the fact that he read my mind or maybe I was just paranoid. "I don't want to ask her out. I don't even like her. Why would I ask someone out if I don't like them?"

He glared over at me like I'd grown four heads. "Bro, you do realize that you just sounded like a pussy, right? Please tell me you know that?

I rolled my eyes.

"You ask a girl like her out for one reason and one reason only. Do I have to spell it out for ya, Lucas?"

"I get it."

"No I don't think you do."

"Shut your trap before I shut it for you," I argued.

He laughed. "Awe, why so sensitive? Are you hiding something?"

"No."

"What? Do you like Alex? Is that what this is about?"

"No," I adamantly repeated.

"Good. She's like our little sister. If you did, I might have to beat the living shit out of you. You know we all would. It's not like that with her, for any of us," he reminded me, adding to my confusion and insecurities of what Alex and I should be to one another.

"I know that."

"I'm glad. She's a kid, Lucas."

"We're all kids," I stated, trying to sway the conversation away Alex without being overly obvious.

"No shit. But an eleven-year-old *girl* because that's what she is, even though she would probably tackle me to the ground before admitting it," he chuckled at the thought and so did I. "To an almost fourteen year old *boy* is way different. She hasn't even grown into her body yet. Trust me, Alex is going to be fucking gorgeous. Which is all the more reason that we have to protect her. You want her datin' some guy like us? You know how we are when she's not around."

I nodded. "Why are you lecturing me on shit I already know? You're beating a dead horse. I'm fully aware. Relax."

"Then ask Stacey out."

I sighed, knowing I didn't have much of a leg to stand on. Everything he said was true. Alex was young and she was like our little sister. I blurred the lines with that kiss and I needed to make my way back over to the side with the rest of the boys.

It's where I belonged.

"Fine. I'll ask her out on a date just to shut you up."

"That's all I ask, brotha'."

The next day I asked Stacey out on a date.

This would be the first time that I walked away from Alex.

But definitely…

Not the last.

# Chapter 4

## LUCAS

"Whatcha' doin'?" Alex prodded, walking into my bedroom as I'm playing with my phone on my bed. It was an early birthday gift. She scooted next to me, moving my arm so that she could lay in the crevice of my chest.

"Nothin' much. What are you doing here? I thought you were going to town with your mom today?"

"We are," she snickered. "But she had to talk to your mom about something important and told me to come wait up here with you."

"Don't want to go shopping, huh?"

She pouted, glancing up at me. "Do I ever?"

"It might not be so bad, Half-Pint. It's not normal that you don't like to go shopping."

She sat up, facing me with her legs tucked under her tiny frame. "Do you?"

"Do I what?"

"Like to go shopping?"

"Hell no." I sat up against my wall.

"Well then. Why would I?"

"Because you're a girl."

She punched me in the chest.

"Ouch!" I rubbed where she hit me. "What was that for?"

"You know why," she giggled, seeing that her weak ass punch had an effect on me, dwindling sideways on my bed.

I shook my head. "You're so violent."

"I learned from you," she justified, pointing at me, sitting upright.

I laughed because it was true.

"You meeting up with the boys?"

"Nah, I'm meeting up with Stacey in a few hours."

"Stacey?" she asked, taken aback. "Who's Stacey?"

"The girl from the beach."

With widening eyes she sat up straighter, trying to appear much older than she actually was. "The big boobed girl?"

I grinned to keep from laughing. "Yeah."

"Why?"

"What do you mean?"

"Why are you meeting up with her?"

I shrugged. "I don't know, we're hanging out."

"Oh."

I raised an eyebrow. "Oh?"

She lowered her head to my comforter and started picking at the seams. She only did that when she was nervous. "Is this a date?" she muffled.

"I guess."

"Oh."

"Why you keep sayin' that?"

"No reason," she lied.

"What's wrong?"

"Nothin'."

"You know you can't lie to me, so why don't you just tell me what the sad voice and sappy face is for?"

She scowled at me. "I'm not lying."

I stood, folding my arms over my chest and cocking my head to the side. She knew I wouldn't let her leave my room if she didn't tell me the truth. I would get it out of her, one way or another.

"I thought you didn't like her. You said you didn't," she finally answered.

"I never said that," I stated, taking in her solemn demeanor.

"Oh."

"Will you stop speaking in code?"

"I'm not," she scoffed, moving her legs to hang over the edge of my bed.

"I told you she's just a girl and she is. That's all."

"Then why are you going on a date with her, if she's just a girl?"

"Because that's what boys do."

Her lips parted, displaying her bright red tongue. She must have been sucking on a cherry lollipop, our favorite.

I almost smiled. "It's not a big deal, Half-Pint," I confessed, rubbing the back of my neck.

She nodded, her eyes shifting to the door behind me.

"Well…" She leaped from my bed to stand in front of me, barely meeting my chest, and I was reminded how small she really was, how young she really was.

"Have fun on your date."

My eyebrows lowered. "Why you actin' like this?"

"I'm not acting like anything," she replied, shrugging, the attitude evident in her tone. "I'll see ya later." She stepped aside and walked toward my door.

"Alex," I called out, forcing in the breath I hadn't realized I held. "You'll always be my brown eyed girl."

## Alex

I stopped dead in my tracks.

"You'll always be my brown eyed girl," he confessed in a tone I'd never heard before.

My heart beat rapidly with each passing second, and the longer I stood there not saying anything the more I felt it.

"I know," I softly spoke, with my mouth dry and my heart heavy.

I didn't know whether to smile with delight over the fact that he would always be my best friend or to cry with devastation knowing that maybe he'd never be anything more.

Would there ever be an Alex and Lucas or were we doomed to be Bo and Half-Pint for the rest of our lives?

"Alex! You ready?" Mom yelled from the bottom of the stairs, breaking the simple words that held us together.

I didn't dare turn around to look at him. I pretty much ran down the stairs and into my mama's car. I spent the rest of the day in town with her.

"Honey, what about this one?" Mom prodded, placing the hanger in front of me.

I eyed it up and down. "It's a dress."

"Yes. It's a very nice dress."

Which actually wasn't that far off from the truth. It was light yellow with spaghetti straps, shorter than I was used to but not entirely hideous. The material was soft at least.

"Okay."

"Really? You're not going to fight me on this?"

"No."

"Are you sick?"

I smiled for the first time since I left Lucas' bedroom. "No."

"What do you want?" she quickly added, making me laugh.

"Nothin', it's a nice dress."

She skeptically looked me over for a few seconds and then nodded to go pay.

"Everything alright?" she asked on our way home.

I shrugged.

"What's going on with you?"

"Why do you think something's wrong?"

"Alex, you let me buy you a dress and I didn't have to bribe you."

I sighed. "Lucas is going on a date," I blurted, surprised by my own honesty.

"Ah."

I met her eyes. "What?"

"So that's what's upsetting you," she stated, looking back at the road.

"It's not upsetting me."

She narrowed her eyes at me.

"Not that much," I added, facing in front of me.

"Those boys are growing up, Alex. They're going to start dating. I mean Lucas will be fourteen soon."

"Yeah so what? I'll be twelve soon, too."

"Right. But it's different for boys than it is for girls."

"What's that supposed to mean?"

"It means that their interests may change."

"That's stupid," I scoffed, disappointed.

"Yeah but your interests will change soon, too."

I shook my head. "I don't think so."

"You'll see."

"Mom, we've been best friends since the day I was born. I've done everything with them. Are you saying that it won't be like that anymore?"

She contemplated what I said. "Not exactly. I have no doubt y'all will always be close. You don't have any siblings, Alex, and I can't tell you how grateful I am that I've never felt guilty about not giving you someone to play with. We didn't have to. You had them boys. All I'm sayin' is that things may start to change on how much time y'all will have for each other."

"Because of girls?"

"Yes, honey, and boys."

I grimaced. "I don't like boys."

She laughed. "You love them boys," she clarified.

"Yes but they're different. I'm talkin' about the boys at my school. I don't like any of them."

"Right. Do you like any of *your* boys? Lucas, maybe?"

I leaned into the headrest. "No."

"No?"

"I don't know. Lucas and I have always had a different relationship than I've had with the rest of them."

I caught her nodding from the corner of my eye. "I know."

"I don't want to lose any of them though, especially Lucas."

"You won't ever lose them. That much I do know. But with that being said, Alex, you need to expand your horizons. I don't want you to regret missing out on anything because you didn't know any better. Familiarity can be confused with something that it isn't. Do you understand?"

"Kind of."

She sighed. "You're young and Lucas is young. You've grown up together. It's normal to feel possessive of him, over all of them."

"I don't want things to change."

"I'm sorry, sweetie, but they will. That's just life, but it doesn't matter because as I said before I know that you will always have them in your life. That I can promise you."

I nodded, shutting my eyes and silently praying she was right.

Especially…

When it came to Lucas.

# LUCAS

"Hey, you listening?" Stacey asked.

"Mmm hmm," I lied. I couldn't stop thinking about Alex. *Why couldn't I stop thinking about Alex?*

"I had a really good time tonight. You think we could do it again?"

"Sure," I simply stated.

We were sitting on the beach, watching the waves hit the shore.

She smiled, leaning into me. "Good. I really like you, Lucas."

I nodded because I didn't know what else to say. She slightly turned, nuzzling my neck with her nose. I felt my dick stir and before I knew it, I turned my mouth to meet hers and we were kissing. It wasn't the same kiss I had with Alex. It was completely different. I didn't really know what to do, but I had seen enough movies to know the logistics of moving my lips with hers. My mind couldn't catch up with the movements of our mouths and the way my dick throbbed with how she felt up against me.

The crazy thing about it was that I didn't like her, I had no feelings for her whatsoever, but I couldn't stop kissing her. My body betraying me, and the more we kissed, the more I wanted.

It was uncontrollable.

The urge.

I loved it and I hated it.

My tongue slid into her mouth, she tasted of mint ice cream. I detested that ice cream. She glided her tongue into my eager mouth and moaned, making my dick twitch from the sound. I desperately wanted relief as she clutched me closer, leaning back onto the sand, pressing my body on top of hers. My insistent hands started exploring and she began rubbing her body underneath mine, making me shudder from the sway of hers. Our bodies took over and it felt incredible, there were no words for the sensations she awakened. For the first time, I understood what Dylan and Jacob were talking about.

How easily it was to get lost in someone with the desire and want my body so hastily craved.

Thank God we were at a secluded part of the beach.

"Damn, boy, get up in there all good like and shit."

My body jolted off of hers, standing. "What the hell, Jacob?" I spun ready to give him hell when I came face to face with Jacob, Dylan, Austin, *and* Alex.

Her head lowered and her shoulders slumped, and I swear my heart stopped beating, swallowing the lump that had suddenly formed in my throat.

"Relax," Dylan interjected, bringing my pissed off glare back to him. "We're just passing through, heading up to Half-Pints restaurant for dinner. By all means, keep goin'." He reached for Alex's hand, and she easily took it, her eyes remaining on the sand, not looking at anyone, especially me. He nodded toward Stacey who was still sitting, unfazed by getting caught.

"Bye, Darlin'." They walked off.

"Where were we?" Stacey purred from the sand.

My stare was frozen on Alex. My mind screamed to run after her.

To do something…

Anything.

It took everything inside me not to run to her, to explain. I convinced myself that I was overreacting. I didn't owe her an explanation.

*Then why did I feel like I did?*

She still hadn't looked up, trailing close behind Dylan, her small hand in his. She appeared tinier among the boys, sticking out like a sore thumb.

Our Half-Pint.

*My* brown eyed girl. Sad.

My gaze shifted to Stacey not being able to look at Alex any longer. It hurt too much. "Come on." I extended my hand out in front of her. "I'll walk you home." I couldn't get her home fast enough.

"Okay." She smiled, not picking up on my sudden change of mood or composure in the least. I left her on her doorstep and I could tell she wanted me to kiss her again, but I didn't. I couldn't.

By the time I made it to the restaurant it was near eight. The boys were playing pool in the back with no sign of Alex.

"Hey," Austin greeted.

"Where's Half-Pint?" I immediately asked him, trying to keep my emotions in check.

"She said she wasn't feeling good and went home."

"Oh. How long ago?"

"Not too long after we got here. Her mom took her home, her dad's still around here somewhere."

I nodded. "Who's winning?" I tried to seem nonchalant. The boys didn't need to know the turmoil I felt.

"The champion," Jacob announced, looking smug as shit. "We're almost done, play me next."

I shook my head. "Nah, I gotta head home."

"How was Stacey? From the looks of it, you two seemed cozy," Dylan chimed in, grinning like a fool.

"I'll see you guys later." I ignored him and left.

I pedaled my bike as fast as I could to Alex's house, knocking on her door.

Her mom answered. "Hey, sweetie."

"Hey, is Half-Pint around?"

She frowned. "Oh I'm sorry, Lucas, she isn't feeling well. She went to bed as soon as we got home a little bit ago. I'll let her know you stopped by. Your mama is inside though with Lily. Do you want to come in?"

I shook my head no. "Can you let her know as soon as she wakes up? I really need to talk to her. It's important. Can you tell her to call me?"

"Will do." She stepped back and closed the door.

I took a shower and went straight to bed, trying to block out the look on Alex's face and failing miserably in doing so.

It wouldn't be the last time I hurt her.

This was just the beginning…

# Chapter 5

## LUCAS

I usually hated Sunday mornings. Everyone dressed in their Sunday best to attend service at the only church we had in town. I dressed in my usual black slacks and gray button down with a tie firmly knotted around my neck. I was already hot and we hadn't even left the house yet. Thank God I didn't have to wear a suit jacket. It was way too hot outside. Alex always called me to make sure that I was awake so I didn't have to face my mom's wrath about not getting up on time and not taking service seriously.

She didn't call that morning.

I contemplated whether to call her or not but decided against it since I would be seeing her soon anyway. The car ride was inexplicably slow and I sat next to my baby sister Lily, she was eight and for the most part never really annoyed me. I thought about Alex the entire way to service.

Her face.

Her lips.

Her eyes.

"Lucas, you listenin'?" Lily asked, taking me away from my thoughts.

"Hmm?"

"I said, are you alright?"

"Yeah I'm fine."

"You sure? You're actin' funny."

"I'm good."

"Okie, I thought maybe you were coming down with the same thing Alex got."

That made me turn to look at her. "What?"

"Half-Pint." She rolled her eyes, thinking that's the reason I was confused.

"Yeah, I know. What are you talkin' about?"

"She looked like you do last night. I thought maybe—"

"You saw her last night?" I interrupted.

"Yep. Mama and me were at the restaurant when her and the boys showed up. She looked really down like she got sick or something. Her mama took her home and we went with them. She usually at least tries to play with me, but this time she didn't say a word, she just went right to her room and went to sleep. Mama and Mrs. Collins were making tea and she asked me to take her up some medicine and water." She hesitated for a few seconds distracted by the kids running out of their cars to service.

"Lily."

"Oh." She shook her head. "Her face was all red and her eyes were watery. She said she didn't feel good, but it looked like she was crying to me. Just sayin'."

The wind was knocked out of me and I was finding it hard to breathe and gather my feelings on what Lily had innocently shared. I caught my mom's eyes from the rearview mirror, and for a moment I thought she knew. The knowing look on her face made me tear my gaze from hers, not wanting to answer any questions that were imminent in her stare. I stepped out of the car first and they all followed, slowly treading behind them, looking around for Alex. She usually waited for me at the front entrance so we could walk in together and sit with the boys in the back.

She wasn't waiting for me, and it only added to my anxiety and apprehension of what the hell happened.

I immediately found her when I walked in, except she wasn't sitting with the boys. She sat with her parents, beside her mom, but that's not what shocked me. What stunned me was that she wore a light yellow dress and her hair was down. I don't think I ever saw her hair down unless we were in the water, and even then she quickly piled it on top of her head with a hair tie. The long shiny dark waves flowed swiftly down her back and I found myself wanting to run my fingers through it to feel if it was as soft as it appeared to be.

*How had I just realized her hair was so long?*

Once I found my footing I made my way to the boys who were all staring as intently at Alex as I was. They all looked my way and I shrugged, answering their confused stares that I didn't know what was up either. Service ended and we all gathered outside, waiting for her family. She was the last to walk out behind them and I exhaled a breath I didn't realize I held until I saw her.

She looked...

She looked like a *girl*.

Not just any girl, a beautiful girl.

"Half-Pint—"

"Alex," she corrected me.

"Excuse me?" I countered.

She smiled at all of us, picking up our jaws from the floor.

"My name's Alex," she simply stated, smiling.

"Since when?" I asked, not knowing the girl in front of me. She even sounded different.

"Since birth," she sassed, looking at only me.

Dylan cleared his throat, bringing her stare back to all of them. "You look nice, Alex."

I narrowed my eyes at him. *Why was I the only one pissed off about this?*

"Thank you," she replied, blushing.

The rest of the boys followed suit, acting as if our lives hadn't just changed drastically. They fawned over her like they would any new girl that would come around us. Except this wasn't a new girl, this was our Half-Pint. I didn't care what she wore or who she pretended to be. I knew who she was on the inside and on the inside she was *mine*. The shark tooth necklace that still hung around her neck proved my point. It helped ease my desire to drag her away and call her out on this bullshit.

I backed away from them not wanting to make a scene, but mostly I backed away from her. The more I looked at her the worse I felt. It was a continuous, unforgiving feeling in the pit of my stomach. I had done something wrong, and it caught up with me. I'd never felt like that before, and all it would take was for her to look at me for one second, for one damn second and she would see it.

We all went back to her restaurant, exactly the way we had every Sunday. The Collins' provided a huge Sunday spread, being their busiest day of the week, bringing in people from South Port, the next town over. Everyone told Alex she looked beautiful, grown-ups, old people, shit even boys from our school.

I hated it.

I hated the attention she was getting. I hated the stares that were suggestive and not very subtle. I hated the dress she wore and I hated that she smelled so damn good that all I wanted to do was wrap my arms around her and never let her go.

*How could I feel that way? We were so young.*

But mostly I hated the fact that she ignored me. She wouldn't meet my questioning eyes and I was sincerely about to lose my shit. My temper was looming, and I was ready to drag her out onto the beach and yell at her.

*Why did I want to yell at her?*

I didn't eat a bite of my food and when she asked for a glass of water with lemon instead of cherry coke that we always drank I seriously almost yelled at her from across the table.

*Was she provoking me?*

"Lucas," Jacob called out from beside me. "Come with me outside."

I stood, still glaring over at her, but everyone seemed to have her attention but me.

"What the hell is your problem?" he questioned, as soon as we were away from prying ears.

"Nothin', what's your problem?" I argued, needing to take my anger out on someone.

He put his hands out in front of him in a surrendering gesture. "I'm not the bad guy here. But it would take a fool not to realize that you're pissed off about Alex."

"Her name's Half-Pint."

He narrowed his eyes at me, stepping closer. "Listen to me because I will only say this once. She's growing up, Lucas. Did I think it would happen this quickly? No. I thought we would at least have one more year. But we're all changing too Lucas, and she's always wanted to be one of us. She doesn't want to get left behind. Does it suck? Yeah, it fucking does. I'm not gonna lie to ya, but this is her way of doing that. Come on give her a break. She looks great. I'm happy for her, we all are. Now lock up your shit and be happy for her, too."

"Don't tell me what the fuck to do, Jacob," I gritted out.

He jerked back. "You're actin' like you're jealous, Lucas."

"I'm not," I simply stated.

Complicate Me

"Good," he merely replied back.

We stood there squaring off, neither one of us backing down. If Jacob thought he could pull that big brother shit on me, he was dead wrong and had another thing coming. It may work with Alex but not with me. He didn't need to be telling me what to do when he had no idea what the hell occurred in the first place. This wouldn't be the first time that Jacob pulled this bullshit on me. I would get used to it throughout the years, the older we got, the worse it became. Dylan and Austin wouldn't be that far behind either, all jumping in on something that was none of their fucking business to begin with.

She didn't need protection.

Especially not from me.

"What's going on?" Alex questioned, drawing us away from our intense exchange and making us both turn to face her.

# Alex

I went home that night after seeing Lucas with Stacey and looked at myself in the mirror, and for the first time in my life I didn't like what I saw.

I didn't look like any of those girls that hung around the boys, not even close. I wasn't girly like them. I didn't move like them, I didn't even talk like them. I was on the other end of the spectrum, the one that put me in the "Little Sister" box. After I picked apart everything I wasn't in comparison to what they were, what they offered, I lay down in my bed and tried not to think about Lucas and that girl.

The way he touched her.

The way they moved in sync with one another.

The way he kissed her.

The sounds she made echoed in my head. It vibrated so damn loud that all I wanted to do was scream to drown out the noises. I couldn't get it to stop and it didn't want to. It illustrated what Lucas made her feel, the way he touched her with such determination and abandonment made me sick to my stomach. It appeared as if they were made for one another, both of them touching parts of their bodies that made me blush just thinking about it.

*Why did I have to be such a little girl?*

*Why did I have to be so young?*

I didn't realize I was crying until I felt the tears falling down the sides of my face. He hadn't done one of those things with me.

Not one.

I thought our kiss meant something. I didn't understand how to play those games, how to say one thing and act another. Maybe that's what boys did? Acted one way with you in private and then another one out in public.

*That's not Lucas, is it?*

The confusion and unanswered questions pegged me, engulfing me like the waves of the ocean, taking me under and not allowing me to breathe until the traitorous waves were ready to let me go. The exact same ones Lucas rode with such purpose and resolve. The irony was not lost on me. I lay in bed with nothing but my thoughts, they were coming one right after the other, it was a non-ending assault of torturous questions and what ifs and I couldn't get a break in between. One would form before the other even fully surfaced.

I drowned in them.

If things couldn't get any worse my lower abdomen cramped, a new, unfamiliar pain enveloped my core. I went to the bathroom and right there before my eyes was the evidence of my very first period.

"Oh no…" I breathed out. "Mama! Mama!" I screamed.

She ran into my bathroom and behind her was Lucas's mama.

"Oh my God, honey, what's the matter?"

And then I broke down. I was emotionally spent, and there were no hiding the fervent feelings that were boiling all around me waiting to erupt like a volcano. I started bawling. The tears were uncontrollable and it was all too much to bear. I cried for everything that happened, and for everything I didn't understand. I cried for the feeling of deceit, and the loss of an emotion, that I desperately wanted to hold onto. The memory that hung around my neck stung, it burned badly, leaving behind a trail of sadness, despair, and betrayal.

It was the first time Lucas had ever hurt me, and I hated that more than anything else. All the other stuff I could endure, but knowing that he caused me pain.

The boy I grew up with.

The boy I loved.

The boy that promised me he would never hurt me.

My best friend. My boy. My Bo.

Lucas…

"It's okay, Alex, calm down," Mama coaxed. She helped me finish in the bathroom and then we walked into my room.

Mrs. Ryder sat on my bed. "Congratulations. Welcome to womanhood," she celebrated.

I leaned into my mom, needing the support and comfort.

"Is this about my boy, Alex?"

I looked up at my mom and she nodded in reassurance. I lowered my head, shrugging.

She sighed. "You know your mama and I have actually been talking about this for a very long time."

I immediately looked up at her.

"Yes. That's right." She nodded. "This isn't much of a shock to us. My boy has been smitten with you since the moment you were born. I remember when your mama was pregnant, he would go up to her belly and say that it was his baby in there." They laughed, no one had ever told me that before.

"He loved you before you were even born, Alex. He just knew you were going to be a girl. Every time we corrected him he would vigorously shake his head saying girl. He's growing up, honey, you both are. I know it may hurt now, and you may not understand what is happening, but it's part of life. You both need to try new things, make new friends, go places, be teenagers. Let other people in besides those good ol' boys of yours. You've been attached to those boys since the day you were born, just like they are to you. Life is too short for you to ever question that something better could have come along. Do you understand?"

I sadly smiled, wiping away my tears. "You don't want Lucas and I together?"

"No, honey, I don't want either of you to settle down until you know what else life has to offer, and if one day you find your way back to each other then you know. You know it's for sure. There will be no doubts and no regrets."

I lowered my head. "Yeah," was all I could say.

"Now," Mama interjected, picking up my chin. "Enough of this crying, Alex, I think today is a great day." She clapped her hands. "You want to know why?"

"Why?" I chuckled.

"Let's celebrate! Because you're a officially a young woman and I think that maybe you should consider—"

"Being a girl," I interrupted.

They beamed and we spent the next hour giving me a makeover.

I never imagined I would get the reaction that I got from the boys. They all seemed pleased and satisfied, almost as if they'd been expecting it to happen.

Except Lucas.

I ignored him, mostly because I didn't know what to say or what to make of his overbearing demeanor toward me. It burned a hole in my side and I wasn't going to let him affect me when I felt so pretty. This was all new to me, especially that reaction. I watched Lucas and Jacob from afar, and I could see both of their pissed off faces from where I sat at the table.

"What's going on out there?" I asked Dylan.

He shrugged. "Guy stuff."

I scooted my seat out.

"Half-Pint, don't get involved."

I walked toward them before the last word left his mouth.

I felt their hostility as soon as my sandals hit the sand. "What's going on?"

They both spun, facing me.

"Nothin'," Jacob announced, his attitude calming.

"It doesn't look like nothin'." I paused, taking in Lucas's heated composure but not toward Jacob, toward me. "What?"

The glares in his eyes were intimidating to say the least, and all it did was add to the confusion that had been brewing between us. Except this time Jacob witnessed it. At least I thought he did. I could feel his pissed off stance and he wasn't even touching me. Everything was directed at me. The eye of the storm was right in front of me, and his stare held mine until he couldn't anymore and then he receded, walking away from me for the first time. Which did nothing but enrich the hurt in my heart.

"Stay away from him till he calms down, Half-Pint."

I glanced at Jacob. "What's wrong with him?"

"Don't worry about it." He grabbed my chin, locking my gaze with his. "You look really pretty."

I smiled. "Thanks. I feel, I don't know, different I guess. I'm still one of you. You know that right?"

He smiled back at me. It comforted me in a moment of pure chaos. Lucas had taken his hurricane with him, but this time Jacob held me down and I wasn't dragged along with him. It wouldn't be that way always, and somewhere along the way I learned to appreciate it when I could.

"Of course. Except now you'll be much nicer to look at."

I punched him in the chest.

Laughing he said, "Ah! There she is, finally making an appearance under all that hair." He put his arm around my shoulder. "Come on, let's go finish eating."

I spent the rest of the day with the boys, minus Lucas. No one talked about the fact that he wasn't around. Dylan walked me home and before I opened the door, I felt him. The wind picked up, his presence was all around me. I didn't have to turn around to know that he waited for me, and he had been waiting for me for a long time.

That night would lead to many more firsts that only added to our complicated love.

# Chapter 6

## LUCAS

She descended down the stairs. "Hi," she shyly whispered when she stepped onto the last step.

I reached out my hand for her. "I want to show you something."

She placed her hand in mine, and I helped her onto the handlebars of my bike. She tucked her dress in between her thighs and nodded when she was ready. We rode a few miles from her house, heading in the opposite direction we usually traveled. I parked my bike near the back of the abandoned house, making sure no one would see it.

"Where are we, Bo?" Even though she wore a dress, she still jumped off the front of my bike, making me grin.

"Come on."

I led her up the wooden stairs, having to shove the patio door a little to get it to open, it made a scraping sound on the floor, the hinges old and rusted. I stood by the door wanting to take in her surprised expression. She slowly treaded all around the room, her eyes fluttering every which way. Alex loved the different architecture when it came to the homes that were right on the water. There was nothing else like it in Oak Island, we were known for our beachfront properties. I knew she would love the open floor plan, the bay windows toward the water, the tray ceilings, and the open decks throughout the entire house. Anywhere you stood in the three-story house you could see the water.

Her face really lit up when she saw the fireplace, they were a rare find around here.

"Wow. Whose house is this?" she asked, her voice echoing on the vaulted ceilings.

"No ones."

She glanced over at me, baffled. "No ones? The house is almost done. Why would someone leave it like this?"

"My dad said something about it being a new construction property and they ran out of money so they abandoned it."

"Oh." I could see her mind spinning, and I knew it had nothing to do with the house.

"You look beautiful," I stated, taking her away from her thoughts, hoping that it would work. I didn't want to have it out with her, not here. I wanted this to be our safe place, where we were away from the world and everything that went along with it.

"I know I didn't say it earlier, but that doesn't mean it's not true."

She lowered her head, all of a sudden shy. "Thanks, Bo."

"I'm really sorry, Half-Pint."

She immediately raised her staggered eyes to me. "What are you apologizing for?"

"What am I not apologizing for?" It came out as a question but it wasn't.

"Do you like her?"

"No," I replied, shaking my head, silently hoping she would believe me.

"You don't have to lie to me. You're allowed to like girls, Bo. I mean she's pretty and stuff."

"You're pretty."

I could tell I caught her off guard. We didn't have this type of friendship, where I would call her pretty, and apologize for things I may have done that could have caused her pain. She was one of the boys, once we argued it was done and over with. The dynamic of our friendship geared into new territory that we were both unfamiliar with, and as soon as I saw her wearing that dress, I knew it. After spending the day by myself, and having to be alone with nothing but my thoughts, I realized that's what bothered me the most about seeing her look so different.

We were all growing up and that included Alex, which was the hardest pill to swallow.

For a while we just stood there, neither one of us talking, trying to appreciate the silence when we could. The voices in our minds sedated, perhaps comforted by one another's presence.

She would tell me later in life that nothing calmed her more than my arms around her, and if I had known that then, I would have held her every time she looked at me with sadness or disappointment. And maybe it could have helped heal the wounds that I cut along the way.

The broken heart I shattered piece by piece, bit by bit, with nothing but my actions and at times my words.

When she finally walked out onto the deck that overlooked the water, I followed close behind, taking the comfortable silence with us. There were so many things I wanted to say but couldn't, it would be a never-ending pattern between us. What could either of us say that would even make sense? We were both still so young, we barely understood what the hell flourished between us. There was no one we could discuss it with but each other, and that was easier said than done.

"Why were you so upset today, Bo?" Her stare remained toward the waves of the ocean, making it easier for her to open up to me.

I opened my mouth to say something, anything, but I quickly shut it. The words just not forming fast enough for me to answer.

"It's hard to realize that things are changing, huh?" she stated as a question, appearing much older than she actually was.

"Yeah," I weakly muttered.

"I never thought..." She shook her head, gathering her thoughts. "I don't know what I thought, all I know is that I don't want to lose you, Bo, I don't want to lose any of you." Her eyes locked with mine. "Especially you," she added in a softer tone.

"Me too," I whispered, tucking a piece of her hair behind her ear. "One day—"

"I know," she interrupted. At the time I didn't think she did, but that's another thing I grasped later. Alex was aware of it all. It was me who wasn't.

"I asked her out on a date because Jacob, I mean the boys, it's just..." I mumbled, the words still not forming the way I wanted them to.

She smiled, breaking the intensity of our stares. "My dress is really soft. I don't think I've ever felt material this soft before. I like it. I mean I don't fill the dress out like those girls—"

"You're perfect."

Her eyes lowered, but her face didn't. "I'm still one of the boys, Bo. I don't want you worrying yourself over nothing. I haven't changed. I promise."

"It doesn't feel that way to me."

Peering back up at me with the most sincere, warm, welcoming eyes. "I'll always be your brown eyed girl, Bo."

She put her arms around me, her tiny frame hugging mine. She fit perfectly, melting against my chest. Our hearts placed beside each other, and for the first time that day everything felt right.

"I know," I whispered into the side of her face, kissing her cheek. Breathing in the scent of her vanilla shampoo and sunscreen, they quickly became my new favorite smell. "They're just girls, Half-Pint."

Having her in my arms made it easy for me to find the words to express the truth.

It made no sense to me, nothing did.
*When did things get so confusing?*

# Alex

I wanted to cry…
*Why did I want to cry? I hated crying.*
I bit my lip to keep from crying.
*When did I turn into this girl?*
*The one who wears dresses and cries, and has all these emotions that are hard to comprehend and follow.*

I pulled away first, needing to secure the bit of control I still had over myself. I didn't want to cry in front of him, I would always do it by myself. The hold he had on me when he was around, and the lock that was in place when he wasn't, was enough to have me weak in the knees and heavy in the heart.

I reassuringly smiled, gazing all around the back of the house. "I really love this house," I said, trying to lessen the intensity boiling between us.

His stare followed mine. "I'm glad you like it because my dad says it's probably going to be one of those properties that just gets looked over and sit here empty for years."

"That's a shame."

"I don't think so. I thought it could be ours."

I raised an eyebrow. "Ours?"

"Yeah, I mean maybe this could be our place. You know, where we get away from everyone."

"What about the boys?" I asked, uncertain.

"What about them?" he replied, with certainty. "Ours, Half-Pint. As in yours and mine."

"Oh,"

"Oh?"

I chuckled, leaning my back against the railing. "Umm yeah. I really like that idea."

He was all grins and mischievous eyes. "Good because I'm full of them."

And just like that...

We were Bo and Half-Pint again, spending the rest of the evening the way we always had, pretending that nothing changed, and knowing in our hearts.

That it had.

***

School was back in session and tomorrow was my first day of middle school. Words couldn't express how nervous I felt about finally being back together with my boys. All of us under the same roof, although they were in eighth grade and Austin was in seventh. We spent the rest of the summer together and for the most part things remained somewhat the same. Except there were girls around, many more than there had been in the past. Even though the boys didn't take any of them seriously, I knew there would come a day where they would, and it got closer with each passing week.

I became a really good liar.

I smiled when I was supposed to.

I laughed when I needed to.

And I played nice with all the girls because I had to.

Even with the girls that hung around Lucas.

It was easy to hide my feelings. To hide the way I felt inside. To hide my emotions from the truth I thought would be spilling out of me, but no one ever called me out on it.

Including Lucas.

So I just listened.

And watched

And kept pretending…

Lucas and I spent a lot of time alone in *our* abandoned house. It was easy to get lost in each other when there was no one else around. Not having to worry about those who didn't understand our closeness, our connection.

He turned fourteen, and I swear he grew overnight. He started to look like a man. Okay, maybe not a man but definitely not like the boy he used to be. His appearance might have changed on the outside, but on the inside, he was still my Bo.

He was still mine.

"Are you ready for school tomorrow?" Dylan asked, sitting beside me on the beach in front of my parents' restaurant.

"I guess as ready as I'll ever be."

His shoulder bumped mine, teasingly. "Have you decided what you're wearing?"

"Just because I dress like a girl doesn't mean I act like one."

"No shit," he laughed. "You're going to be twelve in a few weeks. Our Half-Pint's almost a teenager."

I sighed, pushing my feet into the sand.

"What's with the sighing?"

"I don't know."

"Yes, you do."

I shook my head, bringing my knees up and hugging them to my body. It was then that he followed my stare, which was intently placed on Lucas and Stacey. They were walking next to each other on the shoreline and every so often she would casually touch his chest, flirting.

"She's just a girl, Half-Pint," he stated like he knew I needed to hear it. "Can I ask you something?"

"Of course. You can ask me anything."

"Do you like Lucas?"

My mouth dropped and immediately looked at him, shocked. "What?"

He held my surprised gaze, not holding back the sincerity in his eyes. "Do. You. Like. Lucas?"

"Of course not."

"You sure about that? We don't lie to each other, right?"

I felt like this was a test. "No, I don't like him. I love him. I love all of you," I reaffirmed. "It's just weird to see him with a girl, that's all. It's weird to see all of you with girls."

He narrowed his eyes at me, almost as if he could see through me, and was able to read the truth that I so desperately tried to hide. I turned my face, looking at the sand instead.

"Good," he simply stated.

"What's that supposed to mean? I'm not good enough for Lucas or something?"

"More like the other way around."

I bit my lip to keep from looking at him and asking any more questions.

"You're our little sister, Half-Pint, no one will ever be good enough for you. I don't mean anything against Lucas, but Stacey is more his speed."

"Yeah…"

"When you're older you'll understand what I mean by that."

"I understand now," I whispered to myself.

"Do you?"

I glanced at him. "Sex, right?"

His eyes widened.

"I'm not *that* young," I reminded.

I swear the boys thought I was still six years old in pigtails with training wheels on my bike, which I only allowed on there for a few days. I was adamant that I would ride my bike like they did theirs and I skinned my knees more times than I could count, so they started carrying Band-Aids in their pockets for me. I rubbed the scar on my right knee. It was the same scar that Lucas bandaged up for the first time.

Exactly like my love for him…

It never went away.

61

"Obviously," Dylan replied, pulling me away from my memories. "My, my, little Half-Pint, I think maybe we've underestimated you."

"Seriously? I found your Playboys when I was ten. Did you not think I went home and asked my mama about it? I mean I didn't rat you guys out or anything, but I needed to know, and I knew you guys wouldn't have told me."

"Damn straight."

I laughed at his bluntness. "It's not a big deal. I get it."

"Do you now?" he baited.

"I do."

"Just so we're clear when it comes time for you to—"

"Dylan!" I shouted.

He didn't falter. "We will beat the living shit out of him. That — I can promise you, so you may want to think about *that* for his sake at least."

"Oh my God, that's such a double standard."

"Call it how you see it. I don't give a shit."

"You know this whole big brother stuff is gettin' kinda' old." I pointed in between us. "I can take care of myself. You're getting as bad as Jacob. I'm just going to scuff it up to testosterone."

He cocked his head to the side. "What do you know about testosterone?"

I cocked my head back. "What do you know about periods?"

He laughed big and wide and clapped his hands. "God, I love you."

I rolled my eyes. "Yeah… yeah…"

"I meant what I said before, though."

I tore my eyes from him and back to Lucas. "I know."

And I did.

# Chapter 7

## LUCAS

"You ready?" I asked.

"Yeah. I just need to go to my locker. I forgot my Algebra book. She gave us a ton of homework to do over Christmas break," Alex replied.

"I'll walk you."

"You don't have to. I'll meet you guys by the bike rack."

I nodded, walking away. "Okay, hurry."

Four months went by and it was officially Christmas break. We had two weeks of no school and no drama. Having Alex in the same school as us proved to be eventful, not only was she developing in all sorts of places, she was also coming into her own. She started wearing makeup, and I despised it. The first time she walked out of her house wearing lipstick, I was literally off my bike and over to her in three strides, wiping the peachy color right from her lips.

The boys hollered, "Hell yeah," as they witnessed me doing it, and she didn't speak to me for the rest of the day. Saying some shit about me embarrassing her and not letting her grow up. I didn't pay her any mind because, for one, she could never stay mad at me, and for two, I wouldn't allow her to stay mad at me. We pretty much beat the boys off with a stick. They knew Alex was off limits before she even walked through the doors on the first day of school, but that didn't stop some of the fuckers from trying to get her attention.

"Hey, baby," Stacey greeted, coming up beside me and nuzzling her arm around mine.

"Hey."

"I thought this day would never end. Finally! Christmas break."

Stacey and I weren't serious, and we weren't exclusive either. I guess you could say we were dating. She tried to make me jealous with different guys an infinite amount of times, and I always blew her off each and every stint. She could do whatever she wanted, and I told her that often. All it did was confirm what the boys and I already knew about her, and as shitty as it sounded, it worked for me.

"What do you want to do over break?"

I shrugged. "I haven't really given it much thought."

"Oh, well then maybe I should think about it for us."

"Or let's just play it by ear."

"Okay…" she muttered, holding me closer.

"Where's Half-Pint?" Jacob asked as we walked up to the bike rack.

"She had to get her Algebra book from her locker. She said she would meet us out here."

"She's going to be a while," Stacey smugly informed, baiting me.

"What's that supposed to mean?" I questioned, eyeing her.

"Oh, well, I saw Gavin cornering her—"

"Cornering her?" Dylan interrupted, stepping off his bike.

"Jesus calm down, guys, they're just talking. Leave her alone."

Austin raised an eyebrow, rounding the bikes. "I'll go get her."

"No one needs to come get me," Alex chimed in, strolling up to us. "He was just asking me for the assignments that needed to be completed durin' break. No need to come and scare him. Trust me, boys know I'm not to be messed with, y'all have laid down the law." She rolled her eyes.

"What's your problem?" I asked.

"What's yours?" she argued, sitting on her bike.

I couldn't tell if she was pissed because of the way we protected her or because Stacey was still wrapped around my arm. I assumed it was a little bit of both. Stacey had a way of making herself seem more important to me than she truly was, and it always happened to be when Alex was around.

"I'll see you later, baby." She tried to kiss me on the mouth, but I turned my face at the last second, and she kissed my cheek instead.

"Half-Pint," I coaxed, getting on my bike, trying to get her to look at me.

"What? I'm here. Let's go."

She was the first to take off and I pedaled up beside her while the boys rode way in front, even after all these years she still couldn't pedal as fast as us.

"Are you going to talk to me?"

She glanced at me, annoyed. "Why wouldn't I talk to you?"

"I know you better than that. Give me some credit."

"Fine," she scoffed. "I think it's ridiculous that you boys guard me like rabid dogs, I mean you pretty much pee on me to keep boys away and it's not fair."

I laughed. I couldn't help it, she couldn't say things like that and not expect me to laugh.

She glared at me.

"What? Oh come on I'm sorry, I didn't mean to laugh.

"Yes, you did."

"Maybe. A little bit. Like half a cup."

She grinned, staring back in front of her to avoid smiling at me. I told you she couldn't stay mad at us, especially me.

"It's still not fair," she repeated, the attitude in her tone calming.

"I never said life was fair."

"What if I did that to you? Huh? What if I made sure girls wouldn't talk to you? What if I told Stacey to go fly a kite or something?"

"Fly a kite? That's the best you got?" I teased, knowing that she didn't cuss. I don't think I had ever heard a cuss word come out of her mouth before.

"Bo, you know what I mean. You wouldn't have it. You would put a stop to it immediately. You all would. It's not fair that the rules are different for me."

"You're a girl," I simply stated.

If she weren't riding her bike, she probably would have tackled me to the ground because I called her one. Even though she dressed like one, it still didn't give us the right to say it to her. The heated scowl she shot in my direction was enough for me to know that she was past her breaking point of not being taken seriously.

But again I didn't give a shit.

"I don't know what you want me to say, Half-Pint."

"Say that you'll let me grow up."

"We do."

She frowned.

"Sort of," I mumbled, my eyes shifting every which way.

She sighed. "I'm never going to experience anything because of you boys."

"Excuse me? What are you bickerin' about over there?" I trailed closer to her, if I wanted to I could reach out and pull her hair from her face. She always wore it down now, she never put it up and I'd be lying if I said I didn't love it.

"Never mind." She pedaled faster, trying to get away from me.

At least that much I knew.

We caught up with the boys and I couldn't stop thinking about what Alex implied. She was making new friends outside of us, girls, never boys, and I wondered if that had something to do with it. I realized girls talked about that kind of stuff. Maybe they had said something to Alex about *experiencing* things. I mean sixth grade was when most of our friends started kissing, I was the only pussy that waited until seventh.

Though I had already kissed her.

*But not that kind of kiss... Was that what she wanted?*

There was no way in hell that she was going to kiss another boy, especially that sort of kiss.

*What do I do?*

"Lucas!" Alex yelled.

"Hmm," I peered up at her from the table at her parents' restaurant. We were eating lunch. We usually ended up here after school to eat before heading home to do our homework. We ate at school, but that didn't stop us from being constantly hungry. It was Christmas break and we didn't have anything but time.

"Where did you go?" she asked.

"What?"

"Just now. You seemed lost in thought or something."

Everyone looked at me so I smiled. "I'm good."

We finished lunch and the boys wanted to surf, we left our boards in the office at the restaurant. It made it easier for us to hit the waves whenever we wanted, versus having to go all the way home to get them. Alex said it was too cold outside to sit on the sand and watch us like she usually did and decided to go home to start on her homework instead. Saying she didn't want to worry about it for the rest of the break.

"I'll ride back with you," I said, nodding to her. "I'll be back once I get her home."

The guys nodded, understanding, and headed toward the water.

"You don't have to do that," she informed, taking my stare from them to her.

"I want to."

She rolled her eyes. "I'm not a baby. I can make it home by myself. I can take care of myself."

"What's with the attitude?"

"You just don't get it." She shook her head, walking away from me.

It was the second time that day that she tried to get away from me and it only pissed me off. Her moods were changing faster than her damn dresses.

I couldn't keep up anymore.

I ran, kicking up sand with my sandals to catch up to her, tugging her by the arm to stop and face me. "What's your problem?"

"You! You're my problem," she shouted near my face.

"What the fuck did I do? I'm just taking you home."

And then she pushed me, like full on shoved me and I barely wavered, which only infuriated, and then she pushed me again. My eyes widened, surprised and partly amused with her feisty spirit that always did things to me.

I grinned and tackled her to the sand, laying right on top of her and holding her in place. "Do you need a cuddle? Is that what this is about? Do you need a hug? I give really good cuddles and hugs," I teased in a high-pitched voice, holding her tighter.

"Oh my God, Bo! This is cheating," she laughed, unable to resist my charm.

"See all you needed was some attention," I proudly stated.

"Get off!" She thrashed.

"No."

"Lucas Brody Ryder…" she warned.

"Just because you call me by my full name doesn't mean I'm going to listen to you. That only works for my mom."

"Then get off of me."

"Not until you stop whatever hormonal shit you're going through right now."

She gasped.

"Wrong thing to say?" I taunted. "How about this?" I reached down her side and tickled where I knew she hated, right under her ribs, making her whip around and laugh all at the same time. "Are you done? Is it over?" I tickled the other side.

"Stop!" She laughed out, trying to catch her breath.

"Say the magic words."

"Yes! Yes, I'm done," she exasperated.

I instantly stopped, leaning back to sit on my knees, and she took the momentum of my movement to push me, making me fall in the sand.

"Jerk!" She stood up, glaring down at me with a satisfied look on her face that she made me fall over.

"You're going to pay for that later," I grinned.

She rolled her eyes again and reached her hand down to help me up. It took me a few seconds to actually trust her to not shove me down to the sand again, also contemplating on whether to drag her down onto the sand with me. But she was already smiling and I didn't want to break the current shift in mood.

We rode our bikes in comfortable silence and when I didn't turn down her street, I saw her smiling from the corner of my eye.

I told you.

She was all about the little things.

*Alex*

I just couldn't stay mad at him.

He made it absolutely impossible for me not to laugh and he knew it, too. Which only made it worse. It was like adding fuel to the fire, making it bigger and wider with each flare of gasoline.

When I saw that he didn't turn down my street and kept riding in the direction of our abandoned house, I smiled.

There was no helping that either.

The times that he chose to be with me over the boys warmed my heart, especially when he preferred me to surfing.

We parked our bikes behind the house and ran up the stairs. Over the last few months, we had turned it into our own little paradise, bringing blankets and pillows to throw on the floor, candles for when it got dark. Sometimes Lucas would even bring in wood from outside to turn on the fireplace. We had magazines, board games, snacks, and water. Everything we needed was there.

I loved it.

He handed me a bottled water to drink and then I passed it back to him so he could, too. I laid down on the blankets and pillows and beheld the vaulted ceilings with a content sigh.

"Whatcha' thinkin' about over there?" he questioned, sitting down facing me.

"How much I love this place."

"Good."

"I want to get married here."

"What?" he chuckled.

"You heard me. I want to have my engagement party here and I want to get married here. And then I want to buy this house and raise a family here," I firmly stated.

"Aren't you a little young to think about stuff like that?"

"No. I think about stuff like that all the time."

"Oh yeah?"

"Mmm hmm…"

"Who you marrying?"

I immediately held his amused gaze. "What?" It was my turn to say.

"You heard me," he replied, throwing my own words back at me. "Who you marrying?"

"Oh," I breathed out. "I don't know."

He raised his eyebrow but didn't call me out on my lie. "Don't you think that maybe you should *experience* things first?"

"How do you know I haven't?" I provoked, wanting to wipe the smug look off his face.

"Because I know."

"Whatever." I looked away.

"You want to know how I know?"

I kept my stare on the tray ceilings, swallowing the saliva that had pooled in my mouth, and hoping that it would calm the fluttering feeling I had suddenly formed in my belly. I shrugged because I couldn't speak. My voice would giveaway how I felt.

"I know because I would remember it, just like I remember our first experience. The same one that's hanging around your neck."

My heart pounded with each word that fell from his mouth.

"Do you want me to?"

"Do I want you to what?" I replied, already knowing what he meant but needing to hear him say it.

"Do you want me to kiss you?" He paused to let his words sink in. "Really kiss you?"

My mouth parted and my chest rose and descended with each breath I took. I found myself nodding before I gave it any more thought, ignoring the voice in the back of my mind that screamed at me that this was a bad idea. He bent forward and rested on his hands and knees, his face, his lips, coming toward me and making me tightly shut my eyes.

Waiting.

A million thoughts went through my head, but the second I felt his lips on mine they were all gone in an instant.

Nothing else mattered at that moment.

# Chapter 8

## Alex

I had no idea what to do, and my heart drummed so fast that I swear he could hear it. I never thought I would be more grateful for the fact that I laid down. Knowing that if I were standing my knees would have given out from the pounding in my chest. It was the most overwhelming feeling I had ever felt. As if reading my mind, he slowly opened his lips, and I followed his lead, parting mine in the same rhythm he was. Our mouths moved in sync with each other, like we had been doing this all of our lives.

At least it felt that way for me.

His tongue touched my lips and it was the craziest sensation. I pulled back my tongue and he took it as an open invitation to gently push his into my mouth. He tasted of Cherry Coke and Fruit Stripe bubblegum, as he sought mine out with his, turning the kiss into something more. I'm not quite sure what that was, other than an explosive moment and memory in my life. It was wet and making sounds that were unfamiliar, but it felt amazing and stirred emotions that I didn't think were possible. That I didn't even think existed. If I thought I was confused before, well, then this, this added a whole new element and spin to it.

In those minutes, I didn't care because…

It felt right.

*We* felt right.

I didn't know it then, but that's when I fell in love with him.

He pecked my lips one last time and gradually pulled away from me, leaving me breathless and winded, with incoherent thoughts running rapidly in my mind. When I opened my eyes he smiled, big and wide above me, and the intensity of his gaze was once again familiar. It was the same stare that was for me, and only me, the same one from the beach. His eyes never appeared that way with Stacey, and I knew because I'd watched. It was the only thing that comforted me when I wanted to fall apart.

"There," he stated. "Now you can say you've experienced things."

This wouldn't be the first time he laid claim on me, and it was far from the last.

# LUCAS

We graduated eighth grade. Only Austin was left to watch over Alex for one more year, and then she would be alone again. Two more years until we were all under the same roof and school. Our friendship stayed the same, but the feelings we had for each other grew in ways that were far more complex. After that kiss there was no going back, and that was probably why I did it in the first place. I claimed her.

Summer came and went and so did another school year, and then another summer. Before we knew it I was sixteen, and Alex was about to turn fourteen. It was her last year in middle school and we were in tenth grade, Austin in ninth. I went to get my driver's license on my birthday with Alex impatiently waiting in the sitting room with my mom, and the boys waiting at the beach to celebrate. When I told them I passed my test she jumped in my arms, shrieking and acting like a girl. My mom smiled, and we all walked outside. Parked right out front was a silver Chevy Silverado with my dad in the drivers' seat.

I instantly looked at Alex who smiled and enthusiastically nodded her head, turning to my mom who was holding up keys.

"No?" I softly asked.

"Happy birthday, baby," Mom replied, placing the keys in my hand.

I was shocked as shit that they bought me a truck. It was very unexpected, even though I had been hinting that I wanted one. Our boards would fit perfectly on the bed and it had enough room to fit the boys and Alex. Now that I had a truck we could try different beaches to surf. Dylan got a black Jeep for his birthday, and Jacob got a classic black Ford Mustang that we spent hours fixing in his garage.

"I can't believe you got this truck! This thing is a beast, Bo!" Alex excitedly shouted while I drove.

She looked so tiny sitting in the seat beside me. She wore a black dress that seemed more like a baggy shirt on her. She wore dresses all the time now, but they never clung to her body, still a tomboy at heart. I would say her style was sort of like a hippy, and the makeup on her face was always minimal. She didn't need it. She was naturally beautiful with her dark brown, waist length, wavy hair. It was as soft as it appeared to be. We still spent every second we could alone in our abandoned house, but we hadn't kissed again.

"Where are we going?"

"I'm kidnapping you for the day."

She giggled. I loved hearing her laugh.

"It's not kidnapping if you tell me first, besides it's your birthday shouldn't I be the one kidnapping you?"

"I want to spend my birthday with you, that's what I want to do."

She blushed, it was subtle but I saw it.

We pulled up to our abandoned house and I grabbed her hand before she went up the patio stairs.

"Stay here." I went upstairs and grabbed the blanket and picnic basket that I stole from my mom earlier that day. I left it inside for us. "We're always in there," I stated, answering the question that appeared on her face as she followed me down to the beach.

The house came with a private beach and no one could see us without trespassing. I laid out the blanket on the sand and she sat down, helping me take out the sandwiches, chips, and waters from the basket.

"I can't believe you did this."

I shrugged. I didn't want to make a big deal about it. I wanted to do something nice for her, so I did.

"You even used the crunchy peanut butter. Your mom doesn't even buy this kind."

I grinned.

Complicate Me

We ate our food in silence but every so often I heard Alex take a deep breath. I knew she was content. In the grand scheme of things this was a very simple surprise but to her this was huge. This was worth everything and I wanted to make her happy, that was my present. We spent the entire day talking about meaningless things and when the sun began to set I laid down extending out my arm for her to lay on. She snuggled up beside me.

We watched the sunset in comfortable stillness with the waves of the ocean receding on the shoreline. I couldn't help but think about the next time...

I would have her like this.

\*\*\*

Dylan was exclusively dating this girl named Aubrey. She had blonde hair and bright green eyes, and her body was exactly like the ones he admired in those magazines all those years. Jacob dated Ava, who had red hair and blue eyes, and she was much more petite than Aubrey, who was Jacob's style — she wasn't as tiny as Alex though, she was still our Half-Pint. Austin was a player and that surprised all of us. He had a different girl around him every time I saw him. They flocked to him like bees to honey.

There was a birthday party waiting for me the next day at Alex's parents' restaurant. I hated being the center of attention, but I was a good ol' boy and played my part. Stacey was there, and we were still playing the same old game, and just like before, it worked for me.

"Stacey's eye fucking you from across the room," Dylan chuckled, hitting the solid six ball in the corner pocket.

"No shit," I replied, casually looking around for Alex.

"So what are you waitin' for? She's like a bitch in heat. I can smell her from here."

I hit the stripped five ball in the side pocket.

"She'd let you hit it tonight. I'm predicting that she may already be waiting for you, too. You know, birthday present and all."

Jacob raised a questioning eyebrow.

"God, Dylan, do you have to be so crass?" Ava asked, annoyed. "How does Aubrey put up with you?"

"I have a big dick," he stated.

I shook my head, shutting my eyes. I swear he did it just to fuck with her.

Ava was very sensitive. I found Alex talking to Aubrey by the bar. She really liked her, more so than Ava. I think it was because Ava was really whiney, but Lily was by Alex's side. My baby sister was ten and looked up to Alex for some reason, she followed her relentlessly, and I knew a part of Alex really loved that. I saw her trying to teach Alex how to play her guitar a few times, but Alex couldn't carry a tune. Lily on the other hand, her voice was a gift and the talent she had with her guitar excelled everywhere she played.

"You wouldn't be talkin' that way if Half-Pint were here," Ava declared.

"That's because she's a lady."

"Cut the shit, man, you tryin' to cock block me?" Jacob joked, making Ava slap him in the chest and left.

"Thanks, man."

"Stop being such a pussy. Tell Lucas to grow a pair and get balls deep into Stacey already. Damn, man, you're already doin' everything else with her, what's one more thing?" Dylan snidely alleged.

We had messed around a few times, she had blown me and I had fingered her, but I wouldn't go down on her. It was too personal, even though she begged me for it. Alex didn't know that, at least I didn't think she did.

"Why don't you worry about your own dick?" I eyed him.

"Because I love ya and I want you to get *your* dick wet."

"Right..."

"I mean check out Austin," Dylan nodded behind me.

I turned to find him making out with some chick. "I swear he better be using rubbers, he's going to get an STD or shit get someone pregnant."

"Legit," Jacob stated.

"So how was it gettin' your cock sucked?" Dylan blurted, making me look over at him.

"What?"

"Your cock, Lucas, you can't tell me you didn't love it. Now times that by ten and that's what it feels like to sink into a warm pussy. Lose your goddamn virginity already, you're making us look bad."

"He kinda has a point, Lucas, what are you waitin' for? You got a girl who doesn't even care if you want to fuck her seven ways from Sunday with no commitment. Git 'er done," Jacob added.

I locked eyes with Stacey from across the room. She sat on a barstool sipping her water with hooded eyes.

I nodded to the boys. "Yeah," was all I could say.

It wouldn't be the last time I thought with my head and I'm not talking about the one on my neck.

# Alex

"How's school going, Alex?" Aubrey asked as we stood by the bar.

"Good. My classes are killer but so far, so good."

I really liked Aubrey. She was sweet and down to earth. Dylan started seeing her exclusively a few months ago. She was fifteen and her body was ridiculous, I guess she resembled Stacey in that aspect. They both looked like they should be in nudie magazines. Although you would never be able to repeat that after talking to her, she didn't act that way one bit.

Stacey, on the other hand, was a different story. She didn't pretend to be anything she wasn't already called to her face and behind her back. I never understood Lucas's attraction to her, other than she gave it to him for free. Why buy the cow and all that. I hadn't a clue how far they'd gone. I didn't ask and he didn't offer. It wasn't discussed. The boys were good about keeping things behind closed doors, seeing as we didn't go to the same school and all, but come next year that would change. It made me nervous just thinking about it. Stacey and I weren't friends, we barely even spoke, but I knew her role in Lucas's life and she knew mine.

End of story.

Ava was dumb as hell and I couldn't see the appeal of her either, but Jacob didn't seem smitten with her so I didn't feel like I had to worry about her. It was more of a passing kinda thing. Jacob was hard to please, and every girl that came in his direction realized it and then moved on. It became difficult for him to hold down a steady girlfriend, although I knew in my heart that eventually he would meet the right girl. It would be about timing for him, and that proved to be true when we were all older.

I wanted Aubrey to stay around, though, but I knew how Dylan was. I mean not personally because he guarded his crass and vulgar side when I was around. I wasn't ten anymore, but I had heard enough things to know that there were two sides to him: one when I was around and one when I wasn't. Aubrey put up with him and God knows I commended her for it. It took a lot to settle the bull inside of him. She had subtle ways of calming him like rubbing the back of his head. She loved his long hair. However, I thought maybe there were two sides to him with her as well, one that we saw and then one when they were alone.

Now Austin, he was a hot mess. I think it caught us all by surprise. I didn't know what was up with that boy, and a huge part of me knew he didn't either. I had heard our mama's yell at him one too many times to wrap it up and think with the head that was on the upper half of his body, not the lower. I laughed just thinking about it. Austin and I were closest in age and it wouldn't be until the boys left for college for us to truly form a bond without them around. I understood Austin in ways that the boys didn't, he was a lot like me in the sense that he wanted to be one of them, possibly losing himself in the process.

I would turn fourteen in a few weeks and I still didn't have any life experiences outside of the boys. I hadn't dated anyone, kissed anyone *else*, or even been on a date. All the boys on the island were too scared to come near me because they knew I came with baggage.

Four of them.

My boys grew up. And by that, I mean they looked like men, tall, muscular and broad. They had the whole bad boy, intimidating thing down. One would think they had rehearsed the part their entire lives, or something. They protected me even more than they had when we were growing up, and it got to the point where I just gave up. It wasn't worth it to me, having them all in my life was enough.

Especially Lucas.

Complicate Me

The mere thought of them leaving in two years, and just having Austin for one more after that, it killed me every time it crossed my mind. I hated knowing that things would once again change.

Lucas and I were the same as we'd always been. We spent every chance we could alone in our abandoned house. It was our special place and no one could take that away from me.

From us.

I had a torn emotion in my heart. It was the same one that's been there for so many damn years. A piece of me sustained the hope that maybe one day, there might be a chance for us. Exactly how our mama's had told me a few years back.

I waited. Maybe someday there would be a place for us outside of our abandoned house.

Where he could hold my hand.

Where he could kiss me whenever he wanted.

Where he could be mine and I could be his.

Where he could tell me he loved me the same way that I loved him.

*Waiting.* That's all I ever did.

Little did I know that life had a funny way of keeping you on your toes and making you see the reality of the world. I desperately and urgently tried to ignore what had been staring me in the face all along.

As I was about to walk out of the bathroom stall, the restroom door opened.

"I think tonight's the night."

I recognized her voice immediately, stopping me dead in my tracks.

Stacey.

"Oh yeah? What makes you think that?" another girl replied.

"Because we've done everything else. I know he wants to fuck me. He's hard every time I'm around,"

I had to sit down on the toilet, my legs unable to hold my shuddering body.

"How is he?"

"Amazing! Of course, I taught him everything he knows. His cock is fucking huge, Mallory! It would definitely hit all the right spots, I can barely take half of it in my mouth."

My hand rose to my lips, swallowing down the bile that threatened to escape.

"He's a dirty boy, too, the shit that comes out of his mouth when he's fingering me and I'm sucking his dick, Jesus! He's ruined me for other guys." They laughed, loud and throaty.

"Tonight's the night. I know it. I'll call you tomorrow and tell you all about it."

I heard them walk out the door and it rattled when it closed. My body instinctively spun and heaved up everything I had eaten and drank. It came out in one swift motion of opening my mouth, disposing of the toxic words that I overheard.

Over and over again until there was nothing left inside of me, including my heart. I spit into the toilet and wiped my lips with the back of my hand. Opening the door, I went right for the sink to splash cold water all over my face, hoping that it would hide the truth that I had been denying for the last several years.

I'd been lying to myself and to everyone around me. It was all a dream, a hope. It was a young girl's fantasy.

Lucas wasn't mine.

And he had never been. I stood there for a long time, dreading the reflection that would be staring back at me. I avoided the mirror and walked out of the bathroom instead, finding them immediately. I watched Stacey lead Lucas out of the restaurant and onto the beach.

I was no longer the girl waiting.

I was now...

Broken

# Chapter 9

## LUCAS

Stacey walked beside me on the beach, hugging her body firmly around my arm. Her attempts of trying to hold my hand over the last few years were taxing, and she finally gave up. It was dark out, but the full moon illuminated the entire beach, producing a soft glow around us. No one was on the beach. We were alone.

"Come on," she baited, pulling me under the pier. She laid a towel on the sand, laying her body in the middle propped up on her elbows.

Peeking up at me through her lashes, "Don't you want your birthday present?" she rasped, spreading her legs open, showing me she wasn't wearing any panties.

I watched her every move. Stacey was never subtle, and it only made things much easier for me.

"This doesn't change anything," I reminded her, sounding like an asshole, but I'd rather she knew what she was about to get herself into than lie.

I would fuck her if she let me but that's all it would be. Nothing more, nothing less.

"I know," she stated with hooded eyes and a confident demeanor.

"I don't have a condom."

"I do."

Reaching for my hand she lured me onto the towel, sitting her body on top of my hard dick. I gripped her waist when she started to gyrate her hips in a back and forth motion, leaning forward, close to my face.

"That feel good?" she teased, swaying her hips slower and steadier.

"It would feel better inside you."

She seductively smiled and slid down my body, stopping when her face was in front of my zipper. Grinning up at me with glazed eyes she unbuttoned my pants and then lowered the zipper, freeing my cock and putting it into her awaiting mouth. I watched her suck my dick like she had something to prove, enjoying the sensation she stirred in my balls. She unwrapped a condom and placed it on the tip of my head, rolling it down in one swift movement. Confirming what I already knew, she used me as much as I did her.

She climbed up my body with a slow, steady stride, till she hovered above me waiting for me to make the next move. I didn't falter. Grabbing my cock I angled it toward her opening. My eyes shut as I clutched her hips, gliding her down my shaft, making my head roll and my back arch. The feeling was indescribable, way better than having her mouth wrapped around me. With my eyes closed it made it easier to pretend she was someone else, even though I knew she wasn't who I desperately wanted her to be.

I felt her lips on my throat, licking and sucking all over, intensifying the sensitivity of being balls deep for the first time. I groaned loud and hard. Panting and trying to control the pace of her riding me, she took it as a sign to move faster, grabbing the back of my neck for good measure. She wanted me to look at her. I could feel her sex driven glare on my face. She moaned louder and heavier when I didn't open my eyes, kissing my mouth, beckoning me to open.

I didn't, pulling my face away.

It fueled her fire to work me over harder and more demanding, each sway of her calculated hips hitting every spot that drove me closer and closer to release. I couldn't hold back any longer, it felt too fucking good.

"I'm going to come," I huskily groaned.

"So come."

I came so fucking hard I saw stars behind my eyes, my body spasmed uncontrollably. Every inch of me perspired. My chest heaved as I lay there catching my breath and steadying my heart. After this experience it only made me want Alex more. I couldn't imagine what it would feel like with her.

"Want to do it again?" she moaned, resting above me.

I flipped her over. "Fuck yes."

Complicate Me

The second time lasted longer than the first. Stacey told me exactly what to do for her to get off, which felt un-fucking-believable on my cock. I tried not to picture Alex's face but it was pointless.

When we finished, we went back to the restaurant. The boys were still playing pool, grinning like fucking idiots when they saw me walking up.

"Have a good time?" Dylan implied with raised eyebrows and a cocky smile.

Jacob laughed while looking at his phone. "Not bad, I was expecting you to last a lot less."

They each handed Austin a twenty.

"Are you fucking kidding me?" I argued, looking only at Austin.

"What? Why are you pissed at me? I'm the one that rooted for you. Hence, I'm forty dollars richer."

I tried not to laugh as I shook my head, eyeing around the room. "Where's Half-Pint?"

"She left after you left with Stacey, she said she didn't feel well," Jacob replied with a shrug, chalking up his stick. "I offered to take her home, but she said she wanted to be alone or some shit like that. I don't know, I didn't argue. You know how she is these days. I can't deal with all the girly hormone shit. She texted me when she got home. That's all that matters."

I rubbed the back of my neck, feeling the muscles tense immediately. "Yeah," I sighed with a dry mouth and a pounding heart. I needed to get the hell out of there. I could feel the panic taking over. My skin crawled and my nerves were on edge. I knew I needed to leave before I freaked the fuck out, and the boys noticed. Stacey said she was tired and I used it as an excuse to take her home. I drove in a haze after I dropped her off, parking my truck down the road before I even noticed where I was. My feet moved of their own accord up the street and to the driveway, reaching the last porch step of our abandoned house.

My heart dropped. It shattered right then and there on the ground below me. My whole world seemed to come crashing down on me in a matter of seconds. Everything I thought I had under control, everything I wanted to believe, all of it... gone.

I saw her.

And I knew.

It wasn't hard to put two and two together. I don't know how she found out, but all that mattered was that she did.

My brown eyed girl sat on our blankets with her arms wrapped around her knees, hiding her face. The tiny frame that I adored so much shook uncontrollably, only heightening the deepest sobbing that escalated with each passing second. It was such an intimate moment, not to be shared with anyone, especially me. Alex didn't cry. I watched her bawl for the first time in my life. I had never seen anyone cry like that before, and it shook me to my core, slicing me whole and making me feel like I was dying. Carving a memory that I would take to my grave.

There was no going back…

No erasing.

No do-overs.

No deleting.

What I witnessed tonight would be my purgatory. I would now close my eyes and forever see her falling apart in front of me. Shattering before my very own eyes and I found it hard to breathe.

Hard to move.

My feet were glued to the goddamn floor as she continued to weep, sob, bawl, violently sucking in air that wasn't available. I accepted it all, each tear that fell from her face becoming pieces of me. Circulating through my veins and blood, it flowed endlessly, a river of her sadness and sorrow and of my broken promises. No beginning or ending to her cries, just an infinite current, flooding the hole where my heart should be. The shadow of her trembling petite body reflected off the walls, leaving a trail of regrets in its wake.

Mine.

Hers.

Ours.

Growing up in a small town you overheard a lot of things. People talking, stories told, town gossip. You listened a lot. You learned a lot. Tourists, townies, friends, and especially family all shared wisdom and advice that you think you will never need.

Bunch of bullshit.

They say you have that one moment in life where things could have been different, that one moment that changes the course of your life or the direction you could have taken. That one moment that could forever change you and everything you wanted to be true, everything you wanted to believe in.

One simple decision could alter your entire future.

My entire world.

I would forever remember this moment for the rest of my life. This is the moment that changed everything. This is the moment where I took another direction, another road that led me to my own demise.

My own regrets.

I should have walked in there. I should have apologized. I should have begged for her forgiveness. I should have promised that I would never hurt her again. I should have done whatever it took to make her look at me the way she had our entire lives.

But I didn't.

I did none of those things.

Not one.

Nothing was said between us.

No words.

No actions.

I was a coward and couldn't do it. I couldn't see her like that. I couldn't look into her eyes and know that I had hurt her, that I had disappointed her. That I ruined her love and lost her respect for me.

The boy who promised he would never hurt her.

The boy who swore he would always protect her.

The boy who vowed he would never let anything happen to her.

That same boy was me.

I was the reason she was bawling.

I was the reason she was hurt.

I was the reason she was broken.

She knew the truth. It had finally caught up to me. I shattered her illusion that I was hers. I ruined the one good thing I had in my life. The girl that owned my heart was bleeding out for me in a way that I had never seen before. The house was no longer our safe place.

I had brought my hurricane with me…

I couldn't risk the possibility of losing her permanently if I walked in there and admitted my truths. She wouldn't love me anymore, she wouldn't look at me the same anymore, and she wouldn't be mine anymore.

My brown eyed girl.

The girl that I had loved all of my life.

The same girl that I would love for the rest of my life.

*Alexandra.*

I gave her the only comfort I could in her moment of despair. I turned around and left. I walked down the stairs and got into my truck. I turned the engine on and drove my sorry ass home. I took a shower and never once looked at myself in the mirror. I pretended that nothing changed. That I didn't cause her pain, and that she didn't know the truth. That I didn't see her sobbing and that she wasn't even bawling to begin with. That we were still just best friends, and that she was my girl and I was her boy.

My Half-Pint and her Bo.

It was better than knowing…

I. Ruined. *Us.*

# *Alex*

"Are you okay, honey?" Mom asked, walking into my bedroom.

"Mmm hmm," I mumbled, lying in my bed with the covers pulled up to my chin. I hadn't moved since I got home the night before.

"You're not dressed, Alex."

"I don't feel so good."

She felt my forehead. "You don't feel warm."

I shrugged. I didn't feel like moving, I barely felt like talking.

"What happened last night? I saw your face when you came home. I heard you crying all night but I left you alone because I wanted you to have your privacy. Now tell me please." She sat beside me, rubbing the back of my head.

"I don't want to talk about it. I'm sorry, Mama."

She frowned. "Is it about Lucas?"

I slightly nodded.

Complicate Me

"Baby—"

"Please. Please don't make me talk about it. I don't want to cry anymore. It is what it is."

She sighed. "You know those boys are going to want to come check on you when they don't see you at service today."

"I know."

"Are you ready for that?"

I nodded again.

"I know it hurts now, Alex. Trust me, honey, I remember what it was like being your age. It's probably one of the hardest times in a young woman's life. Not being able to understand the emotions that you feel so deeply in your heart. It will get better. I promise you that everything happens for a reason, and one day you'll understand what that reason is. Even if it feels like you're dying now."

I opened my mouth to say something.

"You're so young. You both are," she added, taking my will to say anything.

"Yeah…"

"I love you, Alex, and I will always be here for you. Even if you think that I will be upset with you, I am always your mama, and nothing you can ever do or say will change that. Do you understand me?"

"I do."

She smiled. "Rest and shower. Try to eat something. I'll keep the boys away as long as I can."

"Okay."

She kissed my head and left my room. I don't know how long I stayed there, wrapped in my own cocoon. The tears were gone. I used them all. Nothing would take away what I already knew and I hated that more than anything. I'd rather not know. It was easier to pretend.

I wanted to stay there.

I got up, took a shower and dressed. Patiently waiting for the boys to arrive to give a performance of a lifetime.

Where I was his Half-Pint and he was still my Bo.

# Chapter 10

## Alex

I watched them all exit Lucas's truck from my bedroom window, my heart rapidly beating through my ears. Lucas was the last to round his truck, a bag from my favorite donut shop in his hands. He appeared the same boy as always, and I would be lying if I told you it didn't sting that he didn't just know. That he couldn't feel that I was hurt.

*How stupid is that?*

I took a deep breath as I heard the pounding of their steps coming up to my bedroom, each one louder than the next, mimicking my heart in every way, shape, and form.

"I can do this," I told myself, putting on a brave and casual face.

I heard a knock on my door.

"Why you knockin' on the door?" Austin probed.

"She's a girl, you fucking idiot," Dylan replied annoyed.

I rolled my eyes, chuckling. It eased the pain I felt in my core. "Come in," I called out.

Dylan walked in first followed by Austin and Jacob.

"I told you she was faking," Jacob stated, sitting beside me, tugging me over to his side. "You cheater!"

Dylan plopped down at the foot of my bed and Austin leaned against the headboard. Lucas was nowhere to be found.

"Why'd you lie?" Jacob asked, kissing the top of my head.

"I didn't feel well."

"You look pretty. Girls don't look pretty when they aren't feelin' well," Dylan chimed in, looking smug and grinning.

"Girl problems," I stated, knowing it would make them uncomfortable.

"Ugh!" Jacob backed away and leaned on my window. "Enough said."

"Where's Lucas?" I blurted, adjusting the tone of my voice, picking at the seams of my bedspread to avoid their eyes.

"Who the fuck knows," Austin informed. "He was behind me."

"It's hot as shit outside, let's stay here and watch movies all day. Your mom said we could order stuff on Pay Per View," Jacob said, none of them paying me any mind.

"Half-Pint," Dylan peered up at me through his lashes. "Want to go make us some popcorn and get us some drinks," he requested in the softest voice.

I smiled. "Sure."

I heard them arguing about which movie to watch as I left my room. We were watching a man movie with or without my consent. I eagerly made my way through the house, hoping that I wouldn't run into Lucas alone. I quickly put the popcorn in the microwave, setting out two more on the counter. The boys could eat.

Everything.

"Need any help?" I startled when I heard his voice from behind me, spilling the soda on the counter.

"Shit! Sorry." He swiftly grabbed paper towels and wiped up my spill.

I kept my gaze on the counter, serving the rest of the drinks, silently praying he couldn't hear my heart that was pounding out of my chest. It was weird to be that nervous around him.

I didn't like it.

"No worries," I said, trying to keep my voice from breaking. "Where were you? You just snuck up on me."

"I brought you some donuts." He ignored my question and handed me the bag.

"Glazed?"

"Of course."

I shyly smiled, still not meeting his intent gaze that was settled on my cold and distant demeanor.

*Why was he looking at me like that? Maybe he always looked at me like that.*

"Umm, you can help with the drinks." I twisted the cap back on the liter and spun to check the time on the microwave.

"Alex." He gripped my wrist, locking me in place, using my name that sounded so foreign coming out of his mouth.

I slowly met his stare. "Yeah," I casually reacted, pretending that it hadn't affected me as much as he saw it did.

His mouth parted wanting to say something, but nothing came out. He looked tired, and it only fueled the truth to what I knew he did last night.

With her.

I instinctively pulled my wrist from his hold. "What?"

It didn't shock him. My reaction, and it only confused me more on what was going on between us. I couldn't begin to recognize the look on his face. He looked sad and I didn't understand that either, but he quickly smiled, trying to hide the fact that I noticed it.

"I love you, Alex," he whispered like he needed me to hear it. "You know that right?"

I lowered my eyebrows, feeling somewhat uncomfortable, my stomach tossing and turning. He smiled sweetly, and I thought for a second I saw something behind his eyes, but just as fast as it appeared, it was gone.

"I know," I simply stated.

He jerked back, hurt, that I hadn't said it back. In that moment, I didn't want to ease his questioning stare. I wanted him to hurt. Two wrongs don't make a right but go tell that to someone who felt the way I did. They'd laugh in your face.

He bit his bottom lip contemplating what to say. "She's just a girl, Half-Pint, just a fucking girl," he breathed out, and I never wanted to punch him in the face as much as I did in that second.

I didn't even know what to say or how to respond to that. I could see his mind reeling, debating on whether or not he should say what he thought, what he felt. I could tell that a lot weighed on his mind. I wanted to ask him, but I knew I wouldn't get the answers I sought. It only reaffirmed what I said earlier, what I knew to be true, and over the next few years it would become like the melody of my favorite song, playing on a broken record. The boys never thought about the consequences of their actions. They acted on pure impulse. Never contemplating that it could hurt someone in its wake. And that wasn't just Lucas.

It was all of them.

"Half-Pint," he softly spoke.

89

"Stacey's just a girl. I get it. But what does that make me, Bo? Just another girl?"

He sternly shook his head. "You know that's not true."

"Do I?"

He looked deep into my eyes and spoke with conviction. "You're my brown eyed girl, you always will be. I would never hurt you intentionally. That's the last thing I want to do, and I'm sorry if I have."

I bowed my head not able to look into the depths of his truths any longer. It was too confusing, and I was emotionally exhausted. I didn't want to play these games anymore, I didn't know the rules, and I had no idea how to win. And a huge part of me hated him for that. I would have played this game until the end.

Even if it meant…

I would lose.

# LUCAS

"I know, Bo, I love you, too," she recited as if it caused her pain to say it.

There was no going back. All that was left was to move forward, praying that we could get back everything we never had out of our abandoned house. This added to the unanswered questions and unsaid emotions that were placed in between us, stirring the pot for one day to boil over and scar us with wounds we may never be able to heal from.

*\*\*\**

The school year passed in the blink of an eye, once again summer vacation. Alex's last summer before she entered high school with the rest of us, going into her freshman year, Austin into his sophomore year and Jacob, Dylan, and I into our junior year. Alex and I slowly but surely found our way into a new normal. We had become quite the chameleons. We still spent every second we could in our abandoned house, and over the course of a few months the same adoring look that was just for me found its way back into my presence.

I stayed away from Stacey as best as I could. Though she always found me. A fucking spider I couldn't get away from, her webs were around me even when I wasn't looking. Jacob was single, again, Austin still being *Austin*, and Dylan surprisingly still with Aubrey.

This was the summer that changed it all.

Alex was fourteen, shy of turning fifteen in a few months. Sometimes I would watch her from across the room and the mere vision of her left me breathless. She had turned into a beautiful girl, there was nothing that resembled a little girl anymore. Wearing a little bit more makeup here and there, her eyelashes appeared fake they were so damn long. Her pouty lips more enticing with the glossy shine she applied on them.

She started wearing shorts, crop tops, off the shoulder tank tops, showing more skin, belly, and legs than I wanted her too. Her hair hung long and loose down her back or those messy buns on top of her head. When we stood close together I could smell the cherry, flavor she put on her lips, and it took everything in me not to kiss her, not to claim her lips with mine.

One evening we were hanging out in her bedroom, the boys left and it was just her and I. She went to the bathroom and I don't know what came over me, but I went into her closet and grabbed all of her new clothes, throwing them in the garbage can by her desk. She yelled at me and told me to mind my own business. She was growing up with or without my approval and that I wasn't her daddy to tell her what she could or couldn't wear. She'd never spoken to me like that before, and that shocked me more than anything. She kicked me out of her bedroom. The next day she wore an outfit so revealing it made me want to throw her over my shoulder, carry her home and lock her in her bedroom.

A part of me knew she did it on purpose. She wanted to provoke some kind of emotion out of me, wanting to make sure I noticed her changing.

When I called her out on it she said she wanted to find her own way, her identity, outside of us boys. Or some shit like that, I stopped paying attention after she pissed me off saying she was going bikini shopping with her mom that weekend.

All of our families were pretty well off. Not to sound conceited, but none of us had to work, that's just how it was. Alex chose to work, she asked her parents for a waitressing job at their restaurant and they excitingly jumped on it.

Again, we didn't discuss it. Not even when we were at our abandoned house. When I asked her why she hadn't mentioned it to me, she said it slipped her mind. The truth was she knew I wouldn't like it and she didn't want to fight with me. We had been bickering enough. I didn't understand why she wanted to spend most of her summer working when we could have been hanging out, exactly how we always had. That was the point of summer, to get to spend more time together and do whatever we wanted.

She decided to work full time, as in forty hours a week, basically working every day, and long ass eight-hour shifts. We spent most of our time surfing or hanging out at the restaurant while she worked. At times, it felt like nothing had changed. Other than the fact that she took our orders and served us food, always serving me first, and I would be lying if I said I didn't love the fact that she fed me. Sometimes without me even putting in an order.

"My feet hurt," she whined, laying down on the blankets and pillows of our abandoned house. She had worked another eight-hour shift and it was already almost nine o'clock, her curfew was soon.

"You should quit," I simply stated, grinning and putting her feet in my lap to rub them.

She giggled, "No." She hated her feet touched, ticklish to no end.

I massaged them anyway. "Anything interesting happen today?" I asked.

"You would know, you spent the entire day in there," she mocked in a condescending tone, so I tickled her foot.

"Stop!" she shouted, laughing. I went back to rubbing them, prepared for the next sassy remark.

"Maybe you should get a job."

"Nah, then who would feed me?"

She grinned.

"No funny stories?"

"Nope. Nothing I can think of, ask me again when I'm not so tired," she yawned.

"You work again tomorrow?"

"Why do you ask when you already know?"

"That's it."

I dropped her feet and made my way to her ribs, where I knew she hated. She thrashed, screaming and laughing all at the same time. I sat on her thighs and gripped her wrists, placing them above her head. She whipped around a few more times to no avail and finally gave up, laughing too hard to fight. I laughed too. She was contagious. We both found our bearings and it was then that I realized our compromising position, and by the look in her eyes she did, too.

I smiled, looking down at her while she was gazing up at me with a look that I couldn't quite read. There was emotion behind her eyes and it was the first time I had sincerely seen her guard come down since *before*. I pulled her hair out of the way to see her face. It did it to me every time. My hand caressed the side of her cheek and I fucking knew I was sending the wrong message, goddamn it, I couldn't help myself.

I grabbed the back of her neck and brought her up to me, she came effortlessly. Her lips were just as I remembered, if not fucking better. Tasting of cherry flavored lip-gloss, and it stirred my dick in ways that now the mere smell of it would arouse me. She knew Cherry Coke was my favorite, and at that moment I realized she did that for me. I sought out her tongue before she had the opportunity to find mine.

She moaned in my mouth.

Both my hands found the sides of her face and her hands found my hair, pulling at it. I took in the feel of her pouty lips while framing her face that I adored so much. Moving my hands down her body, fuck if she didn't feel unbelievable. Her dress had hiked up and her thighs were exposed, her skin was soft and silky-smooth.

I needed to stop...

We needed to stop...

I wanted nothing more than to keep going. I wanted to be with her, but shit she was barely almost fifteen, it couldn't be this way. I wasn't going to let desire change everything that I worked so hard to get back. Our lips were devouring each other as if we were both making a memory to take with us, not knowing when another chance like this would happen again. I wish I could describe the intensity that I found myself feeling with her in my arms. Only I couldn't even do it justice. I couldn't even put it into words what I felt in my heart.

What had always been there.

It overpowered me. This was the third time I let it take control and a huge part of me wanted to throw caution to the wind and just go with it.

I didn't.

I had enjoyed the sensation of her lips against mine one last time before I pulled away and she whimpered at the loss.

"Alexandra," I breathed out, inches away from her mouth. My forehead placed on hers with my hands holding me up on the sides of her face.

She immediately opened her eyes. They appeared dark and dilated. It was the first time I had called her by her whole name.

"Lucas," she panted back, luring me in again. I softly pecked her lips, rubbing mine back and forth on hers.

"Please," she huskily pleaded, her voice soft and torn.

*What was she asking for?*

*Did she even know?*

"What do you—"

Her cell phone rang, cutting me off, both of us jumped at the sound with me flying off, and her reaching for her phone.

"Mom," she answered. "Yeah no, I know. I know, Mom, I'll be home soon. Okay love you, too." She hit end and sat up against the wall as our eyes locked from across the room.

Neither one of us said anything. Our intense gazes spoke for themselves.

## *Alex*

"I gotta go," I said, breaking the silence.

He nodded. "I'll drive you home."

"Okay." I got up first and he quickly followed.

We rode in dead silence on the short ride back to my house. He parked his truck out in front but didn't turn off the motor, the diesel engine vibrated beneath me.

*Or maybe that was my body that shuddered?*

"I'll pick you up in the morning," he announced, breaking the silence.

"You don't have to." Most of the time, he was the one who dropped me off and picked me up from work.

"I want to."

"I'll see you in the morning." I opened the door about to step out, but he gripped my arm making me turn to face him.

"Sweet dreams," he smiled, lovingly.

"You too."

I made my way up the steps to the front door and then to my bedroom. I looked out my window, knowing he was still there. Once he left, the wind around me stayed, the emotions and confusion wrapped around me, engulfing me.

The hurricane left.

Except this time…

It took me with him.

# Chapter 11

## Alex

A few weeks went by. The boys were surfing, but it was around the time they would be heading back soon.

Hungry.

I put all their orders in and went to take care of the new table that was outside on the deck. Amber said it was a party of one, so I carefully placed a glass of water, chips and salsa on the tray with my eyes intently watching the movement of the glass. I hated using this damn thing.

It wasn't the tray this time, just my plain ol' clumsiness as I accidentally hit the glass, knocking it over and into the customer's lap.

"Crap! I'm so sorry!" I ran to get more napkins and when I came back he stood, wiping off all the water from his board shorts. It was then that I noticed how tall he was, as tall as my boys.

He hovered above me. "It's okay, accidents happen," he said, sitting back down and looking up at me for the first time.

He seemed around my age, bright green eyes and blond hair, fair skin. A dimple on each side of his cheeks, I noticed them and he wasn't even smiling. The complete opposite of Lucas, but I still found him very attractive.

I blushed when I realized I hadn't stopped staring at him. "Sorry." I bowed my head, cleaning up the mess from the table and handing him the napkins. "Your lunch is on me."

"That's not necessary." His voice was deep, also like the boys. With a crooked grin exposing the dimples in his cheeks, catching me off guard, he asked, "What's your name?"

My hand wiped small circles on the clean spot while I tried like hell to regain composure. My name? What was it? I could only think of one thing. "Half-Pint!" I yelled out in realization.

My new friend laughed a cute, raspy laugh while I felt the crimson burn in my cheeks, knowing they were visibly glowing.

"I think you misunderstood. I was asking for a name, not a measurement."

I felt the red color leaving my face when I laughed, too. "Yeah, sorry. Everyone calls me Half-Pint."

"Cole, Cole Hayes," he nodded with an extended hand and the same boyish grin, exposing the cute little dents in his cheeks again.

"Alex, my name's Alex," I reaffirmed as my small hand slipped into his. I could still feel the damp, wrinkles in his palms from surfing in salt water all day. It felt like Lucas's hand. The unfamiliar handshake was a nice change of pace. I couldn't remember the last time I'd shook someone's hand. Maybe the Pastor from church? This handshake was different. It was nice. I let my hand linger in his while the name Cole rolled silently off my tongue.

"Alex? What's it short for?"

"How do you know it's short for anything?" I questioned with my hand on my hip, rag in hand, still holding his hand, or was he holding mine? I think we both held the grasp.

"You're too pretty to have a boy name."

That's when I pulled my hand away. That's when I tried to be cool, keep my eyes from expanding, and reel in the crimson burning my nose, hoping like hell he didn't notice.

"That color of red looks really nice on you," he acknowledged in a teasing tone.

I grinned, peeking up at him through my lashes and catching my bearings. "Alexandra, Alexandra Collins."

He smiled, big and wide. It lit up his entire face. "Well then see that's a beautiful name, it fits you. Nice to meet you, Alexandra Collins."

I nodded, not being able to form the words to describe what his flirty banter did to me.

"You from around here?" he asked, leaning back into his chair with his arms casually placed on the sides.

"Yeah born and raised. My parents actually own this place."

"I'm here on vacation. Well actually my parents just bought a beach house a few miles down the road so I'll be here every summer until I go away to college, I guess."

97

"I know," I blurted out, immediately shaking my head in astonishment of my crappy flirting skills.

His eyes widened, surprised, making my belly flutter and my palms sweaty.

"No, I mean I know you're not from around here. I would remember you."

He grinned, all knowing.

"No... not in that way... I mean... just in general..." I stuttered. "You know because I live here... and it's a small town... and everyone knows everyone... not in a stalker... crazy girl kinda way..." I sighed from my own mumbled banter. "I'm going to stop talking now." Highly embarrassed with my babbling.

"How old are you?" he replied amused.

"I'll be fifteen in a few months. You?"

"I'll be sixteen in a few months. Freshman?"

"Going to be. Sophomore?"

"Soon to be," he admitted at the precise moment his head cocked to the side and his eyes scanned my body. For the first time, I felt like the center of someone's world, someone besides my boys.

He smiled with a dimply grin. "I like fresh meat."

"Me too, motherfucker," Lucas roared from behind me, making me spin so fast it may have caused whiplash. I should have known better, but I guess I was gluten for punishment. I saw the look in his eyes. The eye of the storm stood before me, but this time it wasn't directed at me.

It was directed at Cole.

This wouldn't be the first time and trust me when I say, it damn well wouldn't be the last.

He put his arm around my shoulders, tugging me into his body. I immediately placed my palm on his chest in a calming gesture. It usually worked, and for the first time. It didn't. "Bo," I softly warned as I looked up at him with pleading eyes.

He grinned not paying me any mind with his intent stare focused solely on Cole. "Let's get one thing straight so we don't get off on the wrong foot or anything. You already made an asshole of yourself on your board the other day. But seeing as you clearly don't know the rule of cutting another man's wave, it's the same as fucking with another man's girl," he paused to let his words sink in.

"We clear?" he challenged with raised eyebrows and a confident demeanor.

I took a deep breath while shaking my head. If I hadn't been embarrassed enough before, this definitely took the cake.

"She your girl?" Cole responded with not a hint of intimidation in his voice.

"Damn straight," Dylan declared, standing beside Lucas. I knew Jacob and Austin weren't far behind.

"Alex here is off limits," Jacob added, his arms folding over his chest, walking up next to me.

*See? Told you.*

I never wished for the ground to swallow me whole as much as I did in that second.

Cole stood tall, firm, and wide. Not backing down in the least, and I swear I thought this boy must have a death wish or something. No one squared off to my boys.

No one.

He didn't falter. "Well seeing as *Alexandra* here didn't tell me she was off limits." He arched an eyebrow. "Or that she was *your* girl," he retorted only looking at Lucas, who I swore was ready to jump over the table and pounce him like a lion. The only reason he didn't was because I was still firmly placed on his side. He wouldn't have let me go even if I wanted him to.

"Until *Alexandra* tells me otherwise, I'll be seeing her around," he added once again, emphasizing my name like he knew it would piss Lucas off.

He provoked him.

I didn't understand at the time what happened, other than normal testosterone fueling through the air. I realized later that this is where the animosity between Lucas and Cole began, this is where the line was drawn and I had to choose a side. I didn't. I couldn't. I would spend years trying to remain in the middle, neutral to both of them. At least I thought I did. Lucas never saw it that way, saying I always leaned toward Cole.

He backed away, but not before he flaunted a smartass smile for the boys and then a kindhearted one for me. If I noticed it, I knew damn well my boys did, too.

Especially Lucas.

Complicate Me

Cole left, Austin sneering as he walked past him. I watched him leave with scornful eyes, and anger quickly replaced the embarrassment that I felt in my core. I was livid, and as more minutes passed it only added fuel to the fire I felt for the boys.

Particularly Lucas.

I instantly pushed off of him. He staggered a bit and looked at me like I was crazy. The eye of the storm now directed at me. I didn't care. For the first time, I let my emotions get the best of me and they would each hear the wrath of my reaction.

"Who the hell do you think you are?"

Their eyes widened and their faces frowned, a domino effect of confusion and shock from my outburst.

"This. Ends. Now. Do you understand me? All of you?" I shouted while putting my hands on my hips, coming to an upright position to accent my pissed off composure.

"Half-Pint," Austin mumbled.

"No." I fervently shook my head. "Don't Half-Pint me. I'm sick of this. There is not ONE boy in this town that will even talk to me. Not one! They're all scared of you, and it's not fair. How dare you embarrass me in front of him?"

Lucas scoffed, "Who the fuck cares about him?"

"I do!"

His eyes narrowed at me with hurt and sadness all in one.

"I want a friend. I want a guy friend outside of you. Outside of all of you." I glared at each of them, one right after the other. "He didn't do anything wrong, he was friendly and being nice. He wasn't hurting me for you to act like that. For any of you to act like that. I'm a big girl. I'm going to be fifteen in a few months and you keep treating me like I'm five, I'm over it. I can make my own decisions. I don't need any of you to babysit me or tell me what to do." I stood taller, clenched fists at my sides.

Lucas mirrored my stance and Dylan reached out for me.

I backed away, placing my finger out in front of me. "No! I'm not kidding. You can all do whatever the hell you want. You can date. You can kiss. You can even have sex! And I don't say a damn thing. I have accepted that you're growing up, and I'm still there for you when you need me. I'm not going anywhere. I will always be your Half-Pint, but you can't do this to me anymore. It's not fair," I argued, my trembling voice breaking. My throat burned and tears crept into my eyes so I blinked them away, folding my arms over my chest to keep from shaking.

"Fine," Jacob stated.

"Fine what?" I snapped.

"I understand where you're coming from." He cleared his throat like it pained him to say that. "But. We're doing it to protect you, Half-Pint, that's all we ever do. It's not coming from a bad place. Boys are assholes and they fucking suck. Do you understand that?"

I shrugged, not wanting to admit that he was right. Instead I met Lucas's heated glare, hoping that he realized he was one of those boys, and by the look on his face he knew what I thought.

Jacob exhaled a deep breath and stepped toward me. "I get that you want to grow up. It's just a little hard to see it. You've been following us around since you could crawl. Okay?"

"It doesn't matter."

"It does to us," he stressed.

"We will always protect you. It's in our nature. We will take it down a notch. That's the best I can give you, Half-Pint," Dylan added while glancing at the guys and then back at me. "Happy?"

I sighed defeated. "It's a start I guess."

Jacob kissed the top of my head, Dylan pulled me into a tight hug, and Austin rubbed my back, grinning and tugging on the ends of my hair before they made their way back inside. I was left with Lucas, who hadn't moved or said one thing since I yelled that I cared about Cole. Knowing it had nothing to do with Cole.

It was the fact that I said I cared about someone...

Who wasn't him.

# LUCAS

I needed to be alone with my thoughts.

This wasn't going to end well if I didn't control the rage I felt for her sticking up for some fucking douche that acted as if he owned the ocean. Riding up and stealing another surfer's waves.

Complicate Me

There aren't many rules to surfing, but you respect each other's breaks.

Plain and simple.

I didn't know what possessed me to act like that.

Yes, I did.

Although the encounter didn't go as I envisioned it. I was blinded by rage and panic of having her flirt with someone who wasn't me. The urge to mark her overwhelmed me, and I found myself digging my nails into the palms of my hands to keep from shaking the shit out of her. I wanted to remind her that she was mine. I couldn't seem to control myself, or the rapid thoughts that circulated my mind. She belonged only to me. As stupid as that sounds, that's how I felt. I didn't want her to be friends with another guy, and the reaction that she just pulled on me was complete fucking bullshit.

Neither one of us dared to say a word, knowing that nothing could take away my desire to claim her as mine. Alex knew me like the back of her hand and vice versa. I was jealous and she was resentful, two emotions combined that only led to disaster.

"Tell me, *Alexandra*, do you like your new friend?" I viscously mocked.

Her eyebrows raised, the shock evident on her beautiful face making me regret my words almost instantly. "Half—"

"Not as much as you like Stacey," she countered almost knocking me on my ass.

"Leave Cole alone, ya hear?" she added, not breaking the intensity of our stares.

"Or what?" I scowled through gritted teeth.

"Lucas," Jacob hollered from inside.

I turned to find him staring us both down, taking in our heated standoff with eyes that realized more than I wanted him to. "Come on," he said with a nod while opening the door wider. The cool air brushed against my heated skin and helped ease the fact that I wanted to hit someone.

Mostly Cole.

I didn't turn back around. I just left.

All I achieved was adding to the times that I would walk away from Alex.

# Chapter 12

## LUCAS

"What the fuck was that?" Jacob asked as he grabbed my arm, stopping me to face him when we were outside.

I aggressively pulled my arm away. "Don't worry about it."

He jerked back while cocking his head to the side and spoke with conviction. "We're all pissed, Lucas, why don't you calm down before you do something you will regret later."

"What do you want?"

He didn't miss a beat. "Are you jealous, Lucas?"

"No," I lied with a straight face.

"It looks like it, and from what I overheard, it fucking sounds like it too. Let me remind you that Alex is our little sister. You do remember that right? She's not Stacey."

"No shit."

"Then I'm going to pretend that I didn't see what I'm assuming."

"Don't fuck with me, Jacob," I snapped.

He put his hands in the air out in front of him in a surrendering gesture. "Half-Pint is off limits, to all of us. Especially you."

I scoffed. "What the fuck is that supposed to mean?" I replied through gritted teeth. My fists clenched at my sides and my muscles tensed. I could feel my temper looming. It took everything inside me not to put my hands on my best friend. But this wasn't the time or the place. It would take years for Jacob and me to throw down though it being for a whole different reason.

"Do you even have to ask me that? You're not good enough for her. You know it and I know it. You're going to hurt her if you haven't already."

I swallowed the saliva that had pooled in my mouth, trying like hell to not take his words to heart, but I couldn't help it.

Everything he said was true. I had hurt her in ways I promised I never would. Immediately the memory flooded my mind of watching her fall apart in the abandoned house we called our safe haven. It was as if I stood there all over again and not in front of Jacob. It replayed in my mind causing me to feel the shame and remorse for the piece of shit I knew I had been.

Or possibly still was.

"I love you, Lucas. But I will knock you the fuck out if you don't put your cock back in your pants and start thinking with the head on your goddamn shoulders. We clear?" He acknowledged with a nod.

I decided to ignore his threat to break the tension between us. "What did you want?"

I wasn't scared of Jacob.

"You want to direct your anger at someone? Well, I got the perfect guy." He grinned while snickering, slapping me on the arm, and hauling me over to his chest in a lighthearted manor. "Let's catch up with the boys."

We trailed behind a few blocks until we caught up to Austin and Dylan. Not just them, but Cole too. They stood in front of him, almost caging him in while he leaned against a fence with his foot propped resting along it, his arms crossed over his chest. He wasn't afraid of us, nor was he intimidated. That much was clear.

We gathered next to all of them with our bodies firmly facing Cole. You would have thought we were having a fucking pow wow with the way his demeanor carried. Not a thread of worry in his eyes or in his stance, he was as cool as the ocean water. This guy could fight. That much was also obvious.

"Seems like we all started off on the wrong foot," Jacob recalled in a throaty tone, breaking the silence but not the intensity.

Cole cocked his head to the side with a toothy grin. "Oh yeah? You mean that's not the general welcome around these parts? Damn," he sarcastically stated.

I chuckled. I couldn't help it. "Cute," I snickered as I eyed him up and down, ready to punch the smart ass fucking grin off his face. He realized it. I was never one for being subtle.

He unyieldingly arched an eyebrow. "I try to be. Alexandra sure seems to think so," he snidely insinuated only provoking me further. If I didn't hate him so much already, I probably would have shaken his goddamn hand.

Dylan placed his palm on my shoulder, sensing that I wanted nothing more than to take his sorry ass out. That wouldn't score me points with Alex though, and that's the only reason I kept playing nice. But if he kept luring me like that I wouldn't give a fuck anymore and take the bait. Alex would forgive me eventually, and I would have the pleasure to fuck up his pretty boy face. He walked a thin line and he knew it, part of me realized that's what he intended. He wanted me to hit him for whatever reason.

Through the years, Cole would prove to be smarter than I ever imagined.

"What Jacob here is tryin' to say, is that you're only going to be around for the summer, I highly advise you to reconsider where you stand," Dylan warned not letting go of his tight grip on my shoulder.

"And where is that?" Cole wittily replied.

"You don't fuck with Half-Pint and we don't fuck with you," Austin chimed in, treading near his face.

Cole smiled with a nod. "Can't we all just get along?"

Now it was my turn to smile. "We will as long as you know where you stand. Don't fuck with her and there won't be any problems."

"Huh," he breathed out, narrowing his eyes at me and striding toward me till we were inches apart. "And what if she fucks with me? What then?" he whispered to close to my face.

"You son of a bitch." I shoved the shit out of him before the last word even left my mouth and his back slammed into the fence. "Want to try that again?" I threatened, while lunging at him but Dylan and Jacob grabbed my arms.

He put his hands up in the air, laughing. "Now this is what I call a fucking welcome," he yelled out in a high-pitched voice. "By all means boys. Duly noted, I'll make sure to not *fuck*," he paused, emphasizing the word with wide eyes, "with Alexandra." He clapped his hands together, moving away. "Now if you'll excuse me, I have some waves to catch, and I'll be sure not steal any of those either." And with that he turned and left.

"At least he has balls, I'll give him that," Austin boasted.

Complicate Me

I roughly flung my arms out of Dylan and Jacobs holds. "Fuck him," I called out loud enough so he heard me.

"Relax," Dylan coaxed. "I'd rather her be hanging out with someone like him than a goddamn pussy who can't protect her."

My face scowled and my blood fumed. "Are you for real?" I hissed.

"He's right," Austin stated. "Let it go. He knows what's up. We said our peace. Get your shit together and cool off."

I shook my head at all of them, seething. "Un-fucking-believable." I turned and left, not bothering to hear any more of the bullshit spewing from their mouths.

I staggered around endlessly for a few hours and then ended up in the only place I ever felt complete.

## *Alex*

It was still fairly early by the time my shift ended. Lucas wasn't parked out in front of the restaurant like usual, and I would be lying if I said I wasn't disappointed. I headed to the only place I knew I would find him.

He lay against the pillows while he threw a tennis ball at the wall in front of him. His stare remained at the task at hand as I walked inside and sat on the blankets beside him, facing him. Dream On by Aerosmith played on the radio. Neither of us said a word, and I swear it felt like hours had gone by. I tried to remain patient. Soundlessly taking in the words of the music around me. It seemed fitting.

I couldn't take it anymore, my frustration getting the best of me. "You're not going to say anything?" I asked, breaking the deadly silence that consumed my very being.

"What would you like me to say, *Alexandra*," he replied with his stare intently placed on throwing the stupid ball.

"An apology maybe?"

"I'm not going to apologize for protecting you," he simply stated once again throwing the damn ball back at the wall.

"That's not fair."

He shrugged not paying me any mind. "I never said life was fair."

I scoffed as my head shook, baffled. "It's so easy for you."

"And what would that be? The fact that I have to watch you grow up, knowing that it's only a matter of time before you really start *growing* up," he harshly rasped while he angled his head on the wall. Throwing the ball much harder now.

"Bo," I whispered my head bowing, hoping that this conversation wasn't going where I thought it would. "I don't know what you want me to say. I don't know what you want me to do," I spoke honestly.

Everything was so confusing. So overwhelming. I wanted to go back when we were just kids and nothing else mattered but playing and laughing. Enjoying spending every second together, before emotions and feelings took over and nothing made sense anymore.

Before we started growing up.

"It doesn't matter what I want. It's what you want," he alleged, his voice broken and torn.

That was what made me look up at him. "What's that supposed to mean?"

"You know."

"Remind me then," I challenged.

"You just want to hear me say the words, Half-Pint, and I'm not going to because then I would have to lock you in this house. And we both know that's not going to happen."

I sighed, "Bo, I've accepted that you've grown up. I accept everything you do and I'm still your brown eyed girl."

He threw the ball a few more times, contemplating what to say, I was sure. It echoed through the room, mirroring my tolerance for his next words to me.

"That's exactly it. I fuck, Half-Pint."

It fell from his lips so easily, making me loudly gasp, surprised as hell. He's never had the audacity to admit that to me, and for some reason I had the feeling that he was aware that I already knew. He would have never spoken to me like that otherwise.

"I don't care about anyone other than you," he followed, still throwing the damn ball against the wall. Which now mirrored my heart. I hated everything he shared because I knew he meant it and all it did was add to the pile of confusion.

For us...

For me...

"You're not like that. I know it and you do too. So when the time comes, you won't be my brown eyed girl anymore. You'll be his, and that's the truth between us."

I sat there blindsided with a parted mouth, taking in every word as if he recited poetry. It flowed through my mind making its way to my heart where he would forever be engrained.

"You're a good girl, Alexandra. That's what makes you my Half-Pint. You're the calm to my storm. It's always been that way," he paused to let his words sink in. "You're my refuge."

Tears fell from my eyes, down the sides of my face, and into a puddle where his emotions now lay beside mine. I couldn't stop the tears, and for the first time I didn't want to.

So I said the only thing that I knew to be true. "I love you, Bo," I wept my voice breaking.

He hit his head against the wall, the ball no longer flowed through the air, but it was tightly gripped in the palm of his hand. His eyes shut like what I just expressed caused him pain. It only made me cry harder.

Then the ball unexpectedly hurled through the air, hitting the wall so hard it broke through the drywall. He immediately stood and was over to the door in three strides, opening it and stopping right before he stepped out onto the deck.

With a bowed head and soft voice he said, "I love you, too." And then he was gone.

Only adding to the times...

That he walked away from me.

Lucas always comforted me. With his arms, his words, his expressions, even when he was hurting me. He was as much my refuge as I was his. I lay there for the rest of the evening, staring at the hole in the wall and letting the music lull me.

Waiting.

I heard the door open and close. I felt his presence as he sat beside me gently lifting my head into his lap. I closed my eyes while he lovingly stroked my hair.

Softly humming…

My Brown Eyed Girl.

# Chapter 13

## Alex

I watched him walk in from the corner of my eye. It had been a few days since I first saw him. He sat out on the deck, and I made my way out there, tray in hand. I placed it on the table, and he smiled the same dimply grin that made my belly flutter and my palms sweaty.

"The boys didn't scare you off, huh?" I joked with a hint of amusement in my voice and a hand firmly positioned at my hip.

"I like to live life on the edge." He leaned back in his chair as he looked up at me with a slight glimmer in his gaze. "You're too pretty to stay away from."

The crimson red crept along my cheeks, immediately making me feel hot all over. I ignored his comment and moved the glass of water, with the chips and salsa from the tray to the table, not meeting his fixated glare that was intently placed on my flushed face.

"I really need to stop blushing around you," I admitted, handing him the napkins.

"Please don't," was all he said.

I smiled, peeking up at him through my lashes.

"So, Alexandra—"

"You can call me Alex."

"Can I now?" he teased. "What if I don't want to?"

I raised an eyebrow, trying to hide the smile from my face.

"Alex is a boy name and you Darlin', are no boy."

I giggled and it seemed foreign coming from my body. I sounded like a girl, and I tried to pretend that I didn't love that.

"Besides, Alexandra is a beautiful name and it suits you just fine."

I nodded while I pursed my lips, making him cock his head to the side. "Are you enticing me, beautiful girl?"

"Wow," I breathed out. "You are quite the flirt, huh? This work for you back home?"

He smiled, big and wide and folded his arms over his chest. "I don't know, is it working for me now?"

I smiled back, shrugging. "Where you from anyway?"

"You change the subject when you're shy and you ignore compliments, good to know. I'm from California."

I smirked. "Ah, hence the surfing."

"Hence she says," he teased again.

"Are you done?"

He shook his head with a proud look on his face. "I haven't even started, Darlin'."

"Where in California?"

I could see that he wanted to call me out on the fact that he was right about everything he claimed. "Santa Barbara." But he didn't. "Ever been?"

"No. I've never been anywhere before."

"Really?"

"Yep."

"Well coming from someone who has been everywhere, there's something to be said about a small town girl."

I jerked back with lowered eyebrows.

"In the best possible way that is," he added after taking in my grimace. "This is the first time I've been to Oak Island, though."

"You should check out the pier or umm, the lighthouse."

"You should show me," he quickly followed.

"Excuse me?"

"You heard me. I mean you're my only friend and all."

"I find that hard to believe," I stated with a grin.

He put up three fingers. "Scouts Honor."

I laughed. "What would you like to order?"

He grabbed the menu, looking at it for a few seconds and moving his head side-to-side to the music playing from the speakers. "I'll take the gator bites and a cheeseburger with curly fries."

"Coming right up."

"And, I'll take you as a tour guide for a day."

I peered up at him while writing his order on my pad of paper. "I work every day this week."

"Next week?"

"I don't know yet," I lied.

"Yes, you do. Oh, come on, don't make me beg."

I narrowed my eyes at him in laughter.

"It's not a date if that's what you're thinking. Not that I would mind that, but I just think we should get to know each other before you fall in love with me."

My eyes widened and my mouth dropped.

"You'll see," he simply stated.

I shook my head because quite frankly I had no clue how to respond to that, and I wasn't going to pretend that I did. I spun and left him sitting completely pleased with the effect that he had on me. There was no hiding it.

Cole Hayes was something else.

I just hadn't figured out what that was yet.

# LUCAS

We sat inside at our usual table, sitting directly across from where I could see Alex. I watched her talking to Cole, anxiously wanting to know what went through her mind. What she thought about. What she felt. What she wanted. I imagined it had something to do with the pretty boy who sat in front of her. I ignored the plaguing assumptions and directed my attention back to her.

The way she blushed.

The way she smiled.

The way she pursed her lips when she was nervous.

How her head would tilt back when she laughed, always laughing with her entire body that had Cole quickly mirroring her contagious laughter. How her hand would instinctively find her cocked hip, waiting to emphasize her sassy comments and witty stance. All the feisty mannerisms that made her who she was, all the little things that I loved so much about her, Cole witnessed with a fascinating regard of complete and utter devotion. He couldn't look away even if he wanted to.

And he didn't want to.

He was completely mesmerized with our Half-Pint, wanting to know more. Wanting to know everything. Both of them entirely wrapped up in each other, oblivious to anyone or anything around them.

As much as I hated seeing her flirt with someone who wasn't me and trust me, I fucking despised it. I couldn't take my goddamn eyes away from her. My gaze solely focused on her and her alone. I barely paid any attention to him or at least I tried not to. The crazy thing about it was that I watched her hundreds of times, shit it may have been thousands by that point. I often wondered if she knew half of what I truly took in, my eyes could sense her presence anywhere. I gravitated toward her. She was like a magnet to me. It had always been that way, especially when we were kids. At times, I felt like it was mutual, that we were connected in a way that neither one of us understood. But as I sat there taking her in, watching her every move, I would be lying if I said it didn't make me question the bond we had.

*Was it just in my mind or was it actually real?*

I couldn't be around them for very long, the jealousy that washed over me was hell. The constant subtle body language between them taunted me from across the room. I wanted to walk over and tell Cole to back the fuck off. My possessiveness could be felt around the room. It was that thick and consuming, blinding and overwhelming. I drowned in it. I couldn't put it into words or coherent thoughts. I felt it in my very being. It flowed through me like the waves of the ocean, dragging me under until I couldn't breathe.

I knew what she meant to me.

But for the first time I sat there and watched her through different eyes. It was like admiring a whole new person, someone I saw for the first time. I couldn't fathom how that was even possible, we grew up beside one another our whole lives. How was I just now noticing the shift between our Half-Pint and Alexandra?

*How did it take me this long?*

No longer the little girl with pigtails running after us, insistent that she would do everything we did. Dressing like us, and acting like us, it didn't matter what it was, she'd always been one of the boys.

One of us.

Complicate Me

Right before our very own eyes, the feisty, shy, adorable girl, the same one who would tackle you to the ground if you ever called her one, acted like a real girl. Somewhere along the line she shed her Half-Pint skin and slowly transformed into her own being. She became Alexandra. She didn't need the boys or me. She could stand on her own and be her own person. It took me seeing her with Cole to realize and acknowledge it.

She grew up.

As much as I wanted to go over there and stop whatever spark ignited between them, I didn't want to interrupt seeing her blossom. Seeing her appear so different but still the same, if that made any sense at all. It only added to the pile of things I loved about her.

I caught Cole's demeanor every once in a while, taking everything in and cherishing every second of it. She had the same effect on him that she had on us.

Especially me.

Jacob's glare was seen out of the corner of my eye, it was the exact same stare I gave her, them. As soon as she walked back into the room our eyes locked across the distance. The connection we always shared found its way into both of our bodies, almost like it was ingrained in us. Her apprehensive, almost questioning gaze immediately spread across her face, making me lower my eyes to my menu. I could play off staring at her, but there was no way in hell I could hide my natural response to her at that moment. So, naturally I pretended it never happened and Jacob hadn't noticed when I knew damn well he did.

"Hey," she announced with a steady voice when she reached our table. "Good waves today, huh? It's windy out. I put your orders in, they should be out soon."

I nodded while I played on my phone. "What did douchebag want?"

"Be nice," she warned in a lighthearted tone.

I looked up at her and smiled. "I'm always nice."

She smiled back, her face sedated. "I'm going to check on your orders."

We ate our food and played some pool to let it digest before heading back out. The swells were getting bigger and higher.

"I'm going to the bathroom, I'll catch up with you guys," I said after we paid our bills. Jacob lingered for a few seconds but didn't call me out on it, nodding his head and following the rest of them out.

I saw her walking across the room into the hallway. My feet moved forward as if being pulled by a rope, and I found myself following her. She made her way to the restroom, and I was grateful it was secluded in the back of the building, because I waited for her.

"What did he want?" I immediately questioned when she came out of the bathroom.

She gasped, putting her hand on her chest. "You scared the crap out of me."

I had reached for the side of her face before reason and doubt took over, my fingers grazed her cheek, and I tucked a misplaced hair behind her ear. Her lips parted and her chest rose.

"You look really pretty today. I wanted to tell you that. Your hair is getting so long." It was almost down to her waist, she wore white jean shorts and a crop top that showed a little bit of her belly when she moved fast. The restaurant called for casual beach attire, so her parents never made the staff wear uniforms. They dressed how they wanted.

"Thank you," she replied almost out of breath. I wanted to know that I had an effect on her as well. I wanted to know a lot of things. I took my hand away and slipped it back in the pocket of my board shorts instead.

She cleared her throat. "What did who want?"

"Oh yes, the douchebag. What the fuck did he want?" It came out harsher than I wanted it to sound.

She cocked her head to the side. "He wanted to order food. I'm his waitress remember?"

"You're not his anything," I crudely stated.

Her hand found its way to her hip. "I am the restaurant's waitress, so therefore I'm his. He wanted to order food. You know the reason people come into the restaurant is to eat. I take their orders, put them in with the cook, and then bring them back out to serve. Pretty standard stuff, Bo, you've watched me do it for how many weeks now?" she mocked, catching me off guard.

"Better take the sass down, Half-Pint."

Complicate Me

She raised an eyebrow, stepping toward me. "Or what?"

It all happened so fast. I barely had time to register what occurred. My mouth moved while her eyes connected with mine. I could feel her breathing on my lips and the smell of cherry lip-gloss and Cherry Coke assaulted my senses. I placed my hand on the nook of her neck and pulled her closer to me, the touch of her breasts against my chest was an unwelcoming sensation that I didn't need in my already fucked up mind.

The next thing I knew, her soft pouty lips were pressed up against mine. Her mouth slightly parted and with the tip of my tongue I lightly touched her lips, gliding my tongue along the gloss-scented coating. It was over before it even began when I begrudgingly drew away, not before claiming her mouth one last time and enjoying the sensation that only she stirred within me. Our eyes opened at the exact same time, the hooded gaze I had grown to love carved deep within her pupils, mine mimicked hers, I was sure.

"Stay away from the douchebag," I ordered, grinning, my hand still clutching the back of her neck. "Unless you want me to remind you again?" I challenged, hoping she would say yes.

She immediately closed her eyes not wanting me to see her truths.

"That's what I thought," I chuckled, tugging her toward me and kissing the top of her head. "I'll see you in a bit."

I knew one thing was for sure...

Game on motherfucker.

*Alex*

I watched him leave as my fingers brushed along my lips where he had just licked. Lucas was always in control, even when he wasn't. He must have seen something that had shaken him enough to want to *remind* me of what we were to each other. I stood there with my erratic breathing and my heart pounding waiting until I couldn't see him anymore to move.

*What the hell was that?*

I don't even think he knows.

I shook my mind off the lingering thoughts and emotions, needing to get back to work but taking a few minutes to compose myself before I made my way back to Cole's table.

"You ok?" he asked as I bussed the table.

"Yeah," was all I could say.

"You sure? You look flushed."

I nodded not meeting his eyes.

"I guess I have that effect on you."

His words made me look at him, confused. "What?"

"And I make you speechless," he cockily stated with a grin, exposing the dimples that instantly made my palms sweaty.

I laughed I couldn't help it. "Sorry to say, it has nothing to do with you."

He put his hand over his heart in a dramatic manner. "Ouch. A guy can dream, can't he?"

I smiled, shaking my head and continued to clear his table.

"So about next week. What time can I pick you up?"

"I didn't say yes," I reminded, not meeting his prying eyes but feeling them precisely on me.

"You didn't say no either."

I sighed, taking in a deep breath. "Let me think about it."

"You sure are putting a lot of thought into us hanging out. You're making me think you don't like me."

I narrowed my eyes at him and he smiled, giving him the exact reaction he wanted. "You do like me, don't you?"

I cocked my head to the side with a penetrating stare.

He put his hands in the air in a surrendering gesture. "I need to hear you say it or else I may never recover. Do you want that on your conscience?"

I rolled my eyes, grabbing the tray and placing it on my hip. "I don't think you need anyone to over inflate that ego of yours."

He let out a rough deep laugh. It was one of those laughs that formed in the bottom of his belly, then rumbled its way up and erupted from his mouth. "Damn, Alexandra, you're just making me fall for you more and more. Is that your plan? Seeing as mine is backfiring."

I ignored him again. "Here is your bill." I placed it in front of him and walked back inside. I needed to readjust myself from Lucas

117

and Cole. They overwhelmed me in ways I wasn't used to, ways I didn't understand. For some reason, I knew he wasn't the type of guy to hear no very often. I didn't want to lead him on. By the time I wandered back to his table he was gone, all that sat there was a $20.00 tip firmly placed under the black receipt holder.

His name and phone number written across it.

# Chapter 14

## Alex

As soon as my shift was over I walked out to a beautiful burnt sky. It held the promise of a calm night over the horizon. My eyes shifted away from the mystical colors to Lucas, waiting for me across the street in his parked truck. My foot hit the running board and my hand landed in his. We pulled in unison, Lucas, helping me with the leap.

"Hey," I greeted.

"How was the rest of your shift?" he asked, shifting the gear into drive.

"Went by fast. Why didn't you come back in?"

Our eyes locked and a satisfied grin quickly appeared on his face. "You know why."

I kept his intense gaze for a few seconds, trying to read his amused expression that made my heart skip a beat. Not wanting to break the calm that was displayed all around us, I decided to turn my head and look out the window. Sometimes it was better not to disturb the storm that followed him everywhere. We had driven in silence for a few minutes before I noticed he missed the turn to my house and then again to our abandoned house.

I finally asked, "Where are you going?"

"To South Port," he simply stated.

"To town? For what?"

He ignored my question.

"Are the boys meeting us there?"

"No."

"Then why are we going?"

He cleared his throat like his mouth had become suddenly dry. "I'm taking you out," he rasped, holding onto the steering wheel tightly. "Me and you," he added.

"What about the boys?"

"Fuck them."

"Oh…" I stayed silent for another few minutes and finally blurted, "Like on a date?"

He smiled as his grip made its way to my upper thigh, squeezing it firmly. I squirmed and giggled.

"Put your seatbelt on," he ordered, still not answering my question. It didn't matter I already knew the answer. I'd known before I even asked.

We pulled up to Putt-Putt Golf. Lucas jumped out first and helped me out of his truck when I opened the door. "Thanks," I half-whispered.

He'd done this several times, except this time he hadn't let go of my hand. I followed close behind him as he led the way, cherishing how he guided me effortlessly. I enjoyed the feel of his huge hand. It was so bulky in mine. Hoping we could stay in this moment forever and not let it pass us by. Secretly praying we would get a chance to be like this. Always. I tried not to think about all the things that awaited us when we stepped back into Oak Island, our families, and the boys mostly. I lived in that second with him. Where we could just be Lucas and Alex, loving each other's company and not wanting it to end.

We played two rounds of Putt-Putt and he won both freaking times. I hated playing games with him, he never let me win and it infuriated me to no end. I think he did it on purpose, just to get a rise out of me and see me act adorable.

His words, not mine.

We strolled down the beach, hand-in-hand until we came up to an ice cream shop. He ordered two scoops of vanilla adding peanuts, my favorite, and chocolate with fudge, his favorite.

"I have some change in my truck," he told the girl behind the counter.

"It's fine." I reached into my pocket and pulled out my tips. The twenty-dollar bill fell to the floor, and standing at attention was the name Cole and his phone number, fiercely burning against the ceramic tile.

Lucas and I both stared at it like it was diseased infected, and the mere thought of what was to come made my stomach hurt. He bent down, grabbing the twenty-dollar bill and placed it into his back pocket. For a quick second, I wondered if he was actually going to give it back to me. When I looked up, I saw the answer to my question on his face. I paid the girl and then he reassuringly grabbed my hand again, this time much tighter than before. He found a secluded spot on the beach where we could take in the waves of the ocean while eating our ice creams, even though my appetite had become almost non-existent.

We sat side-by-side, leaning into each other.

"He asked me to be his tour guide for the day," I divulged, wanting to break the tension between us.

"Are you going to go?" His tone was neutral.

I was surprised by his response. I expected a lot worse. "I don't know," I honestly replied.

"Would it matter if I told you I didn't want you to go?"

I glanced at the side of his face. "Are you telling me that?"

"What if I was?"

I bowed my head and stared at my cone, it started to melt down the sides and drip onto the sand. "That's not fair."

"Do you like him, Alex?"

"I don't know him, Lucas," I countered, throwing his name back at him.

"Do you want to get to know him?"

"He's nice," I said loud enough for him to hear.

# LUCAS

It was like taking a knife to the heart. "He's a fucking douchebag," I stated, remembering the way he squared off to me, provoking me.

"You don't know him, either. You're not being nice."

"I don't give a shit what I'm being. The guy's a fucking douche. I don't like him, and trust me the feeling is very much mutual."

"How do you know that?"

If he hadn't mentioned our encounter to her then neither was I. "I didn't think you found pretty boys like him attractive," I said, changing the subject.

She shrugged.

I hated all this lingering bullshit placed in between us. I didn't know how to express myself into words without getting pissed off and letting my temper get the best of me.

"Did you take me out because of him, Bo?" she murmured, not taking her stare away from her cone that melted everywhere. I grabbed it and licked all around the edges, making it good as new and handing it right back to her.

She shyly smiled. "Thanks." Immediately licking where I just did, making my dick twitch. It was so innocent, she didn't even realize the effect it might have on me. All it did was reinforce the fact that she was still so fucking young. I had to stop watching her and shake away the thoughts, but I didn't want to answer her question either. It wouldn't come out the right way. The truth was he did have something to do with it, but not in the way she would interpret it.

She was mine.

I didn't want to share her.

Not with Cole.

Not with anyone.

*How do you explain something you don't even understand?*

"You take Stacey out," she said, pulling me away from my thoughts and making me look at her again.

"Not like that."

"Like what then?"

"She doesn't matter," I firmly stated.

"You always say that."

"It's the truth."

She sighed and then opened her mouth to say something but quickly shut it.

"Say it," I ordered in a serious tone.

"It's nice having a new friend."

My head jerked back and I narrowed my eyes at her. "What's that supposed to mean?"

"It just means that it's nice meeting new people. All I've ever had is you boys, and sometimes I've felt left out, is all."

"When?"

She bowed her head, looking at her cone once again. "Dylan has Aubrey, Jacob has different girls all the time and don't even get me started on Austin," she hesitated for a few seconds, "You have—"

"You," I clearly asserted. "I have you."

She finally looked up at me. "Do I?"

I didn't falter. "Always."

We stared at each other for a few minutes, neither one of us saying anything, but I knew hundreds of thoughts ran rampant through our minds and there was much more we wanted to express. When you're that young, you don't realize how short life truly was. You think you will have all the time in the world to be and do whatever your heart desires, it will eventually get there. It's bound to happen.

One day.

Two simple words that meant everything.

In the back of my mind I always thought our time would come, it was only a matter of time. When we were older, when we understood what we meant to each other, when our parents would understand, when the boys could understand.

When… when… when…

Our relationship was filled with what ifs, and maybe some days…

It was complicated.

It was messy.

It was us.

I couldn't take her in small doses and I couldn't take her in large ones. Nothing was ever enough. As we got older, it just piled on and before we both knew it, we went from hundreds of things to say to nothing. The pile became a mountain of endless questions and not enough answers.

As any sixteen-year-old boy would do, I ignored the warning signs and this was the first one that would lead to many. So I did the only thing that came naturally to me, I lunged on top of her and she shrieked, catching myself before all my weight fell on her. I gazed into her serene eyes before kissing her cheeks, her chin, her forehead, and then the tip of her nose.

"You're heavy," she laughed, trying to squirm her way out of my hold.

"Nah."

"I can't breathe."

"That's because you're laughing. Why ya laughin' if you can't breathe?" I teased, moving my hand to her ribs.

"Don't," she warned.

"What are you talkin' about?"

"Bo, I will hurt you."

"Nah." I tickled her anyway.

"This is torture!"

"It's not torture when you like it."

I held her down and started tickling her everywhere until I found her sweet spot, it was right in her inner top thigh. I dug my fingers in and tickled the hell out of her, she screamed, kicked, and laughed all at the same time. Her laugh was fucking contagious and I finally had to let go, falling over on my back laughing. She immediately gasped out of breath, and I grabbed her hand kissing it and laying it back on my chest.

We laid in comfortable silence for a long time.

"Bo..."

"Hmmm..."

"I'm going to show Cole—"

"Shhh, let's just lay here okay?"

"Okay," she half-whispered.

I had to let her grow up, but it didn't mean I had to fucking like it.

# Alex

A few days had gone by before I saw Cole again. He was dressed in slacks and a button-down shirt with a tie when I watched him walk into the restaurant with an older man that I assumed was his father. They sat inside instead of his usual table on the deck.

"Hey," I greeted.

He gave me a simple nod and then looked down at his menu. Which was odd but I didn't say anything about it.

"Would you like to hear the specials?" I asked them.

M. Robinson

"I don't have time to hear the specials. We will take your soup of the day and some salads, can you put a rush order on that. I don't have time to waste," the man demanded.

"Oh. Umm, yeah. Would you like—"

A scowl appeared on his face as he looked up at me. "No, I would not. Run along. Put our orders in."

My eyes widened and I looked over at Cole who had his head bowed with shame, but he didn't say anything. Not one word.

I nodded and backed away to go put in their orders. The rest of the lunch went exactly like that. Cole wouldn't meet my eyes and the man he was with was rude and mean, although he did leave me a thirty-dollar tip on a twenty-dollar meal. Several hours had past when I saw Cole sitting outside on the deck in his usual seat. A huge part of me didn't want to acknowledge him at all, or even serve him for that matter, but I decided against it.

As soon as he heard the door open he looked up and we locked eyes.

I reached his table. "What can I get you?"

"I owe you an explanation."

I shook my head. "You don't owe me anything."

"My dad, he's well, he's... fuck, he's an asshole."

I raised my eyebrows, surprised with his stammer.

"My mom is better but not by much. My parents, they're just pretentious and self-righteous. They treat everyone like that, it's not personal."

"Why—"

"Why didn't I say anything?" he interrupted. "It's not going to change, it's better when I ignore it."

I nodded, not knowing what to say or do.

"I meant it when I told you I don't have a lot of friends, and all the so-called ones I do have aren't anything to brag about. My family has a lot of money and I've been everywhere, Alexandra. You seem real and honest, and I haven't really ever met someone like you."

I weakly smiled.

"I would love for us to be friends. I know I need one and something tells me that you do, too."

"I'd like that, Cole."

125

"Good."

"So, I'll take you up on your offer to show you around. I mean if you still want me to?"

"Of course."

"I have off tomorrow. My dad has a golf cart that we could use, it makes things much easier than walking around."

"That sounds perfect."

I wrote down my address on the pad of paper, ripping it out and handing it to him.

"That's my address. Let's say around noon?"

"I'll be there."

"Now. What can I get you?"

He stood up. "You gave me what I wanted." He slipped the piece of paper in his pocket. "I'll see you tomorrow."

I watched him leave with anticipation and sadness. I felt bad for him. There was more to Cole than meets the eye and I knew right then and there.

That we had that in common.

# Chapter 15

## Alex

"Please don't embarrass me," I repeated for the tenth time to my dad.

"Why would I embarrass you? I'm a cool dad."

I looked over at my mom as she leaned against the kitchen counter, taking in the desperation that was probably clearly written across my face.

"Mom…"

She smiled. "Alex, you're going on your first date—"

"It's not a date," I interrupted.

Her eyebrows lowered.

"I'm just showing him around."

She raised an eyebrow.

"It's not like that," I clarified.

She folded her arms over her chest. "When a boy asks you to hang out with him, that meant a date in my time. What's the big deal? You're allowed to date, sweetie, you're going to be fifteen in a few weeks."

"Speak for yourself, Jana, I need to make sure this boy knows that he can't mess around with my daughter. He's only here for the summer. I know what those kinds of guys are interested in," Dad chimed in, making me bow my head.

"Please don't embarrass me," I repeated again.

"Nathanial…"

He spun to look at her. "What? Jana, you know I'm right."

"Not every boy is like you, honey," she stated, teasingly.

"I should call the boys and tell them to—"

"NO! No calling the boys. Mom!" I whined.

My eyes widened as I heard the knock on the door.

"And he's early, I like him already," Mom said, grabbing Dad by the arm so that I could go open the door instead of him.

Complicate Me

The anxiety crept higher and higher with each step I took as I made my way to the front door, but it only became worse when I saw Lucas standing there.

"What are you doing here?" I blurted.

His smile disappeared. "Well hello to you, too."

"No, I mean we didn't have plans."

I tried to ignore his questioning stare. "Since when do we make plans?"

"Right..."

"What's up with you?"

I reluctantly met his gaze. "Nothing."

"Are you going to let me in?"

"Umm…"

I felt my dad's arm go around me as he pushed the door open further, allowing more sunlight to come in.

"Alex here is just nervous that I'm going to embarrass her on her date today."

Lucas raised his stunned eyebrows. "Date?" he frowned, and for a moment I held his intense glare before I couldn't take it anymore and had to look down at the floor.

My dad followed. "They don't know about your date?"

"I told you it's not a date," I muttered.

"You know this guy Cole?" Dad asked Lucas.

I stepped away, avoiding any further conversation by escaping to my room. It didn't take long for me to hear the light tapping on my door before he walked in. I kept my attention to my closet, pretending I was still deciding what to wear. Lucas's arm grazed mine as he pulled out a cream dress.

"I love this color on you. I'm sure Cole will, too," he alleged in a tone I couldn't place.

I didn't know if he meant it in a condescending way, and when I raised my eyes to him, he lowered his gaze. I fought hard with myself, trying not to be the one to break the focus. Instant anger overpowered his demeanor as he looked back up at me and I held his stare. I wasn't about to back down. Not this time. Something in the way his eyes glared at me with his heated composure radiating all around me caused me to feel something. Something familiar, yet I couldn't put my finger on it. The feeling was new. A fulfillment I couldn't explain or even understand for that matter. I felt pleased. Gratified by the fact that his fire was being fueled by me.

I didn't understand the strange vibes searing between us, it boiled to the point of discomfort. The feelings I had, what he provoked and stirred within me, what he always did to me. No one could ever explain or understand what it was. How it happened. No one else could do this.

It was only Lucas.

Always Lucas.

Not one other soul had this pull.

On me.

On him.

On us.

My glare slowly moved away from his and toward my closet. With all the attitude I could give. And I didn't even know why. Why did I feel like this was a turning point?

"He's just a boy, Lucas," I assured him as he had for me time and time again.

I wasn't trying to be mean or maybe I was, but the recognition of my words on his face answered my doubt. His eyes flickered with rage and a familiarity. It made me feel satisfied for some reason, I never wanted to hurt him. At least I didn't think I did. Though at that moment it felt nice for him to be on the other side of the fence looking in, and maybe for the first time he would feel what it was like in my shoes.

"I thought it wasn't a date?" he snapped not missing a beat with frustration spreading across his face.

There was no room for me to walk past him and he wasn't moving his stance either.

"Excuse me, Bo, I have to go change. I think you're right about the dress," I crudely replied, wanting to get more of a rise out of him.

How did we always go from one to ten in nanoseconds?

He narrowed his eyes at me. I saw irritation and annoyance quickly replacing the anger and confusion. Neither one of us spoke for what felt like several minutes but was probably just seconds. When the doorbell rang I tried to step aside but he blocked me in with his daunting, bulky stance, his folded arms over his chest only accenting his large frame over mine.

"You didn't answer my question."

He already knew the answer, but he wanted to hear me say the words. Again. And for the first time I didn't want to give him the reassurance.

"You heard me the first time and the second," I simply stated.

He cocked his head to the side. "This the way you want to play it, *Alexandra*?"

I didn't know what the hell he vowed, but I couldn't falter. "I have to go. I'll see you later, *Lucas*." I pushed him aside with my shoulder and walked into my bathroom to put on the dress he so scornfully told me to wear.

# LUCAS

I placed the twenty-dollar bill on her bed, except this one didn't have Cole's phone number on it. I threw that one in the fucking garbage, not that it mattered she was still going on a "date" with the douchebag. I knew what he tried to pull, I didn't trust him as far as I could fucking throw him. I decided to walk through the kitchen and go out the back door to the pool. I could leave by the side gate. My truck was parked in front of the house, but at least this way I wouldn't have to look at his fucking pretty boy face.

I stood outside in the backyard, the place that held so much of my childhood memories, and I tried desperately to ignore the bitter feeling that formed in my stomach. I heard the door open and then close and for a split second I thought it was Alex, choosing me over him.

It wasn't.

"Are you okay?" Alex's mom questioned, standing beside me, her arms folded over her chest like mine. Except hers were in comfort, mine were in aggravation over the fact that I caused this. It was my fault. I was more pissed off at myself than anything else, but it was easier to blame Alex.

I shrugged not knowing what to say.

M. Robinson

She softly smiled over at me and it reminded me of Alex, except it didn't provide the security I needed, that's only something she could do.

"I've seen Cole around the restaurant a few times. He seems like a nice boy," she sincerely expressed.

I knew what she tried to do, she wanted to ease my worry that Alex was being taken care of, but all it did was add to my insecurity that maybe she was right. And I didn't want to like Cole, not now. Not ever.

"Appearances can be deceiving."

She took in my words for a moment. "You know we all grew up together and then we all had kids together. When I was your age, I thought I was in love with your dad."

"What?" I replied, stunned. My parents had never revealed that to me.

She smiled, relieved. "Don't look so surprised, Lucas. You've seen your dad. Your mom and I were best friends. She knows. But in the end the best woman won. I realized that it was just a childhood crush, I ended up with the man I was supposed to be with."

I shook my head, baffled and speechless of what she shared. I wasn't expecting that. "What are you trying to say?"

"That everything happens for a reason. You'll realize that when you're older."

"Why doesn't anyone want Alex and I to be together?" I finally asked. It was the first time I acknowledged that I actually felt something stronger than just friendship with Alex and her mom didn't even seem phased. It was like she already knew and was more shocked at the fact that I finally admitted it out loud.

"You're young and she's even younger. I think that everything will work out the way it's supposed to. In the meantime have fun, summer is almost over."

I nodded. "Yeah." I wanted to say more, but it wouldn't change anything, it wouldn't prove anything that she didn't already know.

For years to come, I would think that our mothers were one of the biggest obstacles to us not being together, and I would learn way too late that it was the exact opposite.

131

She smiled again. "I'll see you later, honey." She kissed my head and left me with nothing but the empty feeling that I would also carry with me for years to come.

I did the only thing that made me forget…

I went and picked up Stacey.

## Alex

"Your dad is intense," Cole exclaimed as he drove the golf cart toward the lighthouse.

"Sorry about that," I replied, thoroughly embarrassed. Lucas's truck was still parked in front of my house when we left, but he was nowhere to be seen when I walked back downstairs.

"What are you thinking about over there?"

"Nothin'."

He raised an eyebrow. "You know when you lie your voice changes. It does this low pitch thing."

I already knew that. Lucas reminded me often. "Are you always this perceptive?" I teased, bringing the attention back to him.

"It's a curse."

"Oh yeah? Why is that?"

"By the way, I know what you're doing. Just in case you don't realize that I'm aware of you trying to change the subject." He flashed me one of his full-on dimple smiles I had become familiar with. "My parents are both lawyers."

"Ah," I replied, ignoring the first part of what he said.

"They work all the time, and it's one of the reasons they decided to buy a house here. Trying to get in some family time before I go away to college."

"Makes sense. Why Oak Island?"

"My mom loves North Carolina. She used to come here in the summers when she was a kid, they passed through here a few times so she has fond memories."

"But this is your first time here?"

He nodded, grinning at me. "Definitely not the last."

I rolled my eyes, sitting sideways so I could give him my undivided attention. "Okay, buddy, new rule."

"Oh yeah?"

"Yes. This." I pointed from him to me. "If it's going to work, this flirting thing you got going on, it's got to be taken down a few notches."

"How many?"

"Like all of them."

"I can't commit to that."

"Cole…"

He chuckled, making his dimples prominent and enticing, I wanted nothing more than to reach over and touch them. I blushed just thinking about it.

"I love it when you say my name."

I slapped his arm. "Stop that."

He laughed. "Alexandra, why do you want me to stop it? I like you. I've been pretty upfront about that. When a guy likes a girl, he flirts with her. It's in our genes. We don't know how to be any other way."

"That's bull honky."

He laughed again. "Bull honky? What happened to bullshit? Is that how you talk around these parts, Darlin'?"

"Darlin'? Now I know I'm not all fancy and from California like you are but I do know that 'Darlin'' is a Southern term. Now, who's fakin'?"

He glanced over with a mischievous stare. "You caught me. Can't get anything past you, huh? I'm trying to impress you, is it working?"

I giggled. I couldn't help it. "I'm here, aren't I? I'm kinda digging you calling me Darlin', no one's ever called me that before."

"I'm almost certain no one's ever done a lot of things to you before," he hesitated. "And I'll tell you what, I really love that."

"Yeah… yeah… yeah… just drive, Casanova." I sat forward.

We arrived at the lighthouse. Cole took some pictures, and he made me pose for him for some of them. I'm usually not much for photos, but I enjoyed being the center of his attention.

"The view from up here is amazing. It's my second favorite thing about Oak Island." He leaned against the railing and I followed suit.

"It is pretty ridiculous. I haven't been up here in a long time."

"That's a shame."

"Yeah," I replied, taking in the fresh air and the smell of the ocean. The breeze was a nice change of pace from the hot, humid summer. I forgot how much I loved it up here.

"Aren't you going to ask me what my favorite thing is?" he asked, moving a little closer to me, causing his cologne to instantly assault my senses. It was difficult not turning to him just to breathe him in.

"I don't know, are you going to say something cheesy or flirty? Or are you going to be honest?"

"I'm always honest."

I gave him a skeptical look and he held up three fingers again like when we first met, making me smile.

"You, Alexandra, you're my favorite thing about Oak Island."

Our eyes connected, and for the first time I didn't have to question him.

The truth was written all over his face.

# Chapter 16

## Alex

"So, tell me something about yourself that no one knows," he inquired.

"Hmm…"

"Not even Lucas," he added.

"Now that's a hard one, there isn't anything Lucas doesn't know."

"I find that hard to believe."

"Why is that?"

"Because you're here with me. That tells me there's a lot that Lucas doesn't know about you. If he did, you wouldn't be here."

I nonchalantly shook my head. I wasn't ready to let him in like that, not this fast. I could lie to you and tell you it was because I didn't trust him, but that wasn't it. Cole was as sincere as they come. Over the years, our friendship would develop in ways that would have him replacing Lucas.

The truth was…

I wasn't prepared to let that happen so soon.

I shrugged and he accepted my silent request by not pressuring me to give him more than I already had.

"Let's talk about you," I reiterated, challenging him to see if he would let me in right from the start or if it would also occur over time.

"I'm an open book, ask me anything."

*Well that answers that.*

"You said you didn't have many friends. Why is that?"

"Starting off with the big guns, eh?"

"Maybe."

"Alright." He nodded. "Duly noted. This last year was my first year at a real school, well a private school anyway. Before that, I was homeschooled. My parents wanted me to have the best education, so I wasn't surrounded by kids my age unless I was going to charity functions or stupid shit like that."

"That sounds sad."

"I could say the same to you."

I was taken aback. "To me? I have lots of friends."

"Do you? Because I've only met or seen you with four."

My eyes moved all around me, contemplating what he insinuated.

"I told you, we're more alike than you think. Something tells me you already knew that, too. Or else you definitely wouldn't be here."

I glanced over at the side of his face and he appeared deep in thought.

"Cole."

He turned to face me.

"I think I'm going to like us being friends."

"I know I'm going to want us to be more," he simply stated.

"Duly noted." I grinned followed by a quick nod. "I'm hungry. Let's go get lunch."

He trailed close behind me and I knew he wanted to grab my hand, I could sense it. I think that's why I kept them folded over my chest. I didn't want to give myself the option.

Of letting him.

It didn't take long for us to get to my parents' restaurant. I showed him a few more sites on the way there and we laughed the entire time, enjoying our banter and not taking the seriousness of our conversation from the lighthouse with us.

I saw them as soon as we walked into the restaurant and I should have known better. I did it to myself. Again it had me contemplating whether I did it on purpose or not. Subconsciously wanting to hurt Lucas.

"Half-Pint," Dylan hollered, waving me over to their table. Aubrey sat beside him. Jacob was next to her with Macy, a girl he had started seeing. Across from them were Austin and some girl I had never seen before, but right in front of Dylan sat Lucas with Stacey firmly wrapped around his arm. I swear she held him tighter when she saw me.

"Come on," I said to Cole, who immediately grabbed my hand, leading the way to their table. I watched Lucas' glare go from him to our interlocked hands.

To be completely honest, I was shocked as hell, too. Cole knew everything without me ever having to tell him, and I learned it at that very moment.

*If he could see it and he had just met me then why couldn't Lucas?*

"Hey," I greeted to everyone, averting my eyes from Lucas whose scowl burned a hole at my side.

"Well... well... well... lookie here, our Half-Pint's on her first date," Jacob announced, smiling as big as the Cheshire cat.

"It's not—"

Cole wrapped his arm around my shoulder pulling me into his side. My hand instinctively went to his chest, while he kissed the top of my head as if he had been doing it our entire lives. At that moment, it felt sincere and loving, almost like it was one of my boys doing it. I loved the feeling it gave me, providing a comfort that I was safe from anyone just like with them.

"It's not going to be the last either," Cole interrupted, taking me away from my thoughts and continuing to bait Lucas.

That much I did know.

"It's alright, Half-Pint, I can feel your anxiety from here. Your mom already informed us that we're to be nice to Cole and that you were on a date. Can't say I'm not hurt that you didn't tell us yourself," Dylan exclaimed, dramatically placing his hand over his chest.

Aubrey slapped him on the back of the head. "You leave her alone, Dylan McGraw! Or else you're going to have to deal with me, and we both know that you won't win that," she chastised.

I couldn't love Aubrey more than I had in that second.

"Alex, why don't you join us, let the boys here get to know Cole," she added.

Dylan didn't correct her, which I found odd. He never let Aubrey have the last word. I wondered if they had fought about this before, I always knew Aubrey had my back, but I never guessed how much until we were older.

"Maybe another time, I'd like to have Alex to myself on our first date and all," Cole responded, making all the girls swoon at the table.

"I thought it wasn't a date," Lucas chimed in out of nowhere. All eyes moved to him except his were directly pointed at me, and I connected with his intense glare. It made my heart pound and my mouth dry. I prayed that Cole couldn't feel my body shudder, but when he held me firmer, I realized he could.

"At least that's what you said this morning. *Twice*, I believe," Lucas goaded, only looking at me even though it was meant for Cole.

I didn't know what to say, and everything I wanted to reveal would only embarrass Cole and he knew it. It was always a tug of war between them.

"Bo," I warned in a pleading tone.

# LUCAS

I grinned, knowingly eyeing Cole. "Just repeating your words, Half-Pint. Don't want Cole to get the wrong idea."

The tension radiating between us was too much to bear and everyone at the table could feel it. For the first time, I didn't give a flying fuck if the boys suspected something. If he thought he could lay a claim on her in front of me and expect me not to call him out on it, then he had another thing coming.

"Is this your girlfriend, Lucas?" he asked, smiling at Stacey.

And the motherfucker went there.

She giggled. "Hi, I'm Stacey, we don't need to put labels on things to know how we feel about each other." She kissed my shoulder.

Cole nodded, mockingly. "Right... nice to meet you, Stacey." He then turned to Alex. "I think you said you were hungry, let's go feed you, shall we?" He looked back toward the table. "Nice seeing you all again."

"I'll see you guys later," Alex half-whispered, being led away by the fucking douchebag. I wanted to punch that smug pretty boy face once and for all.

Nobody said anything about the altercation, it's almost like they knew better or something. I tried not to watch them for the rest of the day, but I couldn't help myself, my eyes gravitated toward them. Every time he grabbed her or touched her I wanted to hurt him. His hands were on her constantly, and at times I thought she tried to back away but couldn't for very long. She liked his advances on her and that's what killed me the most. She knew I was there.

*Was she purposely trying to hurt me?*
*Had I done that to her with Stacey?*

In my mind, the answer was always no, but what if she saw things differently? How did I not notice that?

I hadn't seen anyone ever have an effect on her as he did, and I hated him even more because of that. She was attracted to him and the easy manner they had with each other made me sick to my fucking stomach. She wasn't allowed to have that connection with anyone but me because in my mind and heart I never had it with anyone but her. It was always her. She had to know that.

*How could she not know that?*

So I patiently waited till it was my turn and there would be no holding back my goddamn tongue this time. I would tell her how I felt and what I wanted. I was over playing these fucking games where we thought about everyone else, except what we wanted. I didn't care about the consequences of my words or my actions. In the end, I would have her and that's all that truly mattered to me.

When they left, I stayed around for a bit and then dropped off Stacey. Giving him plenty of time to take her home and for her to get to our abandoned house. I just knew she would be there. She had to be. That was the point of us. I ran up the porch stairs ready to bare my heart and soul with her. Ready to take her in my arms and tell her that we were done with the bullshit.

That I loved her.
That I always loved her.
That I would always love her.

When I shoved the door open, it made a loud banging sound off the receding wall and I swear it mimicked my fucking heart. It gutted me and almost brought me to my knees. She wasn't there. I looked everywhere and there was no sign of her being at our abandoned house at all, it wasn't like I had missed her or anything, she was just never there. I couldn't fathom how that was even possible, especially after our afternoon encounter.

*Did she not care anymore?*

*Was I that easy to replace?*

The more I thought about it, the worse it fueled my anger and temper. The worse the hurricane that lived inside of me built, becoming something unstoppable and unforgiving. It took me right along with it. I couldn't control it. The thought of them being together and her not caring about me anymore raged inside of me, it seared to the point of pain. Hours went by and still no sign of her. She didn't rush to see me like I assumed she would. I wasn't even on her mind.

Cole was.

Finally I exploded. Since I couldn't hit him, I punched the wall as hard as I fucking could. The drywall crumbled all around my wrist, blowing a hole directly in the wall. When I pulled my hand out, it hurt like a son of a bitch. I shook off the pain and wish I could tell you that I felt better, but I didn't.

I felt worse.

The blood from my knuckles slid down my arm and when I heard a loud gasp from behind me. I didn't have to turn to know who it was, but I did.

Alex lunged into action, grabbing a towel from the floor and wrapping it around my hand. "Oh my God, Bo, what were you thinking?" she fumed.

I forcefully pulled my hand away from her touch. It burned, fueling only the fire inside of me. The already burning flames didn't need more gasoline. She had to feel them. They surrounded us in a fit of despair and desperation.

She raised her stunned eyes to my face.

"What the fuck do you care?"

"What?" she half-whispered, stepping back.

I should have left. I should have never spoken to her the way I was about to, but I couldn't help myself. I wanted to hurt Cole, and since I couldn't do that, I did the next best thing.

I hurt her.

I wanted to ruin the memory of her fucking date with him at all costs. I had no excuse for it, other than the fact that I was young and stupid. I had too much time to think about them, too much time to dwell on how much I fucking hated him. Too much time to focus that she wasn't here, when she was supposed to be, and too much time to concentrate on her not being here for me.

For us.

She was with him. It gripped inside and all around me.

I could see it, feel it, and breathe it in.

I suffocated in the knowledge that I felt her slipping away from me, right from my grasp that I held so tightly around her heart. It hammered in my core, from my head down to my toes, leaving nothing but a loss of what I thought we were to each other. It made me believe things that I prayed not to be true, but every time I wanted to express the sincerity of what I felt to be real, of what I wanted so badly, I remembered them laughing and flirting blatantly in front of me and I drowned in an emptiness of resentment and fury. Adding to the facts.

I couldn't take it out on Cole.

I couldn't take it out on myself.

I couldn't take it out on the boys or our families.

All that was left was her.

She stood before me exactly where she belonged, and all I was about to do was push her further away.

The exact fucking way I always had.

It was just too much. I didn't know any better. I reacted and it formed into chaos, so much fucking confusion I couldn't see straight. I never meant to say things that would make her cry.

Or maybe I did.

*I don't know.*

"You heard me. Where's Cole, *Alexandra*?"

"Bo…"

"Don't. Where were you?"

She bowed her head.

"ANSWER ME! Where the fuck were you? I've been here for hours waiting for you. What, Alex? Am I not important to you anymore? Do I not matter now that Cole is around?"

She shook her head, still not looking at me. "That's not true," she muttered, only pissing me off further.

"At least look at me when you're lying."

Complicate Me

She immediately raised her teary eyes to me and they glimmered with a burn I had never witnessed before, and for the first time I didn't want to comfort her. I didn't want to ease the worry that was clearly written across her face. All I wanted to do was add to it.

"Did you do it to hurt me? Because if that's what you wanted then you succeeded."

"I would never hurt you, Lucas, you know that. You're upset and you're being mean."

"I don't give a fuck what I'm being. You knew what you were doing today and then not being here when you knew I would be waiting. Explain that. Who's being mean now, huh?"

She frowned. "That's not true."

"Then prove it. Stop seeing him."

She shook her head again. "That's not fair. He's my friend."

"You don't even know him," I roared.

"I know enough. You have Stacey—"

"Fuck. Her."

"You already do that!" she shouted back at me. "Did you do that today, Bo? Huh? Did you have sex with her today?" Tears fell down the sides of her beautiful face and it was now my turn to bow my head.

"Exactly! You can't have it both ways. It's not always about you. I have never told you what you could or couldn't do. How dare you make me feel bad for having a friend? I didn't do anything with him. We didn't even kiss. You were so torn up about it, Bo, that I bet the first thing you did when you left my house was go sleep with Stacey! How is that fair to me? How has that ever been fair to me?"

"Because I don't fucking love her, Alex! I love you!

## Alex

I jerked back, winded. "Then you have a real awful way of showing it."

His eyes widened with more fury that should have scared me, but it didn't, it was the exact opposite. If he wanted to have it out with me then he didn't get to play this card on me, I wouldn't deal with his double standard rules.

"I fuck her! That's what I do, and I have more emotion in a goddamn handshake with you than anything I do with her. She knows it. I've never lied to her and I've never lied to you about it either. She's. Just. A. Fucking. Girl! How many damn times do I have to remind you of that?"

"Do you think that makes it any easier for me? That it magically makes it better because you don't love her or care for her? No, Lucas, it makes it worse. I don't want to lose my respect for you, but when you say stuff like that, I do! You sound like a guy and that's not who my best friend is," I honestly disclosed.

It felt so good to finally be able to say that. I had been hiding it from myself for so long.

"I hate to break it to you, Half-Pint, but I am a guy. I know my reasoning may suck for you, but that's all I got. I want you to stop seeing him. He's an asshole and he's using you. He's leaving in a few weeks. What do you think he's going to do when he goes back home? What, *Alexandra*, you think he's going to stay faithful to you? You're smarter than that."

I sadly smiled. "Am I not worth it, Lucas? Am I not worth someone staying true to me?"

He breathed out. "Don't twist my words. You know I didn't mean it like that."

I stepped back, needing to get away from him. "I don't know what you mean anymore, and maybe I never did. For your information he's my friend. I won't use him like you do Stacey. I'm not like that and I never imagined you would be either."

"That's not fair."

"Life's not fair," I threw his own words back at him. I wanted to leave and I think he sensed it because he gripped my wrist, tugging me closer to him.

"Let go of me."

"Fuck no. You're just going to run. Where you running to, Half-Pint?"

"You're being unreasonable."

"No shit. I'm aware that I'm an asshole, I'm aware that I'm giving you a double standard, I'm aware of it all, but I don't give a shit. I can't do this with you anymore. This back and forth shit

143

between us is too much and I'm over it, so choose, Alex, choose a side and fucking stay there."

"That makes no sense. He's my friend!"

He pulled me closer till our faces were an inch apart. "What. Am. I?" he asked with conviction.

My mouth opened to say something, anything, but I couldn't find or form the words. They weren't spilling out of me as they were before.

He shook his head, aggravated. "Don't make me ask you again," he warned through gritted teeth.

"I don't know what you want me to say," I honestly replied.

"I want the truth. What am I to you?"

I should have told him. I should have laid everything out for him. It could have changed everything, but it infuriated me that he didn't know what he meant to me and that he had to ask in the first place. How could he not see what Cole could? Was he that blind? He knew I loved him, we said it to each other all the time. I wanted to be with him, he had to know that, too. Right?

I blamed him for so many things that happened between us, and so many things that didn't. If I would have told him, it may have changed so many other things that still hadn't happened between us.

But I didn't.

I was upset.

I was hurt.

I was confused.

I wanted *him* to hurt. Exactly how I had. The pain overruled reality. In fact it won in the end. I did the only thing that made sense to me, in a moment that was driven purely by the emotion of an almost-fifteen-year-old girl.

I looked him straight in the eye and said, "It's complicated."

In a matter of seconds, I witnessed so much emotion pass through his gaze and clarity for what was to come seemed to quickly follow. His guard came up: a reaction I had never seen before directed right at me, and a wall so thick that it crippled me in ways that immediately had me regretting my words. I wish I could have taken them back, but I couldn't, and a huge part of me didn't want to.

Try understanding that because I didn't.

He immediately let go of my wrist, and I instinctively stepped back and away from him.

He lifted his chin and stood taller in a proud and malicious manner. "Is that right?"

I reluctantly nodded. I couldn't back down. I was too far gone. If I did then he would have won, and I was exhausted from him constantly winning all the time. All I wanted this to be was a give and take, but instead it turned into a power struggle.

"Then that answers that," he simply stated, causing my body to internally shudder. He could have seen it if he wanted to, he could have seen past the lies and the façade I desperately tried to portray. At least in my mind he could, and it made me question the sincerity of our friendship, of how much he genuinely knew me, or was I what he needed to see?

I wanted to ask him so many things. I wanted to know what he thought, what he felt, I wanted to know what he wanted from me...

It was as confusing as it was consuming.

Plain and simple.

"We're best friends, Bo," I reassuringly stated, but not sure for who.

He nodded, looking toward the door. I hated that he expected me to leave, or maybe he just wanted me to go and couldn't say the words out loud. It hurt my heart in ways that made me think I would never recover.

"I'll see you tomorrow. You'll come for lunch at the restaurant?"

All he did was shrug, making me feel worse.

"Okay," I half-whispered.

I don't know how the tables turned and how we went from one thing to another. I never understood how that always ended up happening. I guess old habits die hard. I had taken one last look at him before I turned to leave.

"I'll drive you. It's late," was the last thing he said to me.

As we drove away, I couldn't push away the feeling that things were never going to be the same between us. Even though he drove me home, it didn't give me any solace to our current situation.

Complicate Me

And I realized that this might have been the last time that we would found refuge in our abandoned house.

# Chapter 17

## Alex

Cole and I had spent more time together before he left to go back home, but he made sure that we exchanged every form of contact possible. He texted me all the time and at first it was weird. But it didn't take long for me to get use to his good morning and good night text messages and everything else in between.

We were more than halfway through the new school year, and I couldn't believe how fast summer approached. It felt like I could blink and it would be here. Though being in high school with my boys had been the same, but different. Something changed when they saw me with Cole, in some ways it was a blessing in disguise, in other ways it was a disaster waiting to happen, but that only related to Lucas.

The boys were still overprotective, but it lessened with time. They no longer threatened boys not to mess with me or talk to me. They didn't even flip out when I talked to a boy anymore. They seemed at ease with the fact that I grew up and could make my own decisions based on what I felt was right for me. I expected it had something to do with Cole coming into my life, and I appreciated that the most.

Lucas, well Lucas and I, we changed again. Never in my wildest dreams did I imagine our relationship where it currently was. After that night at our abandoned house, he started to pull away from me. He hung out with Stacey more. In fact, he hung out with a lot of girls more. The rumor around school was that he made his way through the entire cheerleading squad and then some. It was so hard to ignore it when it was blatantly flaunted in my face daily. He turned seventeen and I turned fifteen, and we were drifting away from each other in ways I wasn't expecting or prepared for.

The boys noticed it, too, but they never said anything.

At least not to me.

## Complicate Me

We hadn't been to our abandoned house since that night. I went back a few times after work and other normal times, with the hope he'd be there waiting for me. He wasn't. Not once. I finally gave up and stopped going.

It was easier that way.

In some ways, Cole replaced Lucas in my life. We were becoming close. We talked about anything and everything. Cole was sweet and understanding. He made me laugh with his relentless flirting, which I grew to love. It became a nice distraction from missing Bo. I liked that someone doted on me in ways Lucas never had. In the back of my mind, I wondered why. Girls like that kind of stuff, and I was no exception to the rule. Cole and I were just friends, even though he said he wanted more. I didn't want a long-distance relationship, and I knew he didn't either, regardless of what he said.

"You okay?" Aubrey asked as I watched Lucas cage in some random girl with his built frame, on what I assumed was her locker.

My boy grew up, too. He was broader, taller, and more masculine. He had this certain swagger about him that made the girls at school throw themselves at him. It wasn't anything new, but for the first time he jumped on them, literally. It wasn't just Stacey anymore.

I hugged my notebooks closer to my chest in a comforting gesture. "Yeah."

"He's a guy, Alex, he's just being a guy."

I glanced over at her, surprised. "What?"

She reassuringly smiled. "I know, Alex. I've known for a long time."

My eyebrows lowered in confusion. "You have?" I softly spoke, not believing what she shared.

"Of course, it's hard to miss. The only reason the boys miss it is because they choose to. They ignore what is blatantly in their faces. You guys aren't smooth about it. You never have been."

I jerked back, stunned and relieved at the same time. *Why was I relieved?*

"I still don't know what actually went down between you guys, but it's obvious it was bad. You barely talk to each other, and when you do neither of you makes eye contact. It would take an idiot not to notice."

"Yeah," I muttered, taking a deep breath and contemplating whether I could be honest with her or not. "I wish I could tell you what happened between us, Aubrey, but I don't have a clue." I decided I could and by the look on her face, she wasn't one bit surprised.

"Everything just became complicated. It started before Cole, and then he broke the camel's back. He's always been possessive of me. All the boys have."

She nodded in agreement.

"It's different with Cole. I don't know why, but it is. We're just friends and he couldn't handle it. He told me I had to choose, but I didn't understand what I was choosing. He didn't promise me anything. If he would have told me that we were going to be together then maybe that would have changed things, but I still don't think so. I hate the fact that he was bossing me around. Especially since I've never done that to him. I've let him do anything he's wanted, even with me..."

She sighed, bracing herself. "Did you?"

"No. We've only kissed."

"Phew," she breathed out. "That would have been—"

"I know," I interrupted, and I did.

"This thing between us has been going on since we were kids, and then it turned into something neither one of us understood like it became bigger than us. Does that make any sense? Because I don't understand it."

She smiled, support evident in her eyes. "You love each other, that much I do know."

"I thought love was supposed to be easy? It's not easy, not even a little. I mean you and Dylan make it look so simple."

She laughed, shaking her head. "Trust me, Alex, nothing is easy about our relationship. You know how Dylan is. Fuck, you probably know him better than I do. He's an asshole."

I laughed with her.

"But he's *my* asshole," she added.

My hand clutched my shark-tooth necklace as her words settled in. A sense of longing fell over me.

"Give it time. I know that the boys have a lot to do with him and your guys, whatever. They don't like it, and I know they've given him shit about it. Plus," she emphasized, "you talk to Cole constantly, and that boy is gorgeous."

I grinned. "He's alright. Don't tell him that, he'll get a bigger head than he already has."

"Are you excited to see him again?"

"I am. He's been a great friend."

"Not anything more?" she asked with a mischievous smirk.

I rolled my eyes. "No, we're just friends."

"Hmm…"

"What?"

She shrugged. "Nothin'."

"Doesn't sound like nothin'."

"I know that Lucas is doing what he wants, and I think that you should, too. That's all." She knowingly shrugged again.

"What makes you think I'm not?"

"Alex…"

With wide eyes, I nodded. "I am."

"If you say so."

"I am, Aubrey," I argued.

She put her hands up in the air in a surrendering gesture. "Listen, just know that I'm always here for you. I don't care what it's about. I'm not going to judge you, and I'm not going to tell Dylan or the boys either. I promise." She stuck out her pinky and I smiled, locking my own around it.

"Thank you, Aubrey. You have no idea how much I needed that. I haven't been able to talk to anyone about this."

"Not even Cole?"

"Not really, but I think he knows."

"Yeah the only ones that don't seem to know are your good ol' boys."

I sighed as we both looked over at Lucas, who was now sucking face with the same girl.

"Ugh! He's an asshole," she breathed out.

"Legit."

She linked her arm with mine, turning us around to walk toward the doors to leave. "Come on, no need to watch the shit show that he so desperately wants you to see," she dramatically stated.

"You think?"

She shook her head and glanced over at me. "No, doll, I know. You have so much to learn about boys, Alex, so much," she exasperated.

Maybe she was right.

And it only added to the sting I felt in my heart.

# LUCAS

I knew she watched from afar. She was always watching from afar. It made it easier for me to behave the way I was. Bad. It was a mixture of being torn, confused, angry, and just plain hatred. Not toward Alex but for the situation at hand.

No, I'm lying.

I fucking hated Cole.

Maybe a part of it was also spite and heartbreak. Things were never the same after we left our abandoned house.

I was over the games.

I was over the bullshit.

I was over the back and forth mess between us.

I needed to feel in control again, so I did the only thing that I could. I pulled away from her. It made things simpler that way. I didn't have to watch her and Cole become closer, but looking away sure as shit didn't take away the pain it caused me. I despised him. I loathed him now more than ever. He took her away from me, and I never thought that would happen. The boys never called me out on the fact that I went from just having sex with Stacey to sleeping with any girl that would open her legs to me.

And trust me they did.

It took away the emptiness I felt in my heart. The space that seemed hollow without her.

"You smell nice," I murmured to the side of Celeste's neck with my lips.

She giggled. They always giggled. High school gossip ran rapidly and my reputation grew overnight. I never felt bad about what I did. They knew what I wanted and pretty much threw themselves at me. I didn't do relationships, they knew that too.

Complicate Me

"What are you doing tonight?" I asked, trailing soft kisses down the spot under her ear.

She shivered. "Anything you want."

I smiled against her skin. "Good, I want you." I pulled back and brought my mouth up to meet hers. She tasted like cherry lip-gloss, which immediately made me think of Alex. I couldn't get away from her and a huge part of me didn't want to. The bulge forming in my pants was from the taste of the lip-gloss, not this girl.

It was Friday and the end of the day, teachers wanted to get the fuck out of here faster than the students. Or else I may have gotten in trouble for sucking on her tongue on school property, which happened before.

A lot.

"Come on," I whispered into her mouth, grabbing her hand and tugging her with me.

I caught Alex and Aubrey walking side-by-side a few feet in front of us, and I would be lying if I said it didn't kill me to not be the one walking by her instead of Aubrey.

But that was another time.

We weren't there anymore.

I walked faster and with purpose, and I felt Alex's eyes burning a hole in my back as we made it out to my truck. Celeste jumped in, and I followed suit. I tried not to acknowledge the sad look on Alex's face as we drove away.

We went back to her house and got right down to business once we entered her bedroom. Good thing her parents weren't home. I kicked the door closed with my foot as I took her in my arms. Laying my body on top of hers, we started to make out on her bed. Which quickly led to her only wearing her bra and panties and me with no shirt.

I cupped her breast through the lace material and she moaned in my mouth, beckoning me to linger.

"Is this okay?" I groaned, asking her anyways. I wasn't a total asshole.

"Yes…"

Her bra came off, and I softly made my way down to her breast, licking her nipple before sucking it into my mouth, making her back arch off the bed.

My assault continued toward the edge of her panties. "What about this?" I rasped, peering up at her, faintly blowing on her other nipple.

She nodded, not being able to form words while she licked her lips from the delicious torment I incited through the lace of her panties. I pushed aside the silky fabric, touching the moisture that pooled in between her folds.

"You're so fucking wet," I breathed out, repositioning my body on top of hers and shoving my tongue into her awaiting mouth.

"Play with me," she encouraged against my lips, and I did just that.

I stimulated her clit with the palm of my hand, getting her ready before I pushed my index and middle fingers into her tight heat, fighting the urge to not give her the shocker.

"That feel good?"

"Yes," she purred.

I finger fucked her until she shuddered beneath me, closer and closer to the brink of climax that I delivered.

"Do you have a condom?" she huskily whispered. Her head rolled back while her hips rocked back and forth fucking my fingers.

I didn't have to be asked twice.

She came hard and fast, exactly how I craved. I sheathed myself, not bothering to completely take off my jeans. I flipped us over so that she was now on top ready to ride me. She effortlessly slid herself down my shaft.

"Fuck," I growled, big and throaty, gripping onto her hips and gliding her the way I wanted.

She placed her hands on my chest, and I loved feeling the weight of her against my ribs. It made it much easier for her to ride my cock.

"Fuck, that feels good," I groaned, making her smile. She bit her lower lip, and I shut my eyes. It didn't take long for me to picture someone else.

I don't have to tell you who that was.

There were times when this happened. As always, it was replaced with images of her with someone else, someone that wasn't me. The thought was always too much to bear. It released a primal urge to literally want to fuck her out of my system, and heart. I immediately opened my eyes and peered back to the reality playing out before me. It was simpler.

"Where did you go?"

I shook it off and flipped her over to thrust her harder and with more determination.

"Don't worry about it, baby."

I kissed her just to feel anything other than what was going through me. Angling her leg higher I tried to hit the sweet spot against the head of my dick. It always made them come, taking me right with them. She shivered and pulsated, as her pussy gripped my dick like a goddamn glove, I thrust in her a few more times. We simultaneously found our release together, falling right on top of her. With my body sweating and my balls empty, I decided to spend the rest of the afternoon.

Wrapped inside her pussy.

# Chapter 18

## LUCAS

Alex working at the restaurant was supposed to be a summer job, but we were more than halfway through the school year and she was still working there. Not sure exactly why she still did, but I assumed it had something to do with me.

At least I hoped it did.

I started looking at colleges to apply to. After much thought and serious consideration, I decided that I wanted to get the hell out of Oak Island and North Carolina in general. I didn't foresee anything changing between Alex and I. I imagined it would be easier if I didn't have to see her every day. I knew her and Cole were getting closer because the boys talked about it. For some unknown reason, they fucking liked him, too. I figured it was only a matter of time before they started dating.

I sure as shit wasn't going to stand by and watch that happen. One more year and I could get the fuck out of here, away from her and the inevitable fact that they might actually end up together.

I sat looking at colleges with the boys at our usual table, even though I tried to avoid being in situations where we were near each other. I expected the boys to call me out on it, but they never did. I blamed it on us being busy with our own lives and deciding where we would be going to college since it was fast approaching.

"Hey," Alex said to all of us, but I couldn't look up from the catalog in front of me. There was too much that would be written all over my face. I felt her eyes on me nonetheless.

Maybe she didn't have that problem.

It hurt either way.

"I'll put in your usual's," she added.

"Don't bother with mine. I'm not hungry," I replied, turning the page and not paying her any mind.

She didn't say anything, but she didn't have to. I already knew what she thought. She knew I loved it when she fed me, I told her often. When I heard her footsteps leave I finally looked up and right at Aubrey, who sat in front of me, scowling.

I raised an eyebrow and cocked my head to the side, and she challenged me right back like she *knew*. I immediately looked over at the boys, alarmed that they were staring at me the same way but they weren't. I locked eyes with Aubrey again and she shook her head no, silently answering my question.

"I'm going to go to the bathroom," she said to Dylan, but it was really meant for me.

I waited a few minutes, debating on what to do. In the end, my curiosity peeked more than my reasoning, and I followed her down the hall.

"Stop being a dick to her," Aubrey roared from behind me. She hid behind a blocked wall by the payphone. No one could see us unless they needed to use the phone.

"What the fuck are you talking about?" I questioned, taken aback.

"You know what I'm talking about. Stop being an asshole for no fucking reason, Lucas. Do you not realize that you're losing her more by doing so? You're just pushing her into Cole's arms, you fucking idiot!" she shouted too damn close to my face.

My eyes widened, she had never spoken to me like that. Come to think of it, I had never heard her speak to anyone, including Dylan like that.

"I know, okay? I'm not stupid, and no Alex didn't tell me. I've known pretty much since Dylan and I started dating."

"Does Dylan—"

"No. None of them do. I know how he would feel about it, though. I mentioned it one time randomly, and he threw a fucking fit about it. Saying some shit about how it would be incest and wrong. I don't know, I tuned him out half the time because I was so pissed he felt that way in the first place. I've been around the boys to know that they would not have it, especially Jacob. I can't even mention your names in that way without pissing him off. He thinks she deserves Prince Charming, and you're not him." She crossed her arms and glared me up and down.

"But now that you're acting like a dick, I kind of agree with him. You wouldn't be treating her like this if you loved her the way I know you do."

I scoffed. "Don't talk about things you have no clue about, Aubrey."

"I don't? Really? This started after Cole came in the picture. You lost your shit and now you're not speaking, and you've become a total man whore and it's disgusting. Alex isn't even dating him," she justified by stomping her foot on the ground.

"They're just friends. She watched you for years having sex with Stacey, and now she's watching you have sex with half the female population of our school. How is that fair to her?"

"Aubrey," I warned. She pushed my last nerve.

"Don't Aubrey me! You're being an asshole, and she doesn't deserve it! I'm rooting for you guys, I really am. But, the more you keep acting like this, the more I want her to be with Cole, and I don't even know him, Lucas. I know you!" She shoved her finger in my chest.

"And the Lucas I know wouldn't be acting like a fucktard, like you are. Get your shit together or else you're going to dig yourself into a deeper hole and not be able to find your way out." She took a deep breath, composing herself and then turned around and left.

I stood there completely stunned for a few seconds. I knew how the boys felt about it, but her knowing is what shocked me. Had we been that transparent? I thought about the last few months, how everything she said was true. In the back of my mind, I always knew that. I walked back to the table with a heavy heart and a guilty conscience. Alex laid all of our orders on the table. When I sat down, she was about to leave.

"I changed my mind."

She stopped dead in her tracks, turning to face me. The surprised expression was evident on her face when she realized I held her stare. I don't remember the last time I truly looked at her. Her hair was longer, lighter from the sun and had a tint of red in it. She wore more eye makeup, more than I had ever seen her wear before. She appeared older in some ways. Her lips were still glossy and shiny, just the way I remembered them.

Complicate Me

I immediately remembered the taste of them.

She appeared sad, and it was then that I sincerely grasped how much of what Aubrey argued was true.

"I'll take my usual, Alexandra."

It was the first time I called her that in a natural way. She somehow managed to grow up during the school year, which was almost over.

My Half-Pint was gone…

Though it made me upset.

I also realized my brown-eyed girl was still here.

That was clear as day.

# Alex

I wearily smiled. "Coming right up."

I didn't think twice about it. I didn't want to get my hopes up only for them to be shot down with disappointment. I wasn't expecting anything to change between us just because he ordered a meal from me. He could have just been trying to be friendly or cordial. The boys left, but he hovered around until the end of my shift.

"How you been gettin' home?" he asked as I looked up at him after clocking out on my timecard.

"My bike, sometimes one of the boys pick me up, or my parents," I shyly responded, bowing my head not knowing how to feel comfortable in my own skin.

"I can take you home. We could put your bike in the bed of my truck."

I thought about it for a second. "Umm, you don't have to."

"I want to."

That had made me look up at him. "Why now?" I blurted.

He grimaced, it was quick, but I saw it. "Can't we just start over?"

"I don't want to start over, Bo."

His eyebrows curled toward his nose, only this time he didn't try to hide it.

"You've been ignoring me for months. I mean the school year's almost over and you've maybe said a handful of words to me. Only when the boys were around, so I know it wasn't for me."

He softly chuckled. "Still the same blunt girl as always, I see."

I didn't falter. "Did you think I would change? Am I supposed to?"

"I don't know, Alexandra. I really don't."

"Why do you keep calling me that?"

"It's your name."

"Not to you."

His head cocked to the side and one arm folded over the other in defiance. His eyes shifted up to the ceiling briefly and then to me. The sneer on his face accented his rebellious stance and so did his words.

"Just to Cole then," he coldly snickered.

I didn't want to play this game with him. I'd rather him continue to disregard me than to have him hurt me on purpose.

"I don't need a ride. Thanks anyways. I guess you could go back to chasin' tail and ignoring me."

"Is that what you want?" His demeanor changed again, and I swear the wind picked up around us even though we were inside, and I knew that wasn't possible.

I stepped back, walking away. "Bo wouldn't have to ask me that. When you find him, you let me know." I turned not waiting to see the expression on his face.

It was easier just to leave.

The hurricane behind me.

***

"I plan to kidnap you the entire summer. You are aware of that, right?" Cole reminded over the phone.

I laughed. He had been repeating this a lot over the last few days and it never got old. It still made me laugh. He always made me laugh.

"I thought the point of kidnapping was not to tell anyone?"

"This is a different kind. I need you willing, Darlin'."

159

I rolled my eyes even though it still made my belly flutter when he called me that. "Whatever."

"Alexandra, is that hesitation I hear in your voice? Don't pretend you're not excited to see me. I know you are."

"Oh do you now? Why is that?"

"I can tell. I have powers when it comes to you. You were made for me."

I shook my head, amused. "God, laying it on thick tonight, huh? Are you bored, Cole?" I asked while rolling onto my belly and elbows, and putting my cell phone on speaker.

He chuckled. "Oh, I'm laying it on somewhere—"

"COLE!" I blushed.

For some reason I knew he was rolling onto his back. Maybe it was because of the way his tone changed, it was heavier. He let out a big, throaty laugh.

"I like you, Alexandra. When a guy likes a girl he pays attention to the little things, and you, Darlin', are very easy to read. As much as you want to pretend that you don't feel something for me, I know the truth and one day, I'll prove it to you. I'm not going anywhere, I'll wait as long as it takes."

I beamed. I couldn't help it.

"You know the first thing I'm going to do when I see you?"

"Flirt with me?" I sassed.

"That's the second. The first is to pull you up into my arms and spin you around until you tell me to stop. Will you tell me to stop, Alexandra?" he rasped.

My heart pounded in my chest with heavy thumps, and I rolled onto my back in some awkward position. My eyes landing on his, sitting right on my nightstand, wrapped in a black frame. The photo of Lucas and I stared me right in the face.

"What time do you land?" I asked, changing the subject. I had to.

"Two in the afternoon and you already know that," he paused as he debated on what to say. If there was one thing I knew about Cole, it was that he always spoke his mind, no matter what.

"What took away my happiness, Darlin'? I can hear it in your voice."

Sometimes I hated that he was so perceptive.

"Is it Lucas?"

Over the past few months, I started opening up to him. I told him as much as I could about Lucas and I. He always listened, never saying anything bad about him. I wouldn't let him if he tried.

"Something like that," I simply replied. "I'm fine."

"Now that I'm aware of."

I giggled. I loved the ability of being able to go from a serious conversation to a light one with him. It was never like that with Lucas.

"I'm really glad I met you, Cole."

"Good, so I'll see you tomorrow?"

I nodded even though he couldn't see me. "You land at two o'clock, and I will see you at two forty-five at the lighthouse. I'm bringing lunch and a smile."

"Promise?"

"Cross my heart."

"Sweet dreams, Darlin', and by that I mean me."

"Goodnight, Cole," I chuckled.

I instinctively grabbed the picture of Lucas and me from my nightstand as I hung up. We talked when we were around the boys. And he said hello when he passed me in the halls at school. But that pretty much summed up our relationship. School had been over for two weeks now and nothing really changed between us.

I hated it. I hated it so much. The worst part was that there was nothing I could do to fix us. His extra-curricular activities seemed to die down or maybe he hid it from me. I silently hoped it had something to do with me, and what I had said to him.

That maybe I made a difference in how he acted. I wasn't giving up hope, but I wasn't going to hold my breath either. At times, I swore I could feel his eyes on me or maybe it was just wishful thinking. I would be lying if I said it wasn't easier to distract myself with Cole. Everything with him came easy. I truly loved that about him. Cole was a nice change in pace from the hurricane that constantly surrounded Lucas.

I wish I could tell you that my feelings for him went away, that I woke up one morning and they had vanished. Gone like the wind. They didn't. I started to wonder if they ever would, and to be honest I wasn't prepared for them to leave me anyway. It had become a part of me. He was ingrained. Etched somewhere deep in my heart. Every day it got a little easier not having him around me, but then there would be times like this where my heart physically ached for him in ways that made it hard to breathe.

I hit send on my phone before I even realized it, and then I heard his voice.

"Alexandra?" he answered. It only added salt to my open wounds when he addressed me by my full name. Which was the complete opposite feeling when Cole called me that. I loved it.

"Hey," I breathed out.

"Are you okay?"

Silence.

"You haven't called me in a long time," he added, his voice breaking.

More silence.

"Are you there?"

"Yeah..." I started to panic. I wasn't prepared for whatever attitude he would throw toward me. I didn't know what to say. "I'm sorry I called. I'm sorry for bothering you." I was about to click end.

"I'm not," he stated, making me hover my finger over the button.

"Do you want to hang out tomorrow? I miss you," he paused, letting his words sink in. "I miss us," he coaxed, catching me completely off guard.

"I could pick you up. Our abandoned house probably misses us," he chuckled, trying to break the tension. Though I could hear the strain in his tone. "I could pick you up around two."

My heart dropped.

"Half-Pint..."

It now shattered, along with my hope for things to change.

"Please. I'm sorry for everything. You know that, right?"

"Wednesday," I blurted with my heart in my throat. "You could pick me up from work."

I immediately noticed that his breathing became heavier, deeper. He hesitated for a few seconds. Talking to Cole on the phone for months made me realize how much you could learn about a person just by being on the phone with them.

"Why not tomorrow?"

"Bo," I pleaded. I didn't want to tell him.

"Why. Not. Tomorrow?" he demanded, stressing every word.

"Cole gets into town tomorrow and I promised him—"

He scoffed in disgust, cutting me off. "Is that right? Well then by all means, *Alexandra*, I wouldn't want you to keep Cole waiting or anything. Seeing as he's so important to you."

"That's not—"

"*I*... haven't spent time with you in months. Months. Fuck," he seethed. "You know what? Fuck it. Have a great time."

"Bo—" The call ended.

And for the first time I felt like it mimicked our friendship.

# Chapter 19

## LUCAS

When I saw her name come up on my phone, I thought that maybe something would give and we could find our way back to each other.

I'm a fucking idiot.

Cole.

It was always fucking Cole.

I wasn't first in her life anymore, and she couldn't spell it out for me any clearer if she tried. It was evident.

"Are you alright?" Stacey asked, pulling me away from my thoughts and walking toward me.

I smiled and pulled her closer. "I am now."

After Aubrey had confronted me that afternoon, I decided to change my ways. At least around Alex I would. I didn't flaunt my conquests in front of her. I also didn't parade all the pussy that was thrown at me. I didn't even try to get laid as often. If it happened, it happened. I didn't go looking for it like I did before. Girls would still talk about me, but at least she didn't have to be as exposed to it like before.

As more time went by our drift became bigger. I didn't know who she was anymore, and I had no one to blame but myself.

We tend to hurt the ones we love.

I had to learn that the hard way.

Cole was officially coming back to town for the summer. I would see them together everywhere. The only way to prevent it, was to lock myself in my bedroom for the whole summer. I thought about doing it once or twice, I'm not going to lie. This next year would be my last summer before college. I applied to several out of state schools and had already heard back from a few with "Congratulations, you've been accepted" letters. But, I didn't commit to any of them yet.

I told everyone I hadn't chosen one because there was so many to choose from. In reality, it all came back to her. Every time I thought about not seeing her, it was hard to breathe. It was easy to contemplate leaving, pulling the trigger, though that was a whole different story.

"What are you thinkin' about over there?" Stacey rasped against my neck with her hand moving to my cock. We were sitting on the bed of my truck at a party in the woods. Anyone who was anyone was there, including the boys. Alex never came to these things even though the boys begged her to tag along. She would reply with "Nah, that's not really my thing."

She was a good girl, always had been. I prayed she always would be.

That was one of the things I loved most about her.

I pulled away from Stacey, needing some space from the daunting thoughts that plagued my mind.

"What? Am I not good enough for you? Huh? Now that you have half the school fawning over you?" she spewed.

I rolled my eyes. "Whatever. I don't have time for this shit." I jumped off the bed of my truck.

"Lucas! What the fuck?"

I stepped toward her, my mouth close to hers. "Don't," I warned.

She spitefully narrowed her eyes at me. "Going to see, *Half-Pint*?" she mocked in a condescending tone. "Oh yeah, she has better things to do now and they don't include you. Why would they? When she has someone who looks like Cole by her side." Her eyebrow arched when she realized her words were getting to me, even though I tried to hide it. I couldn't, I never could when it came to Alex.

"Maybe I should go play with Cole. If he's good enough for her, then he damn well would be good enough for me."

I maliciously smiled. "Well God knows if I had to choose between you and Alex, there wouldn't be a choice."

She laughed viscously, a cackling sound I felt deep in my bones. Nothing could have prepared me for her next words.

"You're a fucking idiot. What do you think you've been doing all these years," she paused to let her words linger, "*Bo*?"

Complicate Me

I jerked back like she had just punched me. The truth of her words just about knocked the wind right out of me.

"What? You think you haven't? You're a fucking fool. Sorry to break it to you, but, Lucas, you have been choosing me over Alex for years. Fuck," she sneered. "And this last year, you've been choosing every other girl, but her. So get off your high horse, suga', the only one that's been hurting her is you."

I stood there in a trance-like state. "That's not true," I muttered through my teeth, barely believing it myself.

She let out a loud laugh with her head falling back. She laughed at me because she knew as much as I did that my words were nothing but lies.

"I'm not the villain in this story, Lucas. You are."

I instinctively stepped back to catch my bearings, but it was too late. The quicksand of her words took me under. I gripped the side of my truck to steady my composure. It didn't help. Stacey's words caused a domino effect of memories and mistakes hitting me like a thunderbolt.

Every time I left with her.

Every time she saw me with her.

Every time I told her she was just a girl.

Every excuse. Every explanation. Every lie.

It engulfed me, hurting me in ways that I assumed I hurt her. I found it hard to move.

For the first time…

I was slapped in the face with my own hurricane. The winds turned against me and I didn't even fight it. I let it take hold. I deserved it all.

"She'd be stupid to choose you over Cole."

I peered up at her through my lashes. "Get the fuck away from me," I ordered with my head cocked and heated eyes.

She smiled, big and high. "Truth hurts, doesn't it?" And with that she turned and left.

I don't know how long I stood there replaying everything she said. All of it just sort of mixed together, causing a typhoon of regret. Before I knew it I was at our abandoned house, staring at the hole in the wall that I had caused. I hadn't been back there since that night. I pushed her away like I did my feelings.

At the end of the day, I was left infinitely and utterly alone and I had no one to blame but myself.

# Alex

Summer was in full swing. I couldn't believe we were already halfway through it. It seemed like it was just yesterday that we walked out the doors of school and into summer break. As always, the restaurant was packed and I worked all the time. There were only two months out of the year that Oak Island had a high season for tourism. Cole spent most of the time surfing while I worked, along with the boys. Lucas also hung around a lot more than he used to.

It was like having the old Bo again. I got so used to seeing him surf with the boys that I started putting in his order for lunch without him having to ask me. He always met my eyes when he came in. Lucas tried to talk to me at least a few times a day, asking me how I was, how my day went if I needed anything. I don't know what caused the 180-degree change in his attitude toward me, but I appreciated it nonetheless.

Girls still flocked to him, he was a magnet to the opposite sex, but he didn't pay them any mind. I hadn't seen him hanging out with anyone other than the boys. Sometimes I would catch him talking to Aubrey, it always seemed as if they were in some deep conversation, but never around the boys. It only happened when it was just the two of them. There were several times that I wanted to ask Aubrey about it, but I decided against it at the last second. I didn't want to rock the boat.

We weren't Half-Pint and Bo anymore, but at least he was cordial now.

"Hey," Lucas greeted, nudging me with his shoulder and pulling me away from my thoughts.

I nudged him back. "I didn't see you standing there."

We stood in the sand where I watched them surf all the time. Cole wasn't as good as Lucas, but he wasn't that far behind either.

Lucas was always the best surfer among the boys, and they knew it too.

"Do you have time to sit for a bit?"

I glanced over at him, smiling. "I do."

He returned my smile and nodded toward the sand before sitting down. I followed suit. We both sat with our knees up and our arms lying across them, side-by-side. Our shoulders touched and I immediately felt his warmth roll down my body.

"How's your day going?" he asked, looking at the ocean. I wondered if he watched Cole.

"Good. Busy."

"You like busy, though."

I softly chuckled, "I do. How's your summer going?"

"Nothing too exciting going on."

"I know, you're here every day," I blurted, my cheeks reddening the second the last word came out of my mouth.

Looking at me with a fascinated regard, he grinned and nodded. "That I am," he simply stated.

"So, are you excited about turning eighteen soon?" I questioned, changing the subject.

"I guess. You excited about turning sixteen soon?" he answered, throwing my question back at me.

"I'm excited to drive. It would be nice not to rely on someone to get everywhere. I'm kinda over my bike."

"I could... I mean... I... umm..." he mumbled.

"You could what?" I was never one for patience.

"I could drive you to and from work? You know, the way I used to."

"Why? Why now?"

He sighed, defeated. "And we're back to this again."

I shook my head, dumbfounded. "What do you expect from me? I wish I could just let things go and we could magically go back to what we used to be, but I'm not made like that, Lucas. You know that. I need to know why now? I don't understand how you can go from ignoring my existence, to offering me rides, and not expect me to question your timing."

He kicked the sand around below his feet. He did this when he was nervous. "I don't know what you want me to say, Alexandra. I really don't."

I ignored how normal my full name sounded from his lips. I ignored the way it made me feel because if I didn't, I wouldn't have been able to go on with this conversation. It would end how they always had. Bad.

"Tell me the truth," was all I replied.

He gazed out at the ocean again, as if it pained him to look at me and tell me what he had been trying to hide for so long.

"Everything got so confusing. One day I woke up and I wasn't a kid anymore, but you were. I know we're only two years apart, but that's a long gap when you're that young. You may not be able to understand that, but that's how it felt."

"I'm not a kid anymore."

He grimaced, his shoulders slumping forward. His eyes shut and he sucked in a deep breath, collecting his thoughts of what he wanted to say to me. "I know. I missed you growing up. Or maybe I didn't. I saw it happening and it didn't matter because I couldn't handle it. You wanted what we all did, to have *experiences*. I've known you your entire life and it was hard for me to see you as anything other than my brown eyed girl."

"I am—"

"You're not," he scornfully interrupted. "You haven't been for a long time."

"That's not fair."

"I never said life was fair."

I hated when he said that to me. Now more than ever, but I let him continue with what he needed to say. If he was opening up to me, I wasn't going to begrudge him that.

"I'm not going to lie to you, I see you sometimes and I have no idea who you are anymore. I mean you're still my Half-Pint but at the same time you aren't. I don't know if that makes any sense, but it was so much easier when I didn't have to look at you. I fucking hated it. I still hate it, but it was easier in some ways and harder in others."

"Do you not want me to grow up?"

"I never really thought about it. When it started happening it was like taking a knife to the heart, it still is. I'm sorry I don't have a better explanation for you. That's all I got."

"So now what? What happens now?"

He shrugged still not looking at me, even though he could feel my intense stare on his face. It's almost like he feared if he said anymore it would change the calm that was placed in between us.

"Cole and I are friends. We're just friends," I found myself saying.

His jaw clenched. "For now. Cole will always have you in a way that I can't. There's no history there. No baggage. It's new and untainted. We have so many barriers placed in between us and I don't know how to remove them." He finally peered back over at me with a sad smile that I'm sure I mirrored. "Do you?"

I bowed my head. I didn't.

"Yeah," he added.

We sat there in silence for I don't know how long. This was the most we had spoken to one another in a year. There was still so much that was left unsaid between us.

*How long would it go on like this?*

"I love you, Bo."

He reached over and grabbed my hand, bringing it up to his lips to tenderly kiss my knuckles. "I love you, Half-Pint."

I didn't know what the future held for us.

But, at that moment I didn't care.

We were trying to find our way again and that's all that mattered.

# Chapter 20

## LUCAS

Summer was almost over.

After our talk on the beach, I took Alex home from work a few times. It helped us. I wanted so badly to take her to our abandoned house. A part of me knew she wanted that, too. I was terrified that if we went there, our complicated relationship would follow us. I didn't want to ruin whatever progress we had made.

Our friendship wasn't anywhere near what it used to be, but it was something for now.

She and Cole spent a lot of time together. I saw them everywhere. My eyes tended to gravitate toward her, even when I willed them not too. I never talked to him, even though the boys did. We ate lunch with him a few times and I played nice.

Not for him.

For her.

I spent the morning arguing with my parents over the fact I still hadn't decided on what college to attend. If I didn't respond soon, I would lose the opportunity to attend. I'd end up at Wilmington University.

*Would that be so bad? I didn't know…*

By the time I made it out to the beach, it was after lunch. I saw the boys as soon as I placed my board on the sand. They had been out there for hours already. Alex was on the restaurant deck with Cole standing in front of her, caging her in with his arms against the wall. She looked so tiny, gazing up at him. She seemed completely comfortable in her own skin. From Cole's body language, it was obvious what he wanted.

Her.

He said something that lit up her entire face, the same way it used to for me. The glimmer of her lip-gloss reflected against the sun, making her mouth appear more inviting and enticing. I gripped my surfboard so fucking hard that my knuckles turned white. Jealously quickly escalated through my entire body in response. He may have a lot over me that I couldn't compete with, but I did have one thing going for me that he never would.

She was mine first.

I must have made a loud noise when I picked up my board because our eyes locked despite the distance between us. Cole rapidly followed her stare. He scowled at me but shook it off pretty fast and tugged her face back to him with his thumb and forefinger.

I gripped my board, making my way to the ocean. I would take out my frustration on the waves. I paddled out a few yards and found a steady rhythm as always. Nothing compared to the feeling I got riding the water with skill and stride that I acquired throughout the years. As I caught my first wave, I saw pretty boy out of the corner of my eyes, paddling into it and cutting me off. I rode the wave as close as possible to him, made a firm left turn and sprayed him as hard as I possibly could. Narrowly dodging him, making him fall back into the wave, as I continued riding on.

The fucker did it on purpose.

That much I was sure of.

"What the fuck is your problem?" I yelled out, paddling up to the tail of his board.

"Can't handle some healthy competition, Lucas? I already stole your girl, so I guess not."

"Fuck you!" I roared.

"Ooohhh, touchy subject."

I turned to face him as we both paddled out past the break. "Not at all, seeing as you're just friends. At least that's what Alex keeps reminding me of," I maliciously spewed.

He narrowed his eyes at me and didn't falter. "At least I'm something to her. Can't say the same for you."

I jerked back and he saw it. Grinning he said, "It's about time someone puts you in your place, I don't mind being the man that does so. Pick a wave. I'll meet it. I'll pick another and we'll see if you can. Let's see who can really ride better." I could tell he was sore from me spraying him and making him drop back out of the wave.

I shook my head in disbelief. "Fuck that. That's dangerous, there's too many surfers out here today," I reasoned, looking around us.

He snickered not looking around us at all. "Always knew you were a pussy, no wonder Alexandra came to me."

I scoffed in disgust not backing down now more than ever. "I'll go first."

He smiled, a big toothy grin showing his stupid fucking dimples that I wanted to fuck up. "Lead the way, *Bo*," he triggered with wide eyes.

It took a few minutes before I found the wave and nodded toward it. He didn't miss a beat, immediately paddling out. We both rode the waves with perfection and precision of an experienced surfer, except at the last second he cut me off again. I realized right then and there he played dirty. We went back and forth a few more times, each wave bigger than the last. Since I knew how he competed, I kept my distance so that he couldn't get close enough to cut me off again. It didn't take long for the other surfers to grasp what we had going on and they swiftly made their way out of the ocean.

Before we knew it, it was just the two of us. I looked out toward the beach and saw a crowd had gathered. We were too far out for me to see if Alex was among them, but something in my gut told me she was. It just gave me more determination to make Cole look like the asshole I knew he was.

We played this back and forth for what seemed like forever with neither one of us backing down. The waves were getting bigger and heavier. Clouds began to form above our heads. Rain was fast approaching, with high winds only inciting the seas.

Cole's turn was up and when he nodded toward the pier it took me a second to understand what he suggested.

He must have seen my trepidation. "Aww! Come on, Lucas, if I can do it, you can."

"You're insane. The waves are too rough. It's too dangerous."

"No shit. That's the point. Whoever rides the wave under the pier the slowest stays away from Alex."

I shook my head. "I'm not agreeing to that."

"Scared you'll lose then? Come on, I know you want me gone. I'll back off if you win."

"She means that little to you?"

He smiled. "I know I won't lose. She means that much to me. Can you say the same?"

I knew in the back of my mind it was a bad idea. I also knew that I wouldn't back off even if I lost, though he didn't need to know that. If there were a chance that winning would make Cole go away, then I would fucking jump on it.

I cocked my head to the side and then nodded for him to lead the way. He did. My heart beat out of my chest with every wave we had to duck dive. In a matter of minutes, the winds picked up. The wash off the back of the waves sprayed hard into our eyes, making it that much more difficult to reach our destination.

Once we arrived, my skin felt chills due to the wind and rain that mercifully pounded into my flesh. I was ready to get the fuck out of the water. By the look on Cole's face, he was too. "First one to make it under the pier the fastest wins," he reminded.

All I did in response was nod my head. My lips felt chapped and dry.

We jockey for the wave trying to find the best break spot. We both managed to catch the wave, but Cole was in the best position. I didn't let that deter what I needed to do, even though I knew I might get fucked. As I approached the pier, I strategically laid out how I would avoid the pylons as I chased Cole under the pier. At the last second, he purposely cut back and stalled, leaving me with nowhere to go.

I tried to bail off the back of the wave but clipped the pier on my way out, catching my right foot on the barnacles. Immediate pain rushed through me, burning like hell. I had no time to contemplate how bad my foot was because I needed to get the fuck out of the way of danger before the next set of waves took me underneath the pier.

I jumped on my board, using all my strength to paddle my way out from under the pier and let the white water drag me back. By the time I reached the shoreline everyone had ran toward me to help. As panic and chaos ignited all around me, all I wanted to do was pass the fuck out from the blinding pain in my foot.

I didn't even wait until I reached the sand before I rolled onto my back, desperately trying to catch my breath and govern the

M. Robinson

burning sensation that elevated from my foot through my entire body.

"Oh my God! What the fuck were you thinking, Lucas?" Jacob yelled, kneeling beside me and placing my head on his lap. The rest of the boys gathered around me, but I didn't see the one person I wanted to.

Alex.

"Have you lost your goddamn mind? Do you have any idea how dangerous that was? Jesus Christ, Lucas, you could have died," Dylan scolded, lifting my foot, that was now drenched in blood.

"I'm a doctor," some man chimed in, pushing aside Austin and Dylan.

*Thank God.*

After he checked my foot, he called 911 stating I needed stitches. Dylan was able to get pain medication from the restaurant. I swallowed them whole and with no water. The crowd tapered after several minutes and it was then that I saw Cole hovering above me, looking down at me with worry and guilt all wrapped up in one on his face.

Not even a second later I saw Cole literally being shoved sideways and into the sand, his big, bulky frame falling over into a patch of water. I immediately turned my neck to find its source of strength.

"Are you freaking kidding me?" Alex barked at him with her hands out in front of her. I had never seen her so pissed before. It took me a few moments to realize that she was the one who knocked him over.

"Darlin'—"

"Don't, Darlin' me. I saw you, Cole! I saw you provoke him. You knew! You knew what he would do! Why? Why would you provoke him into something that could get him killed!"

"That's not—"

"I'm not stupid! You stopped! You stopped right in front of him and he had to jump off his board to miss you or even worse hit the pier! Oh my God, Cole! How could you?" she wallowed with tears falling down the sides of her beautiful face.

Complicate Me

I looked back at Cole who had his hands up in a surrendering gesture and for the first time I felt bad for him. I don't know why I did, I just did.

Love makes you do crazy things. I guess in part I knew he loved her, and that won out in the end.

"Half-Pint," I coaxed and she instantly spun, her anger now directed at me. Which was not what I expected.

"You!" She pointed at me with a stiff finger and a heated composure. "Don't, Half-Pint me! Why would you listen? Why would you be so stupid to put yourself in danger? What do you have to prove to him? Nothing! Not one damn thing, Lucas!" She stomped her foot, her body shaking. "You could have been killed. Do you not realize that? You could have died and I would have watched it happen. How could you do that to me?"

I jerked back, my own eyes filling with tears. "I'm sorry," was all I could say.

She wiped her face with the back of her hand. I knew she hated to cry and to have people watch her breakdown almost killed me in itself.

"You always say that! That's all you ever say and nothing ever changes! Not one thing! I'm over your fair weather apologies that mean nothing. You never think about me! You don't care about what I think or want! It's always about you!"

Her words cut me in ways that made the burn of my foot seem like nothing in comparison. "It was just a guy thing. A stupid fucking guy thing," I muttered, looking over at Cole who seemed amazed that I didn't sell him out.

She stepped back, staring back between the both of us. "Like your, 'She's just a girl,' thing?" she scoffed in frustration, vigorously shaking her head. "You two can have each other."

"Alex," I called out as she ran away from us. Aubrey quickly chased right behind her.

Cole and I just stared at each other before her mom stepped out of nowhere. I hadn't even notice she was there. I saw the disappointment clear across her face, making me feel like a bigger piece of shit than I already felt.

"Lucas Brody Ryder," she scolded and I winced.

"I don't know what happened out there, but I do know that my daughter was worried sick the entire time. Jesus, Lucas, I have never seen her so scared before," she sighed and I bowed my head.

The shame was too much to bear.

"I am so disappointed in you. So disappointed." She handed me her cell phone. "You need to call your mama. The ambulance will be here soon."

I grabbed the phone not being able to look up at her. I hit send and it rang three times before she answered. I know because I counted.

"Hey," she greeted.

"Mom," I said with a voice I didn't recognize. The comfort in her tone brought me to my knees and I flipped out. Of course that caused her to flip out.

"Lucas? Lucas, honey, is that you?"

"Mom, I'm in trouble."

"What do you mean you're in trouble? What did you do?"

"I hit the pier with my surfboard," I explained with nothing but dread in my voice.

"Why were you under the pier with your surfboard?"

"I don't know." I shrugged even though she couldn't see me. "I'm sorry."

"Lucas, where are you?"

"At the beach, by the restaurant. The ambulance is on its way."

"Ambulance?" she shrieked. "What's going on? Oh my God, Lucas, never mind. I'm on my way." She hung up.

I handed the phone back to Alex's mom still not meeting her intense judgment.

"Cole, you need to call your parents." She handed the phone to him next and I immediately saw the fear in his eyes.

"He doesn't need to call his parents."

They both looked over at me, shocked and dismayed.

"I'm hurt, he's not," I simply stated.

"Lucas, he needs to be punished for his involvement in this. You both do."

"I'll be fine. No need for both of us to get in trouble."

She nodded in understanding. "Okay. I'll go wait for your mama out front.

She left and the boys instantly hovered above Cole, who still hadn't moved from his spot on the sand.

"You better stay the fuck away from, Alex," Jacob warned, ready to strike if needed.

"Leave him alone."

They all turned to me. "You can't be serious?" Dylan chastised.

"I am. Leave him alone. It's between him and I. Now give us a few minutes before my mom gets here and I'm grounded for the rest of my life."

They all shot him dirty looks but took in my request and left.

"Man, I appreciate—"

"Shut the fuck up," I interrupted, catching him off guard. "I don't like you, you don't like me. That much is obvious. I didn't do this for you. I did it for Alex. As much as I hate it, she needs you in her life. You're her friend in ways that I can't be. At least not now."

"I love her, Lucas."

I nodded. "Me too. I hate that you're around. I hate that she relies on you and no way am I saying I want you anywhere near her. And trust me when I say I don't fucking like you, but who knows when I'll be allowed to see the light of day again. So, take care of her this summer."

"You have my word."

"Now get the fuck away from me before I change my mind."

He stood, peering down at me with one hand behind his neck. Rubbing the tension and anxiety that radiated off of him. "Lucas... I didn't... I mean... I was running on pure adrenaline. I never thought... I mean..." he paused, trying to find the words to say to me. When he finally breathed out, "I'm sorry."

I nodded again and with that he left.

I sat there thinking.

Not about Cole, or the pain I was in, or even how much trouble awaited me.

Alex and how everything she said.

Was right.

I didn't give Cole the approval to be with her. I would never do that, but for the first time I thought about what she needed and right now.

She needed Cole.

End of story.

# Chapter 21

## Alex

I stood there on the sidelines with my heart in my throat. I had never been so scared before. I knew when Cole left to go back into the ocean something was bound to happen. I felt it. I never thought that he would be the one to initiate it. He seemed more mature than that. When I watched him go straight to Lucas as soon as his surfboard hit the water it was like watching a train wreck happen right before my very own eyes. I couldn't look away, even though everything in my mind told me to.

It played in slow motion, each second worse than the last.

I watched them fight for my attention and now I watched them fight for my love. How did things get so complicated? I never thought that I led Cole on. I was always honest with him. We were friends. He was what I needed this last year. I didn't have to share him. I didn't have to argue with him, and I didn't have to explain anything to him. It was easy. We were simple. That was the beauty behind us. As I watched him provoke Lucas in ways that he knew he wouldn't back down, I felt as though I failed. I couldn't keep any of the men in my life from chaos.

And it made me wonder if I was the hurricane not Lucas.

The more they ambushed and goaded each other, the worse the winds picked up around me. Like the Universe insinuated what I felt, was right. The boys paddled out of the water and came running directly toward me. In that second I didn't have to wonder if they knew.

They just proved it to me.

They hovered around me like I was a glass doll that was about to break. Each of them offering reassurances that it would be okay, but I knew in my heart.

It wouldn't.

My heart dropped when I saw them paddling toward the pier, nothing good could come of it. I swear I stopped breathing the moment Lucas jumped off his board to avoid hitting Cole or worse the pier itself. My whole life flashed before my eyes.

A life without love.

A life without happiness.

A life without Lucas...

It took everything in me not to run to him. I was terrified he wasn't going to come back up, that the treacherous waves had taken him under and I was never going to see him again. That this was the end of our story. When I didn't even feel like it started in the first place.

I was in a daze when I watched him ride the white water back onto the shoreline. The boys ran to him and I should have too, but I couldn't get my feet to move from the place in the sand where I stood. It offered a false security that if I moved I would crumble.

Right then and there for everyone to see.

When I heard the doctor say he needed stitches and an ambulance had been called it added to the worry and hurt that I felt all around me. Hearing the boys yell at him that he could have died, that it was so dangerous, what was he thinking...

It reaffirmed all my fears that flashed before me in the blink of an eye. Everything hit me at once. All the emotions that I felt throughout the years erupted and crashed into me, exactly how the waves did to him. It was one right after the other. I drowned in them.

He lay there trying to catch his breath and calm his surroundings. I ached the same way.

I never felt so exposed, so vulnerable and I hated it. At that moment, I hated him.

For everything he had ever put me through and for everything he still hadn't...

When my glare shifted to Cole, he hovered above Lucas with worry, concern, and guilt written all over his face. I just reacted. I let my emotions completely take over and I booked it. I ran as fast as I could toward him with all the strength I could muster and I pushed him. The way his large frame fell into the sand mimicked the way my heart dropped when I thought I would never see Lucas again.

The words spewed out of my mouth, one by one, and I had no control over them. They came off my lips effortlessly with tears fast accompanying them. It infuriated me further that I broke down in front of my boys, and a bunch of people I didn't even know.

Adding to the pain they both caused me.

I said my peace to both of them and ran. It was fight or flight and once the fight was over, I fled. I ran away like the scared little girl they made me feel I was.

"Half-Pint, slow the fuck down," Aubrey yelled from behind me.

I immediately ceased, dead in my tracks. She lost her footing, almost falling over me from my sudden change of pace.

"Don't call me that," I immediately reprimanded.

Her eyes widened as she steadied herself and found her composure. "Alex," she coaxed with sad eyes and a frown on her face.

"Why would he do that to me, Aubrey? Why?" I pleaded while my heart broke into a million more pieces.

"Oh, Alex, come here." She pulled me into a tight hug and I let her. It was nice to have someone comfort me for a change.

"They're just being stupid fucking boys. That's all. They would never want to hurt you."

I fervently shook my head on her shoulder, fresh tears falling down my face. "That's not true! Lucas hurts me all the time. When is it ever going to stop, Aubrey? When is it going to be enough?" I sobbed.

"Oh, Half-Pint," she wallowed.

"Please don't call me that anymore, it hurts so much when you call me that."

She rubbed my back, trying to soothe me. "Shhh… it's okay, it's over now. He's fine. Lucas is going to be fine."

"It doesn't matter, nothing is going to change. Not one thing. I hate Cole for what he did to him. I hate him so much right now. I hate both of them."

"I know and you have every right to. But it will pass, I promise."

"It doesn't feel that way," I bellowed as the hurt in my chest dispersed throughout my entire body. I couldn't stop crying, my body shuddered with tears.

I hated that the most.

Aubrey just let me cry for as long as I needed. When I finally opened my eyes, lifting them up, I locked intense gazes with Cole. Who appeared exactly the way I felt.

I pulled away from Aubrey and she combed her fingers through my hair, away from my face. Her eyebrows lowered and her lips pursed when she met my eyes, following my stare that was locked with Cole's. She looked back and forth between us and I nodded my head, giving her silent approval to leave. She did but not before she kissed my head and warned Cole with an angry glance that had him wince and nod his head.

We stood there staring at each other for I don't know how long. Time just seemed to stand still for a minute.

"I fucked up," he confessed, breaking the silence. "I fucked up really bad. I'm sorry, Alexandra."

I didn't move. I didn't say anything. I just sort of stood there and watched him, trying to accept his sincere apology that sounded more like words than anything else. When he realized he wasn't getting what he needed out of me, he stepped forward and I instinctively stepped back.

He bowed his head with understanding. "I wish I could tell you why I did it, but I don't know the answer to that," he sort of mumbled. I saw his chest puff out as he sucked in a big breath of air, almost like it was the first time he started to breathe again.

"Yes, I do. I'm lying. I don't want to lie to you anymore." He took a few more deep breaths and then lifted his sorrowful eyes to me. If I wasn't so pissed at him, I probably would have felt sorry for him.

"I like you a lot, that can't be a surprise to you. I tell you all the time. You don't really talk about Lucas, but I see the way you look at him. You look at him the way I look at you. I see it all the time." He shrugged, appearing defeated. "I snapped. I hate that he has you and I don't. I hate that he treats you the way he does and you're still there for him. I hate that I don't ever know where we stand. And I hate more than ever that we may never have a chance to find out what this thing between us could be."

Silence.

"Darlin', I'm sorry. It got out of hand. One thing led to another and accelerated at warp speed. Before I knew it he was jumping off his board and into the ocean. I feel awful, but there's nothing I can do to change what's been done. All I can do is apologize to you, and hope you believe me. I would never want to hurt you, and I know somewhere deep inside. You know that."

More silence.

He sighed and his shoulders slumped forward. "I know you feel something for me, but you won't give into it. Part of me understands and then another huge part of me doesn't. What do I need to do? I'll do anything."

My expression hardened. "Stay away from me, Cole."

He violently shook his head, stepping toward me again, except this time I didn't step back.

"You don't mean that. You're mad at me and I completely deserve it, but you don't mean that."

I willed myself to breathe because my heart raced so profusely. It resonated in my temples. "I need some space from both of you. You need to respect that."

"For how long?"

"Does it matter?"

"It does to me."

I crossed my arms over my chest in hopes that it would make me appear more confident. I sure as hell didn't feel it. Every fiber in my body seemed tense and clenched, it was hard to feel anything other than the pain they both caused me.

"I'm so fucking sorry. Please believe me," he bellowed as if he could read my mind. His eyes gleamed and his lips shook as he said it.

I could feel my resolve breaking. "You hurt me," I simply stated, trying to remain strong.

He winced and shut his eyes. "I know."

"How can I trust you to not do it again?" As soon as the words left my mouth my heart sped up, anticipating his response.

"I can't promise you that I won't fuck up again. I'm not perfect and I'm not going to lie to you by saying I am."

I didn't have much time to appreciate his words because my attention turned to Lucas's mom who walked behind the two paramedics supporting Lucas, one on each side of him. I'm sure he refused to be placed on a stretcher.

He frowned when he saw me. I could physically feel the anguish radiating off of him and onto me. Our connection had always been like that. Unlike Cole who had to tell me his regret and remorse, I could actually sense Lucas's.

It was a part of me.

We were a part of each other.

As much as it confused and overwhelmed me, it provided the comfort that I needed at that moment. His soft baby blue eyes were calm, his hurricane once again sedated. I nervously shuffled around, the mere presence of him causing me to feel everything that I desperately tried to hide.

The boys were staring at us.

Everyone was staring at us.

While I stared at the center of my existence and vice versa, stirring open wounds that would take years to heal, for both of us.

I wish I could tell you things changed after this.

They didn't.

This was the beginning of the end for us. Except it wouldn't be Lucas's fault.

It would be mine.

# Chapter 22

## LUCAS

"Mom, I told you I'm sorry! How many times do I have to repeat it?"

"Boy, do NOT raise your voice to me."

I bowed my head. "Yes, ma'am."

"How many times do I have to cover for you, Lucas? I had to lie to your father, again," she emphasized.

This was the first time she had spoken to me in three days. She barely said a word to me on our way to the hospital. Sixty stitches later and a laceration diagnosis, my foot was pretty much fucked. I had crutches that I've barely used because I haven't moved from the spot on my bed. The pain has been almost unbearable, but the painkillers had helped. I hated taking them. They made me pass out and when I fought it, I was fucked up, literally.

I had to change the bandage once a day and I couldn't put any pressure on it for a few weeks, not that it mattered because I was on lockdown until the end of the summer. Mom didn't tell my dad what happened, she just told him that I got tossed off my board and my foot slammed into a rock. He gave me a lecture that I swear lasted five hours, but it didn't matter. I was so fucked up on pain medication that I felt like I watched a cartoon in live action. My mom said she hadn't told my dad the truth because she didn't want him to worry about another thing.

I'm not sure what that meant, but I went with it nonetheless.

We always had a special bond. She hid things from my dad several times over the years. This wasn't the first time, and I'm sure it wouldn't be the last. After I explained to her what really happened between Cole and me, and why I got injured in the first place. She stopped talking to me. I apologized profusely every time she changed my bandages on my foot, which only seemed to infuriate her more. She could barely even look at me when she changed them.

She brought me food, medicine, and water. Again, barely regarding me. I wouldn't say she had been mean to me, but she sure as shit didn't baby me like I assumed she would.

"If you weren't so careless and competing with Cole, you wouldn't have anything to apologize for, Lucas."

I sighed, annoyed. "I'm aware of that, Mom, thank you so much for reminding me."

Her eyes immediately went wide, clenching her jaw.

"I'm sorry," I instinctively blurted.

Her expression softened as she sat down beside me on the couch. Being in the same position on my bed for the last three days started to depress me. She said she would help me into the living room but not before she ordered me to shower. She said I smelled like shit and that's a lot coming from my mom who barely ever cursed to begin with. I argued with her that I didn't need her help, she rolled her eyes at me. Ignoring my plea, she placed a bench in the shower, so I could sit down and not have to worry about putting pressure on my foot or getting it wet.

I kept my boxers on the entire time while she washed me. When she tried to reach into my boxers to wash me there, I refused. She claimed it wasn't anything she hadn't seen before, reminding me that she used to change my diapers. I was a grown ass boy now and that wasn't happening. She sighed, shook her head and turned her back, as I washed my own cock and balls. Then she helped me out of the shower, and into my bedroom. It took me about an hour to try to take off my wet boxers and put on new ones. Again, she tried to assist me and once again I had to remind her I wasn't five anymore. She got bored of waiting and left me alone until I was done. I hollered for her to come back to help me get dressed the rest of the way.

It was a mission to say the least.

"What on earth possessed you to do something so dangerous, Lucas? Do you have any idea how much worse this could have been? You could have been paralyzed! You could have died, ugh! Every time I think about what that boy provoked you to do, it makes me want to call his parents to give them an earful."

I lay back against the pillow, my pain pill finally kicking in.

"Lucas! Are you listening to me?"

"Mmm hmm," I mumbled, glancing at her to prove it.

"Why won't you let me call his parents? It's not fair that you're the only one suffering for what he provoked."

"I know."

"No, you don't. Or else you would let me call them," she justified, folding one arm over the other on her chest.

"It's pointless. It's done."

"If you say so. Have you talked to Alex?"

"You know I haven't."

She wearingly smiled. "She'll come around."

"I don't know about that one."

She caressed the side of my face. "Honey, all of this is hard for her, too. You are both so young and I hate to say this, but it might be better like this. At least for a little while."

I pulled away from her hand. "Why does everyone keep saying that?"

"Lucas," she warned, hostility evident in her tone.

"I'm serious. I'm not a kid anymore."

She narrowed her eyes at me.

"Alright." I nodded. "I'm still stupid, but I'm not a kid. I'll be eighteen in a few weeks and she'll be sixteen. Don't you think we're old enough to choose what's right for us?"

She adamantly shook her head. "No. I don't. I'm sorry, Lucas."

I bowed my head, defeated. She gripped my chin with her thumb and index fingers making me look at her.

"You have so much more life to live. This is your last year of high school. Alex still has two more years after you're done. Do you think it would be fair to her for you to start something and then leave? Do you think it's fair that either of you would have to base your decisions on one another? You should be able to do whatever you want before you settle down, with anyone," she added, causing me to flinch.

"I have nothing against Alex. I love her like she was my own. If you two end up together, then I would be the happiest mom in the world. I just want you to be sure. Both of us do."

I knew she spoke about Alex's mom. I didn't have to ask whom she referred to.

"Trust me. Resentment can ruin the strongest relationships and I would hate for that to happen to the two of you just because you jumped into something so young before either of you got to experience all of what life has to offer. Do you understand?"

*No.*

But I nodded anyway.

I sensed she knew I lied, so I gave her a half-ass smile in hopes the conversation would be over. Lily walked into the room, announcing that she was hungry. Mom got off the couch to go make us some lunch and I closed my eyes.

Lily slapped me on the chest.

"Ow!" I opened my eyes, placing my hand on the spot she hit. "What was that for?"

"You're an idiot," she simply stated.

"Why?"

"You know why…"

I cocked my head to the side. "Can you stop speaking in code? I obviously don't."

She rolled her eyes and shook her head. "I know you love her and I know she loves you, too."

I sat there dumbfounded, staring at my eleven-year-old baby sister. For the first time she appeared much older than she truly was, instantly reminding me of Alex at her age.

"Lily, you're too wise for your years."

She proudly smiled. "Duh."

I laughed.

"I don't like Cole. He looks too much like Ken and I'm pretty sure Ken's gay. Alex doesn't really look like Barbie. She needs someone that looks like G.I. Joe. You kinda look like him, so that matches better."

*And out goes the older theory.*

"That made absolutely no sense."

She punched me again.

"Stop hitting me!"

"Then you shouldn't have taught me to hit."

"Oh my God, Lily, you need to go away. You remind me too much of Alex and I really can't think about her right now."

"That's because you're a dumb boy. If you would just tell her you loved her and wanted to be with her then… voilà," she exclaimed with her hands out in the air. "Problem fixed."

"There's way more to it than that, kid."

"Nah uh. Love is easy. It's you that's making it hard."

There were times like these where I wished I had her optimism. She had always been like that. Ever since I could remember, my baby sister looked at the glass half full, rather than half empty.

"One day I'm going to fall in love and he's going to love me fearlessly. He's going to protect me and fight for me. He won't care about what anyone thinks, because he's not a dummy like you are. We're going to be happy because all you need is love. You should really learn that, Lucas." She shrugged. "Just sayin'."

I chuckled. "I really hope that, Lily, if he's not then I'm going to kick his fucking ass."

Her eyes widened and she giggled with her hand over her mouth at my crass words.

"Now, go away. I want to take a nap."

She obliged and kissed my forehead.

I closed my eyes and tried to let slumber take me over.

When it did.

I dreamed of *her*.

# Alex

It had been three weeks since Lucas's accident and I still hadn't said a word to him. I knew how he was because Lily kept me updated. School started in a few short weeks, so I drowned myself in work and told my parents to give me extra shifts at the restaurant. Cole came by every day. He surfed, ate lunch and often waited till my shift was over just to be able to talk to me for a few minutes before I went home.

I was still pissed at him but each day it became less and less, toward both of them.

"There's a new movie playing at the theater," Cole commented while I cleaned up his table.

"Oh yeah?"

"Yeah. I thought maybe you'd want to go watch it with me? What do you say?"

"I'm kinda tired, Cole. My feet are killing me, and all I really want to do is take a bath and watch TV."

He nodded, understanding. "I could go rent a movie and we could watch it, together."

I peered up at him through my lashes. He had one of those grins again, the one with his dimples smugly on display.

"You're never going to give up, are you?" I teasingly asked.

"Not in my nature."

"I don't know, Cole."

"It's just a movie. I'll sit on another couch, you won't even have to touch me, look at me, or talk to me."

I laughed. "Then what's the point?"

"To be near you."

I laughed again. "Still saying all the right things, I see."

"You got me on one of my good days."

I cocked my head to the side and placed my hand on my hip. "Do you ever have a bad one?"

"Everyday these last three weeks has been a bad day."

I instinctively stepped back, putting some space between us. "I just don't think I'm ready for all that. I'm sorry."

"I deserve it. I leave in two weeks, and I'd love to spend more time with you before I go."

"You'll be back," I reasoned.

"I will, but it doesn't mean I don't want to see you before I go."

"Maybe," I breathed out, not giving in but not declining either. "Okay?"

He nodded as he stood. I think he wanted to leave before I changed my mind.

"I'll see you tomorrow," he said.

I watched him leave and then made my way toward the boys and Aubrey.

"Anything else before I clock out?" I asked them.

"You look tired, Half-Pint," Jacob noticed. He was never one to hold back what he thought.

191

"I am tired. It's been a long day."

"Is that the only reason?" Dylan chimed in and my eyes immediately shifted to Aubrey. Who looked as nervous as I appeared.

"Would there be another one?" I challenged, needing to hear his response to my question.

"You talk to Lucas?" Austin asked, bringing my attention to him.

"No."

His eyebrows lowered in a curious yet serious manner while he glanced at the boys before saying, "Maybe you should."

I didn't falter. "How's he doing?"

"Don't pretend like you don't know," Jacob accused only staring at me.

I placed my hand on my hip, leaning all my weight into it. "What's that supposed to mean?"

"You tell us," Dylan countered.

"Boys!" Aubrey scolded, but none of them turned to look at her. Their intense glares placed on me. I felt like I was on trial or something. Every move I made or anything I said would receive an objection.

"Stop ganging up on her," Aubrey yelled out, sticking up for me. But even I didn't back down from their glares.

"Mind your business, baby," Dylan ordered in a husky tone I'd never heard before.

"We've given you weeks, Half-Pint, and you haven't said a word. Is there anything you need to tell us? Or do we need to keeping assuming?" Dylan proclaimed.

"You know what they say about people who assume," I sassed, and I could feel Aubrey smiling behind me. It gave me the courage I needed to keep going and for some reason, I felt she knew that.

Jacob stood first and the rest followed, their large frames towering over my small one.

"Get your shit together. Ya hear me?" Jacob insinuated something that I couldn't place my finger on, but his tone left me contemplating what he really meant.

I nodded even though I didn't understand. "Loud and clear."

"Good, while you're at it give Lucas a call. He needs a *friend*," Austin implied, accentuating the last word.

"He's got you boys," I simply stated.

"He. Needs. You. As a *friend*," Dylan coaxed, also stressing that word. He pulled me over to him with his hand on the back of my neck and kissed the top of my head, murmuring, "Don't lie to us again."

I lifted my face to look at him but I was too late, he already turned to leave. Jacob hugged me next, tight and securely around my waist and Austin followed suit. They trailed after Dylan toward the pool table.

I turned to Aubrey when they were out of earshot. "What the hell was that?" I questioned, surprised and utterly perplexed with what just happened in the last five minutes.

"I wish I could tell you. Dylan has been pissed at me since the accident and I didn't even do anything. I swear he knows that I knew or something. He smells it on me like a bloodhound."

"Have they talked to Lucas?"

"I mean they have but they haven't. I don't know. It's weird. It's obvious they know something's up. I think they're hurt that they're just now figuring it out. I'm not really sure, it's very confusing."

I swallowed the saliva that had pooled in my mouth. "What should I do?"

"Fuck if I know."

I shrugged, glancing over at them with her. "I guess I didn't even notice they had been acting weird toward me. I've been too caught up in work and trying to ignore everything else around me. Is it bad?"

"It's not good. Maybe talk to Lucas and see where that goes. All I know is they've been keeping their distance from him."

My eyes widened, stunned. "Really?"

"Yeah."

"I don't want that. I don't want to cause a rift between them. Not ever."

She nodded. "I know you don't, but you've always been the glue that's kept them together, Alex, you know that right?"

I didn't.

And it made me feel worse.

As I looked back over at my good ol' boys, it was the first time I realized that it wasn't just about Lucas and me anymore or maybe it never was? It involved all of us in some way, shape, or form.

I never wanted to come between them and I knew what I had to do.

Even though the thought alone.

Nearly killed me.

# Chapter 23

## LUCAS

It had been a month since the accident and I finally moved around without the crutches. Not for very long but it was progress nonetheless. When I heard the doorbell ring I figured it was the boys. They hadn't been around a lot since the accident. I figured they were just busy with summer. I didn't blame them for not wanting to hang out with a crippled that couldn't leave his house. My mom was out for the day and my dad was at work.

When I heard the knock on my bedroom door, I realized it wasn't the boys because they would have just walked right in. That only left one other person.

"Lily, go away! I'm not playing Barbie's with you again, that was a one-time thing."

The door opened and Alex stepped in smiling like a fool. I hadn't seen her since the accident. She wore a white crop top with black cotton shorts. Her hair sat on the top of her head in a messy bun with pieces scattered and falling around her face. I knew she didn't do that on purpose, she probably just slept with her hair like that and didn't bother doing anything with it when she woke up.

Her sun-kissed skin and her glossy lips immediately did things to my cock, which had me reaching over to grab a pillow to cover it.

"Barbies?" she teased with a cocked head and arched eyebrow. "You never played Barbie's with me," she giggled, and it felt incredible to hear her laugh again.

My day drastically changed from bad to amazing.

"You didn't have Barbies, but you did play G.I. Joes with me," I stated, mirroring her smile.

"That's because he blew stuff up and it was cool. Barbies are stupid."

"In my defense Lily got me at my all time weakness. Being lonely and fucked up on pain medication will make you do things," I shared as a joke to keep the momentum of our light banter going, but when her smile faltered and she frowned. I knew I fucked it up.

"I'm not lonely anymore. You're here now," I reassured, hoping to see that smile that lights up her entire face again.

She softly grinned, it wasn't the one I wanted to see, but she still looked beautiful.

"How are you feeling?" she asked, walking toward me. I nodded to the place in front of me on my bed. I slid over putting my back against my headboard to allow her more room.

She climbed up and lay sideways with her head pitched up on her hand, always lying like that. It warmed my heart that she was still able to feel comfortable around me, even though we hadn't spoken in a month and were nowhere near where we used to be.

"I'm good. Better now," I reaffirmed again. I didn't want to put any doubt in her mind that I didn't love that she was here with me.

It's where she belonged.

"You look better. I mean not that I know what you looked like before but Lily—"

"Lily?" I interrupted.

Her cheeks reddened as she peered down at my comforter. She immediately started to play with the seams, her nervous habit.

"Oh… well… Lily has been keeping me updated and stuff." She shrugged. "It's not a big deal or anything. I was worried about you."

If my baby sister were in the room I would have tackled her to the ground and kissed her. I made a mental note to do something nice for her later, even if that meant I had to play fucking Barbie's.

"How often do you talk to Lily?" I asked.

She shrugged again. "Often enough."

"Which is?" I added, needing more information than she gave me.

"Every day."

My eyes widened in shock and I couldn't help the love and fondness that soared throughout my entire body, leaving a sense of longing in its wake. Before I gave it any thought, I grabbed her wrist and pulled her toward me. She came effortlessly. I threw the pillow and placed her on my lap with her legs straddling my waist, it didn't help my over stimulated cock's enthusiasm for her, but I didn't give a fuck.

I wanted to hold her.

So I did.

I wrapped my arms around her tiny frame. At first she stiffened into my embrace unsure of what to do, but it didn't take long for her to soften and wrap her arms around me, laying her head on my shoulder and breathing me in.

I kissed the top of her head like I had done countless times before. It was way too many times to have ever kept count. "God, you feel fucking amazing," I groaned, smelling her coconut shampoo and sunscreen skin.

"You do, too," she sniffled.

As much as I didn't want to pull away from her, I did. I looked into her beautiful watery eyes and asked, "What's wrong?" My heart sped up at lighting speed. Concern and worry were evident in my tone.

She smiled, the same one that ignited her entire face. "I'm happy," she laughed out.

She gazed at me and I knew that look. My brown-eyed girl sat on my lap, placed in my arms, and I couldn't help myself. I knew there were miles of barriers between us, I knew we had every obstacle under the sun against us, I knew that it may have been wrong, but fuck it, it felt so fucking right.

She meant everything to me.

I grabbed both sides of her face, closing the space between us.

I leaned in and kissed her. At first it started innocently enough, but after a couple seconds she parted her mouth and started to move her lips. Her mouth became more demanding wanting me to respond and I gently started to, which earned me a moan from her lips. She tasted like Cherry Coke and cherry lip-gloss. I couldn't get enough. It melted my heart that she still drank Cherry Coke and wore cherry flavored lip-gloss, it was always my favorite and she knew it. Her tongue was smooth and felt like silk. I hadn't kissed her in so fucking long, it felt like it had been centuries since the last time I felt her lips against mine.

Complicate Me

I started to lean forward. I wanted to feel her body beneath mine. The second I was above her, my hand started roaming. It started at her hair and then traveled down to her face. She writhed and moaned beneath me, enticing me to go further. My hand moved to the top of her breast and I could feel her nipple hardening through the flimsy cotton shirt and bathing suit top underneath. She pushed her breast further into my hand and I immediately gripped it harder, earning me another moan.

It was the first time I ever felt her in this way. I subconsciously rubbed my hard cock against her pussy. My thin gym shorts and her slim cotton ones made it easy to feel the friction that ignited between us, it felt so fucking amazing that I did it again. She followed my lead pretty quickly and started rubbing up against me.

I kissed her with all the passion and hunger of a starving man. She met each and every push and pull that I delivered. My hand moved under her shirt and I knew I needed to stop, but I couldn't fucking help myself. I wanted this for so long that I let it take over. At first I caressed on top of her bathing suit but it didn't take long for me to push the material aside and touch her warm perky breast, which felt fucking incredible against my fingers and in the palm of my hand.

Everything with Alex was indescribable. It didn't matter how many girls I had been with nothing came close to this.

*To her.*

It excited me in ways I never thought were possible. The emotions and love I felt for her made everything more real and complete.

Our movements became headier and more urgent since we were both searching for something. When I pushed her shirt up and kissed my way down to her breast, her back arched off the bed. Her hips moved faster against my cock and I kept up the same momentum. I opened my eyes to look at her. I desperately wanted to see her breasts. I cupped it again and it fit flawlessly in the palm of my hand. Her cream colored nipple was just the right size. It was taut just waiting for me to take it in my mouth.

I did.

It was then that I truly noticed how warm her skin felt and how precise her hips rotated against mine. I sucked on her nipple a little harder and she rewarded me with a loud abandoned moan that made me look up at her through my hooded eyes.

Her mouth was parted, her face was flushed, her chest raised and lifted at rapid speed as she fisted my comforter.

*Shit.*

I immediately stopped and pushed myself off her.

"What's wrong?" she said out of breath but not moving.

"Fuck," I yelled out, pushing my hair out of my face and holding it back with my hands.

She inhaled deeply and rapidly, trying to steady her aroused body. "What was that?"

"Fuck!" I shouted out again, only pissed at myself. "I shouldn't have done that."

She instantly froze, as if I had dumped frigid cold water on her. Sliding her bathing suit top over and pulling down her shirt, she closed her eyes tightly as if it pained her to look at me.

"What?" she softly spoke.

"Half-Pint," I coaxed.

"Was I not good?"

"Fuck no," I said too harshly. "That has nothing to do with it. You felt *too* good."

She contemplated what I said for a few seconds. "So did you. I felt like my body was—"

"I know," I cut her off. Not being able to hear her say that she was just about to come.

That I almost made her come.

*I'm a fucking asshole.*

# Alex

I finally opened my eyes and beheld the ceiling. I couldn't look at him I was too embarrassed. Nothing even remotely close to that had ever happened to me before. It was like I didn't have any control over my body, and I rode this high that wouldn't drop.

*What was that?*

Complicate Me

It was the first time I ever felt his manhood. The thought alone caused my skin to burn, igniting the already fuming flames into my bloodstream. Producing a tingly sensation down there, where our most sacred parts had just met. I felt some unfamiliar sensations between my legs. An occasional pulsating in places unexplored. It was also safe to say he felt it, too. The hardness pressing into my ache was a dead giveaway.

"I'm sorry," I heard him say.

"Why are you apologizing?"

"Because it's so fucking wrong what I just did. I would never use you like that. You know that, right?"

I nodded. I did.

"It takes two to tango, Lucas."

"Yeah. But I started it."

That made me sit up and look at him. His hair was a mess and his skin was red all over. It was his eyes that struck out to me the most. They looked the same as they did that day on the beach when we were kids. They looked the same after every intimate moment that we've had since.

My heart lifted. He *did* want me.

"What if I started it?" I blurted unexpectedly for the both of us.

"What are you saying?"

"You heard me."

"Half-Pint, you would never do that," he adamantly stated. "You're not like that."

My face frowned. "Why do you always do that?"

He shook his head, confused. "Do what?"

"That." I stood up and stepped in front of him. "You have put me on a pedestal and you treat me like a doll! You can touch me, I want you to touch me. I am not a child anymore. I want to experience things and I want them to be with you. I'm almost sixteen years old and I've only been kissed by you, it's always been you."

His jaw clenched. "That's not what I meant."

"Then what? What did you mean?"

He sighed, pulling back his hair again. It made his arms appear bigger. The ache between my legs once again made itself known.

"I just meant. You're different and I love that about you. That's all. You're not like the other girls."

"But you want *those* girls," I justified.

"No." He swept a piece of my hair away from my face and tucked it behind my ear. That simple touch had me melting into his hand.

"I want you," he huskily rasped.

I was speechless and by the look on his face he knew it.

"You have to know that, Half-Pint. All I've ever wanted is you. I don't care about anyone else, nothing compares to the way I feel when I'm with you. Or how your skin feels against mine, or how I live to see your face light up for me. It's your innocence, it's your spunkiness, it's the *girl*," he accentuated with wide eyes. "That would *try* to kick my ass if I ever called her one. The same one who grew up before my very own eyes and turned into the most beautiful girl I've ever seen. I fucking love you," he paused to let his words sink in. "I loved you then, I love you now, I'll love you always."

"Bo…"

I soaked up everything he had just shared with me. Every last word. It felt like daggers attacked my already aching skin, especially at my heart. Everything in my body screamed, "Yes do it." It ate me up inside. It was the burden of knowing that if I gave into us, I would be causing a major rift between all of us.

I remembered the conversation from the restaurant as if it was just yesterday. Maybe if I didn't know, maybe if they hadn't warned me. Maybe if I wouldn't of known that Lucas and I being together would cause all of us to drift apart, maybe things could have been different.

*We* could have been different.

But they had warned me. It was my moment of clarity and I wasn't strong enough to inflict any more pain on my boys than I already had. Then we already had. I continued to let Bo say all the things that I waited to hear for so long.

I needed that for myself.

"I'm sorry things got out of hand, but I had to touch you. I had to feel you beneath me. I want to know every part of you, Alexandra. I've wanted that ever since I can remember. But that's not the way it should have happened and for that I apologize. At the end of the day, I don't care about anyone or anything but you."

"You don't mean that."

"I do. The boys, my parents—"

I stepped back away from him and immediately felt the loss. "No. Lucas, I could never. I won't," I babbled. "I mean. I can't. I would hate myself if I ever came between you."

"What are you talking about?" He stepped toward me.

"When was the last time you saw the boys?"

His eyes moved all around the room and then he nervously laughed. "Come to think of it, I guess a few weeks."

"They know."

"Know?" he lingered.

"That's why they haven't been around you. They've been treating me different, too. Aubrey said—"

"Aubrey? You know about Aubrey?"

"Yeah. Do you?"

He didn't have to say anything, I could tell by the look on his face. It all made sense now. Especially the times I caught them in deep conversation.

"You don't think…"

I shook my head. "She would never. But she's right. They don't like it, and I can't be the reason that you would lose them. It would kill me."

"Alex—"

"Let me finish, please."

He nodded, allowing me to continue with what I planned to say in the first place.

"All my life, all I've ever known is you and the boys. I didn't care about anyone else other than *my* boys. You've always meant something more to me, but that doesn't take away from the fact that they mean something to me as well. I love all of you. You're each apart of me. I've realized that this thing between you and I has caused a rift with all of us." I took a deep breath, willing myself to keep going.

"I can't be the cause of that between you boys. Just like you can't be the cause between them and me. They mean too much to me and I know they mean just as much to you."

He bowed his head with recognition that I was right.

"You boys are my family and my heart and soul, Bo. There is no Alex without any of you. Please tell me you know that I'm right, I need to hear you say it."

"I can't, Alex," he murmured loud enough for me to hear. "In the back of my mind I know that you're right." He peered up at me with so much emotion in his eyes that it nearly brought me to my knees.

"But in my heart, in my heart I don't care. I hate myself for that because I should care. I've always been a selfish bastard, and the way I feel about you and not caring about them, it proves that. That's the honest to Gods truth."

I didn't think it was possible to feel anymore shattered than I already had.

I was so wrong.

All he wanted was to be with me. I wanted that more than anything, but couldn't bring myself to do that to my boys. I wasn't made like that, and I would be lying if I said it didn't hurt like hell that Lucas was. At the same time it gave me a satisfied feeling that he could give them up for me so easily.

Without a second thought.

It was followed by raw sentiments that overpowered any other reaction ingrained deep in my heart. Making me feel as if I didn't love him enough, and that in itself was a rude awakening.

"It's too late for us, Lucas," I whispered and I felt my heart breaking into a million pieces.

I would always remember this moment as the first time.

That *I*...

Intentionally walked away from Lucas.

# Chapter 24

## LUCAS

They say time heals all wounds.

That's fucking bullshit.

The school year was just about over, and it was hard to believe that in a few short weeks I would be moving away from Oak Island.

Most importantly I'd be moving away from Alex.

The boys and I were all leaving, except Austin, who still had one more year left of high school. I decided to attend Ohio State. They had a great engineering program. I had a passion for building things, even as a child. Jacob and Dylan got accepted as well, so it didn't take long for them to jump on board. Our parents were spending a small fortune on out of state tuition, but I think they were just relieved that we were staying together in an apartment off campus. Not at the fraternity house we planned to pledge.

Dylan was upset to be leaving Aubrey since she was in the same grade as Austin. I think it bothered him that she seemed so nonchalant about it, but he never said anything to me. He said they were going to try to do the long distance thing for a while and see how well it turned out. She seemed to understand. I could tell he loved her. He possibly loved her as much as I loved Alex. I would be lying if I said it sure as hell didn't bother me that Alex didn't put up a fight against me leaving. For some reason I knew the girl I grew up with would have, she probably would have put up a fight against all of us leaving.

But too much had happened.

We were way past that now.

Jacob wasn't dating anyone, in fact he never dated anyone, so the decision for him was easy. As we got older Jacob still remained single, I mean he dated girls on and off but nothing serious. He said he preferred it that way, and I never pressed him for more information than he willingly shared. Growing up, Austin hated that he was younger than all of us. I think he knew that this day would eventually come, us going off to college together before him. He was a lot like Alex in that sense. Very intuitive and always wanting to be one of the boys. It comforted me knowing that he would still be here to look after her for one more year and then she would really be alone.

For the first time, the future was unknown for all of us. I never imagined that the roads ahead would be as unclear as they were now, assuming they would only get worse as time went on. With each of us taking different paths and going in separate directions that may or may not lead us back to Oak Island. I don't want to say that my mom was right, but I decided it was wise to follow her advice and expand my horizons. Especially after nothing changed when I poured my heart out to Alex. At least not the way I wanted it to. We became friends again, but we hadn't been back to our abandoned house in years. It held too many memories for the both of us and it was easier to sweep everything under the rug.

It took us a few months to get used to this new friendship we evolved into. We were the same but different…

I'm not going to try to understand any of it. She was in my life again and that was good enough for me. I think we were all just ready to try something new and different. I guess you could say things went back to normal.

With all of us.

"Oh my God, will you stop fucking texting Cole for two seconds?" I snarled.

Alex placed her phone in her back pocket and smiled at me. "I wasn't even texting Cole, thank you very much."

"Right…"

Oh yeah, and Cole didn't fucking go away.

"I like the gray sheets, they look better than the black," she stated, taking the black sheets out of my hand and grabbing the gray ones.

She conned me into going shopping for the apartment. We were leaving after the fourth of July and that was only three weeks away. I hadn't given much thought about what I would need but I didn't have to. Alex had done it for me. I could have done this shit in

205

Ohio, I didn't want to lug around any more stuff than I had to, but it made her happy and at the end of the day.

That's all that mattered.

"For the last time, I don't fucking care, Half-Pint. Get what you want, I'm over this."

"We just got here, do you see this list?" She placed the paper in front of my face.

"I've only crossed off two things from the sixty on the list," she informed me, assuming that I would give a shit.

I didn't.

"Oh my God, I'm going to die here."

She rolled her eyes. "Bo, I took off work for this."

"Good. You work too much anyways," I grinned, glancing at her.

"I thought you loved it when I fed you."

I smiled. "Yes. When you feed *me*." I didn't have to say his name for her to know who I implied.

She reminded me often that she and Cole were still just friends. *I believed her because what other choice did I have?*

"Why couldn't you and Aubrey do this?"

She sighed. "Aubrey is having a hard time with all of this."

We walked down the aisle and I looked over at her while she dumped more random shit into the shopping cart.

*Did she honestly think I would dust?*

"What do you mean? Dylan said she's been fine with everything."

She shrugged, grabbing a broom and dustpan that I grabbed from her and placed back on the rack.

"No," I ordered, rolling the cart to leave the goddamn cleaning aisle.

She placed the same dustpan and broom that I just took out of her hands back into the shopping cart, completely blowing me off with a great big smile on her face and a scowl on mine.

*See? I told you things were somewhat back to normal.*

"Alex," I warned.

"What?"

I shook my head. "Nothing."

She placed her hand on her hip, cocked her head, and looked right at me. "You're going to need a broom and dustpan, I know how messy you boys are. I don't want to have to go buy one when I come and visit."

I loved that she was already thinking about coming to visit and we hadn't even left yet, so I disregarded the smartass comments that I really wanted to say.

"I can't believe you boys are leaving me in three weeks," she softly spoke not meeting my eyes.

"We're not leaving you."

"I know."

"We will come back all the time. Ohio isn't that far away."

"It's over a ten-hour drive."

I nudged her with my shoulder as we walked side-by-side. "Look at all the practice you can get at driving. Maybe I won't fear for my life when I'm in a car with you anymore."

She smacked my chest and shoved me away from the cart, rolling it to the next aisle.

I subconsciously looked up at the number above our heads, three. *How many fucking aisles does this store have?*

"I'm a cautious driver," she stated, pulling me away from my thoughts.

"No, you're a scary one."

"How would you know? You never let me drive your truck."

"That's because you can barely see over the steering wheel, and the first time I let you drive it, you popped a curb and scratched my rim."

She scoffed, placing her hand on her chest. "That curb came out of nowhere."

"Right... because that happens all the time. Curbs popping out of nowhere and shit, I'm constantly hearing about it on the news."

She glared at me and I laughed. "I drive in your car enough to know that you can't drive worth shit."

"I just got that car."

"Exactly," I stated with wide eyes.

Her parents had bought her a white Honda Civic a few weeks ago. They thought if they waited until she was almost seventeen to buy her a vehicle, that she would have more time to practice. That she would somehow develop some sort of awareness for driving.

Complicate Me

She didn't.

We stayed in the store for the next three hours. I drew the line when she tried to buy accent pillows for the couch and my bed. She tried to play it cool when she added some of her own toiletries and other stuff that I knew were only for her. I didn't call her out on it because I didn't want her to take them out or make her feel like she wasn't welcome or wanted. As much as she tried to pretend that she was excited for us, I knew deep down she was scared of another change in our short lives. Not just with me this time.

With all of us.

I wanted to reassure her that everything would be all right and tell her anything else I had to say to ease her concern. Except *this* time I didn't want to lie to her, it's what started our complicated chaos in the first place.

Things were changing again.

It was inevitable, just like the days changing and time moving forward.

But I never imagined it would be to the degree that it did.

# Alex

I hated that we grew up.

I hated that we still had so much more growing up to do.

I hated that they were leaving me.

I hated that I felt like I was left behind.

It would only be Austin and me for one more year. Then I would be alone, even Aubrey would be gone.

I hated *that* more than anything.

I tried to pretend that none of it bothered me. That I didn't lose sleep over it, or that it wasn't constantly on my mind. But when I was alone with nothing but my thoughts and nothing to distract me, there was no escaping it. The realization quickly followed. I did have a co-dependent relationship with my boys, and I had yet to figure out if that was a good or bad thing.

I always wanted to be with them.

That's just the way it was.

As a child you don't comprehend how much impact relationships like ours can have on your life and the decisions that you needed to make. Especially when it came time for everyone to go their separate ways. Which was another thing I never considered.

*Leaving.*

My junior year was fast approaching and it was time for me to start thinking about the future.

*My* future.

What I wanted to do with my life and where I wanted to go. My parents told me they would pay for any college of my choice, though scholarships and grants would be easily attainable for me. I was a great student. Made honor roll ever since I could remember. That wasn't what plagued me. I could get in anywhere.

There was a major difference between my boys and me.

I didn't want to leave.

I loved Oak Island. It was home to me. I guess I assumed we would all attend Wilmington University and grow old here like our parents did. When the boys told me they were leaving because they wanted to live in a big city and do new things, I wanted to yell at them the same way I did when we were kids, and they told me something that didn't make any sense, but I couldn't.

It wouldn't be fair to do that to them. I had to let them grow up, exactly the way I always had.

My mom had always told me that boys were different than girls. That we were made differently, and I never considered it to be true until they told me they were leaving so easily. The words flew from their mouths like the waves of the ocean. I pretended to be happy, ecstatic from the news even. My boys knew me well, so when they pulled me into tight hugs my eyes began to water. The older I got the harder it was to hold back my emotions. To keep them hidden like I did when I was a kid.

I guess I really did turn into a girl at some point.

Lucas had been spending more time with me and I knew it was for both our benefits. He would miss me as much as I would him.

That wasn't even a question.

The answer was already ingrained in our hearts.

Complicate Me

I didn't know how long it would last, so I cherished it as much as I could not knowing when it might end. I started thinking about the future and how much it could really change. As soon as thoughts of love with other people crossed my mind I immediately shook it off.

I would rather be surprised than to expect it.

It was easier that way.

Or so I thought...

"Whatcha thinkin' about over there?" Lucas asked while we were watching a movie on his bed.

"I'm watching the movie."

"What's it about?"

I looked from the TV to him. "Huh?"

"The movie, Half-Pint, what's it about?" he grinned all knowing.

"Oh," I smiled. "Is the movie too smart for you, Bo? Do you need me to explain it so that you understand?" I teased to no avail.

"You think that's going to work on me? Give me some credit, Alex. What are you thinking about?"

"Why does it matter?"

He turned to face me. The intensity of his stare causing me to pull my legs up to my chest and wrap my arms around them in a comforting gesture.

"I can't do this with you again," he recalled with a familiar edge in his tone. "I can't lose you again. I won't, Alex. It doesn't matter what happens between us, you have to be in my life and I don't care if it's just as my best friend. Know that I'll take you any way I can. So, please tell me what you're thinking, because I can guarantee you that every answer to your question is a no."

The severity of his words shocked me to my core. Somewhere along the way my boy also grew up.

Into a man.

No longer the boy that I was in love with.

"I'm scared," I half-whispered, and by the look on his face it wasn't what he expected me to say.

"I'm scared that you're moving away and you're going to forget about me. I'm scared that you *all* will. I'm scared that nothing will ever be the same like it was when we were kids. I'm scared that I have no idea what I want to do with my life," I paused to let my words sink in. "But mostly, I'm scared that we're growing up and that *our* paths may never cross through the same direction, Bo. That we're destined to remain in this friendship that I love so much, that I cherish with all my heart. The ups and downs are what make us, Bo and Half-Pint. What if that's all we'll ever have?"

He took in each and every word as if I recited his favorite song and then softly grabbed the sides of my face and looked deep into my eyes.

"I told you every answer was no," he simply stated with a heartwarming look on his face before he leaned in and kissed the tip of my nose.

I wanted to remember this always.

Because what happened next...

I wanted to forget forever.

# Chapter 25

## Alex

It was the Fourth of July.

Southport was the next town over and highway 211 was closed down every year for the Fourth of July Festival. Since 1972 over forty thousand tourists and residents gathered around to enjoy the day's festivities. It was usually my favorite day of the year.

Not this year.

This year, my boys were leaving the very next day.

"Alex, honey, what are you doing here? Why aren't you at the festival?" Mom asked as I cleaned my last table.

"I'm working," I simply stated.

"Alex, you don't need to be working. You're missing the fun, you're missing your boys. They leave tomorrow."

"Don't remind me."

"Oh, honey," she sighed as she grabbed my arm, making me sit with her.

"That's what this is about?"

I shrugged because I didn't know what to say.

"They're going to come back for every holiday and I bet some random weekends, too. You will visit when you can. I promise."

"Right."

"Oh, Alex, at times I wish we would have been more careful with you and those boys."

That grabbed my attention, making me look up at her. "What?"

"You're so attached to them. Sometimes I worry if that's healthy for you."

"I'm fine. I'm just sad, is all. They leave tomorrow and I don't want to ruin their last day here."

"Now you know that's not true. Do you have any idea how many times Lucas has called the restaurant begging me to let you off work? Why did you tell them that we're making you work? That couldn't be further from the truth."

"It was easier that way. If I didn't, they would be sitting here instead of enjoying their last day on the island."

"Easier for who?"

I bowed my head.

"I don't have to tell you, but you know that you're so young. You all are. Honey, your lives are going to go in separate directions eventually, but that doesn't mean that you won't be in each other's lives at all."

"How do you know that?"

"It comes with age."

"It doesn't feel that way to me."

"Just trust me, Alex, for once, I promise. Your heart is here, which is true for all of you. Sometimes it takes leaving to know where you come from. To know where you belong." She wrapped her arm around my shoulder and tugged me closer.

"I love you, but if you don't get the hell out of here right now. I'm going to fire you."

I laughed.

"Now go!" She pushed me off the bench, smiled and left.

I went to the bathroom to change into a bikini under my dress. I let down my hair and put on some mascara, blush, and lip-gloss. After a few minutes I felt better about my appearance and walked out into the restaurant.

Cole sat on the exact bench that my mom and I were just on. I hadn't been spending much time with him since he arrived on the island. I gave Lucas and the boys my undivided attention. Cole never complained about it, he knew they were leaving. We still talked on the phone and texted all the time. He was there for me as he had always been. The past summer's incident was long forgotten.

*Boys will be boys.*

"What are you doing here?"

He grinned, his dimples prominently on full display. "Is that anyway to say hello, Darlin'?"

"Hello. What are you doing here?" I sassed and he chuckled, standing in front of me.

"I'm waiting for you."

I cocked my head to the side.

"I hear there's this beach party in Southport after the festival and seeing as the festival is over and it's almost sunset, I'm assuming the party is just now getting good."

I shook my head, confused. "I'm not much for those types of parties, Cole."

"I'm aware of that, but I'm here now. Don't you want me to have the full Fourth of July experience?"

"The festival is the experience."

"You're the experience. Fuck the festival."

I smiled, blushing. The boy had a way with words that still made me blush like it was the first time I had spoken to him.

I nodded. "Fine."

"Great. My car's out front."

We rode in silence while I tried to ignore the uneasy feeling knowing what awaited us.

Lucas.

# LUCAS

"What are you doing here?" I asked Alex with pretty boy standing beside her. "I thought you were working?"

She looked from me to him even though my eyes were solely focused on her.

"Oh, I was but my mom said to go hang out. It was slow so she said to leave early."

I knew that was a bunch of bullshit. It was the Fourth of July, their busiest day of the year.

"Why didn't you call me? I would have come back to drive you."

"Oh... well... Cole was already there and he wanted to check this out, so I came with him. I mean... I knew you'd be here so..." she said, nervous and uneasy.

"Is that right?" I nodded, taking my stare from her to him. "Thanks, Cole," I said with a wide fake smile. The last thing I wanted to do was spend my last night in Oak Island with this fucking douchebag. "I really appreciate you bringing Half-Pint, but I'm here now so you can go."

"I'm staying," he affirmed.

"Of course you are." I grabbed Alex's hand and turned with him following close behind us.

She tottered close to my ear and whispered, "Be nice, Bo."

I spent the next few hours with her close to my side and with him at hers. I wanted more than anything to be alone with her. As soon as her shift was over she would have walked out into the parking lot with me in my truck waiting for her. I hated that Cole got to her first and my plan went to shit.

I took a swig of my drink and Alex took it from my hand.

"What are you doing?"

She innocently shrugged. "I want to try."

"Half-Pint—"

"Lucas," Cole chimed in. "Let her fucking try the drink. She's not a kid."

I raised my eyebrow at him not backing down. "No shit. Except I'd rather make her a new one, she doesn't drink and mine is really strong."

Alex coughed and wiped her mouth, proving my point.

"I'll make her another one," he argued.

"Hey!" Alex shouted. "I'll make myself one," she announced before walking away from both of us with my drink still in her hand.

"She's not a little girl, Lucas. The problem is you still see her as one. Maybe it's time you realize that."

*Motherfucker.*

I turned to face him, mere inches away from his face. "Who's going to make me realize that, Cole? You?"

"Just sayin', brother."

"I'm not your brother. I'm not your friend. I don't fucking like you! The problem is you need to mind your own goddamn business. It has nothing to do with that. I know Alex like the back of my hand. She doesn't drink. I'm just watching out for her. I'm fully aware that she's not a little girl," I scoffed, glaring him up and down. "And when her body was lying beneath mine, my cock was fully aware of that too."

He jerked back, stunned.

I smiled, angling my head to the side with a smug grin. "I guess *Alexandra* doesn't tell you everything? Aren't as close as you thought, huh, *brother*?"

"Lucas!" Jacob shouted from afar before he could reply.

"Come over here, you fuck and play beer pong! I'm losing because Dylan can't play worth shit!"

I took one last look at Cole who hadn't regained his composure, and I couldn't tell if he was pissed or disappointed, I imagined it was both. I made my way to the boys and we played a few rounds of beer pong just shooting the shit with everyone and trying to enjoy our last night there. My attention was never too far from Alex. I didn't even see it coming, it happened so fast. I looked around and she was gone.

My phone pinged with a text message, as Aubrey's face lit up my screen. I swiped over the icon.

**Aubrey:** *Need you now! We're by the pier.*

I took off like a bat out of hell, not bothering to say anything to anyone or explain. As I'm running, a million thoughts raced through my mind and the minute I saw Alex bent over with Cole holding back her hair, each one of them were confirmed. He looked up when he heard my rapid footsteps in the sand and stepped away from her like he knew.

"Listen, man, it's not what you—"

My fist had collided with his face before he got the last word out. His head whooshed back, taking half of his body with him. He stumbled, shaking it off.

"This is how it's going to be?" Cole asked, spitting blood onto the sand.

"Hell yeah! It's go time, motherfucker. I've been waiting for it."

I charged him, ramming my body into his torso, taking him to the sand. He was prepared for it and instantly fought back. We wrestled around in the sand for a few minutes, each of us trying to get the upper hand on the other.

"You fucking son of a bitch!" I hit him. "You let her get drunk!" I hit him again. "For what, Cole? To take advantage of her?" I hit him twice.

"What the fuck are you talking about?" he yelled, blocking another blow.

"Lucas, stop!" Aubrey shouted, trying to pull me away. "This isn't helping anything! Alex needs you!"

Every angry bone in my body stopped in an instant. We both breathed heavily, sweat pouring from our overheated bodies. I jumped back, removing myself from his body with one last shove, spitting blood to the ground by my feet. The crazed look in my eyes warned him to stop. That's when I saw Alex. She was doubled over, dry heaving into the sand, one hand covering her stomach. Cole was no longer in my sights. I didn't give a shit about him anymore. I wiped blood from my bottom lip and went to her. I went to Alex.

"Jesus, Half-Pint, what did you drink? I just saw you."

"Whatever the fuck was in the punch. It hit her out of nowhere," Aubrey answered.

I glared up at Cole while rubbing Alex's back. "I fucking told you she doesn't drink. Why the fuck would you let her drink this much?"

"She told me she was fine."

I wanted to continue to yell at him and threaten him, but all it would do was reaffirm that he didn't know her. By the look on his face he finally fucking realized it.

"What time is it?" I asked Aubrey.

She looked at her phone. "Almost eleven."

"Shit, she can't go home like this."

"I... don't... feels... so... goods... Bo..." Alex mumbled, leaning her tiny frame against my chest and hiding her face in the nook of my neck. "You... smells... good..."

I chuckled. I couldn't help it, even being drunk as shit and smelling like vomit, she was still adorable to me.

"Don't worry about it. She called her parents a while ago saying that she was crashing at my house."

I sighed in relief and kissed the top of her head.

"I'll take care of her," Cole claimed.

"The fuck you will," I roared, standing up with Alex passed out in my arms. I faced Aubrey. "Thank you."

She nodded. "Don't mention it. Just get out of here before the boys see you and her."

"Will you at least text me and let me know she's all right," Cole hollered from behind me as I walked away.

217

"She's all right. Consider this your text message, motherfucker!"

I gently placed Alex in my truck and buckled her seatbelt. "Baby, what did you do?" I murmured, sweeping all her hair away from her face, making sure it didn't have throw up in it. It was just on her clothes and I needed to get her out of them. I got in my truck and looked at my face in the visor mirror. Not much damage, my lip was a little swollen but not enough to where Alex would notice. I took a deep breath and drove her to the only place that ever felt like home to me.

Our abandoned house.

## Alex

"Mmm," I groaned when I felt something hard beneath me. I opened my eyes to Lucas sitting above me.

"Shit. I didn't mean to wake you."

I laughed even though I was disoriented as all hell. "I'm thirsty."

He handed me a bottle of water. Surprisingly it was cold. I drank half of it down in a few gulps while trying to look behind him. Everything just appeared fuzzy to me. "Where are we?" I asked, squinting my eyes.

"Our place," he simply stated, grabbing the water and taking a few sips for himself. "How do you feel?"

"Funny," I beamed.

"You're drunk."

I frowned and pouted. "Nah uh." If I were standing, I probably would have fallen over. I decided to lie down because the ground was on the move. "What's that smells?"

"You," he laughed, placing a shirt by me.

"I need helps. Will you please help me's?"

He nodded, easing me up. I immediately placed my hands on his chest. "Whoa, tell the floor to stop moving."

He laughed again. It vibrated his entire body. He felt so good that I wrapped my arms around his torso. "You smells good and feels nice. I'm going to stay right here… mmm… kay…"

"I need to change you before you can lay down again."

"In your arms?"

"Of course."

I smiled into his shirt. "Mmm kay." I hugged him tight one last time and stepped away, swaying. I closed my eyes and put my hands up above my head, and he swiftly pulled off my dress.

When I heard him hiss I opened my eyes to find him staring at me with lust and desire. I was drunk, but I could see it clear as day. I don't know what came over me. We were in our place, our home, our safe haven.

Away from everything and everyone.

Away from the lies and the truths.

Away from expectations and insecurities.

Away from it all...

It sobered me up enough to know what I wanted.

*Him.*

I stepped toward him and he stepped back, shaking his head like he knew. "Don't," he warned, in a tone I remembered all too clear.

I stepped again, except this time I reached for the strings of my bikini top.

"Alex," he coaxed with a look I had never seen before.

"You're leaving tomorrow," I stated, untying the strings to my top and then bottoms, letting it fall down my body to the ground.

I stood there in front of him with a familiar yearning in both of our intense stares.

Naked.

Vulnerable.

Exposed.

I whispered, "Make love to me. I'm yours. I've always been yours."

I saw a look of pure unadulterated fear and confusion reflected through his stare as he looked at me. Except he wasn't looking at my naked body like I assumed he would. His eyes never wavered from mine. They were bonded together by the severity of my words and what I wanted.

What I needed.

It all seemed to happen so fast after that.

Complicate Me

He was over to me in one stride, roughly grabbing the back of my neck and colliding my lips with his in the most forceful and passionate kiss…

Of my entire life.

# Chapter 26

## Alex

My boys were gone.

Lucas was gone.

Though Austin remained. A huge part of me was gone, too.

My innocence.

My virtue.

My virginity.

Half-Pint left with my boys. Brown eyed girl left with my Bo.

They left yesterday, and I could barely look at myself in the mirror today. There was no going back for me. I already felt lost and alone without them, without him.

I couldn't believe I lost my virginity like that. I couldn't believe I gave it to him so easily. I couldn't believe it was gone.

Like them.

Like him.

Alex... Alexandra... she remained.

With a choice that I made...

With a guilt that I inflicted...

With a hurt that I caused...

With a regret...

That would forever haunt me.

## LUCAS

"What the fuck, man?" Jacob badgered. "Come out with us."

"I'm all right," I yawned into the couch, channel surfing.

"Are you fucking kidding me? Jesus Christ, Lucas, we've been here for almost four months and all you do is watch TV and go to class."

I shrugged.

He took a deep breath, leaned over and turned off the TV.

"What the fuck?" I shouted.

"Exactly! What the fuck?" he repeated with his arms out in the air. "What's your deal, man? You don't want to do shit. We're in college! A fraternity! Chicks throwing their pussy at you without you even giving them a second glance! What's your problem?"

"Right now? You," I stated, not amused.

"What happened to the Lucas from high school? The one who fucked any girl that would spread her legs for him?"

"I'm over that."

"No shit."

I sat up, shaking my head. "What do you want from me? I don't get involved in your business. Do I tell you not to go out and bring home the randoms you do every night? No! I mind my own goddamn business, the same exact way you fucking should."

"At least someone's getting laid around here. Between Dylan fucking moping around everywhere and you with your..." he pointed at me with his hand. "Who the fuck knows, I'm dying of boredom. These are supposed to be the best years of our life."

I arrogantly smiled with wide eyes. "I'm sorry I didn't get that memo."

He narrowed his eyes at me and crossed his arms over his chest. "This is about Alex isn't it?"

"Don't talk about shit you don't know," I scoffed.

"I miss her, too. We all do."

I wanted to say it was different for me. I wanted to say he didn't understand. I wanted to say I loved her. I wanted to say a lot of things.

Mostly I wanted to tell him to shut the fuck up.

"You're going to see her in a few weeks, we will be home for Thanksgiving break."

Nothing mattered anymore. We both lived two separate lives now, her fears becoming our reality.

"Do you think she's sitting around as miserable as you?"

*I hope so.*

"When was the last time you talked to her?"

"A few weeks ago," I muttered. We didn't talk that often. It was easier that way.

"And what?" he added.

"She said she was fine." And for the first time I believed her. "How often do you talk to her?" I found myself asking.

He shrugged, shaking his head. "A few times a week."

*Ouch.* I tried to pretend that didn't hurt like hell.

"Lucas, I know you and her have—"

"Don't," I ordered, not ready to hear what he had to share.

He cocked his head to the side and sighed. "Don't what? What am I not supposed to say?"

"What you've known all along."

We both stared at each other for I don't how long, time just seemed to a stand still.

"I love you, Lucas. I love her, too. You're my family. She's like a little sister to us, she always has been. Do I need to remind you of that?" he scorned in a tone I didn't fucking appreciate.

I leaned forward, sitting my elbows on my knees. "You mean more than you already have?" I challenged.

He jerked back. "That's not—"

"It's not?" I interrupted.

"No. It's not."

"Could have fooled me."

"What, Lucas? You think you're good enough for her? You think we didn't see the bags under her eyes? The way she looked at you from across the room when all you did was flaunt your pussy party in front of everyone. You think that's what love is? I sure as hell don't. She's a good girl, she always has been. She doesn't need your shit, she also doesn't deserve it."

I sat there speechless. I couldn't form the words that I wanted to express so deeply. It wouldn't change anything. The damage was already done.

He nodded, knowing he got to me. "Exactly."

I took one last look at him, leaned back into the couch, and turned on the TV.

# Alex

"Hey," Austin greeted from behind me. I turned to face him.
"Hey."

He sat down next to me on the bench at the pier.

"Whatcha doin' over here by yourself?"

"I don't know. Sometimes I come here to think."

I hadn't seen Lucas or the boys since Christmas break. They were coming home for spring break in a few weeks, except it was college spring break not high school. So who knew how much time I would get to spend with them. I was excited nonetheless. We hadn't talked about what happened before he left for school. Not one word. It was like it didn't happen, except it replayed in my mind like a broken record. Apparently he didn't have the same problem, but to give him the benefit of the doubt, Lucas always had the ability to hide things better than me. I hoped this was the case.

"About Lucas?"

I immediately looked over at him, stunned and dismayed.

He reassuringly smiled with an arched eyebrow and a mischievous look on his face. "It's okay, Half-Pint, I'm not Jacob or Dylan. All I want is for you to be happy with Lucas, with Cole, shit even with a chick if that floats your fancy."

I chuckled. "No girls."

He laughed. "A guy can dream, right?"

I grinned, nudging him with my shoulder. "How long have you known?"

"Long enough."

I nodded with understanding as I turned to look back out over at the water.

"The boys—"

"I know. In all fairness though, they're just looking out for you. It's what we've always done. It's not coming from a bad place."

"I know."

"I don't think you do, I know you, Alex. I've known you as long as I've known them. You and Lucas have always had a special bond. When I was a kid, I used to be jealous of it, not because I wanted you in that way or anything, you're like my little sister and that applies to all of us. Except you and Lucas complete each other.

You balanced each other out in a way that we all do for one another, but you had your own dynamic going on."

I nodded in understanding. I felt like he wanted to say more to me and I didn't want to ruin it by talking.

"I've always felt like the odd man out with the rest of the boys, I'm the youngest. I guess that's why I try to do everything to the extreme. I need to make up for it or something."

"Austin," I murmured, completely surprised and taken aback. "I never knew you felt that way."

"I'm good at hiding things, we have that in common. The boys have never made me feel like that by any means. It's still there though. You know Lucas always tells me that we're a lot alike, and I never understood what he meant until they left," he paused, reflecting on what he was about to say to me. "Both of us wanting to be one of the boys."

I gazed at the side of his face. "I've never thought that about you. Not ever."

"And I've never thought that about you, but it doesn't change the fact that you felt that way, does it?"

"No," I half-whispered.

He sadly smiled and bowed his head for a few seconds, only looking back up when he was ready. "I graduate in a few months."

"Three months," I stated. I knew because I counted down the days until I would really be alone. It was a ticking time clock in my head.

He glanced at me, smiling, and it eased the worry I felt in my heart.

"You going to miss me, Half-Pint?"

"Always," I bellowed, my eyes blurring.

He wrapped his arm around my shoulder and pulled me into his chest, kissing the top of my head and letting his lips linger. "I will always be here for you, it doesn't matter where I am. I will always take care of you, and I will always love you. You're my Half-Pint," he vowed, his voice breaking.

I sniffed. "Ditto."

"One day we won't care what the boys think about us or what we do. On that day, we will both be extremely happy."

Complicate Me

I wanted to say I was happy, but I would be lying. It broke my heart that for all these years he had felt this way and I had no idea.

*Did the boys?*

"So… it's Saturday night and Charlie's throwing one of his raging parties. Let's go," he demanded, standing up and reaching his hand out for me. "No." He shook his head before I could answer.

"I don't want to hear your bullshit excuses about this or that. You will have fun with me. You will drink. You will dance. You will party. And that's a fucking order."

I giggled and rolled my eyes. "Okay."

We spent the next several hours enjoying the night. It was the first time I could ever remember truly letting loose and experiencing being a teenager in high school.

I laughed.

I drank.

I danced.

I did everything Austin ordered me to do. I loved him even more than I did because of it. I never thought that could even be possible.

"Stop walking so fast," I rambled, holding onto Austin's hand.

"Stop walking so slow," he replied, slightly slurring.

"Hurry your asses up!" Someone yelled from in front of us.

"Where are we going?" I asked, already forgetting what he told me.

"The cops are coming, the party is being relocated."

"Oh yeah," I laughed.

He opened my car door for me and closed it when I was firmly seated inside. He jumped into the driver's side, throwing the car into reverse, and my body jerked forward from the momentum.

"Turn the music on," I heard him say.

I had a hard time finding the knobs, my vision blurry and unclear.

"Half-Pint, you're drunk," he chuckled right along with me.

"I love this song!" I shouted when I found the station I wanted. I started to dance around in my seat, while Austin banged on the steering wheel, dancing right along with me. We stopped at a red light or maybe it was a stop sign.

I leaned back into my seat and lazily looked over at him. "I love you, Austin. I love you so so so much."

He looked over at me. "I love you more. I will always take care of you and don't ever fucking forget that. Now put your fucking seatbelt on."

"Oh yeah," I sloppily grabbed the strap behind my head as the car started to move again. "It won't go in the buckle," I giggled.

"Here." He took it out of my hands. "Grab the wheel."

"Mmm kay." I tried to hold onto it, but the road looked really fuzzy. "Austin, I don't think I should be doing this."

"I'm almost done."

I looked down for a second. At least it seemed that way. "You need to put your seatbelt on, too," I hiccupped.

"Done."

I smiled and faced forward, as he grabbed the steering wheel again. I went back to dancing around and so did he.

"Austin, you pussy, can't you drive faster than that," the car next to us shouted. I squinted my eyes to see who it was.

"If I beat you to the woods, you pay for all the beer."

"You're on!" Austin yelled back.

"I don't think—"

"Hey, what were the rules?" he reminded with a huge smile on his face, he appeared so happy. I still hurt from the conversation we had earlier that I didn't want to dampen his spirits. If he felt anything like how I felt in the last few years, then he deserved this as much as I did.

"To have fun," I beamed.

He turned the radio up louder, and the car accelerated faster. I danced around, trying to pretend that I didn't feel the car starting to recoil from the dirt and grass, making my body jolt around all over. I had waited a few minutes before I pressed my hands against the dashboard, trying to hold my body steady from the impact around us.

"Slow down!" I finally yelled.

"We're almost there!"

My stomach felt queasy, I wasn't having fun anymore. I felt scared, so I turned down the music. "You're going too fast."

"Relax we're fine."

Complicate Me

It didn't feel fine. I didn't feel fine. Panic started to take control and a huge lump in my throat made it hard for me to breathe. I gasped in and out, my chest rising and descending at rapid speed as I took in our dark and dim surroundings. The cars headlights only illuminated a few feet out in front of us, making it hard to know where to go next. Austin swerved left and then right, and for a second I thought he may have lost control of the car, but when I saw the clear path ahead of us I finally exhaled out a sigh of relief.

Except it was too soon.

A tree lay out in front of us a few feet ahead, probably as a result from the last few hurricanes.

"AUSTIN!" I screamed bloody murder. It vibrated throughout the entire car as he looked over at me with regret and sorrow spread all over his handsome face. He slammed on the brakes, but it was too late. We were in Gods' hands now. I instinctively placed my arms over my face to provide a false sense of protection that we would be okay. I swear on everything that was holy I felt Austin's arm pressed up against my chest, trying to hold me in.

*Choices...*

Everyone had them.

The good.

The bad.

The right.

The wrong.

The moment I heard our car crash into a tree my life was forever changed...

Like the accident, my life was on a collision course of choices and like that I had to make a choice.

I put on my seatbelt.

He didn't.

The moment I realized that.

Everything. Went. Black.

# Chapter 27

## LUCAS

I lay leaning with my head against the seat, my legs spread out in front of me and my arms crossed over my chest.

"Honey, you need to go home and get some rest," Mom said.

"I'm not leaving," I replied with my eyes closed.

"Lucas, they don't know when she's going to wake up," she reminded.

"I heard the doctor."

"Lu—"

"Mom," I argued, narrowing my eyes at her.

She sighed and nodded. "I'm going to go get some coffee, do you want anything?"

I shook my head no.

She leaned over and kissed my forehead, whispering, "She's going to be okay."

I wouldn't believe that until she opened her eyes and looked at me. Dylan and Jacob had been going back and forth between Alex and Austin's rooms. It had been three days and neither one of them woke up yet. Austin was in much worse shape than Alex. He flew out the windshield. The doctors had put him in a medically induced coma after they operated on his brain with the hope that it would help the swelling decrease. He suffered severe trauma to the head, he had several broken ribs, burns and deep cuts on his face and chest from the airbag and windshield.

Alex's brain was swollen from her head busting the window. No operation was needed since it was slowly decreasing on its own. Her trauma wasn't as severe as Austin's, but she was still in a coma. The doctor said she would wake up eventually. We just had to be patient. She had four stitches on her forehead and two on her lip. She suffered minor cuts on her face, her arms and around her body. She was bruised everywhere, along with a few broken ribs.

Complicate Me

Her alcohol level was .16 while Austin's was .092, the doctor said they were lucky to be alive.

It was just a waiting game now.

My body was exhausted, but my mind wouldn't stop reeling, I couldn't sleep even if I wanted to. I would remember that phone call from my mom for the rest of my life, like a nightmare I couldn't wake up from.

*"Alex is hurt. She's in the ICU. The doctors say... Austin is in surgery. They were drinking... he hit a tree. They were rushed to the emergency room... you need to come home..."*

Dylan and Jacob heard the news by the time I got off the phone with my mom and we all took the next flight out. People talked about having an out of body experience. You saw it everywhere, on the news, in the paper. It seemed surreal until it happened to you. I moved in an autopilot state of mind, I just needed to get to her. I needed to see her, hold her, and talk to her. I felt like if I did, everything would be all right.

As long as we were together.

When I saw her, covered in bruises, eyes closed, tubes coming out of everywhere and sounds blaring loudly from the machines, that will forever haunt me, I wanted to breakdown. I wanted to switch places with her. I wanted to make her wake up. The only piece of mind I held onto was that she was strong. She would fight. No matter what, she would come out swinging.

I taught her to.

We all did.

What blew my mind was that Alex was drunk in the first place. She never drank, it was so out of character for her. Something must have happened and I hated not knowing what that was. I was pissed at Austin for getting in the drivers seat when he had been drinking. He knew better, and I subconsciously held him accountable for Alex being in this situation in the first place. I tried like hell to not let that influence my anger toward him, but I couldn't help it. He was supposed to take care of her.

*What the fuck was he thinking?*

"Hey," Jacob whispered, walking into her room and coming toward me. "You been in to see Austin lately?"

"Yesterday."

"Lucas..."

"Don't," I snapped.

"We're all upset with him, but shit happens. He would never put Alex's life in danger or his. He was stupid and irresponsible, he's paying for it now." He eyed Alex's bed, machines surrounding her with sounds that told us she was alive. Which was ironic since the beeping noises made me realize the severity of the situation. At least that was how I felt.

"And so is she," I added, making him turn back around to face me.

He begrudgingly nodded and followed it up with a long deep sigh. He knew I was right but couldn't admit it.

"You going home to sleep?" he asked.

"Are you?" I countered.

He nodded again in understanding, putting his hands in his jean pockets, leaning against the wall with one foot over the other.

*Waiting.*

That's all we did.

My mom walked in with Alex's mom and Lily by their side. She was thirteen now and reminded me so much of Alex at that age. She dressed like her, put makeup on like her, was spunky like her. Half-Pint was her hero, and I couldn't have been happier for her to follow anyone else's footsteps.

"Hey, Kid," Jacob greeted. Lily wrapped her arms around his waist, as he tugged her into his side. He placed his ball cap on her head. She was always stealing it from him and I knew he put it on her to make her feel better.

"Hi," she softly spoke.

I smiled at her when she looked at me.

"Are you okay, Lucas?" she questioned. Concern and worry evident all over her face.

"I've been better."

She bowed her head with sympathy, it didn't matter what I told her. My baby sister was intuitive, just like Alex.

"Lily is exhausted. Can you take her home?" Mom asked, pulling all of us away from our thoughts.

"I can't leave Jana," Mom whispered low not wanting to disturb her, even though she wasn't paying any attention to us. She sat on Alex's bed holding her hand.

Complicate Me

As much as I didn't want to leave Alex's side, I knew she would want to have my mom at her mom's side right now, they were like sisters, she needed her.

I was about to open my mouth to say something but Jacob beat me to it. "I'll take her home," he stated.

"You sure? Robert is on call and he won't leave the hospital until something happens with Austin or Alex. Do you mind staying over? Lily can't be—"

"Mom," Lily interrupted, looking embarrassed.

I immediately contemplated what the embarrassment was from. Jacob watched her get her diapers changed.

He pulled away from her before I could give it any more thought and peered down at her. "It's okay, Kid, it's more for my benefit. I don't like to sleep in a house by myself."

She grinned, knowing he lied but appreciated it nonetheless.

"Thank you," Mom mouthed.

He winked at her, as Lily came over to give me a hug. My mom kissed the top of her head and Lily wrapped her arms around Jacob as they walked out of the room together.

I leaned back into the chair and closed my eyes. I had a blinding headache from my lack of sleep. I didn't know when I passed out. I think I was more in and out of consciousness than anything else, but when I slowly opened my eyes wiping off sleep I found Alex staring at me.

I instinctively jumped out of the chair and was over to her in two strides, grabbing her hand and kissing all over it. "Half-Pint, oh my God! You're awake."

Our eyes locked, both of us trying to focus and taking everything in.

"Water," she muffled, pulling me away from my need to ask her a million and one questions.

I kissed her hand one last time and ran to the door, opening it. "I need a doctor! She's up!" I yelled to my mom, Jana, and the doctor who were all standing at the nurse's station.

I told them she asked for water as they made their way into the room. I stood in the back to allow them more space, even though I wanted nothing more than to still be sitting by her side holding her hand. He proceeded to check all her vitals and ask her lots of questions. She seemed disorientated and confused, she didn't remember the accident or getting into the car. He continued with questions she would know the answers to and she passed with flying colors. I didn't get a chance to talk to her before she passed out again. The doctor said it was all completely normal for coma patients to seem out of it and her memory would most likely come back with time.

It had been the longest four days of my life, but I finally breathed a sigh of relief that she would be all right. So I sat back down in the chair.

And once again...

Waited.

## Alex

Thank God I was being discharged, it had been a week since I woke up. The entire team cleared me, including neurology who had been watching me like a hawk. I didn't remember anything. It was crazy how your brain could do that, just block out several hours of your life. Maybe it was a good thing that I didn't remember. When Austin woke up three days ago, he seemed way more disoriented and confused than I was, but the doctor said that was normal, since he had been in a coma for a week and then again from the surgery. He would have some wicked scars. They were keeping him for several more weeks, and I could tell he was over it and wanted to go home as much as I did. He had months of recovery and rehabilitation to come.

I was one of the first people to see him when he woke up, and even though he said he didn't remember anything, the way he looked at me told me otherwise. I didn't call him out on it, but when he asked everyone to give us a few minutes, much to Lucas's dismay, he hugged me and just started bawling.

It was then I knew I was right.

I repeated over and over again that it wasn't his fault, and that it didn't matter. We were alive and I loved him no matter what. His breakdown spoke for itself, he didn't listen to any of the comforts I tried to provide.

233

Complicate Me

It spoke volumes.

I let him cry for as long as he needed. He appeared better when he was done. I told him girls were going to obsess over his scars and now he was really going to look like a bad boy with a record to prove it. I saw laughter in his eyes, but I couldn't get a smile. He asked me what I remembered and I told him I had no recollection of the accident. He apologized several times, saying he would never put me in danger, and I knew that. He didn't have to say it out loud. I reminded him every time.

Lucas hadn't left my side since I woke up. He needed to go back to school, but he said he spoke to all his professors and they knew what happened.

"I'm not sitting in that," I said, looking at Lucas who was behind the wheelchair.

"Why are you being so stubborn?"

"I don't need it. I can walk."

"The doctor—"

"I don't care what the doctor said, Lucas, I just want to get the hell out of here. I never want to see a hospital again."

"Yeah… you and me both."

"I'm going to go say bye to Austin. Come on."

"I'm good."

"Why are you purposely staying away from him?" He wasn't being subtle. I had noticed it immediately, it was like he wanted him to know.

"I'm not. I said bye to him last night."

"You're lying! You haven't left my side."

"I'm not arguing with you, Half-Pint."

I gently folded my arms over my chest, not wanting to give any inclination that I was in pain and my ribs hurt. "Great, seeing as I have no intention of arguing with you, you're coming with me."

"Alex," he warned.

"I know why you're acting this way. I'm not stupid."

He smiled, folding his own arms over his chest, mocking me. "I am fully aware that you're not stupid."

"It wasn't his fault," I stated not being charmed by his antics. "It was an accident."

"An accident he caused."

"He didn't tell the tree to come out of nowhere, Lucas."

M. Robinson

He shook his head with a hard, grim expression. "No, you're right, he didn't do that. He just drove drunk as shit and raced his car through the woods. That makes it much better."

"That's not fair."

"Tell that to the cops, Alex, because he's in some deep shit after he gets discharged from the hospital. He will be lucky to ever drive again before he's twenty-one."

"Exactly, Bo, he's already paying for his bad judgment. I got into the car, he didn't make me," I justified. "He doesn't need to be held accountable by us."

"I can't help it. If something worse would have happened to you—"

"But it didn't. I'm fine. I'll be fine," I argued.

"Tell that to your scars and your ribs, Alex."

I rolled my eyes and placed my hand on my hip, a small smile spread across Lucas's face, but he quickly covered it up.

"I could show you hundreds of scars from growing up with you boys. So please try something else because that weak excuse isn't going to work on me. Didn't you once tell me that scars are awesome and that they tell a story?" I reminded him, cocking my head to the side.

"Half-Pint, you were crying like a baby and it was the first time you got stitches. I had to tell you something," he half-laughed.

"You're coming with me to say bye. You're going to smile and give him a hug. You will also be nice to him when he gets discharged. You're going to go back to normal with him, and if you don't, I'm going to be extremely disappointed."

"Alex…"

"Do it for me?"

He took a deep breath, stepped aside and guided us toward the door, letting me win, but who knows for how long.

Things were awkward between Lucas and Austin. He was aware that Lucas was furious with him for being so reckless and blamed him for the accident. I couldn't help thinking about what he told me at the pier before the party.

We were a lot alike.

The boys got to spend the next few days with me, but Dylan and Jacob had to go back to school. I couldn't handle all three of

235

them hovering over me, so with their parents help they were able to go back. Lucas, on the other hand didn't care what his parents or I said. He always did what he wanted. He stayed through the weekend.

When I turned on my phone and the computer I had hundreds of text messages and emails from Cole. My mom said he was worried sick, and that he wanted to take the next flight out, but she let him know it wouldn't help my recovery to have another person waiting around. She kept him updated and that seemed to appease him. Lucas stepped out of my bedroom growling something under his breath when he saw that I called Cole. I told him what had happened, trying to lessen the gravity of the situation. He said he wanted to take the next flight out to see me but changed his mind when I told him I was fine and I would see him over the summer. He sent an obscene amount of roses, chocolate, and a big Snoopy, which was my favorite cartoon from my childhood, surprised he remembered this from one of our conversations. Lucas threw Snoopy in the back corner of my closet, saying there wasn't enough room for him and the stuffed animal. Then he took the roses out of my room, saying that the smell wasn't good for my recovery, followed by throwing away the chocolate because I didn't like any of those flavors anyway. I let him have his way. I didn't want to argue with him. As much as I told everyone I was fine, I wasn't. I was exhausted and emotionally drained from having everyone in my face over the last few days.

I had a feeling my mom would never let me leave the house again and my dad wouldn't let me drive for a while. Or at least be in anyone's car. Our parents were the best of friends. They were all upset and disappointed with Austin for the accident, but we were young and they remembered what it was like, at least that's what they said.

"Do you want me to get you something?" Lucas asked for the tenth time.

"No. What I want is for you to stop doting on me. When do you leave again?" I teased, knowing he left tomorrow morning and secretly dreaded it.

"I know you're full of shit," he reminded as if reading my mind and I chuckled at the thought.

I glanced over at him as we lay in the center of my bed. "Thanks for being here."

"Where else would I be?" he stated as a question though it wasn't.

I once again beheld the ceiling. "You remember when we were kids and we used to come up with images on the ceiling texture?"

"I remember a lot of things."

"Yeah, your stupid dinosaurs always ate my bunnies. I don't understand why your images were so aggressive."

He was quiet for several seconds and the silence unnerved me. Then he finally said, "I've never been so scared in my entire life, Half-Pint. I didn't know fear like that was even possible."

My eyes fell to my chest from the magnitude of his words. I knew this conversation was inevitable, but as more time went on I believed, no, I hoped that it would vanish. Be lost in the hurricane that surrounded us constantly. I had been avoiding it for as long as possible. I didn't want to hear about what he felt. It hurt too much. I wanted to pretend nothing happened, add it to the pile of regrets, fights, and feelings to sweep under the rug.

"I don't think I would have been able to—"

"I'm fine," I firmly stated, but it didn't matter. I could feel his intense and penetrating gaze on me, it flowed throughout my entire body, pumping right along with my blood and circulation.

"I wouldn't have been able to live without you, Alex."

"Don't say stuff like that, Bo," I murmured loud enough for him to hear.

"It's the truth."

"I'm trying like all hell to not be pissed at Austin, but I can't help it. I'm sorry, Half-Pint. It's going to take time for me to get over it."

"It's not his fault," I reminded yet again.

"I don't see it like that. You weren't the one looking at your body that appeared lifeless. You weren't the one picturing a life without you. You weren't the one praying to every God known to man to let you be okay and not take you away from me."

Silence.

I could hear my heart hammering in my ears and I swear he could, too.

237

"I can't promise you that everything will be alright between Austin and me, but I can tell you that I will try."

I nodded, my mouth dry.

"Alex, I think about that night all the time."

My eyes widened in realization of what he declared and I found it hard to breathe, my broken ribs adding to my difficulty to find a steady rhythm. He wasn't talking about the accident. My mind shifted through hundreds of images of that night at our abandoned house and everything that followed. I forcefully shut my eyes, trying to block out the images that replayed in my mind constantly. Wishing I could forget about it like I did the accident. I would have given anything for that to happen. I didn't want to talk about that.

*Not now.*

"I never meant to hurt you. I'm sorry I—"

"Lucas," I anxiously interrupted. "Let's forget about that, okay? I can't right now." It would lead into too many questions that I wasn't prepared to answer.

*Not ever.*

"I just want you to know that night, it meant everything to me. I don't ever want you to feel that I didn't want—"

"Please." I sat up, moving as far away from him as possible, hoping that the distance between us would affect him as much as it did me. Meeting his eyes with nothing but anguish and uncertainty in mine, I repeated, "Please."

His eyebrows lowered, causing his eyes to narrow at me. "Why?" he asked, instantly standing up.

"Not now." I backed away.

"I don't understand. I'm trying to tell you that I didn't want—"

I placed my hands over my ears like a child and peered down at the ground, blocking out the memories that haunted my everyday existence. "Please, Lucas, I'm begging you. Not now!" I shouted, losing the battle to remain calm.

He immediately engulfed me into his sturdy, comforting embrace, his arms caging me in his safety that I desperately craved. I hugged him as tight as I could, damned be my broken ribs, trying to provide the same reassurance that he gave me.

"Okay, I didn't mean to upset you," he whispered, kissing the top of my head. "I love you."

I took in his words…
I was terrified that he would never look at me the same way.
I was terrified that he wouldn't think of me the same way.
I was terrified he'd find out the truth.
I was terrified to hear him say…
*I hate you.*
Which is why we couldn't talk about that night.

# Chapter 28

## Alex

Austin got better and was on the road to a full recovery. He ended up having to go to summer school because he missed too many days due to the accident. They allowed him to walk at graduation, but he couldn't have cared less. He did it for everyone else, including me. He became withdrawn from life and things that used to make him happy. I thought when he got accepted to Ohio State to follow the boys it might lift his spirits, but it didn't. Not even a little. The judge charged him with a DUI, suspended his license for a year and on top of a hefty fine and legal fees he was to perform an obscene amount of community service, which only added to his reclusive behavior.

Aubrey got accepted to the University of California, I couldn't have been happier for her. She had always been interested in design and fashion. She said her dad lived out there, but they didn't have the best relationship, she hoped this could be a new start for the both of them. She never said anything about Dylan and the fact that he wasn't a factor in her decision-making process worried me.

When she broke up with him a few weeks before she left for California, I knew I was right.

He didn't take the break-up well and that's putting it lightly. He trashed his entire room at his parents house, tore every memory of her out of his life. It looked like a hurricane had passed through it.

The irony was not lost on me.

I had never seen him so upset before, it broke my heart. When he finally talked to me about it, he said she became withdrawn. She wasn't herself the entire summer. They weren't very intimate, she didn't allow him to hold her anymore, and she barely acknowledged or spoke to him, even when they were alone. He said he saw it coming and it led to a huge fight. But, then they had sex and he thought everything would be okay.

She broke up with him the next day.

He told her they would make it work, that he would do anything not to lose her, but she didn't care. Her mind was made up. I was surprised he shared so much with me. Of course, my loyalty was with Dylan, though he didn't want me to lose my friendship with Aubrey. He knew she was important to me. I loved him a little bit more because of it.

Jacob was same ol' Jacob. Single and ready to mingle. The ladies man he was.

I spent the summer with all of them, including Cole. He came around a lot more with the guys. As much as Lucas hated it, for the first time he respected it. Summer went by entirely too quickly and before I knew it, they were gone. School had started again and I was a senior, applying to colleges and getting ready for my future.

I turned eighteen and the boys came home for my birthday, which coincidently landed on a Saturday. They took me out to South Port to a club. I couldn't have hated it more if I tried. I was not the girl that gets dressed up in a slutty outfit and grinds all over random strangers all night. The boys wouldn't have let me even if I wanted to but granted, I had no desire to do so. I learned right then and there that clubs just weren't my thing.

It was a lonely school year for me. I kept to myself, worked a lot, kept my nose stuck in a book and hung out with Lily. It was nice to have a piece of Lucas around, although Lily couldn't have been more different than her brother. They were like night and day. She was way beyond her years of fourteen. There were times that I forgot how old she truly was, and she became one of my best friends because of it. I still talked to Aubrey, we remained close, but we didn't talk about Dylan. She didn't ask and I didn't tell.

Senior prom fast approached which would lead to graduation and I had no idea what college I wanted to attend. Cole went to the University of California with Aubrey and they said they had bumped into each other a few times at parties. Cole pledged Pike and Aubrey pledged Tri-Del, so they ran in similar crowds. They both had been begging me to come visit so that I could fall in love with California and want to attend the university with them, but I always made up an excuse. The truth was…

I applied and got accepted to UCLA.

Complicate Me

No one knew that not even my parents.

Guys asked me to go to prom left and right, but I turned each one of them down. I decided I didn't want to go and I didn't bother buying a ticket. Something held me back from wanting to go and enjoy this special night of my senior year. Something was missing.

When I opened my front door and saw him standing in a tuxedo with a corsage in hand. I realized what it was...

*Lucas.*

# LUCAS

My baby sister became my spy, she kept me updated on Alex. What she did and didn't do. They had become really close in the last year and spent most of their time together. I loved it. If she was with Lily at least I knew she wasn't with any other fucking douchebag that crept around her. It's not like it mattered. Alex was oblivious to any attention thrown her way. The magnetic pull she had toward guys was unbelievable, and I spent most of her eighteenth birthday fighting them off at the club. Her innocence and natural beauty was a lure. They could smell that shit from a mile away.

Lily told me she wasn't going to prom because she wasn't feeling it, I knew it was a bunch of bullshit.

Alex talked about stupid high school shit like that since we were kids. Called them milestones and memories to last a lifetime, shit you read on fucking Hallmark cards and bumper stickers. I called her mom and asked her to buy two tickets for us, making her promise not to say anything to her about it. I took care of the rest. This year had been hard on her. I didn't need Lily to tell me that, I already knew.

It was hard for me, too.

I hated that she was alone.

I hated that I left her alone.

Her mom was more than willing to help in any way she could. Ecstatic that Alex would have a beautiful memory from her last year of high school. I rented a tuxedo that matched this white, lacy, flowing dress that went down to her ankles. She bought it when she was sixteen telling me it was for a special occasion, I still remembered her cheeks blushing as she said it. It wasn't prom attire by any means, but that's who she was. A tomboy at heart. She wouldn't have wanted to wear anything that the stores were selling as prom dresses. It wasn't her style.

I had the entire night planned out, nothing fancy or expensive. She was all about the little things and I knew that at entirely too young of an age. The look on her face was worth a million dollars to me when she opened the door.

That's all the reassurance I needed.

"Bo," she said, surprised. "You look, oh my God, you look amazing. What are you doing here?"

"I randomly rent tuxedos and knock on girls doors, just to see the look on their faces."

She laughed and I followed suit. "I'm here to take you to your prom."

With wide, teary eyes she conveyed, "What? I don't have anything to wear. I don't even have tickets." She looked down at herself. "I mean look at me. I'm a mess."

"I am looking. You're perfect. Put on *your* dress."

She peered up at me through her lashes with a slight grin and rosy cheeks.

"You know the one."

She raised an eyebrow, contemplating what I said.

"I have the rest taken care of."

She smiled big and wide as she shrieked before running up the stairs. I waited in the living room, looking at all our pictures on the mantle. I was in every one of them, along with the boys.

The sound of someone clearing his throat made me turn around. Her dad stood there, tall and intimidating. He had never appeared like that before. I figured he was about to start the "prom conversation." Don't touch my daughter, have her home by a certain time, no drinking, be responsible, and so on.

"Hey, Nate," I greeted. We were on a first name basis with all of our parents since we were kids.

"How's school, Son?" he asked, handing me water.

"Great. Finally finding the swing of things."

"Good. Have a seat, Lucas, I'd like to talk to you for a minute."

"Sure," I breathed out, sitting beside him, turning to give him my full attention.

"I've known you a long time, your whole life to be exact. I can't believe how fast time goes by."

I nodded, taking in his words, mentally gearing myself up.

"Alex hasn't picked a college yet, do you know that?"

I nodded again, except this time I braced myself for what was to come. It wasn't going to be what I expected, it would be much worse. Changing the course of the entire night and everything that proceeded after.

They say everything happens for a reason, that we're destined to meet certain expectations throughout the timeline of our lives. They're inevitable. It's already planned out. If that were true, then this would be the beginning of the end for us.

What happened next…

Forever changed the directions of our lives.

"We keep telling her that if she doesn't decide on something soon she's going to end up at Wilmington. We don't want that for her. She needs to experience new things and grow up, Lucas. It's been a very hard year for her, first the accident, and then Austin leaving, her being by herself. If it hadn't been for your sister, she probably would have never hung out with anyone. I don't have to tell you why she feels close to Lily, now do I?"

I set my elbows on my knees and bowed my head. I knew. I knew it all. I knew everything.

"You know Alex as well as we do. She's stubborn and hard headed. It doesn't matter how many times we've tried to talk to her. She wouldn't listen to us. We've spent the entire school year trying to get through to her, but nothing. It doesn't matter what we say she's going to do what she wants. Did you know she applied and has been accepted to Ohio State?"

I shook my head. I didn't.

"I didn't think so. It's been hard for her mother and me to watch her this year. It would hurt any parent to watch their child suffer from something you have no control over."

I angrily shut my eyes, bile rising up my throat, but I swallowed it back down. I wasn't mad at him. I wasn't mad at Alex.

I was mad at myself. Nothing would change what he expected me to do. It didn't matter. I knew what I needed to do, even though it was the furthest thing from what I wanted. He was right, though. I couldn't ignore the fact.

That. He. Was. Right.

"Except you, Lucas, you have control of it. You're our last resort." His words made a mockery of me and I knew it. My throat burned with the devastation looming.

"I know you love Alex, I know you're in love with her. You wouldn't be sitting here if you weren't. That's why, I know you'll do the right thing and let her find her own way. Not follow yours. Do you understand, Son?"

I slightly nodded, tears pooling in my eyes. I kept my eyes closed, keeping my emotions in check.

"Maybe one day, who knows where life will take you, but now is not the right time. You both have so much growing up to do. She needs to find herself and stop being your Half-Pint. I want my daughter to be independent and make her own choices, decide what's right for her, and she can't do that with you around, Lucas. You know that, right?"

I vaguely nodded again, not being able to form words or even coherent thoughts for that matter. My hurricane finally turned on me, gripping me with the chaos of its forceful truths. Except this time, I wouldn't take Alex with me.

I would set her free.

"You're like a son to me. To both Jana and I. We love you, but we need to do what's in the best interest of our daughter, too. I hope you understand that." His hand seared when he placed it on my shoulder, leaving a scar for the future that didn't include her. "Maybe tonight can be the closing of one door, but the opening of another for her, Lucas. For her," he repeated, driving the nail into the coffin.

I heard the clicking of heels on the hardwood floor and immediately stood, turning faintly to wipe my face. I had never seen her look more gorgeous. The dress fit her exactly how I imagined, loose, but still managing to make her look stunning. Her hair flowed loosely down her face and back. It looked like she just took a brush

Complicate Me

to it. Her makeup was subtle, accenting her perfect, precise features, though I could smell the cherry lip-gloss from across the room.

She was breathtaking.

"Alex," I stammered as she smiled shyly.

Her mom took picture after picture of the last moment we'd be happy together. I made a mental note to ask for one for myself. It would be a night of new beginnings for her and endings for me.

# Alex

"Come on." He placed his hand on the hollow of my back, spreading a warm heat throughout my entire body. He guided me toward the door and to his truck.

I tried to step up on the ladder, but my heel wouldn't allow it. His hand reached out to help me, but I ignored it. Instead, I stepped down and loudly sighed, annoyed. I opened my purse and dropped my sandals on the sidewalk, throwing the heels in the bed of his truck.

I heard him laughing and met his gaze. "What? My mom made me wear those things. I hate them. They're stupid."

He laughed again, nodding in agreement. I jumped in the truck, closing the door behind me. We drove in silence to the dance. Before I knew it, we were walking through the doors of the banquet hall that hosted my prom. Decorations were everywhere and they seemed to go on for miles, as did the crowd. There wasn't a place in the room that wasn't covered in some sort of streamer, confetti, or balloon. We took a traditional prom picture with the photographer, but I didn't get a chance to look at it since Lucas immediately placed it inside his tuxedo jacket. He grabbed my hand and I didn't give it any more thought as I followed him into the ballroom.

We hung out like we always had, laughing and loving each other's company. Austin was right when he said that we balanced one another out, we had our own dynamic.

Always had and always would.

When Lucas said he had to use the restroom, I leaned against the wall admiring how everyone appeared so happy and in love. I wondered if we looked like that, from an outside perspective. I contemplated if this could be a new beginning for us...

My question was answered when I heard Van Morrison through the speakers. I looked around until I found Lucas. There he was with a smug grin on his face, waiting for me to meet him on the dance floor. I didn't have to ask to know he requested for the DJ to play this. They would never play Brown Eyed Girl at my senior prom.

He sang it to me the entire time, spinning me in circles and holding me too close for the rhythm of the music, but the mood changed drastically between us when the soft beats of Stand By Me by Ben E. King played next. He didn't falter. He pulled me tighter into his strong, muscular body, fitting me perfectly in the nook of his frame. He guided my arms around his neck like he wanted no space between us, and then his arms wrapped around me, proving my point.

I laid my head on his chest and he placed his chin on top of my head, softly singing the lyrics to me again. It was around the chorus of the song when something felt different. He felt different.

And then it hit me. I softly shut my eyes with a single tear falling down the side of my face.

This wasn't a new beginning for us.

It was the end.

He was saying goodbye.

# Chapter 29

## Alex

When we got back into the truck, I just knew where we were going. He parked his truck in the driveway, the soft rumbling of the diesel engine hummed beneath our bodies. I stared at the house that stored so many memories of my adolescence. I wasn't a child anymore. I was an adult.

A woman.

"You don't have to bring me here to break up with me, Bo. We're not even together," I stated, never taking my stare away from the house that held my childhood.

"Where are you going to college, Alex?" he asked with a voice so calm it scared me.

"I don't know."

"Bullshit."

I leaned my head against the headrest. "I thought I would go to Ohio State—"

"Why?" he interrupted, holding onto the steering wheel hard enough to make his knuckles turn white.

"What do you mean why? You know I want to be with you boys. I thought we could be—"

"No," he firmly stated, immediately making me turn to look at him.

"No?" I repeated, confused.

"You're not going there because of the boys. You're going there because of me."

"What does it matter?"

"It matters a lot. It matters more than it should. You're following me, Alex."

"So, what if I am."

He let go of the steering wheel and bowed his head in defeat. I wanted to crawl into his lap and make it all go away, exactly how I did when we were kids and he was sad.

"You can't follow me," he let out. I didn't want to hug him anymore, now I just wanted to scream at him.

"You can't tell me what to do!"

He scoffed. "That's all I've been doing, Alex, for our entire lives I have told you what to wear, who to talk to, what to do, it goes on and on. I can't do that anymore. It's not fair to you."

I fervently shook my head. "You don't mean that."

"But I do. You need to experience your own life outside of me, outside of the boys. Damn even outside of this island, Alex."

"I don't want to, that's not what I want. I want to be with you, with all of you. Why are you doing this to me?" I asked, my voice breaking as I wiped away the tears that slowly began to trickle down my face.

He shut his eyes like he was trying to make me disappear. I wouldn't grant him that leniency.

"You're a coward! At least look at me while you break my heart, Lucas! At least give me that!"

He shut his eyes tighter. "I can't," he softly spoke.

"Why now? After all this time! Why now? You owe me that!" Tears flowed freely down my face, I didn't care anymore. I would wear them proudly.

"I'm not good for you."

I bawled, my vision so blurry I couldn't see in front of me. My chest heaving so profoundly that I thought I'd never be able to breathe again. "I thought you loved me. You said you loved me."

"I do. That's why I'm doing this," he swallowed.

"So you string me along. All these years all you do is string me along? For what?" I cried. "For what!" I shouted and it echoed around the cab of the truck.

"I'm selfish," he simply stated and I jerked back, wounded.

I sobbed uncontrollably, I wept so damn hard I felt like my tears would never end. That my pain would never end. I didn't recognize the boy sitting in front of me with a bowed head and distant demeanor.

He wasn't my Bo.

Bo wouldn't allow me to cry. Bo wouldn't allow me to feel anything other than loved. Bo wouldn't break my heart and not have the decency to look me in the eyes as he did it. Making me bleed out through tears of despair and longing for a past that would never be a future, for a promise that would never come true.

Lies.

And more lies.

I hyperventilated, taking one last look at him before blankly staring out the window with a hollow feeling building inside me. The emptiness surged from my heart to my entire body, causing me to feel broken and truly alone. I had nothing left to say, nothing left for me to do. I don't know how long we sat there, both of us lost in our thoughts and disillusions when he put the truck in reverse and drove me home.

He whispered, "I love you. I love you more than I love myself and that's why I'm doing this. It's for you, Alex. It's for you."

He shattered my heart… again. When I opened the truck door, I slammed it in his face.

I shattered…

His.

# LUCAS

The boys went home for summer. I stayed behind and attended a summer session at school. There was no home left for me, I knocked down that house like the big bad wolf I felt I was. I pushed her away and I hated myself for it. She didn't deserve that. Lily told me that she decided to attend UCLA, California. I told her she needed to find her own way, not a place thirty-three hours and 2,260.7 miles between us.

Giving me a fucking equator of distance.

I guess Aubrey and her were going to share an apartment. Dylan didn't bat an eye when he told me. As much as he tried to pretend that he didn't miss her, I knew he was full of shit. He became an asshole to women, a complete and total dick. You would think that would turn women off but it did the exact opposite, they became like a bitch in heat. Constantly wanting more and more of his attention that he wasn't willing to give.

Austin would be coming back with the boys at the end of summer, except he wasn't living with us. He decided to live in the dorms. I subconsciously knew that I was the reason for that. Things remained strained with us, and to be completely honest I didn't give a shit about it. Too many other things plagued my mind.

I sat in front of the TV as I had done so many weekends before, barely watching Sports Center that played in the background of my constantly spinning mind.

My hurricane never let me go.

It was the price I had to pay...

For letting her go.

My phone rang with my dad's face lighting up the screen, I hit ignore and let it go to voicemail, but it immediately started ringing again.

"Dad, I'm not in the mood—"

"Lucas," he said his tone dark and daunting.

I sat straight up on the couch. "What's wrong?"

"You need to come home."

"Is everything alright?"

"I don't want to discuss it over the phone, but you need to come home, Son," he repeated with the same desperate tone.

"I'm on my way."

I grabbed my overnight bag and floored it to the airport, taking the next flight out, which luckily was only a few hours later. I took a cab straight to my house and ran up to the front door, my heart in my throat as I contemplated the urgency of my need to come home.

"Mom! Dad! I'm here, where are you?" I darted toward the living room and found my mom lying on my dad's chest. Completely engulfed in emotions with his arms around her. My head pounded with the same momentum of my heart, and I started to sweat all over.

"What's wrong?" I strained, terrified by the response I would hear.

My mom wiped the tears from her face and stood up to hug me. "I'm sorry you had to come home like this, baby."

I felt her arms wrap around me, and I hugged her back with the same force, her skin clammy and hot.

251

"It's okay. What's going on?"

She kissed my cheek and grabbed my hand, guiding me to sit next to her on the couch. My dad scooted over to allow me more room to sit down.

"Alright, you guys have officially scared the shit out of me. What is going on?"

"Lucas, your mother... your mom..." he sighed, trying to even out his breathing. "She found a lump on the side of her breast." He rubbed his mouth back and forth with his fingers like the words felt dirty coming out of his mouth. "She went to her doctor and they did a biopsy—"

I stood up.

"Lucas," I heard Mom say. It echoed throughout my entire body and vibrated in my core. "Honey, I'm going to be okay. Are you listening to me, Lucas?"

"What stage?" I found myself saying.

They looked at each other before looking back at me.

"Lucas," Mom repeated.

"What. Stage. Mom?"

She bowed her head. "Three."

"Like grandma? How long did she fight for?" I argued, my fists clenching at my sides.

"Four years," she answered, looking everywhere around the room, except at me.

I nodded, remembering how awful it was to watch her die. Slowly taking every part of her, little by little, inch by inch, till she was unrecognizable. It shredded everything within her, her spirit, her will, and her life. I shook my head, not wanting to picture the same thing happening to my mom.

I trembled everywhere. It was uncontrollable.

"Honey, I'm not my mother, and I will fight until I can't anymore. I promise you that."

I eyed her. "Does Lily know?"

"No."

"Does anyone?"

"No. I want to give it time to settle for us. We have some time before I need to tell everyone."

I nodded.

"Lucas—"

M. Robinson

"I can't, Mom," I bellowed. "I can't." I backed away and ran toward the door.

I sprinted as fast as I could.

*"Cancer..."*

It was an endless phrase that repeated itself over and over in my head, a cycle that I couldn't stop over and over again.

*"Cancer..."*

I flew through the air, my hurricane blowing by me, with the sounds of wind bursting around my body.

*"Cancer..."*

My legs felt numb.

*"Cancer..."*

My heart beat out of my chest.

*"Cancer..."*

I could feel my body recoiling.

*"Cancer..."*

I ran faster.

*"Cancer..."*

*Was I throwing up?*

I wiped my mouth and stepped away from the bushes, weeping, sobbing uncontrollably, and sucking in air that wasn't available to me.

*How the fuck could this be happening?*

I needed to talk to Alex. I wanted Alex.

*Oh God! Why?*

I'm not sure how long I stood there and wailed. I think it was quite a while when I had finally shed the last of the tears that were left in me and stared off into nothing, I couldn't move, I couldn't feel, I was numb. I stood there in the dark looking at the place that was ours. I saw shadows from the bay window, then nothing. Darkness. I stepped one foot in front of the other, walking up the porch stairs.

I stopped dead in my tracks when I saw her.

Them.

Cole and Alex.

Kissing.

Him on top of her.

In our abandoned house.

253

Complicate Me

Everything. I. Loved.

Was gone…

# Chapter 30

## Alex

We walked down the beach.

"Darlin'," Cole murmured, sweeping my hair away from my face.

"Hmm..."

"You haven't been yourself all summer. Do you not want to go to UCLA?"

"What?" I stopped and looked at him. He met my stare, stepping closer to me.

"Do you not want to leave Oak Island?"

"What makes you say that?"

"It's like you're waiting for something. Or someone," he intentionally added.

"I need to leave."

"Okay, but that doesn't answer my question."

"This is my home, of course I'm going to miss it, Cole."

"I get it, Alexandra, I really do, but you'll be back, Oak Island isn't going anywhere."

It didn't feel that way to me.

"I've known you for four years, that's a long time. There are things that have happened between us that we have never spoken about. I've respected that because it's what you've needed."

"I know," I whispered.

"Darlin', I love you." He reached for my hands, and I sucked in a breath I didn't realize I held.

"That can't be news to you. I know a part of you loves me, too. It may not be a huge part, but it's there nonetheless." He kissed them. "I want to know you. I want to know every part of you, but you hide from me. You're coming to California with me, that has to mean something. You chose to be near me for a reason, don't you think?"

Complicate Me

I didn't know if he was right or wrong, but I nodded anyway.

"Can you share something with me? Something no one knows about."

I immediately looked behind him and he followed my stare. "What are you looking at, Darlin'?"

I took a deep solemn breath and said, "You want to know me, Cole?"

He spun to face me yet again. "More than anything."

I nodded toward the house behind him and he followed me up the sand to the abandoned home that stored all my secrets. He trailed behind me inside, and I lit the candles that were scarcely placed around the room, creating a soft illuminating allure to the reality of what I had done.

I brought Cole to our house.

Lucas's and mine.

*Ours.*

I had to sit down from the uneasiness in my stomach. From my conscience telling me this was wrong.

I was wrong.

He sat beside me, a little too close for my comfort, but I didn't say anything.

"What does this house mean to you?" he asked.

"Everything," I simply stated.

He nodded in understanding. "I want to make new memories with you here." He grabbed my chin with his fingers, guiding my lips to his and then kissed me.

At first it was soft like he tested his boundaries. I slightly parted my lips and he took that as an open invitation to slowly slip his tongue into my mouth. He tasted of mint and something I couldn't quite put my finger on. He didn't taste like Lucas and he's the only other boy I've ever kissed. It wasn't bad, he was a great kisser, but he wasn't Lucas. Nothing compared to him. I was confused and overwhelmed, but I didn't stop him when he deepened the kiss, tangling his tongue with mine in an urgency that explained how long he waited for this moment.

Which brought on an onslaught of memories.

His hand gripped the back of my neck, gently pushing me onto the blanket and pillows. I placed my hands on his chest but again didn't stop him when he positioned his body on top of mine. I went with it. I let him kiss me. I let him surround me. I let him feel like I was his. It seemed like as more time went on the longer I let him have his way with me.

I tried.

I swear that I tried, but I couldn't. Not now. Not here. Not like this.

I forcefully shoved him away from me and firmly stood up. "I'm sorry, Cole, I'm so sorry, but I can't do this." I opened the door and ran down the stairs, missing the last step and falling flat on my face.

"Shit!" he yelled, darting down the stairs behind me. "Darlin', what are you doing running away from me like that?" He helped me up, but I whimpered when I straightened my knee.

"Come here." He put my arm behind his neck and lifted me up into his arms, carrying me down to the beach as if I weighed nothing where there was more light to see.

"I'm really sorry, Cole, I shouldn't have taken you there. I don't know why I did, but you don't deserve that."

"Your knee is bleeding," he reminded me as he placed me down on the sand.

"I'm fine. Are you listening to me?"

"I'm listening." He swept a piece of hair away from my face. "I'm not going anywhere."

I looked down at my injured knee, another scar to add to my memories, and I wasn't talking about the one on my knee.

# LUCAS

"Another one," I ordered, tapping on the bar.

"Lucas, I could get in a lot of shit for serving you," Stacey informed me.

"Like you give a shit if you get in trouble. Drink with me. I'll buy you all the drinks you want, and I'll tip you nice when we're done."

She grinned, grabbing another shot glass for herself and pouring tequila into both our glasses.

Complicate Me

"You're lucky I just got this job, Lucas Ryder."

"I turn twenty-one in a few weeks, who the fuck cares. This is a dive bar and no one ever comes in here."

"True."

The moment I saw Cole lying on top of Alex, I got out of there faster than a bat out of hell. If they were going to fuck, I sure as shit wasn't going to stand there and watch it. I walked down the street until I saw a cab on the main road, telling the driver to take me to the nearest bar.

Call it fate.

Call it a coincidence.

Call it a fluke.

When I saw Stacey behind the bar, I knew the driver brought me to the right place. I hadn't seen or spoken to her since last summer. Even then it was short and to the point. We hadn't fucked in years, but as I watched her in her tiny jean miniskirt and her tight top with her tits displayed every time she leaned over the bar, I would be lying if my cock didn't stand at attention remembering the feel of her pussy wrapped around my dick.

"What's new?" I asked, staring at her tits, exactly the way she wanted me to.

She leaned forward, pressing them together tighter with her arms as she rested her elbows on the bar. "Same ol' same ol', I'm sure a big college man like yourself has way more stories than a small town girl like me," she purred.

"There's never been anything small town about you, Stacey."

She smirked and her eyes beamed. I hadn't meant it as a compliment, but apparently that's how she accepted it.

"Where's Half-Pint?"

I took my shot, hissing as it burned down my chest and into my stomach. The strong sting of alcohol coated my stomach and set my mood on fire, not that it needed any more ammunition.

"Sore subject?"

I tapped on the bar with my glass wanting another round. She smiled, pouring me another shot.

"This time you have to drink with me, I'm three ahead of you," I informed her, changing the subject.

She clinked her glass with mine before we both drank them down. This time the shot went down much smoother, warming me all over, but I was nowhere near where I wanted to be.

"Is she with Cole?" she grimaced, breathing out the liquor.

"See, the thing about you, Stacey, is that you don't know when to shut the fuck up."

"Ooohhh," she cooed. "Must have been bad. They've been hanging out all summer, like two peas in a pod. I honestly don't see what all the fuss is about, you're way fucking hotter than he is. I never understood what you saw in Alex, she's a—"

"Don't," I snapped.

She shrugged, maliciously smiling as she poured two more shots. "Always her knight in shining armor. I guess some things never changed."

"I'm not here to talk about Alex."

"Then why are you here?"

"To get fucked up."

"With me?"

"Why not."

She pursed her lips and clinked our glasses together again. "To old times then," she stated before we drank them down. "Burns so good," she practically moaned.

We spent the next few hours drinking and shooting the shit. I was beyond fucked up. I could barely see two feet in front of me. The longer I was with Stacey the more I needed to feel her to replace the hole in my chest that was known as my heart. She basically straddled my lap, except her ass sat on the bar and I sat on the stool in between her legs.

I watched with glazed eyes as she placed a shot in between her tits, angling back on her hands and spreading her legs wider for me. She reached for the salt. "Want to do a body shot?" she incited, licking her lips.

*Fuck.*

I looked around the bar and chuckled, my head falling back from the momentum as I stood up. We were alone. At least I think we were. I was so fucked up I didn't give a shit if we put on a show.

She placed her index finger near my mouth. "Suck."

259

I grabbed her palm and slowly sucked on her finger while she bit her bottom lip making my dick twitch. She pulled it away when it was moist enough to dip it in the salt, and proceeded to spread it on top of her cleavage.

"Ready?" she asked.

I leaned over and licked the salt off her breast while lightly sucking and then took down the tequila in one swift movement. She cocked her head to the side with a raised eyebrow, provoking me. If there was one thing Stacey could do right, it was fuck. I paused for a few seconds to admire the view. She seductively licked her lips and started to rotate her hips front and back, just like she would on my cock.

I lunged forward, almost knocking her off the bar. Her body was perfectly aligned with mine as I stood in between her spread legs. She looked up at me with abandonment and yearning. The heated expression was enough for me to lose control. I kicked all the chairs aside and roughly grabbed onto her hips, sliding her ass down to my cock. Her elbows still rested on the bar, holding onto some of her weight while I supported the rest. Her hooded eyes stared into mine and I knew she wanted me to kiss her.

I was fucked up.

I didn't give a shit.

I wanted to feel anything other than what I felt. I placed my forehead on hers, contemplating if I was really going to do this with her. Her lips beckoned mine with just the softest touch and that was my undoing. I plunged my tongue into her eagerly awaiting mouth, initiating a sinful dance of want and need. It went back and forth between us, each giving the other what they craved. She clutched my hair and I pulled on hers, beckoning her head to fall back and give me the liberty to assault her neck.

I inhaled the jarring smell of Stacey, I still remembered it from high school, and I hated it then as much as I did now. I ran my nose up and down from her chin to her collarbone, leaving a wake of desire behind. I urgently and swiftly made my way down to her luscious breasts. Her nipples were hard, waiting for me to take them into my mouth. I sucked and gently bit one while my hand caressed and fondled the other. Her breathing escalated as did mine.

I growled and deliberately unzipped my jeans. My hard cock sprang out from the opening. I slid her panties to the side, not bothering to remove any of our clothing, and with one firm thrust I was deep inside her. We moaned in unison and I didn't falter. I latched on to her hips and fucked her fast, hard and with determination. I didn't take my time with her, I was rough. All I wanted to do was come. My hands went to her ass to thrust in deeper and more demanding. I effortlessly picked her up off the bar and she wrapped her arms around my neck as I continued to slam her up and down onto my cock.

She was tightly wrapped around my body.

She braced her forehead on mine, forcing me to shut my eyes, I couldn't look at her like that. I didn't want a connection with her. This was a means to an end for me, exactly the same way it had always been between us. Within seconds, we were both gasping and breathless for air. Our moans getting louder and heavier, both of us dripping with sweat from the liquor and the haziness of the entire night. Within minutes, neither one of us could take it anymore.

We both came together.

Hard.

And even in my drunken haze…

I saw Alex's face.

# Chapter 31

## Alex

"Hey," Lucas greeted as he walked through my front door.

"Hey," I replied, caught off guard that he was at my going away barbeque. "I heard you were in town."

He nodded. "I've been here a few weeks."

"And yet this is the first time I'm seeing you," I snidely stated, regretting it immediately. "That's not fair."

"I can take it."

I softly smiled, trying to lighten the mood. "The boys are out back."

"And Cole?" he asked, a little too harshly.

"Yes."

"Right..."

"What's that supposed to mean?"

He shook his head. "Not a damn thing, Alex."

My eyebrows lowered, causing my face to frown. "Doesn't sound like it."

"Has he enjoyed you?" he blurted out of nowhere.

I jerked back. "What?"

He chuckled, trying to cover up his abrasiveness. "I just meant have you guys had a great summer? From what I've seen it's been a lot of new things for you. Going to all sorts of places you used to go with me."

I didn't understand what he implied. "We're the same we've always been," I explained.

"Is that right?" he mocked in a condescending tone. "I guess I need to get my eyes checked then."

"Lucas, what are you—"

"Darlin', the burgers are ready," Cole announced, walking in from the back porch. "Lucas," he groaned. "Nice of you to finally show up."

"I didn't get an invitation," Lucas clarified, only looking at me.

Cole stood next to me with his hands placed in his pockets. "Since when is an invitation needed among friends," he added.

"Cole—"

"Alexandra leaves tomorrow with me," he interrupted.

I shut my eyes shaking my head for a few seconds. "And my parents," I explained.

"Is that right?" Lucas drawled out, again.

"Her apartment is actually really nice, Lucas, it's not far from mine. Maybe you can come sometime to visit. I'm sure Alex would love to show you the places I plan to show her."

I glared at him and he innocently smiled, showing off those dimples that I usually loved but wanted to knock off his face at the moment.

"What, Darlin'? I'm just being friendly. Isn't that what you want?"

"I don't give a fuck if you're friendly or not, Cole, doesn't change the fact that I don't fucking like you."

"Lucas!" I scolded, looking at him with wide eyes.

"Oh," he breathed out with a cocked head and an arched eyebrow. "For Cole you give a shit, my how things have changed."

I took a deep breath and glanced at Cole. "Can you give us a minute?"

"Of course." He kissed the top of my head and nodded at Lucas. "Always a pleasure."

"What's your problem?" I asked when I heard the door shut.

He shrugged. "Nothing, *Darlin'*."

"Bo, you know the phone works both ways. I haven't heard from you all summer. You show up to my graduation and barely talk to me through dinner and then you leave the next day. You expect me to invite you to my going away party? Are you for real?"

"You're right. I'm sorry. I hope you've had a nice summer and everything you expected from your first..." he hesitated, much to my confusion.

"From your first day in California," he muttered, but I knew that's not what he meant to say.

"Where have you been? The boys said they've barely seen you."

"Around."

"Lily says—"

"Maybe it's time you stop talking to my baby sister about me."

"What's your problem?" I argued. "Why are you talking to me like this?"

"I'm just saying, Alex, you're going away to college. Big city. New experiences, some you've probably already experienced here."

"Lucas, what are you implying?"

"This isn't the time or the place."

"Oh, now it's not? I always have to march in line with you, don't I? You push me aside when you want, but I'm here when you need me. I'm like your own personal play toy."

"Better mine than his."

I gasped.

"Fuck," he roared. "I'm sorry." He stepped toward me and I stepped back.

"I didn't... I didn't mean that." He reached out for me, making me step back further.

"Is this why you came here, Lucas, to hurt me? You haven't hurt me enough? I'm your own personal punching bag, too?"

"Half-Pint..."

"No!" I stopped him with my hand out in front of me. "You do not get to call me that. Just leave, Lucas. Just leave now. It's what you do best anyways."

Now it was his turn to step back from me. "That what you want?" he tested as if he knew I didn't mean it and I hated him more because of it.

"Yes."

He nodded, backing away. "Have a great time at school."

I barely gave him a chance to finish his sentence before I turned around.

And left.

# LUCAS

My phone rang for what seemed like the hundredth time in the last few days and just like clockwork a text followed. I deleted it without even reading it. I'd done the same thing for the last few days.

"Jesus Christ, Lucas, turn off your fucking phone if you're not going to answer it," Dylan barked.

I did, throwing it on the coffee table and leaning back into the couch. We were playing Halo on Xbox.

"Who the fuck keeps calling you?"

"No one important."

"Obviously not to them, who did you fuck over?"

"No one."

"Bullshit. That's definitely a pissed off pussy phone call, I can smell it."

I chuckled. "How about you get your shit together and play the fucking game."

We played for several hours. It was easy to get sucked into the game and forget about everything else that happened around us. Dylan had his own demons he dealt with, as did I. I watched TV until late into the night, Dylan had gone to bed and Jacob was God knows where. I started to doze off watching Sports Center when there was a soft knock on the door.

I looked at the time on the DVR, it read one fifteen in the morning.

"Hold on," I yelled out, opening the door. "What the fuck are you doing here?" I sneered, taking in Stacey.

"I've been trying to reach you for days, Lucas! Days!"

"Shhh… keep your voice down," I whispered, grabbing her arm and tugging her into the apartment and then to my room. "Talk," I ordered, closing the door behind me.

She spun to face me. "Jesus, I don't even get a fucking hello."

I folded my arms over my chest and leaned against the door. "Fucking is more your speed. Is that why you're here?"

She scoffed. "Don't flatter yourself, Lucas. I've been driving all day." She reached into her purse and took out what appeared to be a stick. "This is why I'm here."

I raised my eyebrows, shaking my head not understanding and she threw the stick at my feet. I looked down at the ground and my heart dropped when I realized what it was. There clear as day it read.

*Pregnant.*

"How do I know it's mine?" I immediately argued, never taking my eyes off the small fucking stick that drastically changed my future in the blink of an eye.

"You're the only person I haven't used a condom with. Or do you not remember that you didn't bother to put one on?"

"Fuck," I breathed out.

"Exactly."

I sat down on the edge of the bed with my elbows resting on my knees, holding my head in my hands. I suddenly had an earsplitting headache. "What are you going to do?"

"Are you asking or telling?"

"Asking."

"I don't know."

As much as I didn't want this to be happening, it was a mistake, an accident. It didn't change the fact that she was pregnant, possibly with my child. I couldn't ignore that. I would man up if I had to.

"I don't believe in abortion, Stacey, and I couldn't live knowing that my child is out there with another family when I'm perfectly able to raise it," I stated, instantly shutting my eyes from the severity of my words. "That's if it's mine."

"It's yours."

"Then a paternity test will prove that."

We were quiet for God knows how long. It could have been seconds or hours, who the fuck knows.

"Did you do it on purpose?" I had to know. "Did you do this to trap me?"

"You're the one who walked into my bar, Lucas. You're the one who forgot to use a condom."

"I could barely fucking walk to a cab, Stacey! I barely remember any of it." My head throbbed and my pulse quickened.

"You know, we could do this together. We could be parents to this—"

"Don't you dare fucking say it. Don't you dare fucking even think it. We have never been more than what you know we are, Stacey, don't pretend there's more here than there truly is."

"That's an amazing story to tell our child one day. You think we should put it in their baby book?"

"If." I stood up and glared at her. "If. It's mine. I will do my part in this fucked up situation. I will be a father to my child whether I like it's mother or not."

"You like me enough to fuck me. You always have. That has to mean something."

I wanted to tell her it's because she's a slut, she's a whore, she spreads her legs to any guy who will look her way. It's what she was good at and she knew it. But I held my tongue, I resisted the urge to treat her like the conniving bitch she was. I knew there was an ulterior motive. She wasn't nearly as fucked up as I was. She barely drank. She did this intentionally and I was the stupid fuck who fell into her trap, but if the baby was mine... then she was the mother of my child, and I couldn't bring myself to say what I really wanted to.

It wouldn't be right.

"How far along are you?"

"My doctor said almost seven weeks. The baby is due April 9th."

It seemed so close but yet so far away. September just began.

"When is the next doctor's appointment?"

"In a month."

I nodded. "I'll be there."

She smiled.

"I want a paternity test done as soon as possible. Do you understand me?"

She grimaced, softly saying. "I'll call the office tomorrow."

I nodded again.

Complicate Me

She tried to open my bedroom door to leave and I shut it. "You're not going anywhere. It's late. You're pregnant. You can sleep in my bed, I'll sleep on the couch."

I grabbed my pillow and a blanket from the closet, immediately noticing it was the one that Alex picked out for her to use.

*Fuck... Alex.*

The realization hit me like a ton of bricks, it felt like the floor caved beneath me. Sucking me in whole and with no remorse.

"You know the bed is big enough for the both of us," she purred, caressing the side of my face and pulling me away from my regrets.

I grabbed her hand. "Not a fucking chance. Get some sleep, Stacey, you have a long drive home tomorrow." And with that I left.

I drove to the nearest bar just to try to get a handle on my emotions and thoughts. The second I saw that positive pregnancy stick I wanted it to be Alex. Images of her showing me she was pregnant with our child flashed through my mind. It was instant and unforgiving. I hated that she wasn't going to be the mother of my child. I hated that I had made a baby with someone else, someone that wasn't her, someone that I didn't love and could barely stand.

*I'm a fucking asshole.*

I couldn't have hated myself more had I tried. There was no coming back from this, only going forward.

I was going to be a dad.

I was going to have a baby.

I didn't sleep an ounce that night. Not one fucking minute. I stared at the ceiling, making images from the texture. I saw bunnies everywhere.

I knew the worst was yet to come.

Alex wouldn't forgive me for this. Not a chance in hell. It was only a matter of time before she found out and walked out of my life.

For good.

*Alex*

My phone rang and Lily's face lit up the screen.

"Hello, it's you," I laughed, waiting for her standard reply of, "Hello, it's me."

"Alex, oh my God! I'm so sorry, how are you? Are you okay? My brother is so fucking stupid. You know he doesn't love her. You know it's a mistake. She's evil and I bet she did it on purpose. I bet she's planned this for years. Ugh! I hate her. I hate her so much."

"Whoa, Lily, calm down. What are you talking about?"

"The baby. I can't believe I'm going to be an aunt to that cunt's child. It should be you, Alex, it should be you!"

I shook my head, utterly confused. "What baby? What are you talking about?"

Silence.

"Lily?"

Silence.

I looked at my phone and she was still on the line. "Are you there?"

Silence.

"Lily, can you hear me? I can't hear you. Are you there?"

"You don't know?" she whispered so low I could barely hear her.

"I don't know what? What's going on?"

"Oh no…"

"You're scaring me. Is everything okay?"

"I'm so sorry, Alex, I thought he would have told you. I can't believe he hasn't told you. I just found out today, but he told my parents weeks ago. They were trying to figure out a way to tell me. I figured you'd know. I called you first. I haven't even called him to yell at him yet. But trust me, I'm going to fucking yell at him. More so now," she rambled.

I sat down on the edge of my bed, barely registering what she said. "Lily…" I lamented.

"Oh, Alex."

"What are you saying?" I murmured, my eyes already filling with tears.

"It was an accident. He didn't mean to do it. He loves you. You know that. You guys are meant to be together. You're lobsters!

269

You're his lobster. Please! Don't lose faith in that. This doesn't change anything."

There was an eerie calm around me that produced a false illusion that everything would be okay.

"Say it. I need to hear you say it."

"Stacey…"

My hand went to my chest as if trying to hold the remains of my shattered heart together.

"Stacey's pregnant, Alex."

I never imagined there could be a pain like this.

I thought I experienced every sort of devastation possible at the hands of Lucas, but nothing came close to this. Nothing compared to this. Nothing prepared me for this.

Not. One. Thing.

"Is it his?"

"You know those tests could be wrong. Sometimes they're wrong, it's not a hundred percent accurate. I read that on the Internet. Want me to send you the link?"

"Is. It. His?"

"Yes," she murmured, loud enough for me to hear, it echoed through the phone.

There was no stopping the tears from falling down the sides of my face, one right after the other. No start or ending to how my tears flowed, they were relentless. I couldn't breathe, I couldn't move, I couldn't think.

"Alex, are you there?"

It was my turn to be silent.

"He loves you. He loves you so much. You're his soul mate and he's yours. You have to believe that. Everyone knows it. That's why she trapped him. She's like the Wicked Witch from The Wizard of Oz. He doesn't love her. She knows that. Do you want me to beat her up? I'll kick her ass after the baby is born. Alex? Please say something."

"I got to go."

"Alex! Alex!" she yelled out, as my hand fell to my lap, I hit the end button on my cell phone. Instantly a picture of Lucas and I was on the screen. I stared at it while my mind was stuck on one word.

*Pregnant.*

My arm shot up and I flung my phone across the room. I watched as it flew through the air, stopping when it connected with the wall. It shattered into bits and pieces, scattering throughout the carpeted floor. I sat there and stared off into space, then looked around my room. There were pictures of us everywhere, presents that he had given me, memories all over, and it made me sick to my stomach to see it.

It was too much.

It was too real.

It overwhelmed me and consumed me.

It hurt me and slayed me.

Like a giant blade was driven directly into my heart.

I reacted.

I leaped off the bed and let the rage, the fury, the craze take over. I went from feeling nothing to an infinite stream of hurt, pain, and emptiness. I had been a ticking time bomb that waited. Exploded.

I was loud, disastrous, and chaotic.

I would take everything in my vicinity with me, like a hurricane whirling around, merciless and unforgiving. It elicited feelings I never thought were possible, emotions that no one should ever have to experience. I felt every loss of breath, every tear, every memory, everything he ever said to me, and everything he ever promised me. It was all lies.

*Lies.*

All of the lies cluttered my mind for my will to keep going, for me to push through. I couldn't keep up with the agony, it clasped onto me like a vice. Taking me deeper underground, where there was no one, but me.

*Alone.*

I darted around my room, my feet stomping everywhere I stepped, leaving a path of destruction in its wake. Throwing pictures, vases, I went after anything and everything I could find. My eyes blurred with nothing but tears. My body twisted with nothing but hate and my desire to fall apart.

"I hate you! I hate you!" I yelled, talking to myself. I repeated it over and over to let it sink into my pores and make it become a part of me. Making me truly believe it, truly know that this was the end.

"Jesus Christ, Alex," Aubrey yelled, running into my bedroom. "What's going on?"

"It hurts! It hurts, Aubrey, it hurts so bad!" I crumbled to the ground and she came with me.

"What? What hurts? Are you okay?" she panicked, trying to comfort me as I sat on my knees with my body hunched over.

"I'm trying to keep from dying… I'm just trying to keep from dying," I bawled, big, huge ugly tears.

She pulled my head into her lap and I wrapped my arms around her waist. "I can't breathe, Aubrey. I feel like I can't breathe," I sobbed uncontrollably.

"Shhh… it's okay, Alex… it's okay, I'm here," she sympathized, her own voice breaking.

I collapsed into her lap. The more I cried, the more I realized, I was no longer.

His brown eyed girl.

# Chapter 32

## LUCAS

When I heard the knock on the door I just knew.

Call it intuition. Call it a sixth sense. Call it being fucking perceptive. I don't give a shit. I knew when I opened the door Alex would be standing there.

Broken.

Hurt.

Devastated.

All because of me.

I took a deep breath, being grateful that no one was home but me. This wouldn't be pretty, not even a little bit. When I opened the door to find her standing there like she hadn't slept all night, I wanted nothing more than to take her into my arms. Comfort her anyway I could, except she would never seek refuge from me again.

I was her destruction.

"Is it true?" she immediately asked, and I shamefully bowed my head.

"Is it fucking true?!" she yelled.

I instantly looked back up at her. I had never in my twenty-one years heard Alex cuss. Not one time. I stumbled back a few feet from the impact of her words.

"You wouldn't be here if it wasn't."

She shook her head and stepped inside, slamming the door behind her. "Oh no, Lucas Ryder, you do not get off that easy. You will say it to me! You will look me in the eye and tell me!" she screamed loud enough to break glass.

I licked my lips, my mouth suddenly dry. With a heavy heart and a guilty conscience I said, "Yes, it's true. Stacey's pregnant and I'm the father. The paternity test proved it."

"Is she keeping it?"

I was shocked that she would even ask me that. "Alex, you know I could never... yes."

"Are you going to marry her?" Her eyes filled up with tears, nearly bringing me to my knees.

"Never, we're not together, this was an accident. I'm going to help her raise the baby, but that's all."

"You say that like it's so easy."

"I fucked up."

"That's all you ever do, Lucas. You're one big fuck up."

I jerked back, hurt. "I needed you, Half-Pint. I needed you so fucking bad. You want to start pointing fingers. Let's start there."

She wiped away her tears and narrowed her eyes at me, offended. "Wow. It's my fault that you can't keep your dick in your pants? Oh no, let me rephrase that. You can't keep your dick in your pants with anyone besides me. With me you can."

"No." I pointed at her. "That's not fucking fair."

"Fair? You want to talk about fair! You have led me on since I could basically fucking walk, Lucas! You string me along. When I finally, finally tell you that I want you, that I need you to please make love to me, to show me what you've been saying to me for so long. I pretty much throw myself at you. What do you do? Huh? What do you do!? You kiss me and look deep into my eyes and tell me that you can't. You turn me down and make me feel like a fool, like a child! Exactly the way you see me!"

"Are you fucking joking? A child? You think I see you as a child? Jesus Christ, Alex, fucking touch my cock and I'll prove to you that I don't see you as a child."

"Too little, too late," she viscously spewed.

I yanked the hair away from my face and held it at the sides of my head. Wanting to tear it the fuck out.

"Why her, Lucas? Of all people, why her?"

"I told you. It was an accident. I was drunk as shit and barely remember any of it," I scoffed, disgusted with myself. "I needed you and when I found you." I stepped toward her, right in front of her face and I was surprised she didn't step away.

"When I found you, you were in *our* house. With *him*."

Her eyes widened and her breathing hitched at the realization of what I said.

"That's right, I saw you. I saw you about to lose your virginity to Cole in our house. The same place I told you I couldn't take that from you. I know I'm an asshole, Alex, I know I'm a selfish fucking prick, I know I've done some really shitty things to you, but goddamn it I couldn't make love to you and then leave you. I was leaving the next day. You were drunk for the love of God. I didn't want your first time to be like that. Do you think I could have lived with myself after doing that to you?" I paused to let my words linger.

"I think about that night all the time.

Every.

Fucking.

Day.

I stopped because I love you. I fuck everyone else because I don't."

She shook her head with a look on her face I had never seen before.

"I didn't, Lucas. I couldn't. Yes, I brought him there, but I didn't sleep with him. We kissed and I stopped him. I actually ran out of the house and fell flat on my face."

I smiled. I couldn't help it. I fucking smiled. My heart soared from the news that she hadn't given herself to him.

"I know this shouldn't make me happy given our circumstances right now, but shit, Half-Pint, I'm ecstatic that you haven't been with him. That you're still—"

She grimaced and didn't even try to hide it. "Bo..."

I shook my head in disbelief. "No."

Our eyes locked. "I was so upset and hurt after you turned me down. I didn't see it that way. You didn't tell me any of those things. All you said was that you couldn't do it. That I was drunk and I needed to sleep it off, that I wasn't in the right state of mind to know what I was asking. We barely talked the next morning. You kissed me goodbye and left. That was it."

I could see the whole night replaying through her eyes, making me relive it all over again.

"After you had left, after all you boys left, I went to work and Cole was at the restaurant. After my shift was over, we went back to his house. His parents were gone."

I shut my eyes not being able to hear the rest but also needing to know.

"We were in his room. I don't even know how it happened. One second we were talking and then the next we were kissing. One thing led to another, it just happened," she bellowed, regret evident in her tone.

"Did he know?" I asked, opening my eyes. "Did he know you were a virgin?"

"He figured it out before it actually happened."

"Cole's not as fucking stupid as I thought."

# Alex

My eyebrows lowered.

"You're connected to him, *Alexandra*. In a way, I will never be to you, and he knows that. He's known that all along."

"I didn't want it to be him. I wanted it to be you."

He didn't say anything, but he didn't have to, his expression spoke for itself.

"Why did you need me?"

"What?"

"That night. You said you needed me. Why?"

He looked everywhere around the room but at me, and when he realized I noticed it he once again met my gaze.

"It doesn't matter. It doesn't change anything. As much as we want it to," he simply stated, sweeping my hair from my face with a sad smile.

"You're going to be a father. You're going to have a baby. Wow," I breathed out. "I knew this day would come, except I always imagined that I would be the one carrying it."

He caressed my cheek as a single tear rolled down his face.

"I can't—" I steadied my voice for what I was about to say. "I can't do this with you anymore. Love shouldn't hurt this much. All you've ever done is complicate *me*." I declared with a stern face, bracing myself for what I was about to do.

I clutched onto my shark tooth necklace, holding it between my fingers for a few seconds to take in the feel of it around my neck. I hadn't taken it off since he gave it to me on my 11$^{th}$ birthday, and the mere memory of it almost brought me to my knees. I roughly yanked it off my neck before I could back out of what I was about to do.

His eyes followed the steady movement of my hand as I placed the necklace in his front pocket, which happened to be on top of his heart. I allowed my hand to linger for a few moments, wanting to remember the feel of him against my hand as his heart beat rapidly, mirroring mine. They had always been in sync with one another. Time, regrets, lies, mistakes, misunderstandings, hadn't made it any less true.

I took one last look at him, wanting to remember him just this way, and sucked in a breath I didn't realize I held. "I'm done, Bo, I'm done," I repeated as more tears fell down his handsome, broken face.

For the first time…

He knew.

That what I said…

Was. True.

# LUCAS

"Damn, man, you sure you want to do this?" Dylan asked as I packed the last of my things.

"What other choice do I have?"

"You don't have to move back home, Lucas. I mean yeah, she's pregnant, but you can finish the school year. Your son's not going to be born until April, it's January." He had just got back from Christmas break. I only went home for Christmas day and then came right back to start packing and take care of any loose ends.

"It just makes sense, man, I need to go. With my mom being sick and Stacey being pregnant, it's the right thing to do."

"Fuck…" He sat on the edge of my bed. "Jacob is barely ever around and Austin is moving in now. He got kicked out of the dorms, and I think he's losing his shit. Did you see him at the kegger? He was on something, that wasn't just weed and booze as he claimed."

"It's his problem."

"He's failing almost all his classes. He never goes."

"Again. It's his problem. Not yours," I stated.

He nodded. "Yeah, I hope he gets his shit together. I'm not going to deal with it when he's living here. Neither will Jacob."

"Austin's going to do what he wants. It is what it is."

"Have you talked to Stacey? Does she know you're moving back and transferring to Wilmington?"

"For the most part."

"She must be happy, she got what she wanted."

"She's the mother of my kid, Dylan."

"Which is why I'm not saying what I really want to."

I zipped the suitcase, placing it on the floor.

"How's your mom?"

"They're going to start the first round of chemo next month. She's as good as she can be. I wish I could say the same for my dad and Lily."

"Yeah, Half-Pint told me."

I glanced over at him. "Alex? She knows?"

"Of course she does."

"Who told her?"

"Your parents over Thanksgiving break. She went home with Cole."

"Cole?" I squinted.

"Yeah, she didn't take the news well. I'm actually glad he was with her."

I hadn't gone home for break. I needed to get all my documents in order for the school transfer.

"Are they together?"

"Not that I know of, but she moved to California, Lucas. You think she did that for shits and giggles? I'm sure he had something to do with it. I wouldn't be surprised if they were together. He's been around for years, like a poor sick puppy dog following her around. At least he's proved himself."

"Fuck him," I roared.

He shook his head. "She deserves to be happy, Lucas. She deserves that more than anybody. If he makes her happy, then that's all that matters to me."

"I should have made her—" I stopped myself from saying what I wanted to.

"You didn't. You never did," he said, already knowing what I wanted to say.

He was right, there wasn't much left for me to say after that. I rolled my suitcase out of the room and placed it by the front door.

"You coming home for spring break?"

"I think the boys and I are going to California. Alex has been begging us to come check it out."

"Aubrey?"

He shrugged. "She's just a girl I used to fuck."

My eyebrows raised, but I quickly wiped the surprised look off my face. "I'll see you." I patted his back.

"Take care, brother."

"Talk soon."

I drove my truck the entire way home listening to Brown Eyed Girl.

On repeat.

# Alex

"Wait, what? Straighten that out for me."

"Cole, that doesn't even make sense," I laughed with Aubrey.

"Oh, it doesn't make sense? I'll show you making sense." He tugged my foot from across the floor, pulling me to him to tickle all over my ribs and under my arms. I shrieked, kicking and laughing all at the same time. He finally stopped his assault with a proud look on his face. I rolled my eyes with a playful smile as he kissed the top of my head.

"I'm going to go order some pizza. Pineapple?" he questioned.

"Duh," I simply stated as he walked out of the room.

"It's nice," Aubrey grinned.

279

I sat up and went back to the coffee table, where our textbooks and notebooks were spread out. We were all studying for midterms that were only a few days away.

"I know I love pineapple pizza!"

"That's not what I'm talking about. It's nice to see you laughing and smiling again, Alex."

I bowed my head, looking at my notebook.

"I'm serious. I know it's been a rough year for you."

"Yeah," was all I could say.

"Have you talked to him? Have you talked to Lucas?"

I shook my head no.

"That's probably for the best. How's his mom?"

"Fighting."

She nodded in understanding.

"Lily is... she's... she's really bad," I stuttered. "You know how she is, such a free spirit, happy go lucky kinda girl. She's fifteen and should be worrying about boys and her learner's permit. Her life's completely changed. I think it's killed some of her spirit."

"Lily is resilient, though. She's a lot like Lucas in that sense. It's a Ryder trait."

"My mom... I mean my parents in general. They're not dealing well with it either. I guess it hasn't really hit me yet. I mean I know she's sick, but I'm not there seeing it happen. I'm here and I feel really guilty about that."

They had told me over the holiday break and as soon as they did. I had a gut wrenching feeling that Lucas was coming to tell me the night he found Cole and I in our abandoned house. Especially after him not sharing it with me during our last encounter at his apartment. He didn't want to add to the pain I felt already, knowing I would find out eventually.

"You being there will not change anything, Alex. Your parents want you here. They told you several times."

"I know that. But she's like a mom to me," I breathed out. "I can't imagine life without her. I don't ever want to imagine it."

"She'll be okay. You just have to have faith."

"I am. I'm trying."

"It's okay for you to be happy. I hate to say this because you know I've always been team Lucas, but Cole he's a good guy. It's obvious he loves you. I think a part of you loves him, too. You have to move on, Lucas has."

My mind processed what she said to me, knowing she was right. "He is a good guy and I do love him, Aubrey. I just don't know if I'm in love with him yet."

"Well, you're never going to find out if you don't try to see what's there. You've kept him in the friend box and maybe it's time for you to take him out of there. I mean you lost your virginity to him. That's got to mean something."

Before I could answer, Cole walked back into the living room clapping his hands loudly, making Aubrey and I jump from the sound.

"I am ready to conquer Physics. Who's with me?"

We both looked at him like he was crazy.

"All right," he stated with a serious face. "Nobody."

We spent the rest of the night laughing, studying and eating entirely too much pizza. Cole crashed on our couch, and for the first time I almost told him to come sleep in my bed.

With me.

# Chapter 33

## Alex

The boys were coming in a few days to visit me in California over spring break. I bought a few air mattresses after I asked Aubrey if it was okay that they stayed with us. She said it didn't bother her and that it was fine. Dylan said the same.

I didn't understand either of them, after this trip I would understand them even less.

"Are you going to help me clean up or you just going to sit there and play Xbox?" I asked Cole who hadn't moved from the couch.

"I knew I shouldn't have let you bring that thing over here."

"Darlin', the guys are coming and you will be very grateful when they're not bored out of their minds because they don't have shit to do. Trust me, they don't want to watch your Pretty Little Liars and Vampire Diaries."

I shook my head. "That's definitely not me, that's Aubrey. I hate it as much as you do. Modern Family and Family Guy are more my style."

"And that's why I love you, Darlin'," he stated as he enthusiastically moved about the couch shooting people.

He said it all the time now, like him telling me he was in love with me on the beach opened the door for him to say I love you whenever he wanted. I would be lying if I said it didn't warm my heart every time I heard that sentiment coming from his lips. I had been giving us a lot of thought since Aubrey and I talked, but I just hadn't worked up the courage to say what I wanted to yet.

"What are you stewing about over there?"

"How do you know I'm stewing?"

"Because you're playing with the seam of the pillow and you only do that shit when you're nervous."

I smiled, laughing to myself. He wasn't even looking at me and he still knew what I did, which helped ease the anxiety I felt about having this conversation with him.

"We need to talk."

"Four words every man loves to hear."

"Cole…"

"Okay." He clicked save on the game and put the controller on the coffee table, turning to face me.

I moved from the armchair to the couch, sitting beside him with my legs tucked under me.

"What's up?"

I took a deep breath. "I've been thinking."

"About?"

"Us."

He grinned, his dimples protruding profusely. "What about us?"

"I think that maybe we could hang out and stuff."

"We do that all the time."

"I mean… in other ways of hanging out. Like dates and stuff."

He chuckled, beaming. "Are you asking me out, Darlin'?"

"Cole," I whined, embarrassed and hiding my face in my hands.

He laughed again but this time it was much bigger and huskier. "Stop," he ordered, pulling my hands down but not letting go of them. "Tell me."

"I just did."

"Why you being so shy?"

"I don't know. Girls aren't supposed to ask guys out, Cole."

"Ah. Well then, let me rectify that. Alexandra, would you do me the honor of going out on a date with me?"

I smirked.

"And then letting me come back to your apartment to make out with you on your couch?" he added.

I giggled, "Maybe."

"Maybe, huh? God, Darlin', I had no idea you'd move so fast. I don't know if I'm ready for this."

283

"In all seriousness, I want to start fresh. I know that may be hard for you to understand, especially because we've already been intimate, but it's what I need. I don't want to talk about the past, I want to date and see where this goes. Can you do that?"

He thought about it for a few seconds before responding with, "Can we talk about it now? Then never speak of it again?"

I nodded. I owed him that.

"That night, it meant everything to me, and it still does. I know it didn't happen under the best circumstances and a part of me feels shitty about taking advantage of you. I wish I could tell you I was sorry, but I'm not. Not even a little, I'm not going to lie to you, Darlin'. I've dated and I've been with other girls, but it's never been anything serious. It's always been you."

I swallowed the saliva that pooled in my mouth, my heart bursting with the devotion and adoration he always had for me.

"I love you. I'm in love with you. I've known that since the first time you basically told me to eat shit."

I laughed and he smiled. "But I'm not stupid, I know you're doing this, moving on because of Lucas."

I bowed my head and he placed his index finger under my chin and brought my gaze back up to him.

"And I don't care. I'll take you any way I can, even if I know I'm the second choice. It's his loss and my gain."

"I do love you, Cole, and that's why I want to see where this can go."

"I want to kiss you so fucking bad right now," he groaned.

I didn't give it any thought. I leaned forward and kissed him.

His lips were soft and smooth. When his tongue beckoned my mouth to open for him, I did, feeling the silkiness of Cole. Only Cole. Our kiss became heady and intoxicating. I felt him everywhere, even though he wasn't touching me and it left me craving more. I never had that feeling with anyone but Lucas, and for the first time it didn't scare me.

I didn't want to push him away. I didn't feel bad. I didn't need to stop.

As our connection deepened, I realized for the first time there was love outside of Lucas, and I was ready to experience that.

With Cole.

# LUCAS

It was spring break and I knew the boys were in California with Alex. I hated that I wasn't there with them. The jealously that radiated inside of me was enough to make me go crazy. I busied myself with helping my mom and Stacey. Getting ready for my son that was due in a few short weeks, my life it didn't seem real. It was like I lived in someone else's life or something, barely recognizing myself in the mirror anymore.

I rented a condo near my parents that overlooked the water. I started working for this construction company that had been established since before I was born, my dad knew the owner. I had a little less than a year before I graduated with a bachelor's degree in engineering. I didn't know what I wanted to do with it. I figured construction was a good place to start.

"Hello!" Mom announced from my front door.

"I'm in here," I yelled out, hearing her footsteps on the wood floor.

"Wow! Look at this," she said, walking around the baby room. "You've gotten a lot done."

I stood, looking around with her. "I don't have anything better to do and he'll be here soon."

"I really love these colors, Lucas, the brown with the soft blue."

I had painted the walls a light blue color and with her help I purchased the dark brown furniture. For someone so small he sure needed a lot of stuff. The baby shower helped Stacey get a lot of things and since my mom had helped her put it together, most people knew our situation and bought double of everything. I was fortunate that there wasn't much more I needed to buy.

I didn't have the heart to send Alex an invitation. I told my mom that, which she understood. It didn't stop Alex from sending a gift, she must have found out from the boys or her parents. The card read to Lucas from Alex, that's it, but when I opened the present it nearly tore me apart. There was a mobile with surfboards, a replica of the board I owned and had been using since I was a kid. She must have had it custom made, along with a onesie inscribed Baby Bo and a shark tooth teething ring. I knew it wasn't malicious, that's not Half-Pint. She was trying to give my son some of our fondest memories. She wanted him to have a part of us and I couldn't have loved her more for it if I tried.

My mom skimmed the mobile with her fingers. "This was really thoughtful of her. She put a lot of effort and care into this."

"I know what you're doing," I stated.

"And what's that?"

"You're trying to imply that she's thinking about me. That she wouldn't have put that much thought into a gift if she wasn't."

She shrugged. "You said it, not me."

"You know, I don't get you. For years you tell me that we can't be together, then you think something like that. You're contradicting, Mother."

She sadly smiled and I immediately felt bad. "That's not what I tried to do, at least not intentionally. I'm sick, Lucas. I'm really sick." The scarf around her bald head proved it. "You learn to look at things differently when something so life changing happens to you. I've made some mistakes and for that I'm sorry."

"What are you saying?"

"I'm saying that shit happens and when it rains it pours. I know you're at a crossroad in your life right now, but that doesn't change the years of memories and love you two have between you. No one can take that away. Not Stacey. Not your son. Not the boys. Not Cole. And especially not me." She stepped out in front of me and placed her hand over my heart. "It's here," and with that gesture she kissed my forehead and left.

I pulled out *her* necklace from under my shirt. My mom was right.

Except that's all they were now…
Memories.

*Alex*

"So you and Cole, huh?" Austin asked with big dilated eyes.

We were at Cole's fraternity party. Dylan was with some random chick, completely ignoring Aubrey like a total dick. He barely said three words to her the entire time they were here and they were leaving tomorrow. As much as she tried to cover it up, I could tell it bothered her. Every time we went out a new girl was hung around his neck. He wasn't very nice to them, and it blew my mind that they still fawned over him as much as they did.

*Girls are weird.*

Jacob was on his phone a lot, constantly texting someone. Stepping out of the room to answer his calls and not coming back inside for a while. I assumed he was with someone, but I couldn't understand why he was so secretive about it. Then again he was still flirting and who knows what else he did with those girls while he was here. So if he was with someone then it wasn't that serious. I tried to ask him one night but he blew me off by changing the subject.

No one had mentioned Lucas. Not one thing. Not one time. I guess we established a new policy, don't ask and don't tell.

Austin, well Austin was just a hot mess. Drinking every day. Partying every night. Most nights he didn't come back to my apartment with us. Granted Dylan and Jacob hadn't either but that was only for a night or two.

"What are you on, Austin?" I sat on the hood of my car with him in front of me.

"Just weed, Half-Pint, relax. You sound as bad as the guys."

"I'm worried about you," I coaxed.

"Don't be, I'm fine. Now, you and Cole? You fucking him?"

I gasped. "Jesus, Austin."

He rolled his eyes. "Oh come on, Alex, we're not kids anymore. I know you get... wet," he crudely baited.

I jumped off my car, walking away from him.

He grabbed my arm a little too hard. "Oh my God, stop! I'm joking. Calm down."

"Let go of my arm."

He did.

"You're lying. What are you on?"

"Ecstasy."

"Why?"

"Why not, Alex! You only live once. Might as well fucking make it count, right?"

"Austin," I murmured, trying to reach for him.

287

"No! Don't look at me like that. I'm having fun."

I disappointingly eyed him.

"Fuck it. I'm out of here."

"Austin," I shouted after him, but he didn't listen. He was gone.

When I told the boys later that night they said they weren't surprised and they've tried to talk to him a few times, but he doesn't care. We had to let him find his own way, as much as I hated it.

"It is what it is," Jacob said the next morning while we were sitting on my back porch, after I tried to talk to him about it again. I didn't understand why they weren't as worried as I was. I guess they just thought it was normal guy stuff, but it didn't feel that way to me, and it would take years for everyone to realize I was right.

"Did you check out what room Dylan came out of this morning?" I questioned with a wide-smile, wanting to lighten the mood.

"No?" he replied with an arched eyebrow and a grin.

I fervently nodded.

"What? They've barely said two words to each other."

I shrugged. "I know. But he definitely slept in her room last night."

"Dylan and Aubrey? You think they...?"

"I don't know, Aubrey's kinda loud."

He busted out laughing.

"Thin walls." I signaled around me with my finger.

"What about you, Half-Pint? You been loud?"

"No!"

"Good. Fucking keep it that way," he ordered with a stern face.

I rolled my eyes and shook my head.

"Cole and you, huh? Don't look so surprised. I saw the subtle looks you gave each other and how he grabs your hand when he thinks no one is looking. I may have seen him lay one on you a few times when he thought you were alone."

I blushed.

"It's okay, I like him. He's good to you and that's all we've ever wanted."

"I know."

"Are you happy?" he quickly followed.

"Given the circumstances. You know Lucas's mom, Lucas…"

"You look happy," he sidestepped my statement. "The rest will fall into place on it's own."

"What about you?"

"What about me?"

"Who's the girl?"

He grimaced. It was fast, but I saw it.

"You don't know what you're talking about."

"Ohhh," I sat up on my feet in anticipation. "You like someone and you like them a lot! If you didn't you would tell me! Oh my God, I'm so excited! Who is it? Do I know her?"

"Half-Pint," he warned.

"Oh, come on, tell me! I won't tell anyone I swear. Please," I begged, pouting with my hands in a prayer gesture.

"It's not like that."

"Ahhh! You love her!"

"Jesus Christ, what the fuck?"

"You do!"

"Alex, you're letting your mind run wild. I'm not with anyone."

"Lies."

"I don't love anybody."

"Lies."

"I'm single."

"Lies."

"There's no girl."

"Lies."

"Stop," he demanded, standing up.

I beamed. "Fine. I'm going to find out eventually and when I do, I'm going to have to approve. I don't want some skanky girl like the ones you're used to dating. The ones you bring around all the time. I can't even have a conversation with them because they're so dumb. That's not fun," I stated.

He ignored me and walked into the house, proving that I was right.

I would learn soon enough how right I was.

# Chapter 34

## Alex

"Happy birthday to you, happy birthday to you, happy birthday dear Mason, happy birthday to you!" everyone sang and he excitedly clapped his chubby little hands together with a great big smile on his face.

It was his 1st birthday party. I couldn't miss it, even though I was barely on speaking terms with his father. Mason looked exactly like Lucas, there was no resemblance to his mother at all, thank God for small miracles. I hadn't seen Mason much, maybe just a few times over the last year when I came to visit. Lucas's mom had sent me a few pictures of him in his Halloween costume and his first Christmas outfit, I never asked her to, but I didn't tell her to stop either. I had seen Lucas maybe a handful of times and we had spoken less than that, it was easier that way. Little by little it started to hurt less and less.

Cole and I were still together. We pretty much never left each other's side. I stayed at his apartment most nights or he stayed at mine. I was happy. I didn't think that would ever be possible without Lucas. I guess in some ways I grew up into Alexandra, leaving Half-Pint behind me.

Though we both did.

Lucas wasn't Bo anymore. I didn't recognize the man before me. He would be turning twenty-three soon, but he appeared much older, I guess fatherhood would do that to you. He loved and adored his son. I didn't have to be around him long to see it, everyone could. When he wasn't with him, the boys said he spent most of his time working, getting his new business off the ground. He opened a construction company that served residential and commercial construction. He hired a few employees but still got his hands dirty. It didn't surprise me, since he was always building something when we were kids. His Legos went on for miles with landscaping, backyards, and driveways. His mom was constantly buying him more so that he could build onto it.

Stacey looked older, too, more mature and grown up. I tried not to pay too much attention to her but I couldn't help myself, it looked like she was a great mom and maybe in some ways this had been a blessing in disguise for her. My mom told me that they did an amazing job at co-parenting, it wasn't like that for the first few months but over time they got the swing of things. Mason seemed like a really happy baby and in the end that's all that truly mattered.

Austin dropped out of college a few months after they came to visit me. No one had spoken to him or seen him. I would get postcards every so often with different postage stamps from all over the world. It gave me piece of mind knowing he was okay for the most part. His parents were devastated at first, but we all knew something changed in him after the accident, in ways that no one knew or understood. There wasn't anything left but to hope for the best and pray that he would eventually make his way back home.

Dylan started at the police academy. He wanted to be a detective, which wasn't a surprise to anyone. The boy had always been a loose cannon. It fit his personality to a T. He had to cut his hair and I knew that pissed him off more than anything. Aubrey started dating some guy named Jeremy. I hated him, he was an asshole and he wasn't very nice to her. We still shared an apartment and he was one of the reasons I spent most of my time at Cole's. I was in my junior year of college and this was her and Cole's senior year.

She started interning at a fashion company called Trendsetters and loved it. I think she was just lonely and Jeremy filled that void for her, the older we got the more reclusive and withdrawn she became. I didn't know what changed. I tried to talk to her about Jeremy, but she shut me down saying that not everyone ends up with their prince charming. After that, I minded my own business.

Jacob was in law school, which again, didn't surprise me. He loved to argue and always thought he was right. Cole was in the same boat as Jacob, he would be attending law school once the year was over, following in his parent's footsteps, who, by the way, hated me. I was a small town girl in their eyes and their son deserved better. I overheard his mother talking about me on the phone one night when we were over for dinner reaffirming my belief.

Cole reassured me that they wouldn't have liked any girl he was with. They were pretentious and he didn't care what they thought, he loved me. Truth was it still bothered me. I majored in business with a minor in finance. I didn't know what I wanted to do with my life and I figured with those degrees I could do anything.

Lucas's mom was still sick but fighting. Every time I saw her she looked worse than the last time though the smile never left her face. I knew she didn't do that for anyone's benefit other than her own. That's just the type of person she was.

"Would you like to hold him, Alex?" Stacey asked, catching me completely off guard. The surprised look on my face must have been evident because she added, "You've been staring at him all day. It's okay if you want to hold him, I think he'd like that."

This was the most Stacey had ever said to me. I nodded in reply. I couldn't find the right words to express how much I really wanted to hold him without it sounding like the overwhelming confusion I felt. I guess we had all grown up, including Stacey. Her gesture floored me, realizing she had turned into a mature woman who put others before herself, finally.

I never thought that would ever happen.

"He looks so much like Lucas, right?"

I nodded again, hugging Mason to my body as he laid his head on my shoulder. I couldn't help it. I placed my nose in his hair and inhaled his baby scent.

"It's not fair that I carried him for nine months and he comes out looking like Lucas." She rubbed his head. "He likes you. He's usually skittish around new people." She softly smiled. "Maybe he can sense your bond with Lucas."

I took in her words and looked down at him, taking in the feel of him lying across my chest. It didn't hurt like I always assumed it would, which is why I kept my distance from him to begin with.

I loved him instantly.

"If you want to see him again, all you have to do is ask. I mean you can stop by whenever, too, when you're in town. To be honest, it would be nice to have the company. I don't have many friends, especially after having him," she chuckled. "He takes up all my time, but I wouldn't have it any other way." She lovingly smiled at him and then at me.

It helped to ease my confusion. "Umm, yeah, I would actually love that. I mean if it's okay."

"Of course. It's good to see you, Alex. I mean Cole always seemed like a nice guy, I'm happy for you."

It was that exact moment that I locked eyes with Lucas from across the room. "He is," I simply stated, rocking Mason in my arms with Lucas looking intently at me. The expression on his face was enough to have me weak in the knees. I knew what he thought. He didn't have to tell me. His demeanor screamed it at me from the distance between us, and the realization of that was also written clear across his face.

"Would you like to put him down for his nap? He's exhausted."

I glanced at her. "I'd love to."

"Okay, great. You can lay him down in Lucas's old room, his pack and play is in there."

"Okay."

When I looked back toward Lucas, he was gone. I quickly peered around the room, but he was nowhere to be found. Stacey kissed Mason's head before I took him upstairs to Lucas's room. I didn't think about either of them, I just wanted to enjoy baby Bo.

"You see this room, Mase? This room is where your daddy and I used to hang out. It holds so many memories, maybe one day I could tell you about them," I murmured to his sleeping body that I didn't want to take out of my arms.

"I hope you do. Either way I'll tell him. Who knows he might have a brown eyed girl of his own one day."

I turned to face him when I heard his voice. He leaned against the doorframe, one leg over the other with his arms crossed over his chest.

"Like father like son, huh?" I grinned.

"One can hope."

"You look good, Lucas. The facial hair suits you. You got this whole pirate thing going on."

"You look beautiful," he voiced with a sincere look of longing in his eyes. He didn't even try to hide it.

"Thanks. I'll be twenty-one soon, I'm getting old," I replied, wanting to lighten the mood. "Do you want to put him down?"

He shook his head. "I'm enjoying watching you hold him too much."

I didn't know what to say so I didn't say anything.

"How's Cole?" he asked in a way to remind himself that I wasn't *his* anymore.

"He's great. He would have loved to be here, but he had to stay behind in California, his LSAT's are coming up. He wants to get into Berkley."

"And you?"

I shrugged. "I'm not quite sure yet."

"Are you planning on staying on the West Coast?"

"I think so. I mean we haven't really talked about the future yet, you know? I guess we will just play it by ear."

"How serious are you guys?"

"Wow, what is this twenty questions?" I breathed out nervously. "How are you? Lily says your business is taking off."

He nodded, but that's all.

"You seeing anyone?"

He shook his head no.

"Well, you know you still have lots of time for that. Women love men and babies so—"

"I have no interest in that, I lost *my* girl a long time ago," he finally spoke.

"Right…" I turned back to the pack and play. "Well, I'm going to put him down. I told Lily I would come hang out with her before I left. I need to head to my parents in a bit. My flight leaves tonight," I rambled, gently laying Mason in the pack in play.

I was about to leave, but he stood in front of me, purposely leaving me no room to move around him.

"It was great seeing you."

I instantly looked down at the ground, anxiously playing with the seam of my shirt. "You, too."

"You look good, all grown up. I've always loved your hair long, I'm glad you haven't cut it."

I nodded, inhaling his intoxicating scent. Combined with Mason's, it was enough to make my heart melt and my body warm that I had to shut my eyes. I hated that he still had this effect on me, and as if reading my mind he pulled me into a tight hug, causing me to freeze upon contact, leaving my arms at my sides.

"I'm sorry, Alex. I'm so sorry for everything I ever put you through. Everything I ever did. I have no excuses for it, but I need to apologize. There were so many times I thought about picking up the phone and calling you, or just showing up on your doorstep. I can't take any of it back, though. I love my son. I couldn't imagine my life without him. I'm sorry I hurt you in the process, I can't say that enough." He kissed the top of my head like he had done thousands of times before.

A part of me had been waiting for this moment. I had wanted it, needed it even. Here I was with his arms around me and it didn't make things any less complicated. My feelings toward him hadn't changed. I was beginning to think they never would.

"I love you. I'll always love you," he murmured so low I could barely hear it.

"I know…" and I did. I pulled away from him but didn't look him in the eyes as he stepped aside for me. I walked to the door but faltered even though everything in my body told me to flee.

"Everything happens for a reason, Bo," I stated, walking out of the room, whispering, "I will always love you, too," but *not* loud enough for him to hear.

I made my way to the bathroom, needing to splash some cold water on my face. I took a good look at myself in the mirror. I felt guilty about my lingering feelings toward Lucas. I thought with time they would go away, they hadn't, but that didn't take away my love for Cole.

Lucas was my past.

Cole was my future.

Plain and simple.

I took a deep breath, looking down the hall to make sure Lucas was gone before heading to Lily's room. Nothing could have prepared me for what I saw when I opened the door.

Lily and Jacob.

Jacob and Lily.

K-I-S-S-I-N-G.

# Chapter 35

## Alex

"Holy shit!" I cussed with my mouth wide open.

They immediately stepped away from each other, both of their hands in the air.

"Oh my God! Lucas is going to kill you. He's going to murder you and hide the body. I'm going to know about it, I'm going to be an accomplice!" I shouted.

"Shhh..." Jacob hushed, pulling me inside and shutting the door behind him. "It's not what you think."

"Not what I think? Did I not just walk in on you kissing Lucas's baby sister? His *sixteen*-year-old sister! Oh my God, Jacob, you're twenty-three! You could go to jail. Please tell me that's all you guys are doing!"

"Shhh… calm down, someone will hear you," he silenced again.

"That's what you're concerned about?!"

"Alex, I love him," Lily chimed in, grabbing my arm to look at her.

"I've always loved him."

"Lillian, stop saying that. You don't know what you're saying. You don't even know what that means," he ordered in a demanding tone like this wasn't the first time he had heard it.

"You love me, too! You just can't say it out loud," she replied, ready for battle.

This was all too much for me. I had to sit down before my legs gave out from under me.

"Stop! I mean it," he urged in a desperate voice.

"Stop what? The truth? You wouldn't keep kissing me if you didn't love me. Who cares about our ages, it's just a fucking number."

"Watch your mouth," he demanded with a finger out in front of him.

"Screw you! You're not my dad. I'm not a child."

"Then stop fucking acting like one."

"Oh my God." The realization hit me. "She's the girl, isn't she? The one from last spring break? Jesus, how long has this been going on?" I asked, my wide eyes going back and forth between them.

"Nothing. Is. Going. On," Jacob gritted out.

"Stop. Saying. That." Lily clenched her fists at her sides, looking from him to me. "Why are you looking at us like that? You more than anyone should understand this."

I immediately stood. "Me?" I argued. "What do I have to do with any of this?"

"You!" She pointed at me. "You love my brother, my brother loves you. You have loved each other since you were kids! The only reason you're not together is because everyone else won't mind their own goddamn business and just let it be. You would think you're related or something. It's so fucking stupid!"

"Lillian, watch your mouth," Jacob scolded.

"Oh my God, fuck you! Are you going to stand there and pretend you're not one of the main reasons they aren't together? You have been butting into their business since the beginning. You all have. I'm over it. It's stupid. They love each other, exactly the way we do! Except you can't get over the fact that I'm Lucas's sister. Who cares? I don't and neither should you."

I shook my head, stepping back.

"You more than anyone can understand what it's like, Alex. Please don't stand there and be all judgmental, age is just a number. I've grown up with these boys as much as you have. It's not like he's old enough to be my father or anything, now that would be gross."

"Lily, it's against the law," I reminded.

"Fuck the law," she let out.

Jacob was over to her in two strides. "I will not tell you again. Watch your fucking mouth."

She put her hands up in the air. "You know what, you two can stay in here and wallow in all this negative energy. I'm not going to stand by and allow it to effect me. I know you'll come find me, Jacob, because you LOVE me! So let's see who's right and who's

297

wrong. I guarantee you that I won't be waiting long, stew on that for a little bit." She turned and left.

I sat down again, resting my elbows on my legs and laying my head in my hands. Neither one of us said anything for the longest time. My head hammered with the silence. I thought back on all the times I saw her take his ball cap off his head and one day he just started putting it on her himself. It was such a meaningless gesture but it seemed to be significant to them.

"I don't know how it happened, Alex. I swear to God I don't. One second she's five years old running around in pigtails and then the next she's sixteen. I tried. I tried like hell to ignore it. To ignore her, but you know Lily, she does what she wants, exactly like her brother. After your accident, she started opening up to me, and I let her because she was a kid and she needed a friend. I liked being around her, she reminded me so much of you. I don't fucking know," he sighed.

"Have you?"

"Fuck. No. All we do is kiss and that sounds a lot worse than it is. We've kissed a few times and it didn't start till her sixteenth birthday. I swear to God that girl is like a tornado and I can't help but be sucked in."

I raised my eyes, blown away from his analogy, it being so close to mine for Lucas.

"I just turned twenty-three and she's going to be seventeen soon. I know that doesn't make it any better, I know it doesn't make it right. Fuck, Half-Pint, she's not wrong. I think I'm in love with her, how fucked up is that?"

I watched him pace around the room until he finally stopped and sat down in the desk chair, facing me, hunched forward with his arms on his legs.

"I have no idea what to say," I softly said.

"I'm sorry, Alex. All these years, all I've ever done is... I mean... with Lucas and you... I just. Fuck... this is my fucking karma."

I opened my mouth to say something, but nothing came out.

"I know, you don't have to say it. I know."

"Does anyone know?"

"Of course not."

"What are you doing in her room? You know that could have been Lucas walking in here. Do you have any idea how bad he's going to beat you for this? Oh my God, Jacob, he's going to murder you."

He lowered his eyes and peered at the ground, rubbing his hair back and forth like he wanted to tear it out. "I know. You have no idea how many nights I've lost sleep because of this. I need to get away from her. It's one of the reasons I'm applying to law school so far away. I need to put distance between us."

"Does she know?"

He shook his head.

"Oh man..."

"I've made my bed and now I have to lie in it. This is the only thing I can do to make things right."

"She's going to hate you."

"It is what it is, I can't keep leading her on like this. I am sending mixed signals all the time, but I can't help it. I can't explain it either."

"You don't have to. I understand."

"Half-Pint, it was never about you. It was Lucas. None of us thought he was right for you. You deserve, you deserve someone like Cole."

"It doesn't matter anymore. It's in the past."

"I'm sorry, I'm sorry if I ever influenced anything that caused you pain. I love you."

I nodded. "I know. Everything happens for a reason," I found myself saying again.

"You're not going to tell—"

"I promise... but if this shit hits the fan, because it's eventually going to, I'm going to claim I didn't know anything. I'll pretend to be just as surprised as everyone else."

He laughed and stood. "I'm going to—"

"Go."

When he left, I realized Lily was right. It didn't take long for him to go after her.

Proving that he really did love her.

After all.

# LUCAS

"Dad, I come to work with you, tay?"

"Hmm, I think you're still too small, bud."

"I not small."

"No, you're not small. You're a big boy now. Momma is on her way here. Oh! I think that's her at the door."

"Momma!" he shouted, running on his chubby little legs to the door.

"Mase!" I warned, coming up behind him.

"I know, I know. Who dis?" he asked through the door.

"It's me, baby," Stacey announced on the other side.

"It's Momma," he nodded like he told me so.

I helped him open the door and he jumped into her arms.

"Oh, little man, you are getting heavy, I'm not going to be able to carry you soon."

"Momma," he giggled into her neck, making us both laugh.

"Okay, okay, I'll carry you as long as you want."

"Come on in."

"Your condo is always so clean, Lucas."

"It helps when you have a cleaning lady."

"Only you could say that and make it sound sexy." She placed Mason on the ground and he took off running toward his room. I knew he wanted to show her the picture that he drew earlier.

"Want a drink?" I offered.

"Sure. I'll take a water if you're offering."

"Water?" I arched an eyebrow. "What happened to the beer drinking girl I used to know?"

"She had a baby and grew up."

I handed her bottled water, grabbing one for myself. We walked out onto the patio as the sunset loomed on the horizon, which always made for a scenic panoramic view over the water.

"This view is so breathtaking. It's been a nice, calm summer. I still have a hard time believing Mason's already three. He's grown up so fast."

I nodded, understanding. Not much had changed in the last two years. My company flourished which seemed to happen overnight. I rented a warehouse in South Port where I designed a few kitchen and bathroom mock-ups for potential clients, and my office manager did an amazing job running things so I could still get my hands dirty. I had several project managers that handled multiple developments, but I couldn't sit behind a desk for more than a few hours without going stir crazy. I belonged in the field and I think my employees appreciated the modesty of it.

The only thing that really changed over the last two years was my mom's health. It disintegrated with each passing day. She hated hospitals and refused to be admitted into a hospice. My dad hired a few nurses that helped when we had to work and couldn't tend to her. It started to get harder though, as much as we tried to ignore it. We knew the end might be near soon.

Alex never moved back home after she graduated from college. Last I heard from Jacob was that she and Cole moved in together. They were renting a house on the beach in California, near Berkley, the law school he attended. I saw her a few times here and there, but we only exchanged a few words, nothing more than standard conversations.

She looked happy.

She seemed happy.

Jacob attended Stanford law school out in California, too, so he saw Alex every so often or so he said. He didn't come home much. School and his internship took up most of his time. He was in a relationship with a girl named Beth that I hadn't met yet. Though he thought about bringing her home for the holidays in the next few months. Dylan was in training for detective and we got together every few weeks to shoot the shit. He dated some girls on and off but nothing serious, I think work took up most of his time and I believed that's the way he wanted it. Now Austin, no one had seen or talked to him in years, other than his parents and those phone calls were few and far between.

"Whatcha thinkin' about over there?" Stacey asked, nudging me with her shoulder.

"Not much."

"When was the last time you surfed, Lucas?"

"Hmm…" I glanced at her.

"Surfing? When was the last time you hit the waves?"

301

"Oh." It took me a minute to think about it. "God, years probably."

"You worry me, between work, Mason, and your mom, that's all you do. It's not healthy. When's the last time you did something for yourself?"

"I spent most of my life thinking about me and it got me nowhere. It's probably a good thing that I take a step back from that."

"Maybe a step back. Not miles upon miles."

"I could say the same thing about you."

"Yeah... about that... I uh... I'm sort of seeing someone."

"Really?" I replied, taken aback.

"It's new. He came into the office for some therapy. He's the new soccer coach over at the high school, he moved here from Florida."

After Stacey had Mason, she went back to school and became an occupational therapist assistant. She said she wanted to do something with her life, for Mason. He needed it and so did she. My dad helped her find a position with one of his physician friends.

I barely recognized her most days she changed so much.

"He's nice, but I don't want to read too much into it. Just in case."

"I understand."

"You know, I used to think we would end up together."

I eyed her with caution. "Stacey..."

"I know. I'm not saying that I still expect that or anything, but a huge part of me wanted it to happen. I hope you don't hate me for what I'm about to tell you. That night at the bar, I wanted to be with you. I knew you were drunk, I knew you were hurting." She bowed her head. "I wasn't that drunk. I wish I could tell you that I regret it, that I'm sorry for trapping you but I'm not. Not even a little and that may make me a horrible person, but Mason saved me. I wouldn't give him up for anything in the world."

I looked back over at the water, contemplating what to say to her. I wasn't surprised by what she admitted. She didn't have to tell me that, I already knew. I had known since the moment she showed me the positive pregnancy stick. I never thought she would actually admit it, though. I guess it showed how much she had really grown up. She was right about Mason he did save her and in a way he saved me, too. He stopped my hurricane, or maybe he was the quiet before the storm. Whatever it might be, he paused the chaos around me, and for that I would always be grateful to her.

"You know we've known each other since seventh grade? Ten years. I can honestly say that I've seen you at your worst and I've seen you at your best. You're an amazing mother. Mason is lucky to have you. We share a lot of memories, some of them better than others, but you're not the same person you were four years ago. I do care about you, Stacey, and that's not just because you're the mother of my child."

She raised her eyes, placing her arms on the railing to look out at the same view I was.

"For what it's worth, I was really fucked up back then. I used my body to get attention and Jesus did I get attention. Growing up I thought I was in love with you and now realize it was more that I wanted what you had with Alex. What she had with all of you. I'm sorry if I fucked that up for you."

"It takes two to tango. And fuck, did we tango."

She laughed. "We were really good at it."

I laughed with her. "That we were."

"Do you miss her?"

I didn't falter. "Every day."

"I bet she misses you, too. She doesn't look at him the way she looked at you. The way she still looks at you. You know she sends Mason stuff all the time.

"What?"

"Yeah. She umm, stops by every time she's in town. She came with Cole once and I could tell he didn't like that she was there to see your son. She didn't let it bother her, though."

"When was this?"

"Last time she was in town."

"Why didn't you tell me?"

"She asked me not to."

My eyebrows rose, completely caught off guard.

"Your mom sends her pictures frequently, Lucas, and she's been doing that since he was born."

My mouth dropped open. "My mom... she's never..." My mind couldn't keep up with the emotions that soared through me.

Complicate Me

"Mason really loves her, but I got to get him home, it's time for his bath. I don't want to get him off his routine."

"Okay." I followed her inside and to her car, buckling in Mason and kissing his head goodbye.

That night when I laid in bed I thought about everything Stacey had shared. I wanted to be happy, but something in my heart wouldn't let me and I would find out soon enough what that was.

# Chapter 36

## Alex

"Oh, God," I moaned, gripping the sheets with my hands.

"Mmm…" Cole hummed as his mouth continued its assault on my core. When I felt his finger enter my opening, my back arched off the bed and my eyes rolled to the back of my head. He moved his fingers deep inside me, hitting the sweet spot that drove me over the edge.

I breathed out my climax while he kissed his way up my body. "I fucking love the way you taste," he groaned before claiming my mouth.

"Darlin', I want to feel you."

I reached for the condom that lay beside me. "Cole," I panted. "Please."

"Alexandra, we don't need it. I'll be careful. Just this once."

I unwrapped the condom and placed it on him, rolling it up his shaft.

"Uh," he growled into my mouth. "That's fucking cheating." He never let up, caging me in with his body as he effortlessly slid inside, causing me to moan upon impact.

"Fuck… you feel so good. How do you feel this fucking good, I was just inside you last night? You were made for me, Darlin'."

He grabbed my hair by the nook of my neck and brought his lips back up to meet mine. He pecked me at first, teasing me with the tip of his tongue along the outline of my lips. My tongue sought his and our kiss quickly turned passionate. Moving on its own accord, taking what the other needed. He never broke our connection as his fingers brushed against my cheek and then down to my breasts. He caressed them lightly, grazing his fingers around my nipples and then along the sides. At the same time, he kept his other hand firmly in place behind my neck. He then rested his elbows around the sides of my face with his whole body displayed on top of me, and immediately lapped at my neck and breasts. I started to rock my hips and he took my silent plea, gyrating his hips and making my legs spread wider to accommodate him.

"That feel good?" he groaned, making his way back up to my mouth.

"You know it does…"

My arms reached around him hugging him against my body, wanting to feel his entire weight on me. He leaned his forehead on mine and our mouths parted, still touching and panting profusely, trying to feel each and every sensation of our skin on skin contact. He put all his weight on one knee and used the other for more momentum to push in and out of me.

"Tell me that feels good," he urged, as close to his climax as I was.

"Yes… God, yes…" I shook with my release, taking him right over the edge with me. He kissed all over my face like he did every time when we were finished. Pecking my lips one last time before reluctantly getting off me. I immediately grabbed the sheets when he was up and moving around.

"Why do you always do that?" he asked, pulling up his gym shorts.

"Do what?"

"That. Cover yourself. I hate to break it to you, but I've seen you naked lots of times."

I blushed.

"Never mind, cover yourself all you want, as long as I get to see your face turn that beautiful shade of red."

"Cole," I squealed into the sheets, leaning over to lie on my side with my head on my arm.

He lay beside me with his arm holding his head up. "So I've been thinking."

"That's dangerous."

He grinned. "I've been working at my parents law firm a few months now and you know how much I despise it. Probably as much as you do yours."

"I don't hate my job." I started working at a marketing company, but it wasn't exactly the right fit for me. I wasn't very good at talking in front of people and it showed with my presentations. "I just don't particularly like it."

"You know my parents are driving me insane."

"Mmm hmm…" His parents still hated me, I think more so now than ever before.

"So I've been coming up with a plan."

"Like a five-year plan?"

"Sort of. Except more like a two year-ish plan."

"Okay?"

"I thought maybe I could open my own firm with three guys that graduated the top of my class with me. They're smart, really smart, been working at top law firms since we graduated a few months ago. I think it would be a great opportunity, for me, for us."

"Yeah, that sounds great, but what do I have to do with that?"

"Well, you have a finance and business degree, I thought maybe you could come run things in the office. Like an office manager, slash finance coordinator, slash *my* sex slave."

I laughed. "I don't know, Cole. I don't think that's such a good idea. I mean us working together?"

"I have another idea. I actually love this one more."

"Okay?"

"I know we're still young, I'm only twenty-four and you're twenty-three, but what if you become Mrs. Hayes and I knock you up with some kids? I was thinking maybe four or five? I was the only child and so were you, I definitely want us to have a huge family."

My eyes widened and I sat up. "What?" I asked, stunned.

He reached into his pocket and brought out a bright turquoise box that read Tiffany's in black bold lettering.

"Oh my God."

"I've wanted to do this for a really long time, Alexandra. I've had this ring for over a year, I bought it when we moved in together. I've been waiting for the right time." He opened the box and the biggest diamond I had ever seen before sparkled bright against the light from the sun.

"Cole…"

He got down on one knee and all I kept thinking was that I was naked and he was proposing with a ring that wasn't me. It had to be at least three karats, and that didn't count all the diamonds around it and on the band.

I never even wore jewelry.

"Cole..."

"Alexandra Collins, I love you. Will you do me the honor of becoming my wife? Will you marry me, Darlin'?"

I looked from the ring to him, back to the ring again. My mind a big jumbled mess. I didn't know what to say, I didn't know what to do.

*Shouldn't I just know? Wouldn't it be instinctual to say yes? Isn't this what every girl wanted?*

My heart was beating rapidly, hammering in my head, and making me feel dizzy. Lightheaded.

"I don't—"

His eyes widened, worry immediately flashed through his gaze.

"I..." I licked my lips, my mouth suddenly dry. "I..." I stammered once again.

"I. Love. You," he emphasized with a look of pure love and devotion and I crumbled.

He was a good man...

He had always been there for me...

He loved me...

He would never hurt me...

I would be safe with him...

Always and forever.

So I shut my eyes and said, "Yes."

Except when I did...

*Why did I see Lucas's face?*

# LUCAS

"Merry Christmas," Mason said to everyone who walked through the door.

It was my mom's idea to host Christmas Eve. She wanted to have everyone there, and by everyone I mean everyone.

Stacey went to her boyfriend's house to spend the night with his family. Things were getting serious between them and I couldn't have been happier for her. Lily got accepted to several colleges, getting a free ride to multiple ones for her talent in music. She decided to attend Wilmington to be close to my mom and Mason. She still lived at home, even though my mom begged her to live in the dorms so she could experience some college life. She downright refused, saying she was needed at home.

"You know Alex is coming, right?" Lily reminded me again.

"Yes. You've told me that once or twice. I'm also aware that she's coming with Cole. Did you forget about him?"

"I wish." She rolled her eyes.

"I thought you liked Cole."

"I do but in the way I like vegetables, just because they're good for you doesn't mean they taste great."

I shook my head. "Where do you come up with these analogies?"

"I'm smarter than you."

I chuckled.

"She's also coming with Aubrey and her boyfriend, Jeremy."

"And to think I thought tonight would be a shit show. I wonder what would ever make me think that?"

We walked into the foyer at the same exact time that the door opened and Mason jumped into Alex's arms.

"Hey, Mase!" she greeted. "I missed you." He wrapped his arms around her neck and she hugged him close to her body, rocking him side-to-side.

It warmed my heart, seeing that our complicated relationship didn't affect her love for my son. The realization only made me love her more if that was even possible.

"Hey," she said when she saw me staring at them.

"Merry Christmas." It was then I noticed that her long hair was gone. It no longer lay down her back. It was the shortest I had ever seen it, a little past her shoulders with layers everywhere that framed her face.

"You cut your hair?"

She shyly smiled, nodding. "Merry Christmas." Not letting go of Mason.

She moved inside, allowing Cole to step in behind her. He seemed as arrogant as ever and I wanted nothing more than to knock that fucking smile off his face. Some things never change. My desire to hurt him was still alive and thriving. Aubrey walked in next with who I assumed was Jeremy. We all exchanged greetings, except I hadn't hugged or kissed Alex's cheek like I had Aubrey's.

I couldn't.

I wouldn't have let her go if I had.

Besides, she held my son firmly in place around her neck where my necklace used to lay. The irony was not lost on me. I didn't need to embrace her for her to feel me. She already held my entire world in her arms.

The night went on with normal festivities, we ate, we drank, and Cole didn't leave Alex's side. When the clock struck midnight everyone celebrated with hugs and well wishes. I decided to be the bigger man and shake Cole's hand.

"Merry Christmas, Cole, I hope this year brought you lots of joy," I acknowledged, expecting him to reiterate the same blessing.

He cockily smiled with those stupid fucking dimples displayed proudly on his face. "Oh it's been an amazing year, and it's going to be an even better new year, Alexandra has already made that happen."

Everything stopped.

Everything.

My breathing hitched, I swear to God my heart stopped beating in my chest, only for a second. A surge of panic flooded my body, my mind, and my soul at precisely the moment my heart started beating again.

Loud and hard in my chest.

Alex looked over at him, eyes wide and full of fear. "Cole," she said in a pleading hoarse tone. She cleared her throat and begged him to stop with that look in her eyes. He didn't even get it. He couldn't read her at all, not like I could.

"We agreed, Cole. You promised," she added with the same desperation in her voice.

Cole's smile beamed with admiration, right down to Alex.

*My* Alex.

At first it was like a movie. When you know something bad was about to happen, the anticipation of knowing what was coming was stronger than the ability to stop it.

I couldn't stop it.

I couldn't stop this.

His hand tucked a strand of hair behind her ear, and his fingers brushed down her cheek. "Darlin', is it so wrong that I want to share and celebrate our news with our family and friends."

A quick grimace crossed her face. It was subtle, but I noticed.

I noticed everything.

The entire room became enlightened to some sort of cosmic energy. I knew everyone was there, that it wasn't just Cole, Alex, and I, even though that's how it felt. It felt like it was just the two of them and me. I didn't want it to be them and me. It was supposed to be *her and me*.

Fuck him.

I tried to swallow away the lump, the one that made me sound like a teenage boy when I asked, "What news?"

My eyes glanced to Cole and I swear he fucking smirked. His eyes darted around the room and he smiled with bright white teeth. Teeth I wanted him to swallow after my fist knocked them down his fucking throat.

Once my eyes landed on hers, it was all over. I didn't need to turn to the clinking to know what it was. Cole raised his champagne glass in one hand and a fork in the other.

The metal clanked off the glass, mimicking a ringing bell. "Excuse me. Hello! Can I have your attention, please?"

The entire room silenced at an eerie speed as he spoke and all eyes turned to Cole.

Everyone's but mine.

Mine stayed intensely absorbed in Alex's. Hers stayed fixated on mine. This trance was different than anything I'd ever felt with her before. We'd been doing this dance with our eyes for as long as I could remember.

This one was definitely different.

This one would hurt badly.

This one would destroy.

Complicate Me

Cole thanked the room for being quiet and spewed his speech. "I would like to start off by saying that Alexandra might be upset with me for spilling the news. She didn't want to take away from the night and the memories of all of us being together, but that's Alexandra, always thinking of others." He reached for her, wrapping his arm around her shoulder and tugging her to the side of his body.

I'm almost positive she sent me a sad smile, but I may have imagined that. Our eyes stayed locked together, nothing or no one for that matter could ever break that between us.

I had that.

It belonged to *me*.

I knew the second the words fell from his lips that would be it. Our glass house would shatter around us. The last tether would be cut for good. The hurricane would stop, no longer wreaking havoc on our souls.

"Alexandra and I are getting married."

And just like that the rope was cut in two.

Her and I.

Him and her.

Cole and Alexandra.

Except it also sliced…

My heart in two.

I spent the rest of the night avoiding her. Avoiding everyone. I was like a ticking bomb, the more I saw all of *my* family and friends rejoice and congratulate them the more I felt like I was going to blow the fuck up. Alex knew, that's why she kept her distance from me.

She wouldn't look at me.

She wouldn't talk to me.

Nothing.

When they were leaving she didn't even raise her eyes to say goodbye, but she made a point to hug Mason tight and let her lips linger more than necessary on top of his head when she kissed him. Cole shook my hand with a smug look on his face like the son of a bitch he was. Jeremy rushed out of the house followed by Aubrey, who appeared like she had been crying when she said her goodbyes. I looked at Dylan for answers. His pissed off expression spoke volumes, but he quickly left right after so I didn't get to ask him what happened.

Lily barely spoke five words all night, which was completely not like her. She loved being the center of attention. I didn't pay too much attention to Jacob and I felt bad that I hadn't gotten to know his girlfriend, Beth. She seemed nice from what I could gather, though.

I spent the night in my old room. I wanted to feel close to her, to us. I tossed and turned all night, not sleeping at all. The words, "Alexandra and I are getting married," played in my mind like a broken fucking record. Every time I shut my eyes, I envisioned her in her wedding dress, walking down the aisle to say, "I do," to a man that wasn't me. I tried to block those images out of my mind and think about all the memories we shared together.

It didn't help.

I became angry, the eye of the storm was gone and I could feel the hurricane inside me begin to build. Before I knew it, the sun was up and I was out of bed, showering and getting dressed. I went down to the beach to get some coffee and as much as I tried to ignore the winds and chaos around me.

I found myself stepping up the porch stairs to our abandoned house.

Stopping dead in my tracks when I saw...

Alex.

# Chapter 37

## LUCAS

She faced the hole in the drywall that never got fixed when I walked in, closing the door behind me and leaning against it. I silently prayed it would hold me up when all this was said and done and all I wanted to do was breakdown.

She didn't turn when she softly expressed, "I used to think that it was Stacey... and then Cole... and then you moving... or it was prom... or me moving... and then lastly Mason..." she rambled as I tried to make sense of what she said.

"I thought that's where things ended between us. Each one of those times, it changed the significant directions our lives took. Each unexpected circumstance and situation, but it wasn't, Lucas, it was that night."

I looked at the hole, replaying that night in my mind.

"The night you punched this hole in the wall, that was the beginning of the end for us. It's still here mocking us." She paused to let her words sink in. I couldn't help but feel that she was right. That night changed everything for us if I would have known then what I know now.

"I hate," she hesitated, contemplating what to say I was sure.

"I hate what Cole did last night, we went back to the suite and argued. It's probably one of the biggest fights we've had. I slept on the couch and I've barely said two words to him this morning. It wasn't about us like he claims, he wanted to hurt you."

"I've always known Cole was an asshole, Alex. I'm surprised it's taken you this long to see it."

She immediately turned to face me. Her eyes were red and swollen like she had been crying all night. It took everything inside me not to go to her.

To comfort her.

To hold her.

"Not like that." She shook her head. "That was cruel. He's never used me for his pride before. He hurt me. He made our engagement become a spectacle, a game."

"A game that he won."

"I'm not a prize, Lucas."

"Then you don't see what we do," I simply stated. "Why do you always show up looking so beautiful that it literally hurts my eyes to look at you?"

Her breath hitched.

"Are you happy? Are you happy with him?" I had to know.

She nodded.

"Is he good to you?"

She nodded, again, her face frowning.

I shook my head in disbelief. "Jesus Christ, Alex, you're literally marrying the first guy that's ever paid attention to you."

She grimaced, making me quickly regret my words. I was about to apologize when she said with her voice breaking, "If that were true, Lucas, then I would be marrying you."

I jerked back like she hit me. "Is that why you cut your hair? Because you don't belong to me anymore?"

"He asked me to marry him and I said yes. I went to the salon the next day and hacked off all my hair. I donated it to cancer patients. It could be their happiness."

I looked at the bright, blinding ring on her left hand. "Where was that rock last night?"

"I had it on, I just turned it over, so the diamond was on the inside of my hand."

"Could he have gotten you a bigger rock? That's not even you, Alex. You haven't worn jewelry your entire life. You're going to marry a man that doesn't even know what kind of ring is *you*?"

She peered down at the diamond. "It's a beautiful ring, Lucas."

"It's a trophy. You're a prize to him. It's also a cock blocker because only a very insecure man buys a woman that kind of a diamond.

She looked at me through her lashes. "Girls like diamonds."

"Not you," I simply stated not needing to add any more.

# Alex

"He loves me and I love—"

"You love the idea of him. You love that it's comfortable. You love that he's always been there, like a sad fucking kitten that you fed one time and wouldn't go away." He stepped toward me and I immediately stepped back. Which made him stop and cock his head to the side. "Scared of me?"

"Of course not."

"Then why won't you let me touch you? Is it because you know everything I said was true? And the second I put my hands on you, you'll know who you really belong to?"

"That's not fair."

"I never said life was fair."

"I hate it every time you say that."

"It doesn't make it any less true, because if it were, you'd be the mother of my son and that ring on your finger would have been placed there by me."

My chest rose and descended with each word that fell from his lips.

"Let me touch you, Alex. Let me prove to you that everything I say is true."

He came at me but this time I expected it, so when my back hit the wall he instantly caged me in with his arms. His face mere inches away from mine, I felt him everywhere. All at once, his scent, his body, his eyes, his mouth, even though the only thing that touched me was his arms.

"Tell me to leave, Alex. Tell me to go. Tell me you don't love me. Tell me that you don't wish it were me that you went to bed with every night and woke up to every morning. Tell me that every time you hold my son you don't envision him as being yours. *Ours.* Tell me you don't want this and I swear I'll leave you alone. I'll let you marry Cole and live happily ever after. I swear to you on my son that I will walk out of here knowing that you're no longer my brown eyed girl."

"Lucas," I warned in a voice I didn't recognize.

"Call me what you really want to." He placed his forehead on mine, bringing his arms closer to frame my face. "Call me Bo," he groaned in a tone that made my stomach flutter and my body warm. His mouth so close to mine that I could feel him breathe on me. As if testing me he licked his lips, slowly, provoking me.

Proving to me that he was right.

I shut my eyes. I had to. The realization was too hard to admit and I knew he could see it in my eyes.

He *knew* me.

"Bo," I panted, my breathing mimicking his. "Please…"

"Please what, baby?" he rasped as if he hung on by a thread. Waiting for me to say the magic words that would set both of us free.

Except not the way he hoped.

"I'm getting married. I'm engaged to another man. I came here today to close the door to us, not to open it again."

It was like a bucket of cold water being poured down his body, he instantly backed away from me. I felt the loss of his warmth, his love, instantly. The damage was done, and the look on his face made me question what I had just done.

*Was I making the right choice? I couldn't hurt Cole. I loved him. Didn't I?*

I stepped toward him but now it was his turn to back away.

"Lucas…"

He sadly smiled. "I have no one to blame but myself. Maybe the better man did win and at the end of the day, as long as you're happy that's all that truly matters."

I forced back the tears that wanted to escape. I would not cry. I was supposed to be happy. Cole makes me happy.

*Then why do I feel like I'm dying?*

"There's nothing left to say. I wish you all the happiness in the world, Alexandra. You deserve it more than anyone I know. I will always, always, fucking love you. No one can take that away from me, not even you."

I blinked away the tears. I couldn't hold them in any longer.

"Congratulations." He took one last look at me and left.

I turned around and looked at the hole in the wall.

It now mirrored my heart.

# LUCAS

I never expected her to not invite me to her engagement party. I just never thought it would happen so fast. Six months went flying by.

I didn't believe it until I saw it with my very own eyes.

*How fucking stupid am I?*

I *saw* my mother helping with the engagement party.

I *saw* the engagement invitation when I held it in my hands.

I *saw* the date.

I *saw* their names.

I *saw* them walking into her parent's restaurant together, her in a white dress, firmly wrapped around him.

I *saw* it all.

It was only then I truly believed it. It was only then that it seemed real. After that everything took a turn for the worst. They say God didn't give you more than you could handle, they say when it rained it poured. They say everything happened in threes.

The cancer.

My son.

Alex getting engaged.

I thought that was the end, but it wasn't. Every day after the engagement party my mom got worse, it had been four months. There was no mistaking it anymore. No wishful thinking or praying.

She was dying.

The doctors reaffirmed that she didn't have more than a few more weeks to live, give or take. My dad called in a few favors and he had one of his alumni take over his patients. He closed his office for the time being. He said he wanted to spend every last second with his wife. My baby sister was beyond devastated. She had always been so positive and cheerful, making lemonade out of lemons and all that shit. To have her breakdown in my arms as we stood around hearing the doctors tell us that her fight was over, that they did everything they could do. All that was left was to make her as comfortable as possible from here on out. They informed us like they had done for a million other families before us, as if it had been rehearsed with no index cards, and they memorized every last word. Every last detail.

I stayed strong because everyone around me, including my father who I had never seen shed one tear before, broke down. The sounds of despair spilling from his mouth made me want to crumble just thinking about it. My mom held him in her arms, like she had done so many times for me as a child, expressing soothing words of comfort that were just a bunch of bullshit. Nothing would be okay after this.

Not. One. Damn. Thing.

I had yet to cry. I hadn't let what I felt brewing deep inside surface. I couldn't allow it to take over. If I did it wouldn't stop. It would take me under and God knows when I would come up again, so I kept going. Concentrated on work, Mason, and my mom. Ignoring everything that collapsed around me.

My family.

My faith.

My love.

I became God's personal entertainment. At least that's how it felt.

"Mom," I muttered, standing at her bedroom door. It became difficult to see her with her eyes closed and not imagine she was gone. She looked gone. No longer the woman who I recognized as my mother, all that was left was the sickness that was taking her away.

"Baby," she murmured like it hurt for her to speak. The machines precisely placed around her only adding to the truth.

I sat on the edge of her bed and grabbed her hand. I don't know what came over me, maybe it was the fact that I knew this would be one of the last times I would speak to her, maybe it was the fact that I knew I needed to say goodbye, or maybe it was just the fucking fact that I knew the end was near. I hunched over, laying my head on top of her still beating heart and bawled like a baby. I sobbed, over and over again. My chest ached and my throat burned. I hyperventilated, sucking in air that wasn't available. She rubbed my back, never once trying to stop my crying or preventing my emotions from running wild.

Complicate Me

"I don't know how I'm going to live without you. I don't know how I'm going to be able to go on. Please... please... God... don't take her away from me," I bellowed in the misery that lay beneath me.

"I will never leave you, Lucas. I will always be here for you. Just because you can't see me, it doesn't mean that I'm not here."

"It's not fair. It's not fair that this is happening." I wept for what seemed like hours. Time didn't stand still. Every second that passed was less time I would have with her and that's what killed me more than anything.

"Everything is going to be okay. I know it doesn't seem like that now. I know it may not seem like that when I'm gone, but I promise you. I swear to you that everything will be okay."

I sniffled, sitting up and she wiped away my tears.

"I love you. I loved you since the moment I found out I was pregnant with you. You lived inside me for nine months, Lucas, the bond that we share is unbreakable. I've heard your heartbeat from inside my body that can never be broken."

I nodded because I couldn't find the words to express how much I loved her.

She placed her hands on the sides of my face. "Listen to me because I will only be able to say it once. Your bond with Alex has so much strength."

"Mom." I tried to pull my face away, but she held me as firm as her weak hands could.

"Everything happens for a reason and I swear to you that me dying is for a greater purpose. Do you understand me?"

I nodded even though I didn't.

"You have to be strong for your dad and for your sister. They're not as strong as you. You have to be my big, Lucas." She hadn't called me that since I was a child and the sentiment almost had me breaking down yet again.

"Promise me that you can do that for me."

"I promise."

"Promise me that you will try not to mourn me and that you will go on with your life. That you will be happy because you know that I'm always with you."

"I promise."

M. Robinson

"Promise me that you will accept any other woman that comes into your father's life."

I shook my head no. "Don't ask me that."

She took a deep breath and said, "Maybe your father was meant to have two soul mates. I don't want him to be alone. Please, Lucas, tell me that you will."

"Okay. I will do it for you."

"I am so proud of you and the man that you have become. I love you so much, so, so, much."

"I love you, too."

She pulled me in for a tight embrace. I hugged her for as long as I could. For every memory, for every promise, and for every new memory she would miss. When I drew away, she stared behind me, and it had me turning to follow her gaze.

Alex stood in the doorway with her arms over her chest, and a look of pure sorrow and grief on her face. Fresh tears pooled in her eyes. She looked so tiny, so delicate, and fragile. She reminded me of the little girl that she once was. Not the twenty-three-year-old woman she was today.

"I came as fast as I could. I'm sorry I wasn't able to come sooner."

"Is Cole with you?" Mom asked, but something told me she already knew.

She shook her head. "He just opened a new firm and he couldn't take time off, he wanted—" she wavered and I recognized that face immediately, which is exactly why she stopped in the first place.

She didn't want me to realize...

That she was about to lie.

# Chapter 38

## Alex

"It doesn't matter, I'm here," I firmly stated, desperately trying to maintain the best poker face I could. Neither one of us said a word as we passed each other by.

"I'll leave you two alone." He closed the door behind him and I stayed rooted where I stood. I was afraid I would break her. I couldn't fathom seeing the woman in front of me, I had just seen her four months ago at my engagement party.

"Sit down, honey, you're not going to hurt me."

I did, placing my hands on top of hers.

"I'm so happy you're here to say goodbye to me."

"Please don't say that," I wallowed.

"It's okay, Alex. I'm not scared of dying. I'm going to a better place with my loved ones that are waiting for me. It's you and everyone else that I'm sad for. It's the loved ones that get left behind that suffer."

"I can't believe this is happening." My eyes pooled with fresh tears.

"So much has happened in these last few years, so many changes. When your mom told me she was pregnant with you, I cried. They had been trying to get pregnant since before I got pregnant with Lucas. Robert actually did the ultrasound to find out if you were a boy or a girl. Lucas sat patiently on my lap waiting, and you can imagine how hard that must have been for him, the boy never sits still."

I affectionately smiled, loving the story she shared with me.

"When Robert read the ultrasound, he swore you were a boy, so we immediately started finding names for you. The moment we found out that you were a girl at the hospital, the very next day your mom and I started to plan yours and Lucas's wedding. We planned out every detail. Even how many kids you were going to have. We spent hours upon hours planning your future together and we loved every second of it."

My eyebrows lowered, confused and torn. "I don't understand. You both have been so adamant on us not being together. Why are you telling me this now?"

"I made a mistake. We made a mistake. I regret very little in my life, I've been fortunate enough to be able to do everything I've ever wanted. Not letting you and Lucas decide what was right for you is definitely one of my biggest regrets. When you're a mother, Alex, you will understand that you want what's best for your children. You want them to see and experience everything they can. You think you know what's best for them. It comes along with the title of being parents. But I don't know everything, no one does. These last few years have been so hard for you, so hard for him, and I can't help but feel responsible for that. We both do."

"My mom does?"

"Yes. She's wanted to have this talk with you and I thought it would be better coming from me. I'm not telling you that you shouldn't get married, Alex. If you're happy, if you truly love him then it doesn't matter what I say. Your heart will speak for itself."

"Yeah..." I bowed my head.

"But, I do need something from you."

I immediately looked up. "Anything."

"I need you to promise me that you will always be there for Lucas. I need you to promise me that you will always look after my boy. He's not as strong as he pretends to be. Stubborn, yes."

We laughed.

"Those boys, Alex, not just Lucas, they're yours. Each one of them has gone their separate ways, and I also feel responsible for that. If we hadn't come between you and Lucas—"

"No," I stated, knowing what she was about to say.

She sadly smiled. "Whether you know this or not, Half-Pint, you're the glue that's always kept those boys together, you're the bond that holds them, and we've known that ever since you were kids."

Tears spilled down my face as I took in her words. They meant everything to me, every last one of them. "My good ol' boys."

Complicate Me

She looked at me with such love and adoration in her eyes and even though she was sick, even though she was dying. I wanted to remember her just this way. "I love you, and I promise you that I will always look after him. Regardless of where we stand, he's my best friend. Always and forever."

"Thank you. I can die happy knowing that my boy is taken care of. That's what every mother wants."

She wiped away my tears and kissed my forehead. I sat with her for a while after she said she needed to rest. I thought about everything she shared with me as I listened to her soft breathing, loving that she looked much more peaceful than she had when I first walked in. It didn't take away the pain I felt in my heart knowing that this would be the last time I would get to be with her. I tried like hell to keep that inside, but I couldn't. I lay down beside her and softly cried.

For her.

For Lucas.

For a past we couldn't change, and for a future I didn't know was meant...

For me.

# LUCAS

My mom passed away five days later, but not before she had time with each of us. Jacob, Dylan, their parents and Lily. Austin was the only one she didn't get to say goodbye to. I'd be lying if I told you I didn't hate him more because of it. The days that followed were filled with people coming in and out of my home. It was the home I grew up in, which now seemed empty and cold. There were endless amounts of condolences and preparations for a day that I just wanted to be over already.

The hours seemed to blend together. I had no idea what day it even was. I continued to be in a fog, a daze and stupefied beyond belief. I hadn't allowed myself to stop moving, I was afraid to. If I stopped moving, I would crash. I couldn't acknowledge anything, not the house that I grew up in, not the memories everywhere I turned. I moved around in autopilot, trying to avoid flashbacks of anything that I held dear to my heart. I just needed to get through today. My only concern was my baby sister Lily. The day our mother passed, I held her until she couldn't cry anymore, until she physically passed out from the exhaustion of her tears.

The first time Mason came running into their house yelling for Gama I almost lost my shit. I tried explaining to him that Gama was in the sky. She was in heaven with the angels. He didn't hear a word I said, and still asked for her every time he was in their house. We decided it was best that he didn't attend the wake or the funeral, so Stacey left him with her mom, while she attended. She hadn't said much to me, only that she was glad Alex was here.

I stood in front of the mirror and tightened my tie, studying my face, searching for something, anything. There was nothing. I was so empty, yet the pain was unbearable.

"You look handsome."

I saw Alex's reflection through the mirror, and I turned around.

"You never knew how to tie your tie, Lucas," she chuckled, straightening my tie. Her hand rested on my chest as she smiled up at me. "You doing okay?" she asked, adding to what seemed like the hundredth time someone asked me. It took everything in me not to throw myself on the floor, curl up into a fetal position and never come out.

I nodded because what else could I say or do?

"I'm here. I'll be here for—"

"Alexandra," Cole called out from the door. "There you are, I've been looking for you all morning."

She spun to face him. "You would know where I was if you had been here earlier," she snapped.

I was surprised by her choice of words and reaction, but I had way too much shit on my mind to contemplate it any more than that.

"I got here as fast as I could." He kissed her forehead, looking at me. "I'm so sorry for your loss, Lucas. If there is anything we can do, please let us know."

I nodded, noting he said, "We." He no longer had to prove anything to me. The proof was on her finger.

"Thanks," was all I could say.

"Are you ready, Darlin'? My cars out front."

"I'm going to ride with my parents and his dad."

"And, Lucas?"

"Yes. We're all going together to the funeral."

"I thought—"

"Like I said, you would have known had you arrived before this morning. She died five days ago. You remember I was the one bawling on the other end of the phone. You do remember, don't you?"

His face frowned in a grimace that didn't seem natural. "I'll ride with you guys."

"There's no room in the SUV, Cole. I didn't know you were coming till this morning. Remember you told me you didn't think you could make it? Something about your firm, you do remember, don't you?" she repeated with the same hard edge in her tone.

They stared at each other for a few moments. Both of them had something in their eyes that seemed familiar yet unrecognizable. Her mom called out our names and I didn't give it another thought after that. Alex sat beside me in the SUV. We were in the second vehicle behind the hearse that held my mom. I blankly stared at it the entire drive, only looking down at my hand when Alex reached for it and placed it on her lap.

At the church, I couldn't make myself walk to the front of that morbid room to see her. I tried. I tried like hell. I really did. I just couldn't do it. I didn't want to remember her lying lifeless in a coffin.

I couldn't fucking handle that.

I stayed standing in the back with Alex by my side. She was with me the entire day. I don't know where Cole was and honestly I didn't give a fuck anyway. Lily sang and played This Little Light Of Mine at the cemetery, a song that our mom had been singing to us since we were kids. I felt a lonely tear slide down my cheek as I watched the silver coffin being lowered beneath the ground. I let my mind contemplate what was happening.

I let my mind and body go to a dark place within myself.

Where my mother wasn't there.

Where Alex wasn't there.

When the funeral was over everyone once again expressed their condolences. I pretended to give a fuck about what they were saying, even though I didn't. I was over it. Just as I was about to walk away someone caught my attention from the corner of my eyes.

Austin.

One single rose was delicately placed on her grave. His shoulders were hunched over, and his hands were buried in his face. I had no idea how long the theatrics lasted, maybe a minute, maybe ten. One minute was the same as the next these days. They all blew. Every last fucking one of them blew. There was a girl standing beside him unlike anyone I had ever seen before, wearing a black knee length skirt with a matching black collared shirt. The sleeves were rolled up and I could see tattoos down her forearms. Her hair was a dark shade of purple and from what I could tell her eyebrow, nose, and bottom lip were pierced.

*Who the fuck was that?*

Austin stood and we locked eyes. He was covered in tattoos. He looked older, taller, and much more broad than I remembered. No longer the boy he was when he left. I hadn't seen him in three years, I barely recognized the man standing in front of me. Alex walked up to him and he eagerly pulled her into a tight hug, picking her up off her feet to swing her side-to-side. When he placed her back down on the ground, she shook hands with the chick beside him. Alex looked so tiny in comparison to her, but it could have been the fact that the girl wore sky-high heels, while Alex was in sandals. They walked toward me together, only stopping once they were a few feet away.

"Hey, man, I'm sorry I couldn't get here sooner. I'm sorry I didn't get to say goodbye," Austin sympathized, but I couldn't tell if he said it for my benefit or his.

I nodded to keep from saying what I really wanted to.

"She was an amazing woman and a mother to us all, Lucas. I loved her very much and I will miss her every day."

"You loved her so much that you're just now showing up?" I snapped, making him wince.

Alex didn't scold me. I guess since it was my mom's funeral I was allowed a fucking hall pass.

"This is Briggs, Briggs, this is Lucas," Austin introduced, placing his hand on her lower back.

"I've heard so much about you," she greeted, smiling. The barbell in her mouth reflected off the sun. I guess her tongue was pierced, too. I wanted to say I hadn't heard a damn thing about you, but this wasn't the time or the place. Plus it wasn't her fault that Austin decided to go MIA.

We met with the rest of the boys back at Alex's parents' restaurant, where everyone had gone after. My mom made my dad promise that he would throw a party after the funeral. She wanted everyone to celebrate her life, not mourn her death.

I stood on the beach with my hands in my slacks, staring at the sunset descending for the night to take over.

Tomorrow would be a new day.

Another day without my mom.

Another day without my brown-eyed girl.

"God, when was the last time we were all together like this?" Alex asked, pulling me away from my thoughts and making me turn around to face her.

"Three years," Austin answered, walking up behind her. Dylan and Jacob quickly followed. We all stood together, each one of us with our own demons plaguing us.

"It's been too fucking long," Jacob chimed in, tugging Alex to his side.

"Jesus... look at those kids surfing. It seems like just yesterday that was us out there," Dylan reminisced, looking at the water with a sense of longing. "How have we let three years go by without all of us being together? We used to spend every second together."

"I know," Alex breathed out. "I can't tell you how much I miss you boys. God... Austin, it's so good to freaking see you." She strolled from Jacob to him, wrapping her arms around his waist.

He kissed the top of her head. "It's nice to be home."

"How are you holding up?" Jacob questioned.

I shrugged. I didn't have anything to say. Not anymore.

"If you need anything we're here," he added.

"I'm going to head out."

"Do you—"

"I want to be alone," I interrupted Alex, turning to leave before I could see the worried response on her face that I knew would be there.

# Alex

We watched him walk down the beach. His slacks were rolled up to his calves with his shoes and socks in his hands. I knew where he was going and it took everything inside me not to follow him.

"How's he really holding up?" Austin asked, holding me tighter like he knew I needed it.

"I don't know."

"Don't worry about it, Half-Pint, he'll come around."

Jacob and Dylan headed back inside a few minutes later and I sat with Austin, admiring the ocean. The waves were calm today and it surprised me, they usually weren't this time of year.

"Aren't you going to yell at me?"

I shook my head. "I think you're too old to be yelled at."

He chuckled. "Never stopped you before."

"Where have you been?"

"Everywhere. You name it, I've been there."

"How?"

"Working meaningless jobs, but I've seen the world, Alex. I've seen it at it's best and I've seen it at it's worst. I've met some amazing people and some really fucking shitty ones. I didn't know, I had no idea she was that sick. My parents told me a while back that she had gotten cancer. I was going to call Lucas, but what would that really have changed? Our friendship died the day I almost killed you."

I winced at his words. I hated that he still felt the wounds that had healed on his body years ago.

"I sometimes check the Oak Island news online. It's random that I came across it. I hadn't checked it in over a year and a half. I woke up that morning with an uneasy feeling. I tried to ignore it but it wouldn't go away. I went online and there it was, front page and everything. Dr. Ryder's wife... yada... yada... yada... it took her dying for me to come home."

*Everything happens for a reason.*

"Are you staying?"

"For a while."

"Who's the girl?"

He adoringly smiled. "That's Briggs. I met her in New York about a year and a half ago."

"She seems… hardcore."

He laughed. "Her bark is worse than her bite."

"You love her?"

"She's hard not to love."

"She trouble?"

"You have no fucking idea."

"Alexandra!" Cole shouted from the deck.

"I better go." I stood, brushing off the sand.

"Don't run away, Half-Pint. I've been doing it for three years and there really is no place like home," he stated out of nowhere.

"Austin…"

"That ring on your finger weighs more than you do."

I eyed it, knowingly.

"Do you love him?"

I nodded because I couldn't say it. *Why couldn't I say it?*

"What about Lucas?"

"Austin," I repeated.

"You know what I've learned these last few years? I've learned that you can't live your life for everyone else. You can't pretend to be something you're not. It doesn't matter if no one understands it, at the end of the day if you're happy then to hell with everyone else. I lived my life for the boys, for you, for my parents. I was never really happy, Alex. I thought I was but deep inside I knew… it's why I left. I traveled around the world to find myself and I ended up back where it all began. All I feel is content. Happiness even." He shook his head, grinning. "I know where your happiness is and I know you do, too."

I looked over at Cole as I took in Austin's words. He stood there waiting for me, and I couldn't help but think how long he had been doing that, waiting.

"You remember how I told everyone, including you, that I didn't remember the accident?"

I froze, gazing back down at him.

"I lied. I remember everything. I remember every fucking thing. I almost killed you."

I bent forward to sit on the balls of my feet in front of him, lovingly smiling, and grabbing the sides of his face. "No, Austin. You told me to put my seatbelt on and when I couldn't do it, you did it for me. Right before we hit the tree you laid your arm over my chest, pressing my body into the seat as hard as you could. You held me there, even though you knew that you didn't have a seatbelt on. Even though you knew I had mine on. It was instinctual for you. You. Saved. Me."

His eyes widened in realization. "You remember?"

I smirked. "I'm good at keeping secrets, too."

"Why?"

"You didn't need anyone else hating you, more than you already hated yourself."

His mouth parted to say something, but I cut him off, "You *did* hate yourself. Welcome home, Austin." And with that...

I kissed the scar on his eyebrow and left.

# Chapter 39

## Alex

Cole flew back to California the next morning and I decided to stay a few more days, much to his disapproval. I hadn't seen Lucas since the funeral. It had been four days when I knocked on his door to no avail. I knew he was home, because his truck was parked outside.

"Lucas?" I announced, opening the door and shutting it behind me.

I slowly walked inside, taking in all the pictures on his wall. I was in several of them, so were the boys, Mason, and our families. I smiled when I saw the picture I had given him for his thirteenth birthday and then again when I saw the one from my prom.

"Hey," I greeted as I made my way into the living room, his back to me as he sat on the porch. He took a sip of his beer, bringing it back down to his lap.

"Lily says she hasn't seen you since the funeral, she's worried. She gave me your address after I told her I would come and check on you."

"I'm not a child, Alex. I don't need you to babysit me."

"I know that. I'm worried about you, too."

He took another few sips of his beer, placed it on the table and came inside. He looked like he hadn't slept or showered in days. "What are you doing here?" he rasped in a lifeless tone.

"I just told you. I'm worried about you and wanted to make sure you were okay."

He sat at the edge of the couch. "How are you doing?"

"Don't worry about me, how are you?"

He blew out a puff of air. His expression told me I should have known this. What was coming, what he was about to say, but I wasn't. I never thought it would come to this or maybe I did and I just chose to ignore it. Sweep it under the rug that now held all of our truths.

"I've been worried about you since you were born. How the hell do you propose that I just stop? You want me to just turn it off, shut it off like a light switch?"

I didn't answer with words, only with my eyes. I couldn't answer that question any more than Lucas could turn off the way he worried about me. His eyes held mine and I noticed a slight shake in his head. An internal fight was clear on his face. "What are you doing here, Alex?"

I didn't know how to answer that either. "I already told you. I love you, Lucas. Why are you talking to me like you're still not my best friend?"

He grimaced, covering it quickly. "Go home, Alex. You need to go home."

"I am home."

"No. You're not. Your home isn't here anymore. Not in this town. Not in the abandoned house. Not here with me."

I stepped back, needing more space between us, even though we were already a room length away from each other. "Why are you trying to hurt me?"

"For the first time I'm trying to do the opposite. All I've ever done is hurt you, with my words, with my actions. I can't do this to you anymore. I need to let you go."

"What?" I frowned, confused and scared. *Why did I feel scared?*

"This." He pointed in between us. "What we've been doing since we were kids."

"Lucas," I coaxed, desperately wanting him to stop what he was about to say, but knowing he wouldn't.

"Go home, Alex. Go home to your fiancé. Go home to California. That's your home now. I'm your past, and you have to let me go. Cole's your future. He's your priority now. Stop worrying about me. I'm not your concern anymore. Cole is. He's going to be your husband, it's time you put him first."

"That's not what I'm doing. I love Cole but you'll always be my best friend, Bo."

"You can't have it both ways. It's not fair to him, to you, or to me. I can't continue to be selfish anymore. I'm not trying to hurt you, Alex. I swear it. I promise you. I'm trying to let you go so you can marry the man you love, so you can have a future with happiness. No more sadness. No more chaos. No more hurricane. No. More. Me."

I sucked in a deep breath, trying to steady my mind. My heart.

"Go home, Alex. Please. Go home to Cole. You're his. Not mine."

I wanted to fight with him. I wanted to tell him that it wasn't true. His words devastated me, but not because they weren't true. They gutted me because they were true, every last one of them. I thought about the years of us playing this back and forth game, the truths, the lies, and the secrets, one right after the other. Which caused a domino effect of confusion, hurt, and of pain and sorrow. Of love and hate.

I loved Lucas, but there were also times I hated him. For what he did and didn't do, but when I pictured my future with Cole I never imagined my life without Lucas being in it. I never realized the severity of me saying yes to his proposal. "I do," meant goodbye to my past. Goodbye to the memories, to the love, to the best friend I had known all my life. To the only other man I've ever loved.

I do was the end of Lucas and the beginning of Cole.

*How had I not realized that earlier?*

I couldn't bring myself to say it, so I just turned around.

To go home.

***

"Hello, it's me!" Lily answered with her standard greeting on the phone.

"Hello, it's you!" I replied with mine. "How are you? How's Nashville?"

"Best decision I ever made."

Lily had dropped out of college after her mom died. She stayed in Oak Island for a few weeks after her funeral and literally packed up her bags and moved to Tennessee. The years of singing and playing the guitar paid off, she got a job at a bar as a bartender and one day they heard her randomly singing. She was now the entertainment two nights a week.

"Have you talked to—"

"No. I changed my phone number remember? He's not going to ask Lucas for it and I already made you pinky swear that you wouldn't tell him. Not that he's—"

"He's asked."

"Oh…" She was quiet for several seconds. "Oh well. That boat has sailed to the Caribbean and isn't planning on coming back. Jacob who?"

"Lily…"

"What? He's the dickwad that brings his girlfriend to our Christmas party and flaunts her in my face. Then he has the audacity to try to be my best friend at my mom's funeral."

"Then why did you have sex with him?"

She gasped. "I told you that in secret and it was never supposed to be repeated. Now go wash your mouth out with soap. It was a moment of weakness. I don't even like him anymore."

I rolled my eyes, shaking my head.

"I don't want to talk about him anymore. As a matter of fact… I don't want to talk about him ever. Let's send him to that island where girls send their mistakes to. Bye Felicia."

I chuckled, hearing her say it with attitude and picturing her jolting her head around.

"Let's talk about your wedding! When the hell are you going to start planning it? It's been six months since my mom passed. I think it may be time for you to jump back into the swing of things. She would want you to be happy."

"I know."

"How's Cole?"

"He works a lot. He's got four cases that are going on now, so I haven't really been spending much time with him."

"So, not much has changed since I talked to you a few weeks ago."

"Not really."

"Why don't you show up at his office naked?"

"Oh my God."

"What? Not like naked, naked, that would be weird. I meant like wear a coat and be naked underneath. Guys like that. Just sayin'."

"It would be easier if I had a job, then I wouldn't be bored all day and waiting for him to come home."

After Cole proposed he told me I should quit my job and concentrate on trying to find something I really wanted to do. I helped getting his office and business off the ground but there wasn't much for me to do there anymore. I mentioned to him that I started looking for another job and by the look on his face he didn't like it. He said he loved me being home, waiting on him, and once we had a baby… I stopped him after that.

"Have you talked to my brother?"

"You know I haven't."

"Right. I guess it's for the best, dad said he's been dedicated to Mason, his company and the house he bought, seems like he's always repairing something."

"A house?" My heart sped up. *He wouldn't… Would he?*

"Yeah."

"What house?"

"I don't fucking know. Some house on the water in Oak Island, I guess it's been vacant for years and it went up for auction. He bought it and is fixing it up."

I had to sit down. My legs couldn't hold me any longer. "Oh my God."

"Oh shit! I gotta go. I'm going to be late for work. Talk soon. Love you."

"Lily! Wait, Lily!" I yelled into the phone but the call had already ended.

I looked around the room every which way as I called my mom.

"Hey, honey."

"Mom!" I shouted not being able to control my emotions.

"What? Oh my God, what's going on? Are you okay?"

"I'm fine. Lucas bought a house?"

"Umm, yeah what? Is that why you're calling?"

"Yes. No. I mean… I don't know. Where is this house? Have you seen it? When did he get it? Is he living there? Is it his or is he planning to flip it?" I asked all in one breath.

"Whoa, honey, calm down."

"Mom, please tell me."

"Okay, umm the house is on the water. It's been vacant for years. They put it up on auction. It was all over town, I mean they had at least seventy people bidding for it that morning. Your dad says he paid way too much for the property, but you know him he's going to do what he wants."

"Holy shit," I breathed out with my hand on my chest.

"Alexandra Marie Collins," she scolded.

"Is he living there?" I asked, not paying her any mind. "Mom, is it his?"

"Honey, of course it's his. Why would he buy a house that's not his? He's living there. He's been living there for the last few weeks. What is going on? I don't understand. It's just a house, Alex."

"No, Mom. It's not just a house. It's way more than that. I gotta go."

"Alex—"

I hung up at the exact same moment that Cole walked through the front door.

"Hey, Darlin'."

With wide eyes I stared at the wall in front of me. I couldn't move. I could barely breathe. I concentrated on just that.

"Is everything alright?" I think he sat down beside me. "Alexandra."

"Cole…" I whispered in a voice I didn't recognize. "Why do you want to marry me?" I finally asked, needing to know. I still hadn't looked at him. It was easier to stare at the wall in front of me.

"What kind of question is that? I love you."

"I know that."

"Then why are you asking?"

"It's a simple question don't you think?"

"I gave you my answer. I love you, that's it, Darlin'."

"Okay, then why do you love me?"

"Is everything alright? You're starting to scare me."

"Cole, please answer the question. Why do you love me?"

"I… I… don't… Jesus… Alexandra. I love you, that's why."

I peered down at my ring. "Do you know that I don't wear jewelry?"

"Of course you do. That necklace. You never take it off."

I shut my eyes. I had to. "I haven't worn that in years."

"What?" He reached for my neck not finding it. "Well, fuck. What does it matter?" he muttered.

"I'm going to ask this one last time and please, please, be honest with me. Why do you want to marry me, Cole?"

"I've waited so long for you. I mean you know that. You're mine."

"I'm your prize," I murmured loud enough for him to hear.

"I didn't say that."

"You didn't have to."

He immediately stood, hovering above me. "What the fuck? Are you testing me? What is this?"

"What if I don't want to stop working? What if I don't want to be a stay at home mom?"

"Alexandra, why are you making problems? I want you to live like a queen. I provide for you and you take care of the home. Those are our roles. I grew up in a house where all my parents did was work. I don't want that for my kids."

I looked up at him. "My?"

"You know what I meant."

I cocked my head to the side with a questioning gaze.

"What? Jesus Christ, I have let you mope around here for months. Not given you any grief for the fact you're mourning a mother that's not even yours. We haven't picked a date for our wedding, and we barely even talk about it. And now I come home to this shit? You have got to be kidding me!"

"Wow, Cole."

"She wasn't your mom. I get being sad, but your mom is still alive. Come on."

I buried my head in my hands. "She was like a mother to me. I can't believe you just said that."

"Darlin'…"

"Don't call me that. Not now."

"I love you. We're together now. I want to move on with our lives. I want to get married, I want to have kids, I want—"

"What about what I want?"

"I thought that's what you wanted, too."

"That night, Cole. The night we had sex for the first time. Did you know?"

"Know what?"

"Did you know I was a virgin?"

"Of course I did."

"No, not right before it happened. I'm talking about the day before or the month before. Did you know before taking me into your room that I was a virgin?"

He sighed and I knew my answer.

"It doesn't matter. I have you. We're getting married. It doesn't change anything. I won. You're mine." He sat down beside me, rubbing my back. "Right?"

I faced him, knowing what I had to do. "I can't marry you, Cole."

"What?"

"I'm sorry. I'm so sorry for everything. But I can't marry you. I should have never said yes. I should have never gone back to your house with you. I should of... I can't change the past, the only thing I can change is the future, and I can't marry you."

He shook his head. "You don't mean that."

"I do. I've never meant anything more in my life."

"I love you."

"I know, but is it because you're in love with me?"

"I don't understand the difference."

I sadly smiled. "You will one day when you meet that person. I'm not her, Cole. You think I am, but trust me, you would know what the difference is."

"It's him, isn't it?" he questioned with a hard edge in his tone.

I bowed my head. "I'm so sorry."

"I can't believe you're doing this. I've spent years waiting for you. Pining over you like a lost puppy. Standing on the sidelines. Shit," he sighed. "I want to hate you. I want to hate you so fucking bad right now, but I can't. All these years, since we were kids I've known. You don't look at me the way you do him. You don't smile the same way. You don't laugh the same way. I thought... I thought that it didn't matter. You would grow to love me, and every time you would say it to me, I swear I tried to believe it. Except that look in your eyes, the one that was for him, I never even got a glimpse of it. Not one time."

Tears fell down my face. "I'm so sorry," I repeated the only thing to be true.

"I never understood your bond, the connection that you hold between each other. It makes no sense to me. Not one bit. I thought I was the better man for you, knowing in my heart I never was. How fucked up is that? I fought for you, knowing I would never win. Knowing I was wasting my time, but I didn't care. I wanted to have you in anyway I could. I don't know if that's love or fucking stupidity." He stood, walking over to the window and I stayed where I was.

There was nothing I could do to comfort him. To make it all right. I hated that I hurt him. I hated that I led him on. It wasn't fair to him, none of this was.

"I never wanted to hurt you, Cole. I swear to you on my life that I never wanted to cause you pain. I can't tell you how sorry I am that you're hurting right now. You don't deserve it. You've been nothing but an amazing man to me, a friend that I needed. I love you. I do. I mean that. But at the end of the day... I have to do what feels right in my heart and it's not us. I'm so sorry. I will treasure every moment we've spent together. I promise you that."

We were silent for I don't know how long. He turned to face me with a look I had never seen before. "We're both to blame. I guess it's one of the reasons I'm drowning myself in work. You haven't looked at me the same since the funeral, and I guess it's why I kept my distance. A part of me knew this was coming. I just thought if I ignored it, it would go away. I could make it go away."

"I don't know what to say."

"There's nothing left to say. I'll move my things into the guest bedroom until you figure things out." He walked toward me and sat in front of me on his heels, wiping the tears away from my face. Both of us knowing...

This was truly.

The end.

*** 

I called my parents the next day to let them know what happened with Cole and I. They weren't surprised. I told them I would be coming home once I straightened everything out. The conversation led back to a change that could affect them and me. They wanted to travel, see different places and mainly just enjoy each other. I asked to buy the restaurant but they insisted on handing it over to me. It was my home. The restaurant, the beach, the boys and our abandoned home that Lucas now had made his.

He didn't know I was back.

Until now.

# Chapter 40

## LUCAS

Four months went by since I bought our abandoned house. It was finally done. I upgraded a lot but there were parts that I kept the same. It still looked like ours, except newer and more modern. I did it all by myself and in a way it was therapeutic for me.

To let go.

I combined my life with her and now my life without her. The past and present, my future was unknown. I sat on the patio from the adjoining bedroom looking out at the water. I started surfing again, mostly at dawn. I needed the quiet that surrounded me and that only morning could bring. It was nice being alone with my thoughts, even though I was alone all the time, especially now that my baby sister was gone. I always felt Alex near me, even being thousands of miles apart. Her presence surrounded me, especially when I was out in the water. The house added to that, it maybe one of the reasons I bought it. I wanted her close.

Jacob went back to California, Austin went back to New York, and Dylan was consumed with work. All I had was Mason. Stacey was engaged to the soccer coach and I couldn't have been happier for her. Mason loved him and that's all that mattered to me.

Everything seemed to go back to normal or as best as normal became.

"Penny for your thoughts?" a familiar voice said from behind me.

I immediately stood, spinning to face her. She looked as beautiful as ever, her hair growing again, midway down her back. She wore a soft yellow dress that fit loose on her body, her feet bare. She leaned against the doorframe, her arms crossed over her chest.

"What are you doing here?"

"I think maybe I should be asking you the same question. I moved back a few weeks ago."

"I go to your parent's restaurant—"

"I told them not to tell you. The boys don't even know I moved back."

"Is Cole—"

She interrupted me by shaking her head no. "We broke up months ago."

"Why?"

"It was wrong to get engaged to him. I should have never said yes, but it's all good now. We're fine, in the sense that we ended on good terms. I don't talk to him, we both prefer it that way."

"Are you okay?" I immediately asked.

She smiled. "Always worrying about me. I'm better than I have been in a long time. Did you know my parents were selling the restaurant?"

"No." I hadn't.

"Yeah… after your mom… they decided it was time to retire. They want to travel, enjoy the rest of their lives."

"That makes sense."

"I thought so, that's why I bought it. Well not really, they essentially gave it to me."

"Why would you—"

"It's home. This is my home, Lucas. It always has been. I never wanted to leave like you boys did, but I'm grateful I did. It gave me a chance to realize that this is where I belong."

I nodded, understanding.

"Why did you buy this house?"

"The same reason you bought the restaurant. It's home to me. It always has been. I couldn't let anyone else have it. It's mine."

"It's ours," she corrected. "You bought it for me."

"Alex—"

"Why do you love me, Bo?"

I chuckled. "What?"

"You heard me."

My feet moved of their own accord, only stopping when I was close enough to touch her. I didn't. The smell of her cherry lip-gloss was enough comfort for me to say, "Since I was a kid you've been the first and last thing I have thought about every day of my life. I know everything about you, your eyes, your smile, your laugh, your sassy spitfire personality, taking no shit from anyone, including me. I lie awake every night missing you, there's this huge hole in my heart where you used to be, and I don't care because it reminds me of you. It doesn't matter where I go, where I'm at, or whom I'm with, you're with me. I love every single thing about you. I love you because I need you. I love you because there is no me without you. I love you because I can't stop loving you, and I would be lying if I said I had tried." I grabbed the sides of her face and she leaned into my embrace.

"You're my brown eyed girl."

Her mouth parted and I glided my thumb across her bottom lip. "I'm not going to tell you it's always been easy because it hasn't, but you've always been worth it. I know I've said this before, but I can't state it enough. I'm so sorry, Half-Pint. I'm so sorry for everything I put you through… Stacey, those girls in high school, the shit with Cole, Mason… I think that covers everything?" I joked and she laughed.

"I'm sorry that I ever made you cry, I'm sorry for all the pain I inflicted on your perfect heart. I'm sorry for ever making you feel like I didn't belong to you. I've been yours for every second, of everyday for the last twenty-six years. I'm sorry for every shitty thing I have ever done or said to you. I hate myself for it. You never deserved it. I can't apologize to you enough. I'm so fucking sorry for everything," I whispered, leaning my forehead on hers. "I want to kiss you so fucking bad right now." I put my arms around her neck and she let me.

I looked deep into her eyes and saw the same intense gaze, staring back at me. My chest rose and descended with each deep breath I took, her heart felt like it beat for me and only me. I knew it.

I brought her lips to meet mine and kissed her.

She matched every beat, every moment, every feeling and emotion times ten. The earth stopped moving and time stood still. With my hands framing her face, I kissed her again, slower, more delicate and defined, less frantic and desperate, but with the same intensity and passion.

"I want you," she moaned.

"Half-Pint," I groaned, claiming her lips again.

"If you don't make love to me I will hurt you."

I laughed against her lips, moving my hands from her face down her body, and gripping her ass to slide her up onto my waist.

She wrapped her legs around my torso, kissing me deeper with a demand I never expected from Half-Pint. I laid her gently on my bed, placing my body on top of hers. It started off innocently enough, but it rapidly turned into something else entirely. Our hands started to roam everywhere, not being able to decide where we wanted to touch each other. When her tiny, delicate hand found my cock, she moaned.

"Fuck," I growled, scooting her up toward the headboard as she stroked me up and down, her hand barely closing around my shaft. I leaned back and helped her take off her dress. My mouth instantly went to her nipples and I sucked them until they were pebbled stones.

"Don't stop," she murmured, pulling down my boxers with her hands and then using her feet to push them the rest of the way down. I kicked them off when they were at my ankles and then took off my shirt.

"Bo," she half-whispered, grabbing the shark tooth necklace around my neck.

"The only time I took it off was your engagement party."

And then she attacked me. Rolling me over to lie on top of me. Kissing me like her life depended on it. My hand found her pussy and she was already soaking wet.

"You're so wet. Who is this minx in my arms right now?" She had grown up, turning into a little vixen that made my balls ache just thinking about it. As much as it hurt me that I wasn't the one she experienced her firsts with, it didn't matter, I was always in her heart and she was always in mine. I was still the first boy she ever experienced anything with and she always remembered my touch.

She smiled into my mouth, knowing what I thought. As if to prove my point, she grabbed the edge of her panties and I helped her take them off, going right back to rubbing her clit again. I couldn't believe I was finally touching, claiming her, and making her mine. Her hips moved against my hand and I had to flip us over, I wanted to savor the feel of her and watch her come apart.

Her fingers clutched the necklace as I started to move faster against her heat. "Yes, baby just like that, give it to me. Give me what I want." I kissed along her jawline, taking in every blush of her face, every moan descending from her lips, every movement radiating through her body.

"Tell me…" I bit her bottom lip.

"I love you. I love you, Bo." Her body tightened so fucking hard and then released with a loud heavy moan. I immediately placed my face between her legs, needing to taste her.

"Oh God." Her legs shivered against my face and when I felt her hand go in my hair, holding me closer to her core, I almost came right then and there. I sucked, licked, and devoured her until she was writhing and begging me to make love to her.

My mind raced as I kissed my way back up to her face. "I need a condom. I don't have one," I groaned, placing my forehead on hers not wanting to stop for one damn second.

"Are you clean? Have you been tested?" she panted, looking into my eyes.

"Of course. I haven't had sex in a really long time, Half-Pint. I haven't had sex since Mason. That's the only time I've ever gone without a condom."

"Wow," she sighed and at first I thought it was from me admitting that I hadn't been intimate with someone in years, but then she said, "You're not going to last a long time at all."

I laughed a deep rumbling laugh deep from my stomach. It shook the entire bed and she smiled adorably at me.

"I've never gone without a condom. I mean I've still been tested. But I've never—"

I didn't need to hear the rest before claiming her lips yet again. "I can't do this. Not like this."

"Please tell me you're joking because this is not the time."

I laid soft kisses on her mouth, lovingly looking into her eyes. It was now or never. "Marry me."

She instantly beamed, nudging her nose with mine. "Are you asking since you know you're not going to last long and you want to seal the deal?"

"You little shit." I tickled her inner thigh and she squealed, laughing and kicking all at the same time. "Of course! Yes! Yes a million times over," she screamed, half-laughing.

I stopped and she caught her breath while I took off her necklace and placed it around her neck, locking it in place. She gazed down at it, her eyes pooling with tears. "It's back where it belongs."

"It's always been there, Half-Pint." I grabbed her leg and angled it upward, bending her knee so that her foot rested on my ass and hesitantly pushed in.

"Oh God," she breathed out. Keeping her eyes open even though they wanted to close.

"You're so fucking tight, you're so fucking perfect."

This was not what I imagined our first time would be like. I couldn't help but love the fact that we were laughing and it was like nothing had changed between us. As if we had been doing it for years, our connection, our bond, and our love, radiating all around us.

She grabbed the back of my neck and kissed me with so much power and passion, I returned it tenfold. I thrust in, little by little, until I was fully inside her, stopping to enjoy and enrapture the wetness, the sensations of Alex.

The feel of her.
The taste of her.
The smell of her.
Her.
Alex…
Half-Pint…
*Mine.*

It was a shock to my core as I was consumed with finally being inside of her.

"Why did you stop?" she panted, kissing all over my face.

"I've wanted this for so long. I just want to remember it, savor every second. I have never felt anything close to this. To you. To us."

"Me neither."

I was inside of her, on top of her, and it wasn't enough. Not nearly enough.

I wanted more.
I needed more.

"Where are you?" she asked.

I placed my hand on her heart. "I'm here."

Complicate Me

She closed her eyes and smiled. We kissed and she moved her hips, I took the silent plea and began to thrust in and out of her. She moved her legs so that they were wrapped around my lower back. Bringing me closer to her, she felt the same way I did, and I swear I could hear our hearts beating at the same rhythm in each other's chests. I rested on my elbows that framed her shoulders, and my hands never left the sides of her face. My thumbs pressed into her cheeks while she hugged around my neck.

We kissed the entire time, not being able to get enough of each other. It seemed like hours went by and the whole world was shut out.

Where it was just the two of us.

And I never wanted to leave.

I leaned my forehead on hers and I didn't even have to tell her to open her eyes to look at me. They were already open, looking lively and thriving and full of love for me. Our mouths were parted, still touching and panting profusely, trying to feel every emotion and sensation from our bodies being one. I swear the pounding of our hearts echoed off the walls. I felt myself starting to come apart and Alex was right there with me, waiting to take the mind-blowing dive together. I put all my weight on my right knee and used the other for more momentum to push in and out. She moved her hands to my back, holding on tight, making my dick shove deep within her core.

"I love you, I love you, I love you," she continually moaned, climaxing all around my cock and taking me right along with her.

I shook with my release and kissed her passionately.

"Bo…"

"Yeah, baby," I groaned in between kissing her.

"You just came inside me."

"Mmm hmm…"

"We didn't use a condom."

"Mmm hmm..."

"You didn't pull out."

"Mmm hmm…"

"I don't know if you are aware of this, but that's how babies are made."

I pulled away, grinning. "I named my son Mason after you."

Her eyes squinted, confused.

"Half-Pint… Mason Jar," I explained, causing her to smile.

"I've been waiting for this for a very long time. Mason needs a sibling. Let's try again."

And we did.

All. Night. Long.

# epilogue

## Alex

"Ahhh!" Baby Bo wailed through the baby monitor.

Lucas fell onto his back. "I'm never going to get laid again."

I giggled, lying on top of him. "He's only three months old. Stacey said that Mason started sleeping through the night around three months."

"Stacey's lying. Mason did not sleep through the night till he was like a year old. Besides I didn't care with Mason. I didn't have my enticing tiny wife sleeping beside me. I brought him into my bed to sleep with me."

"Maybe we should let Baby Bo—"

"Not a chance in hell. I already don't get you alone."

"Then you should have stopped trying to knock me up."

We got married a month after he proposed. It was a small ceremony at our house, the boys, Lily, Aubrey, our parents. That's all we needed. It took me three years to get pregnant, not for lack of trying. I'm pretty sure Lucas lived inside me for the first year, saying he had to make up for lost time. We didn't let the negative pregnancy sticks month after month disappoint us.

It was Lucas's child. It would come when it wanted to.

We went to visit Lily on her twenty-third birthday and Lucas got me drunk off of strawberry moonshine. I still don't remember being intimate, but he swears I had a great time, and apparently I did. Six weeks later I was pregnant, so we brought back a bundle from Tennessee. Lily loves to say that she's the reason Baby Bo was consummated. We named him Bo Savan Ryder, his middle name short for Savannah, after Lucas's mom.

My pregnancy was normal. No complications at all, but by the way Lucas treated me you would think that I was high risk the entire time. He didn't let me do anything, even bought me shirts that said, "If you didn't put it in there, then don't touch it." My mom still laughed about that one. She said that it was endearing the way he protected me, but I just thought he was a pain in the ass.

I watched from the door as Lucas held Baby Bo in his arms, rocking him back to sleep. "I love you so much, buddy, even though you're such a cock blocker."

"Lucas," I gasped.

"Shhh... he's sleeping and he doesn't understand a word I'm saying, but it would be awesome if he did."

I shook my head. "Unbelievable."

He gently laid him in his crib and then looked back at me with a mischievous glare. "Run."

I squealed and took off running.

\*\*\*

The caterers came early the next morning. We were having a party at our house. The boys had finally all come home and I wanted to celebrate. It took years to get to this point. Jacob had moved back a few months ago and Austin did a few weeks ago. When we first told them we were engaged, I expected more of a reaction from them, especially after everything they put us through over the years. We got more of a reaction from them when we told them we were pregnant. Aubrey was probably the most excited with our engagement, other than Lily of course. Aubrey moved back to Oak Island shortly after I did. I couldn't begin to tell you everything my friend went through, breaks my heart just thinking about it.

"Half-Pint," Lucas called out from the bedroom.

"What?"

"Lily's here."

I saw her coming in the front door, Jacob treading shortly behind her. I cocked my head to the side, eyeing her wearing Jacob's ball cap. She hadn't worn it in years. When she realized I noticed she smiled, winking an eye.

"Hey, baby sister," Lucas greeted, pulling her into a tight hug. "Jacob, you pulled in at the same time?"

"Something like that."

I looked back and forth between them, but covered it up quickly when Lucas stood behind me, hugging me against his body.

Complicate Me

"It's really not fair that you look like that, Alex, and you just had a baby. How is that even possible?"

I laughed, I knew she tried to take the attention off her and Jacob. I played along. It didn't take long for everyone to show up. We enjoyed everyone's company, laughing and making new memories to last a lifetime. I looked all around my family and friends, holding my son in my arms with my stepson not far away. The pictures of our childhood displayed all over my walls and mantle. I had all my good ol' boys all under the same roof.

We were home.

Finally, we were all home.

"Are you tired?" Lucas asked, kissing my neck while we lay in bed.

"I'm exhausted. That was a long day. I loved it though."

"I know you did. I saw you getting teary eyed toward the end."

"I've waited a long time for this. I mean, I never thought you and Austin would ever talk again."

"He's my brother, Half-Pint. I loved him even when I hated him."

"I know. I'm just happy that everyone is back. Now they can all get married so our kids can all grow up together."

He chuckled. "I love you." His hand moved beneath my panties.

"Are you trying to get laid right now?"

"What gave that away?" he teased, caressing me.

"Lucas, your sister is here. She's in the guest bedroom."

"So, then you'll have to be quiet. Plus if Baby Bo wakes up she'll take care of him. Now let me in."

"Oh my God."

"I know, I'm awesome." And he was, I came all over his hand a few minutes later, which led to us making love all night.

\*\*\*

"Mmm," I groaned, nesting closer to his embrace the next morning. "What time is it?"

"Early. The sun's barely up, Baby Bo will be hungry soon."

"I should go get him."

"It's okay I'll bring him. I know how you love laying him in between us in the morning."

I smiled.

"I got to go wake my baby sister up. She said she needed to be somewhere early."

I yawned. "Mmm kay…"

He kissed my forehead and I watched him leave, thinking how lucky I was to finally have everything I ever wanted. I looked up at the ceiling seeing bunnies everywhere, waiting for Lucas to come back in so we could play our childhood game that we still played every so often.

He took longer than usual and I was about to go after him when I heard him yell, "I'M GOING TO FUCKING KILL YOU!"

I sat straight up with wide eyes.

Jacob.

# THE END.
For Lucas and Alex.

It's only the beginning or is it *the end* for…
Jacob and Lily, turn the page for the Forbid Me Prologue
(Next in The Good Ol' Boys Standalone Series)

**FORBID ME**
FREE WITH KINDLE UNLIMITED
AMAZON US
AMAZON UK
AMAZON CA
AMAZON AU

Complicate Me

# Forbid Me
## (The Good Ol' Boys, Jacob and Lily)

Prologue

Lily

"Stop," Jacob warned as I tried to pull him closer to me by his shirt.

"Oh, come on, everyone's inside. No one will see us."

It was nightfall. The bright full moon loomed over the horizon like a beacon. We were standing outside on the beach that held so many memories. It gave me a sense of comfort like it had when I was a child. We spent endless nights outside together.

Just. Like. This.

He looked up toward the house behind me. "Kid, I can see them. If I can see them, then they can see us."

I shrugged. "I don't care," I honestly spoke.

"You don't mean that."

"See... there's the problem, Jacob. I've always meant it."

He took a deep breath, his masculine chest lifting before he crossed his chiseled, muscular arms over his chest. The gesture immediately reminding me how they felt wrapped around my body.

"I love you. It's that simple for me." I shrugged again.

"I love you, too. You know that. I've always loved you, but that doesn't change the fact that this is wrong. What we're doing, what we've been doing since you were fifteen behind everyone's backs is fucking wrong."

"Why? Why is it so wrong? I'm not a child anymore. I'm twenty-four years old. I know you're ancient and all, but fuck." I grinned, trying to lighten the mood.

He chuckled, "You little shit."

"We'll figure it out. He has a right to know. They all do."

He nodded, knowing I was right. "I won't lose you ever again. You're mine, Lillian."

The possessiveness of his words radiated all around me. His voice making me feel warm all over.

I beamed, peeking up at him through my lashes. I secretly loved it when he called me by my full name. It made me feel older for some reason. I know it didn't make any sense, what woman wanted to be older? No one would understand until they knew our history and walked a mile in my shoes. It took us a long time to get to this point, but we made it here nonetheless. Nowhere near where we needed to be. God only knows if we would ever get to *that* point.

Have you ever wanted something so badly that it consumed your very being? Something that you could practically taste on your tongue? Something that was all you thought about, day in and day out?

The feeling is so intense that it becomes a part of you. You could feel it under your skin, in your heart, consuming your mind.

That was Jacob to me.

He was my core.

I couldn't remember a time when I didn't want him.

When I didn't think about him.

When I didn't love him.

He put his arms around me, engulfing me in nothing but his scent and strong hold. He towered over me, making me feel so tiny against him. I loved that, too.

I stood on the tips of my toes, nestling my face in the crook of his neck and murmured, "Stay with me tonight." Rubbing my nose back and forth on his skin.

"You know I can't," he groaned. I knew my touch had an effect on him.

"I know you're old and it's way past your bedtime. I mean you are thirty-one after all."

He bit my neck making me yelp.

355

"Watch it."

I giggled, "Stay. I'll let you do things to me."

"Right." I knew he was grinning, I felt it against my cheek. "Because that's a problem. I can't keep clothes on you. All you want is for me to do things to you."

"All the more reason for you to stay."

"Kid, you're staying here tonight, in his house."

"So..."

"So?"

"He won't know, I promise. It will be our little secret," I tempted, using the same phrase I had since the beginning. Since *our* beginning. He pulled away and I followed suit. Jacob looked deep into my eyes with a perceptive smile on his face, reading my mind.

He was everything to me.

My heart.

My soul.

I was his...

My body.

My mind.

It had been and always would be that way.

Except, there was one problem. The same problem we've had since the beginning, and we were about to face it sooner than we thought.

# JACOB

The ocean breeze blowing the thin white curtains did little to cool the heat between us. I swear that girl had one temperature. Hot. Not in a good way either. But damn, she was so fucking adorable when she slept. She was always on my side of the bed, as close to me as possible, half of her body draped over mine. She didn't weigh more than a hundred and five pounds wet, but she always managed to take up the entire bed, no matter what size it was. She claimed that lobsters were supposed to sleep like that.

*I guess we were fucking lobsters.*

I never understood half the shit that came out of her mouth, but I loved her despite it. She was much wiser than her years. No one was like Lily. Trust me I would know. I had fucked enough women in an attempt to get her out of my heart.

No one even came close.

*No one.*

"Hey, you leaving me?" she asked in a sleepy voice. She hated getting up early. The girl could sleep all morning if I let her.

I kissed her closed eyes and tried to scoot away. "Hell, yeah. I should have left last night."

"Where would the fun be in that?" She grabbed the edge of my boxers and pulled me toward her.

"Give me a curl, it's cold."

I hesitantly laid my body on top of hers, caging her in with my arms framing her face. I could never say no to her, which had always been one of our problems.

*One.*

She grinned not opening her eyes. "Mmm... so much better," she sighed contently. "My friend is up." She kissed my neck and along my jawline.

"I have to go."

"No, you have to stay."

"Kid—" She rocked her pussy against my hard cock, breaking my train of thought and flipping me over.

"The sun's not even up yet. I've never seen Lucas get up before noon." She tugged at my boxers, pulling them down and freeing my dick.

I should have thought about how things were different now. Lucas. The house. Everything, but I didn't. I knew in the back of my mind that I would be regretting my decision to not leave, to stay here with her. That was the beauty of Lily, when I was with her nothing else mattered, everything faded to black but her.

Lily was my own personal inferno.

Consuming. Intense. Destructive.

She kissed her way down my chest. Never taking her eyes off mine, she slid my cock into her warm, welcoming mouth. My back arched off the bed and my hand went to the back of her neck, gripping and pushing her throat deeper down my shaft.

"Fuck," I groaned, watching her naked body sway as she made love to me with her mouth. I sat up to get a better view and touch her, but before I even reached for her the door opened and I locked eyes with Lucas.

My heart dropped.

His murderous stare went from me to Lily, who was still...

Fucking. Blowing. Me.

"I'M GOING TO FUCKING KILL YOU!" he screamed while he lunged toward me at the same time.

Lily shrieked, jumping off the bed, allowing me to back away just in time to try and cover her with my body. The sheer white sheet wasn't doing much to shield her naked body. I fucking told her I needed to leave last night. I knew something like this was bound to happen.

"You need to calm down, Lucas," I coaxed with my hands out in front of me, grabbing my boxers from the edge of the bed and throwing them on. Not that it helped our current situation. It couldn't get any worse.

"Lucas, stop it! I love him!" Lily shouted behind me.

*Fuck! Yes, it could.*

His eyes widened and his mouth dropped open, all the color draining from his face.

She didn't falter, not that I expected her to. She never knew how to keep her damn mouth shut. "Lucas, I've loved him since I was a kid. You of all people should understand. Get over it!"

I turned around and glared at her. "You aren't helping," I gritted out.

She shook her head. "I don't care. I love you and it's time he knows! It's none of his business anyway."

"Luc—" His fist connected with my jaw before I even got his name out. My head whooshed back, taking half of my body with it. I stumbled, shaking it off, meeting his intense gaze.

I never thought it would come to this...

*Bullshit...*

Yes, I did.

Which is why I tried like hell to stay away from my best friend's baby sister.

# Connect with M

## WEBSITE

## FACEBOOK

## INSTAGRAM

## TWITTER

## AMAZON PAGE

## VIP READER GROUP

## NEWSLETTER

## EMAIL ADDRESS

# **MORE BOOKS BY M**

## All FREE WITH KINDLE UNLIMITED

## **EROTIC ROMANCE**

### **VIP (The VIP Trilogy Book One)**

### **THE MADAM (The VIP Trilogy Book Two)**

### **MVP (The VIP Trilogy Book Three)**

### **TEMPTING BAD (The VIP Spin-Off)**

### **TWO SIDES GIANNA (Standalone)**

## **CONTEMPORARY/NEW ADULT**

## **THE GOOD OL' BOYS STANDALONE SERIES**

### **COMPLICATE ME**

### **FORBID ME**

### **UNDO ME**

### **CRAVE ME**

### **COMING SOON**

## **THE GOOD OL' BOYS SPIN-OFF**

### **EL DIABLO (THE DEVIL)**

24865038R00199

Printed in Great Britain
by Amazon